Susan Vreeland is the internationally renowned bestselling author of *Girl in Hyacinth Blue, The Passion of Artemisia, The Forest Lover,* and a collection of short stories, *Life Studies*. Her novels have been translated into twenty-five languages. She lives in San Diego, California.

Visit her Web site at www.svreeland.com

Praise for *Luncheon of the Boating Party*

"A vivid novel that brings to life Renoir's masterpiece *Luncheon of the Boating Party* . . . done with a flourish worthy of Renoir himself." —*USA Today*

"Susan Vreeland, like a god, breathes breath into the long dead Pierre-Auguste Renoir. [She] again demonstrates her mastery of historical fiction through which she has already won international acclaim. . . . One of the great pleasures of a Vreeland book is looking at the world through an artist's eyes. . . . Susan Vreeland has once again produced a masterwork, a resurrection of people, events and places long since gone. Like the painters Vreeland writes about, she too is leaving her legacy—some of the world's finest examples of historical fiction." —*The San Diego Union-Tribune*

"Vreeland's vivid imagery makes the reader want to keep turning to the painting's reproduction on the front cover to look for what the text describes, to look again at the expression on a face, the light on a cheekbone, the tilt of a hat. As she slowly reveals the personalities and the relationships among Renoir's eclectic cast of characters, one can't help but try to discern those subtleties in the art itself. The painting literally comes alive, and that, one assumes, was exactly Vreeland's intent. Touché." —*The Boston Globe*

"Ostensibly only the portrait of some convivial Sunday picnickers, *Boating Party* is rife with intrigue as Ms. Vreeland delves behind the scene to reveal daily habits and ways of life among a talented crew of friends and rivals. The reader is made to feel a part of the gossip and personalities." —*The Washington Times*

"C'est magnifique! If a trip to Paris is a bit outside your price range, Susan Vreeland's new novel is the next best thing." —*Parade*

"Vreeland obviously has researched Renoir and his milieu thoroughly." —*The Washington Post*

"A profoundly moving portrait of the creative process and of a community of people who came together for a moment to help create one great work." —*Library Journal*

"The finished product affirms Renoir's credo: 'Art was love made visible.' Vreeland's love for Renoir is made palpable in this brilliant reconstruction."

—*Kirkus Reviews*

"Vreeland achieves a detailed and surprising group portrait, individualized and immediate." —*Publishers Weekly*

"Once again—to the delight of her legion of fans—the bestselling author of *Girl in Hyacinth Blue* (1999) and *The Passion of Artemisia* (2002) imaginatively uses art history as the basis for a carefully constructed historical novel."

—*Booklist* (starred review)

"Novelist Susan Vreeland's prose transports her readers to a real place and time, among people who knew Renoir and his fellow Impressionists. . . . Vreeland's exquisitely wrought, painterly writing, her painstaking research and uncanny grasp of artistic principles combine with a talent for communicating Impressionism's often misunderstood ideas and theories to produce this summer's most satisfying historical novel." —*The Seattle Times*

"*Luncheon of the Boating Party* is Vreeland's most ambitious book yet."

—*The Philadelphia Inquirer*

"Vreeland takes the big, bold brushstrokes of Renoir's personal and artistic oeuvre and displays them with her usual vividness in this eponymous novel. . . . Vreeland brings the era and the complexities of that time to life with sensual and provocative detail." —*The Baltimore Sun*

"Vreeland jumps skillfully from character to character and paints a vivid portrait of the creation of a masterpiece." —*The Christian Science Monitor*

"The beauty of Vreeland's novel is how she shows Renoir coming to terms with his models not merely as models but as people. . . . It's the lives and dreams of these models that Vreeland explores, deftly filling in Renoir's blind spots and spinning a narrative by turns comic and poignant. . . . After the canvas is finished, an art dealer tells Renoir: 'Marvelous the stories you hint at in the interactions.' After reading the novel we can agree: what stories indeed, delicately brushed to life in the pages of Vreeland's novel."

—Ross King, Paris Through Expatriate Eyes Web site

"Vreeland, known for her other novels based on art history, has crafted another masterwork. Her expressive, enviable prose vibrantly imbues both Renoir and his models with life. . . . This novel is a beautiful, lyrical, fascinating portrait of painting, personalities, and a particular moment in the river of time. Very highly recommended." —*Historical Novels Review*

"Susan Vreeland paints a vivid narrative picture of the story behind Renoir's canvas of the same name."
—*ARTnews*

"Many people say they love art, but Susan Vreeland emphatically walks that walk, having spun her passion into a cluster of bestselling novels, including *Girl in Hyacinth Blue,* dedicated to vivifying artists and their work. However, to say merely that Vreeland brings to life Pierre-Auguste Renoir's painting *Luncheon of the Boating Party* in her new novel of the same title is to oversimplify her accomplishment, in much the same way that the title Renoir chose oversimplifies what his picture is about. . . . You don't just read this book: you can sniff, devour, fondle, and listen to it, right along with the characters."
—*Corvallis Gazette-Times*

"Vreeland is at her best when the vivacity and surety of her dazzling prose captures the artist at work. Color, timbre, and mood blend brilliantly into a compelling depiction of the act of painting and representation of a painter as much possessed by his subjects as he wishes to possess them."
—*BC Books: Blogcritics* magazine

"Vreeland is true to what's known about the painter. She writes with the care of a biographer as well as the heart and wit of a poet. . . . 'It's important to see in a thing the person who made it,' Renoir says. . . . In Vreeland's ode to art, forgiveness, and humanity, she reveals an equally lively and lovely soul."
—*Rock & Sling* literary journal

"Susan Vreeland's *Luncheon of the Boating Party* shimmers like the surface of an Impressionist painting. My heart sings with the amazing artistic achievement of the author. Through her words and imagination, I have been allowed to enter the bohemian, artistic life of Paris in the 1880s. I thank Susan Vreeland for enriching my life."
—Sena Jeter Naslund, author of *Ahab's Wife, Four Spirits,* and *Abundance: A Novel of Marie Antoinette*

"As impressionistically dazzling and humane as the Renoir painting that inspires it, *Luncheon of the Boating Party* is itself a true work of art that blends the manifest joys and the impossible longings of life into a single coherent vision. Susan Vreeland has for some time been one of our finest writers, and this is her best book yet."
—Robert Olen Butler, author of the Pulitzer Prize-winning *A Good Scent from a Strange Mountain*

"Vreeland magically transported me into the wonderful world of Renoir and his models. I lived there, tasted and breathed the atmosphere. A rich, compulsive read."
—Edward Rutherfurd, author of *The Rebels of Ireland, Dublin,* and *London*

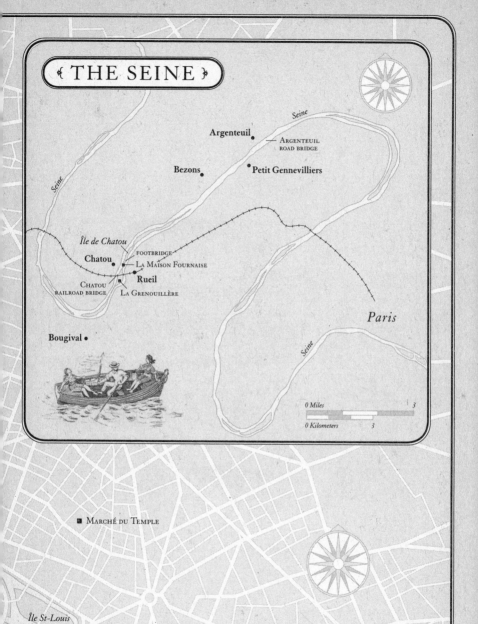

⟨ THE SEINE ⟩

Seine

Argenteuil

— Argenteuil
road bridge

Bezons •

• **Petit Gennevilliers**

Seine

Île de Chatou

footbridge

Chatou •

• La Maison Fournaise

Chatou
railroad bridge

Rueil

La Grenouillère

Bougival •

Paris

Seine

0 Miles   3

0 Kilometers   3

■ Marché du Temple

Île St-Louis

Seine

0 Miles   .5   1

0 Kilometers   .5   1

La Maison Fournaise

Susan Vreeland

Luncheon
of the
Boating Party

{ PENGUIN BOOKS }

PENGUIN BOOKS

Published by the Penguin Group
Penguin Group (USA) Inc., 375 Hudson Street, New York, New York 10014, U.S.A.
Penguin Group (Canada), 90 Eglinton Avenue East, Suite 700, Toronto,
Ontario, Canada M4P 2Y3 (a division of Pearson Penguin Canada Inc.)
Penguin Books Ltd, 80 Strand, London WC2R 0RL, England
Penguin Ireland, 25 St Stephen's Green, Dublin 2, Ireland (a division of Penguin Books Ltd)
Penguin Group (Australia), 250 Camberwell Road, Camberwell,
Victoria 3124, Australia (a division of Pearson Australia Group Pty Ltd)
Penguin Books India Pvt Ltd, 11 Community Centre,
Panchsheel Park, New Delhi – 110 017, India
Penguin Group (NZ), 67 Apollo Drive, Rosedale, North Shore 0632,
New Zealand (a division of Pearson New Zealand Ltd)
Penguin Books (South Africa) (Pty) Ltd, 24 Sturdee Avenue,
Rosebank, Johannesburg 2196, South Africa

Penguin Books Ltd, Registered Offices:
80 Strand, London WC2R 0RL, England

First published in the United States of America by Viking Penguin,
a member of Penguin Group (USA) Inc. 2007
Published in Penguin Books 2008

10 9 8 7 6 5 4 3 2 1

Le Maison Fournaise by Jacques Bracquemond (gravure au burin).
Copyright Association des Amis de la Maison Fournaise, Chatou, France.

THE LIBRARY OF CONGRESS HAS CATALOGED THE HARDCOVER EDITION AS FOLLOWS:
Luncheon of the boating party / Susan Vreeland.
p. cm.
ISBN 978-0-670-03854-1 (hc.)
ISBN 978-0-14-311352-2 (pbk.)
1. Renoir, Auguste, 1841–1919—Fiction. 2. Renoir, Auguste, 1841–1919. Luncheon of the boating
party—Fiction. 3. Painters—France—Fiction. 4. Impressionism (Art)—Fiction. I. Title.
PS3572.R34L86 2007
813'.54—dc22   2006035324

Printed in the United States of America • Set in Granjon • Designed by Amy Hill

To him who is specially hers,
Joseph Kip Gray,
from she who is singularly his,

In memory of his brother,
Michael Francis Gray

To my mind, a picture should be something pleasant, cheerful, and pretty, yes pretty! There are too many unpleasant things in life as it is without creating still more of them.

—Pierre-Auguste Renoir

Whatever you can do, or dream you can, begin it. Boldness has genius, power, and magic in it.

—Johann Wolfgang von Goethe

Contents

1. *La Vie Moderne*   *1*

2. Paris on the Run   *17*

3. To the Left Bank and Back   *25*

4. Reflections on the Seine   *43*

5. Colors, Credos, and Cracks   *50*

6. Looking for Mademoiselle Angèle   *64*

7. *Dans* l'Avenue Frochot   *79*

8. Glorious Insanity   *83*

9. Models, Friends, Lovers   *100*

10. Cork in the Stream   *113*

11. Cycle of Pleasure   *124*

12. Paris Encore   *135*

13. Hats on Sunday   *146*

14. *En Canot* with the Baron   *158*

15. School for Wives   *163*

16. Remembrance of Times Past   *168*

17. The Convocation of *Flâneurs*   *177*

18. In the Time of Cherries   *191*

19. Confession *en Canot*   *203*

20. A Ride in the Country   *209*

21. Circe's Stripes   *215*

22. Moonlight and Dawn   *224*

23. Repairing to Paris   *235*

24. Peaches at Camille's *Crémerie*   *248*

25. The Blue Flannel Dress   *256*

26. *Au* Jardin Mabille   *269*

27. *Allons!* To Work!   *284*

28. An Errand in Paris   *294*

29. *Aux* Folies-Bergère   *300*

30. In a Closed Field   *311*

31. Not One *Canotier* Song   *316*

32. The Deal   *332*

33. Love Made Visible   *346*

34. *À* La Grenouillère   *356*

35. Les Fêtes Nautiques   *366*

36. *À l'Atelier*   *380*

37. So Brief a Pair   *390*

38. The Awning   *400*

39. The Last Luncheon   *405*

40. Incandescence   *423*

Author's Note   *431*

Acknowledgments   *433*

LUNCHEON OF THE
BOATING PARTY

Chapter One

La Vie Moderne

20 July 1880

He rode the awkward steam-cycle along the ridge to catch glimpses of the domes and spires of Paris to the east, then turned west and careened headlong down the long steep hill toward the village of Bougival and the Seine. With his right elbow cast in plaster, he could barely reach the handlebar, but he had to get to the river. Not next week. Not tomorrow. Now. Idleness had been itching him worse than the maddening tickle under the cast. Only painting would be absorbing enough to relieve them both. Steam hissed out of the engine, but it built up inside of him.

He reached down to open the throttle wider. The soft morning light would be flattened to a glare by the time he got there if he didn't let her go all out. The piston beat faster in the cylinder until it became a whir of sound, the poplars and chestnuts along the road a blur of greens, the blooming *genêts* a blaze of yellow, with the blue-green sweep of the river coming closer and closer. A painting! He was plunging into a painting! Down and down he plunged. Warm summer air filled his nose with the fragrance of honeysuckle, and the low-pitched honk of a tugboat urged him onward. At the base of the hill, he checked behind him to see that his folding easel, canvas, and Bazille's wooden color box were still strapped on.

The three-wheeled cycle took the humped bridge at Bougival fine, but the coarse sand on the narrow, connected islands made the front wheel wobble.

All types of *canots*—rowing yoles, sailboats, and racing sculls—tied to posts along the riverbank produced inverted images quivering in the lazy current, deliciously paintable. But not today. They were empty of life. On Sundays, though, every laundress with her chapped red arms, every shopgirl, mail clerk, butcher, and banker, Parisians of all classes took their leisure either on the Seine or in it or along its grassy slopes. La Grenouillère, The Frog Pond, one of the many rustic *guinguettes* along the river that provided food, music, and dancing, had a lonely air about it now compared to Sundays. Then, pleasure-loving Parisians threw off their city restraints and filled the floating café, shouted from rented rowboats, splashed each other in the shallow eddies, picnicked along the bank, drank and danced on the anchored barge—the way he and Claude Monet had painted it a decade ago. They had slapped each other on the back the day they'd discovered that juxtaposed patches of contrasting color could show the movement of sunlit water. What he would give for another day like that one, for that thrill of breaking new ground. Repeating safe, easy methods portrait after portrait, as he'd been doing lately, was suffocating him.

In the distance, a catboat sailing toward him looked like the *Iris,* one of Gustave's boats. He rode toward it. Yes, it was! He stood up to his full height on the foot platforms, twisted to hail him with his left arm, and lost his balance. The front wheel jerked sideways, and the cycle tipped and crashed onto its side. His right hip and shoulder struck sand and gravel, his hand and elbow in the cast taking the fall, his face taking the bounce. The broken smokestack landed on his left leg. His right leg was trapped under one rear wheel, while the other rear wheel spun with a tick, tick, tick. Boiling water splashed and oil leaked onto his pant leg. He struggled to disentangle himself before getting burned. Jesus Christ! He would destroy himself if he didn't start painting soon.

He spit out sand and lay trembling in a cloud of steam, trying to figure out what had happened and watching the glints of light riding the water. How different the colors from this low angle, the contrast between tips of ripples and valleys between them more pronounced now—a deeper forest green for the furrows, with shifting patches of yellow-green and ocher on the humps, and the silver highlights more transparent than he'd ever seen them. My God! To show that to the world!

A throbbing moved up through his legs, hip, shoulder. His right cheek and hand stung. Sand had scoured his palm and left it bloody. He staggered to his feet. Bazille's dear old color box had suffered too—the corner splintered, one hinge sprung, the other twisted. Tubes and brushes lay scattered in the tall grasses, the canvas face down in a muddy patch. The *Iris,* with Gustave oblivious at the helm, was only a triangle of white sail downriver.

Using his left arm and all his weight, he tried to pull the cycle upright, but it refused to budge. The monster weighed more than he did. The front wheel was bent. He could never steer it now. He turned off the oil burner and opened the steam release valve. The hissing quieted to a gurgle. Below the trademark, Peugeot, he saw the model name, *La vie moderne.* Modern life. He chortled. That was the subject matter of the new painting movement, as precarious as the steam-cycle.

He crouched at the river's edge and cupped some water in his left hand to rinse his mouth. A pain shot up his thigh. He splashed his right hand to loosen the grit embedded in his palm. The cool water stung. He crawled through the weeds to gather his brushes and tubes, but couldn't find yellow ocher. If he were well off, or at least stable, he could do without it because he could make it from other colors, but those tubes were almost squeezed flat already. A muttering duck glided between reeds toward a tube of paint. He quacked at it in a tone that said, *Leave it alone.* The duck paddled away. The scent of wild roses assailed him. Any other time, the sight of them would have excited him, their petal faces pale pink and cream like women's cheeks. Like Jeanne's.

At least he'd found his beloved bicycle cap. Now all he needed was to find his way. In painting, in love, in life.

He carried brushes in his right hand and the color box of his dead friend in his left, the lid dangling. He set off limping the ten-minute walk along the wooded strip to the Île de Chatou. Just north of the railroad bridge, he would come to Maison Fournaise, the boaters' *guinguette*—the riverside restaurant, hotel, and boat rental frequented by painters and writers where he had thought to try out an idea on the little canvas.

Up ahead, Alphonse Fournaise, the barrel-chested son of the owner, hoisted a narrow-prowed one-man *canot* off carpenter's sawhorses and over his head as if it were a giant baguette. He ambled to the bank, lowered the boat, and slid it into the water.

"Auguste Renoir, you old fool," Alphonse called. "You've either been in a boxing ring or you fell off your cycle again."

"The latter, of course. I left it in the path just this side of La Grenouillère. The front wheel is bent. There's a muddy canvas there too."

"I'll go get them. Are you all right?"

"I'll find out tomorrow when I try to get out of bed."

Alphonse tied the boat to the dock. "Alphonsine!" he called to his sister who was swimming nearby, and waved her in.

Auguste watched her strong arms propel her through the water. When she climbed up the bank, her swimming costume of striped blouse and knee-length bloomers clung to her curves. Water slid down her shapely legs.

"*Mon Dieu,* Auguste! What happened?" Alphonsine dried off with a towel as he explained. He set down his color box on the table under the trellised arbor and lowered himself gingerly onto the wooden chair.

"I'll get something to wash you."

He felt blood trickle down his cheek. In a moment she reappeared with two basins—soapy water and clear—and two cloths. Spears of light shone through the vine above her and danced in patches on her small mounded breasts. Her nipples poked out like beads under the thin wet fabric.

"Look at me," she said.

"I am."

"I mean look up."

Dutifully, he raised his face to hers. Her skin shone rosy from the sun. Exactly what he loved to paint. Like Jeanne's cheeks, which gave back the light. Jeanne Samary, the darling of the Comédie-Française. She made everyone in Paris laugh. Him too, at one time. He should have brought her here to the country away from heady adulation. Out here, he could have shown her a beauty not man-made, the joys of being an adorer, not merely the adored. Lying on the grass, he could have shown her how light on water breaks up in patches of color. She might have understood his painting of her, how skin really does take on the colors of the surroundings, and it might have all turned out differently.

Like Alphonsine's pink forehead washed with pale green by the vine.

She pressed the warm wet cloth against his face. "You have sand embedded in your cheek. Does it hurt?"

"Only when I look away from you."

Strange pleasure, to allow himself to be so vulnerable. He hoped this would take a long time. A pretty little scowl formed as she pressed the cloth gently against his face to loosen the grit. He tried to relax in order to control the tic in his cheek.

Alphonsine rinsed the cloth and dabbed, snickering softly.

"What's so amusing about a man writhing in pain and about to die?"

"You have a peaky face."

"You have a peachy one."

"Your cheeks go in like saucers, and your nose—"

"What about my nose?"

"It's peaky, that's all. Your face looks weathered."

"Like old wood cracked by the sun? It's an occupational hazard. I paint *en plein air.*"

He supposed he did look like an old fence post to her, with his lined forehead and concave cheeks, deeper when he hadn't eaten well. At least his hair was still brown, though his widow's peak was becoming more pronounced. Two bare troughs on either side of it were carving their way to the top of his head, the reason for his bicycle cap. His eyelids drooped slightly over hazel eyes. Jeanne had called his narrow, pointed nose aquiline, and had thought him handsome, his pronounced cheekbones especially, and so had Margot.

"You're not listening. I *said,* your eyes are always watching," Alphonsine said.

"Sorry. And my face is always twitching. I care more about my eyes."

"Your face is kind of solemn. Are you sad?"

He was, of course, whenever he thought of Jeanne or Margot. "Not that I know of."

"Sit still. Every time you say something, you jerk."

"I can't help it. I'm strung together that way. With piano wire."

Sharp grains scraped across his raw flesh. She began to pick them out with a tweezer. Her face came closer and she worked in one spot, digging with the metal points. "I'm sorry," she whispered. Her lips turned in on themselves and her blue eyes shot through with gold filmed over with wetness. She stopped, her hand resting on his chin, her eyes fixed on his cheek.

"What's wrong?" he asked.

She resumed picking. "They're like metal bits in a soldier's wound."

The tightness in her voice reminded him that she was a war widow. Ten years alone, but still looking young. In her early thirties, he guessed.

Her mother, Louise Fournaise, came outside drying her hands on her apron. "Pierre-Auguste, you had no business riding that contraption with a broken arm."

"Yes I did! It was pure business. It's time I find out what kind of painter I am."

"Couldn't that wait until you walked here like any sensible man?"

He pointed upward with his index finger. "The light, madame."

"Where have you been?" Louise asked.

"My mother's house in Louveciennes." He lifted his cast. "I've been staying there."

"And she let you ride that torture machine? You're thinner than ever. Wasted, in fact. She doesn't feed you?"

Wincing, he tried his most winning smile. "Not like you do, madame."

"So stay to lunch, you rascal." Louise marched back to her kitchen.

Alphonsine squinted as she worked on his face. "You were coming here?"

"Looking for something new to paint."

"Do you remember painting me and your two friends under this arbor?"

"Of course. I remember all the paintings I've done of you. Each one gave me great pleasure. I make it a rule never to paint except out of pleasure."

"I know another place to paint that will give you pleasure. You've never painted from this high place before."

"Let me guess. From the railroad bridge? Do you want to get me killed?"

"No."

"Then from the footbridge?"

"No-o." Her voice ascending flutelike lengthened the syllable into birdsong.

"From the pumping station at Marly?"

She teased him with a moment of coy silence. "When I finish, I'll show you. All the times Edgar Degas has come here, I've never suggested it to him. Only to you."

"Ha! It would have been wasted on him. Edgar paints from his imagination in his stuffy studio and calls it a landscape. It's supreme arrogance to think that what comes out of his brain is more valuable than what we see around us."

"Like this place." She cupped his bloodied hand in hers in the bowl of soapy water. "You have long, thin fingers."

"And you have short, sweet ones."

"Why do you keep your fingernails longish?"

"For protection. I could injure my fingertips and ruin my sense of touch. That would deprive me of a good deal of pleasure in life." Her hands slid over his like minnows. The sensation made him close his eyes a moment. "It's worth the stupid accident," he said.

"What is?"

"Having you do this."

A pink flush crept up her neck to her cheeks that made him want to caress them. Or paint them, which was the same thing, really.

"You have sand in your beard."

"Thank you for calling my measly little fringe a beard."

She dribbled water over it, threading her fingers through his hair. "It's soft. I thought it would be scratchy."

"I made it that way on purpose, to give you pleasure."

"It's nice the way you trim it in a narrow path along your jaw."

She patted his face and hands dry with a blue plaid dish towel and took him by the left wrist which sent a tremor up his arm. "Follow me."

He would skip after her like a young swain if he were able to. His hip ached and his thirty-nine years creaked in every joint as he entered the large restaurant and climbed the stairs to the terrace facing the river.

She flung open her arms. "Paint from here. See what you can see? Both banks, upstream and down." She turned the crank that rolled away the coral-and-gray-striped awning, and leaned out over the railing. "*The floating exhalations from the grass, mingled with the damp scents from the river, filled the air with a soft languor, with a happy light, with an atmosphere of blessing.* Guy de Maupassant wrote that. It's lovely and true, isn't it?"

"Yes. A happy light," he murmured.

Paint from here. He was more than amused. He had been telling himself the same thing ever since Fournaise extended the balcony into a wider terrace three years ago, but he'd always postponed the idea. The perspective would be too tricky. He hadn't known how to convey the sense that the terrace was part of a building and wasn't floating in the sky.

"Someday," he said.

"Why not now?"

He didn't want to admit he didn't know how. "For now, I'm obliged to paint portraits of overbred society women in their fussy parlors." She tipped her head, expecting a reason. "It pays." He swept his arm over the tables and river. "This would be painting just for me. It might not pay a bean."

But what it offered him! Below the terrace, a dozen rowing skiffs tied to bank posts made graceful repeated shapes in the water, and a string of sailboats tied bow to stern formed a caravan from the slanted dock to the floating boat garage. On the eastern shore at Rueil, the white stone inn of La Mère Lefranc with its red-tiled roof caught the light in the afternoon, and on Sundays Parisians ate at tables in the small orchard. Downstream, the Giquel yacht works hung out over the water surrounded by boats, and a few scattered houses were nestled behind market gardens. Upriver, the smokestack of the carriage factory cast an ocher reflection and belched charcoal-colored smoke. Claude Monet would position a sail in front of it. Gustave would ignore the bank and paint from the odd perspective of the needle nose of a racing scull with rowers pulling at their oars. Pissarro, that old Communard, he'd make the smokestack central to the painting, symbol of the proletariat.

And what would he do? How could he portray best this meeting place of city and country? Another riverscape with Parisians in boats? A mix of people eating and drinking? Dancing? Calling down to someone in a rowboat? He envisioned his friends gathered around the tables after a delicious lunch, flushed with pleasure, enjoying a beautiful day, showing what happens here every Sunday. Leisure. *La vie moderne.*

But *how*? He sat down and crossed his legs. That was the more perplexing question, the underlying issue agitating him lately. Impressionist or traditional? It was all tied up with that other question—whether to withdraw completely from the Impressionist circle, continue to submit to the academic Salon and betray his friends, or to return to the Impressionist group he had helped to form. He still hated the term, a slam by that critic Louis Leroy who claimed they were only capable of sketchy impressions, but he loved his friends—Claude Monet, Gustave Caillebotte, Camille Pissarro, Alfred Sisley, Paul Cézanne, and Berthe Morisot—and they'd all accepted the name.

It's just that he didn't want the characteristic broken strokes of Impressionism to dictate his style in everything, particularly figures. Was he an Impressionist at all? If he deserted the cause permanently and painted in a more classical style, what would happen to their unity? The friendships that had kept them going? Who was he really betraying by turning out one society portrait after another? The group? Himself? Both?

Père Alphonse Fournaise, Father Fournaise, a slightly smaller version of his well-fed son, came out onto the terrace wearing a blue mariner's cap, holding a magazine and a baguette under his arm. He set out two tumblers of *petit bleu,* the wine most popular with rowers. "I'm sorry about your mishap."

Alphonsine dabbed at his cheek with the cloth. "It's still oozing. Don't forget what I said. A painting just for you." She went downstairs.

"Did you see Gustave sail by?" Père Fournaise asked.

"Yes, I saw him. If I hadn't, I'd have arrived on wheels and with a face that hadn't been shaved by a cheese grater."

Fournaise unrolled the magazine, *Le Voltaire.* "He dropped this off for you two weeks ago. It has Zola's review of this year's Impressionist show, but it doesn't mention you."

Auguste took the magazine. "That's because I didn't exhibit with them this year. Neither did Monet or Sisley or Cézanne."

"Why not?"

"A rule Degas concocted. If we submit work to the official Salon we can't exhibit in our Impressionist shows too. It was meant as a solidarity measure, but it's having the opposite effect."

"The leaders breaking rank? You're going to let the movement fall apart?"

Auguste drummed his fingers on the table. "That's not my intention. It's just that only a handful of people buy works by painters not in the Salon, but eighty thousand beat down the doors every spring to snatch up works by any old imitator of the past with the cachet of being hung in the Salon."

"Well, read the article and see what Zola says."

He scanned the account of the group as an artistic force, but read more carefully the criticism that Impressionists were too often sloppy, too easily satisfied with work that was incomplete, illogical, and exaggerated.

If one is too easily contented, if one sells sketches that are hardly dry, one loses the taste for works based on long and thoughtful prepara-

tion. The real misfortune is that no artist among the Impressionists has achieved powerfully and definitely the new formula which, scattered through their works, they all offer in glimpses.

"Formula! Formula! Art has no formula. If it did, any Montmartre peddler would be painting pictures. He wants works based on long and thoughtful preparation?" He smacked the table with his palm. "Then he's forgotten my *Bal au Moulin de la Galette*. Six months' work and two preliminary oil studies. You can't lay down thirty heads on a canvas and make it look like a spontaneous moment without *long and thoughtful preparation*."

"No, I guess not."

"Does he think France has turned Protestant, valuing a work by how much the painter sweats in creating it? If an Impressionist settles for a sketch, it's because a sketch serves his particular purpose."

This was souring a beautiful day. He recrossed his legs and read on.

They are all forerunners. The man of genius has not yet arisen. We can see what they intend, and find them right, but we seek in vain the masterpiece that is to lay down the formula. All remain unequal to their self-appointed task. That is why, despite their struggle, they have not reached their goal; they remain inferior to what they undertake; they stammer without being able to find words.

A punch in the stomach. He tossed the magazine onto the table. "I thought Émile was our friend."

"Maybe he still is. Degas was here last Sunday and thought Zola was just challenging the group. Throwing down the gauntlet."

"Degas sees only what he wants to see. There have been signs of Zola's change of opinion before this."

So what was he to do? Let his friends answer the charge themselves? He had enough roiling in his gut without this. His direction. That is, his two directions. A country painter of loosely brushed landscapes, or a city painter of figures in the classical tradition. He loved aspects of each equally. One road might well lead him back to poverty, the other to stagnation.

Auguste looked down through the terrace ironwork. Brawny young Alphonse, the opposite of himself, was wheeling the cycle on its hind wheels. "I think I can fix it," Alphonse said.

"I'd be much obliged. While you're at it, I have a busted color box."

Louise called up the stairs and Fournaise went down. Auguste tipped his chair back against the railing and stared at the empty table. If the rant had been written by Leroy or Wolff or any of the usual critics, he'd toss it off as the same old whine. But Émile Zola. Zola, who had defended the group against old-school judgment-mongers. From him, this was the cruelest cut of all.

Works based on long and thoughtful preparation. Like *Bal au Moulin de la Galette,* his painting of the open-air dance hall in Montmartre. The shadows of two windmills, the tinny music, dust rising from dancing feet, the swirl of muslin dresses, the laughter of his friends, the clink of glasses touching, the lively taste of *piccolo* from the vineyard a block away, the sweet, flaky wine-soaked *galettes,* the fragrance of iris and lavender being ground in a windmill for the perfumers of Paris, the breeze lifting a woman's hair to reveal a graceful neck, dappled light filtered through acacias caressing a cheek, being in love, Margot—yes, all of it pulsing again, *encore.*

An encore. What Zola wanted was just what he needed to do—the major work he'd imagined here for years, *la vie moderne* at Chatou, as *Moulin* had been *la vie moderne* at Montmartre. An encore to *Moulin,* but this had to surpass *Moulin.* If he wasn't going to exhibit with the Impressionists again, he could at least support them by answering Zola's charge with a painting designed to astonish. Figures, landscape, genre subject—all in one. Throw in a still life too. Not just a few figures. A dozen or more, at closer range this time. If he were to abandon Impressionism eventually, he wanted to go out with a bang. But if he were to follow his instinct, he would use a combination of styles. It would be an experiment. The faces modeled with more classical techniques, one hue blending seamlessly into another to create shape, but the landscape and still life in looser, distinct strokes. Every figure, every feature a small painting in and of itself. Ideas came so fast he knew it was the right time to do it. "*The genius has not yet arisen. Zut!* Zola will eat his words."

He sat up straighter. This could turn the tide for him. It could reverse the slippage in sales. Dollfus hadn't bought anything for four years, Duret and Rivière for three, Murer for two. He'd sold nothing to Ephrussi, Deudon, and Chocquet for more than a year. Why?

Because he hadn't been progressing. The technical challenge of this painting would force him to move ahead. But how was he to achieve the perspective? Position the figures? Anchor the terrace? Convey the river below? He read the paragraph again. *They remain inferior to what they undertake.* His arm throbbed, his palm burned. This would be the fight of his life.

The idea was so ambitious that if he couldn't turn out a masterpiece on par with *Moulin,* critics would slice it to shreds. If it only came close it would be ridiculed for its ambivalence of styles or its faulty composition. His sales would drop even more, his career would go backward. He'd be plunged into the poverty of a few years ago. His sense of worth as a painter would crack and he would be afraid to try any other style. So, what now? Dive or stagnate?

He had enjoyed a flurry of success, a few years of financial well-being. He'd bought the Peugeot, sailed with Gustave Caillebotte to the coast, developed a few collectors, but his situation today was uncertain.

How could he pay a dozen models even at the lowest rate of ten francs each per session? What would the work require? Ten sessions, at least. That alone would eat up what was left from Bérard's commission. He would have to rent the terrace if he expected Fournaise to close it off from customers. He'd need a room here to live in and keep the painting in. And the cost of supplies for so large a canvas—probably two or three hundred francs. The commissions he'd have to decline would be a huge loss, and those requests would be snapped up by other painters. No. It was impossible. Claude painting what he pleased without an eye to commissions had always struck him as giddy insanity. *That* he couldn't do. He had his Paris studio rent to pay. It was foolish to consider it.

Alphonsine brought up a plate of green beans, fried potatoes, and *grenouilles,* frog legs sautéed with garlic and parsley, a common dish here because frogs in marshy areas jumped right into your hand. She leaned forward with her elbow on the railing looking at the river. Her breasts hung loosely under her linen blouse and her light brown curls, drying now, moved in the breeze. Her freshness made him feel old. If he was ever going to do this painting, it had to be now.

Fournaise came up with a plate for himself. "You know, Gustave will have stiff competition this year in the sailing regatta. I've seen a new racing sloop pass by which looked like a Series Four. Fast as a swallow."

"It should be an exciting race. You'll make piles of money from the crowd here. When is it?"

"The second Sunday in September. The week after our own Fêtes Nautiques."

Fournaise couldn't have a dozen models and a big painting occupying the terrace during his Fêtes Nautiques, the annual festival of rowing and jousting championships. It would prevent him from filling every corner of his restaurant and grounds with customers. The terrace was the prime viewing spot for the races.

He would just have to finish it by then. But the portrait of Madame Charpentier and her children with only three figures and a hound dog had taken him more than forty sittings. What he had in mind was so complex that he wasn't sure he could make it work at all, much less under time constraints. It wasn't just the Fêtes. Autumn would bring a change of light.

He took a pencil and his small sketch pad from his pocket and scribbled with his left hand. Alphonsine stretched out her neck to watch. "Names?"

"Friends who might be willing to pose."

The wild man Paul Lhôte would, for sure, and if he did, so would Pierre Lestringuèz, his prophet-of-doom protector. Gustave Caillebotte, if he could get him away from the *Iris,* the qualifying races, and his own painting. He would give Gustave a prominent spot in the composition. All that Gustave had done for the group over the years, renting their exhibit space, paying for advertising, hanging the exhibitions, covering Monet's and Pissarro's rent so many times, buying their paintings when they didn't have a sou for a bowl of soup—this would be a recognition of that. It would tell France how important Caillebotte was to the movement.

Who else? Jeanne. With her last portrait, he'd felt he was approaching what he was capable of doing. It was love that did it. He needed to be in love with someone who loved him back, so he would see everything through the atmosphere of happiness. Love always brought about his best work, and this was too big a risk not to be his best. If Jeanne wasn't performing on Sundays, if she was over her pique about his last painting of her, if he could make her see this new one as a valuable means of promotion for her, she might consent, but she'd charge him through the nose—the bigger the image, the more per sitting.

He finished the meal. "What would you think if I painted right here?"

Alphonsine sprang upright.

"Anytime. You know that," Fournaise said.

"I mean a large painting. Lots of people. After one of Louise's savory luncheons. People enjoying themselves full tilt."

Fournaise pushed out his bottom lip. "How long would it take?"

He had to get him to agree before he saw what an intrusion it would be.

"It depends on how often I can get models to come."

"It would make La Maison Fournaise famous," Alphonsine said.

"Why don't you just do the setting here," Fournaise asked, "and add the people in your studio?"

"I can't. I have two rules for myself, and I've rarely broken them. Always paint from life, and don't do anything I don't enjoy. I have to paint it where they'll be living what I paint. Parisians at leisure on the river. The railroad bridge to show how they got here. The light and the feel, right here. I'll rent the space, and a room in your hotel."

"How much space?" Fournaise sectioned off one table at the far end.

"The whole terrace. I can't have people carousing up here while I work. I'll need it during the week too, not just on Sundays."

Fournaise planted his feet wide. His bottom lids tightened. The canny entrepreneur, thinking. In order to build a restaurant, a hotel, a fleet of pleasure boats, a big annual fête, acquire a steam touring launch, and buy up most of the upper island, he'd had to consider all angles of a proposition.

"The whole terrace, then. Until my Fêtes and the sailing regatta."

Not quite two months. It would be tight. "Fair enough."

"You're crazy, you know. You with a broken arm."

True. How was he going to stretch a canvas that large, or even carry it?

"I can paint left-handed. And this cast will come off soon."

"Not if you keep falling on it."

Fournaise called down to his son, "Alphonse, lay off of that."

"I think I can fix it."

"Don't. Wheel it into the boathouse and lock it up." He turned back and put his hand on Auguste's shoulder. "You've got too important a hand to be taking risks with that *engin de mort*."

Auguste reached in his pocket for his wallet, knowing there was precious little in it. Fournaise's hand shot out against his wrist. "Put that away."

Fair enough. Today Père Fournaise was his host. But what about tomorrow?

Chapter Two

Paris on the Run

Moments later, he looked back from the pedestrian bridge and saw Alphonsine on the terrace watching him. He waved, and she called out, "I knew I had a good idea."

It would do her good to think she had conceived of it herself. "Good only if you'll be in it," he called back.

She clapped her hands over her mouth.

The train lurched forward, throwing him back. The half-hour ride from Rueil into Paris always struck him as a phenomenon of speed. He rode in an open-air car in the rear, third class, squinting his eyes against flying soot. The squinting and the speed made the countryside whiz by, transforming market gardens and houses into blurred shapes, momentary sensations of color and light without detail. No wonder he and Monet and Sisley had developed Impressionism. Trains had introduced them to the flash of vision.

Tuesday already. Madame Charpentier's salon day. A few of the people on his models list were sure to be there. Most were working people only available on Sundays. If he didn't get commitments from them for this Sunday, he would lose a week.

He stood up long before the train finished its ten-kilometer run, and was the first one out the door at Gare Saint-Lazare. He went straight to his studio on rue Saint-Georges, where Paris proper gave way on the north to the lower reaches of Montmartre, Montmartre *d'en bas*. He poked his head through the concierge's wicket. Victor, a former caval-ryman now peeling potatoes in his undershirt, twitched his bushy dra-goon's mustache. "Fresh out of the meat grinder, eh?" He slapped the key and a notice into Auguste's palm.

Aching, Auguste climbed the six flights to his studio under the chimney pots. The notice was the landlord's new rule that painters had to pay quarterly in advance. Four hundred twenty-five francs. He yanked books off his shelf and found the jar where he kept some money. Disappointing. What was he? A fool? One tiny consolation. In another jar there were plenty of stretcher tacks.

If he stood on place Pigalle in his homespun painting trousers and canvas shoes, he might look pitiful enough with his broken arm that someone would buy a painting right out of his hands. The people of Montmartre were used to such things. He picked a study of two circus girls juggling oranges.

He took avenue Frochot, a one-block haven of rosebushes and villas, because Jeanne Samary lived there. Someone singing the *Amours divins* aria from Offenbach's *La Belle Hélène* made him pause. It was so lovely that he was tempted to call on her to come outside and hear it too, but thought better of it. He used to be welcomed anytime, by Jeanne or her mother who stuffed his cheeks with sweets, but that was last winter. Liaisons in Montmartre changed quickly.

In place Pigalle he greeted old Père Cachin, the *charbonnier* with blackened skin who squatted by his hole in the ground where he sold lumps of heating coal, grilling charcoal, and artists' charcoal.

"See? I still have your sign," Cachin said and pointed to the card-board drawing Auguste had made showing him in front of his hole with the words *Boutique de Charbon* in fancy script.

"Has it brought you good business?"

"Not so much in summer. But autumn will come." The man grinned his toothless grin. "Days will get shorter."

"That's the last thing I want to hear right now."

At boulevard de Clichy, the southern boundary of Montmartre, he turned left so he could use his left hand to hold his painting outward, sign of its availability. Passing La Libération, Pascal's grim junk shop where the half-blind old man sold used canvases to penniless painters to reuse, he whistled a lighthearted tune to attract attention. An elderly gentleman wearing a bowler, a habitué of the Café Nouvelle-Athènes, gestured with his walking stick for him to stop.

The man glanced at the painting. "Charming. But you're too late. Pissarro has been here already. I just bought a painting from him."

"I don't believe it."

"I had to. He has such a large family, poor chap."

"So, because I've been careful to be without children, I have to starve? I'm in as bad a state as Pissarro, but no one ever says 'poor Renoir.'"

What if someone from the Salon jury saw him peddling? He'd be mortified. It would get around. They would think him pathetic, and they would be right.

He turned the painting inward and headed toward seedy rue Roche-chouart and the Cirque Fernando, a wooden tent-shaped pavilion painted in garish orange, green, and violet, and smelling of hay and horse manure. Inside, a ballerina was practicing her balance on a horse circling the ring at breakneck speed. He inquired after Clovis Sagot, a clown who dealt in paintings on the side.

"He'll be back in an hour," Mademoiselle La-La said.

He hardly recognized the well-known trapeze artist sitting on a bench, knees splayed open, in a nondescript dress instead of hanging by her teeth in an orange tutu the way Degas had painted her, like a slaugh-tered pig in a *charcuterie*. Damned rotten way to make a living.

"You can wait right here." She thrust out her breasts, patted the bench next to her, and made sloppy kissing noises, pointing with her nose to his face. "Kiss, kiss, to make it all better?"

What a tart. Her frizzy black hair, drawn into a puff like a bath sponge, wobbled on the crown of her head. He darted out the door, disgusted with her, disgusted with himself for being a cheapjack. Even Pascal, the junk dealer, didn't cart around his secondhand wares on the street.

He had an idea, one step up from peddling—Madame Camille's *crémerie* across the street from his studio. Once, just this once he'd lower himself, in order to buy colors for this painting that would change everything. And then he'd never have to do this again.

He went in. Camille looked up from drying a cup. "Auguste! What a nasty scrape. You'd think you, a painter, would have a steady hand when you shaved."

"I was in a hurry."

"And when aren't you?"

He sniffed the air. "Patchouli. Don't let your daughters wear it. That perfume makes every floozy in Montmartre smell like rancid pork rind."

"I'm sure they'll appreciate your kind advice. I have some Brie left from lunch, soft but not too runny—just the way you like it."

"Oh, no, thank you."

She leveled a look of exasperation at him. "You can't forget to eat. You're such a beanpole it breaks my heart. It won't take but a minute. Sit."

He lowered his aching body into a chair. It was amusing to watch her ratcheting herself around in the small space behind the counter to work at the stove. Nature had blessed Camille with a rotundity that was ample advertisement for her cheeses and omelettes.

"I know why you came in," she said, her back to him. "It's because now that things are more difficult, with your arm I mean, you've decided to take me seriously and marry one of my daughters." She turned around with a broad grin on her face. "Which one do you want? Marie, the seamstress, or Annette, the shoe shop girl? Either one would be a big help to you," she said in a singsong voice. "It's my dearest hope. Not because you'll secure her a prosperous future, mind you—you're a painter first, last, and always."

"Then why?"

"Because you're so irritatingly lovable. Bohemian to the core, but someday you'll outgrow that, and then you'll be a proper husband, as solid as a paving stone." She set down a heel of bread, a plate of cheese, and a *café crème* on the tin-topped table. "Stop rubbing your nose like that. It's a bad habit. It makes you look like a bundle of nerves. Who's the painting for?"

"Anybody. Would you hang it and see who might come along and want it?"

"Anything for you." She glanced at it. "So sweet. They remind me of my girls when they were that age. How much should I say?"

"If someone offers fifty francs, take it."

"Forty?"

"Take it. Even thirty. It's only a study, but don't say that."

Camille chuckled. "Just think. Me, an art dealer." Her hand rested a moment on her motherly bosom before slinging wide her arm, the flesh under her upper arm jiggling. "La Galerie de la Crème."

"I like it. I could paint a sign for you. *Crème de la Crème.*"

He finished the cheese and *café,* kissed her round cheeks, and ducked out the door. *"Au revoir, ma reine de la crème."*

He left her laughing and jiggling at the doorway.

By God, he deserved a better showcase for his work than a little neighborhood kitchen. And he'd get one too, in the Palais des Champs-Élysées where the Salon was held. He was not destined to end his days as a nobody.

Up the stairs to his studio to change into the gray pin-striped suit his father had tailored for him seven years earlier. He wanted it to last forever now that his father had passed away. He remembered his father's insistence on the highest-quality fabric, and his careful fitting. Putting it on was like donning another self for Madame Charpentier's salon, proper and elegant, someone whom his father would be proud of.

Onward to the Louvre. He bumped into people who looked aghast at his face, swerved into the street around slow walkers, dodged omnibuses, darted in front of mounted gendarmes. Pain shot down his leg. The Louvre, the Louvre.

On the way, he rang the buzzer at the office of the *Gazette des Beaux-Arts* to ask its director, Charles Ephrussi, a friend and collector, to pose. No one answered. He left a note.

He headed toward the river, passing the spot where his family used to live and have their tailor shop, next to the Roman well. As a child he loved to touch its smooth stones and imagine life in Paris so many centuries ago. Gone. Medieval Paris gone too. Razed to lay out Baron Haussmann's grand boulevards, begun under Louis Napoléon as a display of prosperity of the Empire. The new Paris was glorious, yes, but someday people would forget the crooked medieval streets, the Roman well, the history in those stones, just as people in the future would forget how Parisians lived now, and how, in spite of bad times, Paris made itself happy again. That's what he wanted his painting to be. A painting of happiness in his time.

At the Comédie-Française, the concierge recognized him from his many visits to see Jeanne, and let him in the performers' corridor. Auguste wiped sweat from his forehead. Maybe his skinned cheek and broken arm would soften her heart. He knocked at the door of her dressing room and it opened a little.

"Jeanne?" He opened it more.

A man in a crisp linen shirt lounged on the divan. His waistcoat had been flung over Jeanne's rose silk dressing gown on a chair. The memory of its coolness as he'd once slipped it off her shoulders swept over him. The man yanked a fan off the wall where Jeanne had pinned it as a decoration with dozens of others.

"She's not here. Who are you?" the man demanded, fanning himself.

"Pierre-Auguste Renoir. I've painted her many times. Even here, with that fan." He hated having to justify his presence.

The man tossed it onto her marble-topped dressing table and rummaged through her jumble of cake makeup, creams, powders, puffs, and brushes, shoving them about as if he owned them until he found a nail file and went to work on his thumbnail. "I wouldn't wait, if I were you. She doesn't want to see you."

He didn't want to get into a confrontation with this presumptuous parasite. He would not allow himself to be distracted from his focus. At the concierge's wicket, he wrote a note.

Chère Mademoiselle,
Please come to Chatou on Sunday by noon, or earlier, to Maison
Fournaise on the island. If you are willing, I have a painting in

mind that begs for your charms, a *souvenir* for future ages of life as it was lived in the summer of 1880. It is of crucial importance to me, but I can't begin it without you. The time of year forces me to start immediately. Please wear a dark blue dress for boating, and a pretty hat. Do you still have the one you wore at the Promenade de Longchamp, the felt one with feathers and gold braid that makes you look so lovely? We will be outdoors. If you have any feeling left for me, if only the fond remembrance of times past, come.

> *Je t'adore toujours,*
> Pierre-Auguste

On the bottom, he drew the hat, and folded the paper in thirds.

"Please see that Mademoiselle Samary receives this privately." He pressed a fifty-centime piece into the concierge's waiting palm.

He loped into the vast place du Carrousel surrounded by the arms of the Louvre, sacred ground for him. He'd played marbles here as a child, living in the slum of old guardhouses within the arms of the Louvre until Haussmann demolished the eyesore and moved the working class out of the heart of Paris. It grieved him that the house where he'd drawn his first real pictures, on the floor, was no more. But he had lived there long enough to know every inch of the Louvre.

Entering the ground-floor galleries, he felt the calm of the classical marble faces he had drawn as a youth, as familiar as family. He climbed two flights of stairs to the Salon Carré, hungry for what he'd come to see. Not his favorites, Ingres and Fragonard, not even Watteau, whose paintings of *fêtes galantes,* aristocrats of the last century enjoying a day of love on the wooded isle of Cythera, conveyed the mood he wanted. He had painted hundreds of ladies' fans with Watteau's romantic images of Cythera in his younger days. He didn't need to see them again. It was Veronese he needed now, to study his technical achievement.

There it was, *The Marriage Feast at Cana,* ten meters wide and nearly seven meters tall. He studied the angles of the U-shaped table positioned broadside in an outdoor pavilion with richly dressed figures bal-

anced right and left according to the Renaissance ideal, gesturing,
talking, leaning toward one another. And surrounding them—
musicians, jesters, servants, even dogs. The end of the meal, the table
opulent with goblets, grapes, sugared fruit. The wine having run out,
Christ performs his first miracle, turning the water into wine, and it
pours out ruby red from the urns. The festiveness, the wealth of orna-
ment, the splendor of the silks in aquamarine, emerald, carmine, yellow
ocher, had always astonished him.

His would use just one angle of tables. He would emulate the close
overlapping of figures, several conversations going at once, and the fore-
shortening, the most difficult perspective to achieve. He would honor
Veronese, and he would vie with him—and Watteau and Ingres and
Rubens and Fragonard and Vermeer to boot! And he would do it all in
two months. He felt hot with the pressure to get started, and to make it
the greatest figure painting of the whole Impressionist movement.

Only four more days to prepare. He needed to perform his own
miracle.

CHAPTER THREE

To the Left Bank and Back

Crossing the river on the Passerelle des Arts, Auguste was seized by a thought. He was straddling more than just the Seine. The iron and wood footbridge stretched from the Louvre on the Right Bank to the formidable, gold-ribbed dome of the Institut de France housing the Académie des Beaux-Arts on the Left Bank. The new art was a Right Bank school growing out of ragtag Montmartre and the suburban riverside to the west, as far from the classical, tradition-bound Left Bank Académie as it could get. Yet the painting that swirled in his mind, even though modern in subject, required the skill of the classicists. He felt as giddy as he had as a youth the moment before touching the first breast offered to him.

With long-legged steps, he strode through shaded streets of traditional galleries huddled around the Académie, their windows assaulting him with huge battle scenes, teary-eyed Mary Magdalenes, and Roman temples crowded with men in togas. He stopped on rue de Grenelle in front of the Charpentiers' *hôtel particulier,* a mansion eight windows wide and six stories high, all theirs, Monsieur Charpentier's publishing house on the street level, their living quarters above. Open-jawed bronze lions' heads supporting stone pediments roared their displeasure at anyone not invited. Up the marble stairway, he sounded the heavy brass knocker, another lion's head, and noticed that his right hand and wrist had swollen.

"Control your arms," his mother used to say. "Don't slouch. Tall men should use their height to advantage." He put his left arm through the sleeve of his coat and tried to drape it smoothly over his right shoulder.

Salons were a strain on him. There was an annoying proliferation of them lately, most of them hosted by Madame de-This or Madame de-That. He disdained the pretension of names with de or du, as if they were announcing their owner's pedigree like a racehorse naming his sire. Such women hosted political salons, academic salons, literary salons, romantic salons, obsequious salons, critical-of-everything salons, and salon-commentary salons.

Madame Charpentier's tended toward the theatric and literary because Monsieur Charpentier published Zola, the one man Auguste didn't want to see on the other side of this door. Conversation would veer toward Zola's review, and that could get ticklish. Madame needed to round out the arts with a painter of *la vie moderne,* the name of her husband's journal supporting the new art movement. Manet had a salon of his own, Monet was living in the country, Cézanne was in the South of France, Pissarro was too politically radical, so the position fell to him. He and Madame fed each other's ambitions. Her rooms were full of potential clients, so he'd had to learn how to be witty and gallant among the rich and talented, despite his discomfort. He was a craftsman, first and last, and never wanted to be otherwise, but a poor man can't afford shyness.

The butler ushered him in to the sound of many voices and the clink of crystal stoppers in decanters. He passed through the Japonaise room quickly where teethy stone lions were ready to gorge themselves on his thin, available arm.

Upstairs in the silk-paneled drawing room under a window frame carved in a mishmash of cupids and leaves, he spotted his favorite chair, a simple Louis Quatorze armchair with plain blue upholstery. No one ever sat in it because no one thought it would show a person to advantage. He wanted to hug the thing, but instead, he just sat down in it, crossed his legs one way, then the other, and listened to that academic painter in his outrageous plaid trousers, Carolus-Duran, plucking his guitar. Not only had he painted Jeanne in an off-the-shoulder drape, a portrait that got into the Salon and was purchased by the Comédie-Française, but the lucky devil had won the Prix de Rome! Oh, what he, Pierre-Auguste Renoir, could do with that prize, and the trip that went with it, the chance to study the Italian masters. The craving surged in him so strongly that he could taste it, like a full-bodied Chianti on the tongue. With it he could write his own ticket, paint on his own terms, whatever and however he wanted.

At the opposite end of the long room, Jules Laforgue was reading his poetry aloud. It was hard to catch the gist of it, and he doubted if others did, but they applauded when he finished, and Auguste along with them. He had to respect the man for following his own style. He wanted Jules in the painting.

A servant offered him a choice of canapés from a silver tray. He felt like packing all of them into his pockets for later. He took one and surveyed the room for people on his list. Ellen Andrée, the star mime at the Folies-Bergère, a pretty brunette who had posed for him in an elegant café. Good. Not the cachet of Jeanne Samary, a celebrated actress, but still an experienced model. Degas would rage that he stole Ellen from him. Let him stew. The cabaret singer, Yvette Guilbert? Plenty of cachet, but homely enough to sour milk. Leave her to Degas. Léon Gambetta? No. He didn't want a national leader, especially one with an eye patch.

"Pierre-Auguste! Look at you!"

He sprang up from the chair. A pain shot through his hip. Madame Charpentier swooped down on him, rustling her mauve day gown, preceded by her enormous, matronly, mesmerizing bosoms that kept coming closer and closer until they were under his nose. She scrutinized him from head to toe.

"I see that you *half* remembered to put on a frock coat this time." She offered her ruby-weighted index finger for him to kiss. "What happened?"

"I took a job as a house painter because I didn't have a sou in my pocket, but I fell off the ladder." He raised his bent right arm.

"Nonsense. Your cycling cap belies you. Don't you own a bowler?"

"Yes, but I prefer my cap." He grabbed it off his head and tried to flatten his hair over his receding hairline. What a bumpkin he was.

"I have new guests whom I'd like you to meet."

"Potential collectors?"

"Don't gawk. One is looking at you. Not a collector. A potential paramour."

"You know I can't afford one."

Over Madame's shoulder he saw her, a porcelain figurine of a woman expostulating coquettishly to Jules, with delicate hands fluttering back and forth at the wrists.

"I told her she would be fascinated by how you can shift between bohemian Montmartre and the society of Saint-Germain and the boulevards. That intrigued her, so don't disappoint me."

Heat emanated from the young woman's eyes. She smoothed her skirt so that it suggested the shape of her thigh. Such a dress. Pale yellow cupped her voluptuous breasts from below. As joyous to paint as to touch, he was sure, but a taffeta evening dress in the afternoon? The top of her sleeves increased in fullness and projected upward above her shoulder, which gave her the appearance of being permanently startled. There was something about her he couldn't detect that made him wary. Maybe it was the overlarge mouth.

"And the others?" he asked.

"As soon as they arrive I'll introduce you. Monsieur and Madame Beloir. They may be ready to commission you—portraits and something else. If they do, it will be a juicy offer. They were speaking of a series."

"Ah. I'm much obliged," he said before she slipped away to greet others.

Just when he needed money, bless her heart. He caught himself. Was he still a portrait painter, or his own man, painting what he chose? It might be possible to do both—the portraits during the week, and the painting at Maison Fournaise on Sundays. One would fund the other.

He surveyed the room. How was he to ask some of the guests to model, but not all? He tried to follow several conversations—she of the articulated wrists recounting her spring in Italy, a heavily bearded *flâ-neur* trying out his cool observations on the behavior of dancers in the Opéra loges before publishing them in a journal of Parisian life, a portly man saying under his breath, "Now is the time to buy. Even his large paintings are going cheap. I happen to know that a year from now, he'll be fetching high prices."

Puh! As if paintings were stocks or racehorses.

His portrait of Madame Charpentier and her children was hanging between two porcelain plates perched on the ornate black marble mantel. The plates interested him. Had Madame been taken in, or were they authentic Sèvres ware? His china-painting days at Monsieur Lévy's workshop beginning when he was thirteen had taught him the difference. He walked over to them, swaggering a bit remembering that he could turn out eight Marie Antoinette plates in the time other workers took to do one, and he'd gotten forty centimes apiece.

"Examining your work?" Gambetta asked.

He jerked back from a figurine. How did Gambetta know of his humble origins?

"No—that is, I was just taking a look at Madame's china."

"I meant the portrait. The glow of her flesh is positively radiant."

"I hate the word flesh. It sounds like she's a piece of Prussian meat."

"Quite right. We can't say that. Nothing Prussian," Gambetta said. "Inventive of you to have that child sitting on that Newfoundland."

"Remind me never to do another painting with a dog. They make horrible models. This one snored with such unmelodic abandon that I had to time my brushstrokes between them. Whenever one snuck up on me, I ruined something."

"Nevertheless, it's your greatest masterpiece."

"Then put it in the Louvre. You're the Ministre de l'Intérieur. Put it in the interior of the Louvre. Greatest! You think I'll never surpass it?"

"Not at all. I'm sure there are more to come."

"If you really think so, there is something you could do for me." Auguste straightened himself to his full height.

"I will if I can."

"If you could use your influence to get me a post as curator of some provincial museum, one that would pay a few hundred francs a month and not require much of my time—"

Gambetta laughed uproariously. "My dear Renoir, you talk as if you'd just been born yesterday."

Auguste fumbled with his cap.

"Ask me for a job as professor of Chinese or inspector of cemeteries— something at least that has nothing to do with your profession—then I can help you. But if I suggested a painter as a curator of a museum, I'd be laughed out of office."

He broke into a chuckle for politeness' sake. *Zut!* Such a fool he was.

Madame Charpentier strode toward him, her derrière wagging behind her, with the newly arrived couple in tow.

"Auguste, I present Monsieur and Madame Beloir."

Late middle age, genuine smiles, impeccably dressed, the wife overjeweled, the husband's eyes asymmetric, interesting. Typical pleasantries—have wanted to meet you, followed your work in the Salon, liked what we've seen, believe in you—compliments *de rigueur* before warming up to the question.

"We were quite taken with the portrait of Marguerite and her children showing the room, and we'd like to have you paint ours, showing our salon similarly, one of the two of us, and another of our daughter and her fiancé."

"As a wedding gift to them," the wife said.

"Very nice." Auguste sensed a plum.

"The wedding party will be at our estate, so we would like four murals as well," Monsieur said.

"Depicting four views of our villa." The wife's face was full of dewy-eyed hope.

"That's quite a request. When is the wedding?"

"October first," Monsieur said. "We realize there isn't much time. You'll be our guest as soon as you are free to come. That is, as soon as your arm is healed. This is not the place to discuss a fee, but be assured you will be paid handsomely."

Tempting. A solution to his money problems for the moment. But the painting he'd just persuaded himself to undertake hung in the balance. His conviction that now was the time wavered. Only seven or eight Sundays of good northern light. His obligation to support the group. The critics waiting like open-jawed lions for him to fall back to safe commissions. Pouncing on him for small ambitions. Betraying his talent. Stalling his growth with well-hammered shackles. But Madame Charpentier's solicitude for him endangered if he declined. Her continuing sponsorship threatened. All that against the pressure to make this the masterpiece that would declare to the world that he didn't need to do commissioned portraits, didn't need Madame Charpentier's good will. Was he ready for that?

"Where is the villa?" he asked.

"On a cliff overlooking the Mediterranean. Near Cézanne in Aix."

His hope crushed. Impossible to do both. He saw the painting of his heart shrivel.

"I'm sure it's beautiful. It would be a delight to paint in the South of France. I'll let you know before I leave today."

Madame Charpentier was at his elbow. "Pardon me for intruding, but I want you to meet Mademoiselle Cécile-Louise Valtesse de la Bigne."

"Excuse us," he said to Monsieur and Madame of the South.

Madame Charpentier drew him aside. "I had to interrupt when I saw you hesitate," she whispered. "If you decline such a prize, you'll be labeled as persnickety. Who will make you an offer then?"

That could mean she wouldn't recommend him to others. Declining was a rebuff to her.

Madame curled her index finger at the young lady in yellow. He watched her pop up off the sofa, fluff up the frothy cascade of white tulle at her neckline, and sashay toward him. An egg soufflé topped with meringue.

"Cécile, this is Pierre-Auguste Renoir, my court painter," she quipped. "Auguste, may I present Cécile-Louise Valtesse de la Bigne?"

"*Enchanté,* mademoiselle. You have quite a formidable name. A bit weighty for such delicate shoulders to bear."

The name smacked of invention, or purchase. Or, worse, it could have been pirated from the last son of a noble family who lost more than the name under the swift separation of the guillotine. He imagined her grandfather to be the *cordoneur* who pulled the cord that released the blade, and picked up the name as it fell.

"Most people call me Circe."

"Ah, the enchantress who turned Ulysses' men into swine. I shall have to struggle against such vulgar tendencies in this refined company."

"Auguste has the gift of being all things to all people without surrendering his own individuality," Madame Charpentier said.

"Don't lionize me, madame, or I might be forced to compete with those stone lions that are ready to devour me every time I come here."

Cécile-Louise looked at his cap. "It was generous of you to leave off *working* for this occasion."

He put it behind his back. "Only to see you, a buttercup of beauty."

"Madame tells me your paintings have been in the Salon. How lovely to be in the Salon. Wasn't it lovely, Marguerite, when monsieur's painting of you was hanging in the place of honor? The only way for me to be in the place of honor is if you'd paint me, monsieur. You're getting to be quite well known."

She turned from side to side, showing off her figure. "I hope you don't like profiles." She lifted her chin and turned her head. "I detest them. They're so skimpy. Why have half a face when you can have the whole picture?" She framed her face with her hands. "Don't you agree?"

Now he knew to trust his first impression. The mouth was the problem.

"Renoir!" Someone slapped him on the right shoulder. He winced.

"My God, Raoul. I thought you were mayoring Saigon for the Republic."

"I was, winning them over with champagne. I ordered the best. Shiploads of it. Paid for it myself. The prestige of France hung in the balance. *Voilà! Les enfants de la Patrie sont victorieux,*" he sang under his breath to the tune of "La Marseillaise." "Nothing more to do, so I came home."

"Are you free? That is, have you any commitments?"

"Commitments to pleasure, my good man. My boats, my horse racing, and, I beg your pardon, mademoiselle"—his eyebrows sprang up—"my ladies."

"In that order?"

"On most days, at least for now. The regatta's coming up."

"Don't you have to work?"

"I'm on a pension for injuries under the Empire."

Auguste cuffed him on the chest. "Good for you!"

The moment of decision.

What if Monsieur and Madame Beloir turned out to be disagreeable? He'd kick himself for making the safe decision and wasting the good summer light on the Seine by doing portraits. But if the Chatou painting turned out to be a disaster, his reputation would plummet, his confidence would crumple, and he'd kick himself for declining the offer. Southern light was magical, according to Cézanne. He could paint with him there. He'd never been to the South of France. Painting new motifs might satisfy his restlessness. But the motif of the terrace he was building in his mind would be hugely satisfying.

The man of genius has not yet arisen. It was more than just proving Zola wrong. It was a matter of self-respect. Of respect for his own development. If he abandoned the Maison Fournaise painting, how would he think of himself?

As a coward!

"I have a little project, Raoul. Excuse us," he said to Cécile-Louise, who pulled her shoulders back at the affront.

He drew Raoul away, toward Ellen Andrée, and noticed that Raoul's lurching gait was more pronounced now. "Ellen, a delight to see you. May I present the Baron Raoul Barbier, cavalry officer, war hero, statesman, bon vivant?"

"We've just met."

"Good. I was quite taken with your pantomime of the ferryman's daughter in the Folies-Bergère," Auguste said.

"It was only a *divertissement.*"

"Ah, but how you played it! Charming. Gambetta should make the government subsidize the Folies instead of the Comédie-Française."

"I disagree. A national theater for the classics is far more deserving than the popularist entertainments at the Folies."

Her small lips came together primly, definitively, a perfect fit. He patted her cheek. "I wasn't serious."

He beckoned to Jules Laforgue and spoke to the three of them, Jules, Raoul, and Ellen, in a low voice. "I have a project that might happily involve the three of you, if you consent. A painting for which I need about a dozen people to model. At Chatou, the Maison Fournaise. Do you know it?"

He could hardly believe what he was saying. Twenty-four hours ago he would have shouted across the room to Monsieur and Madame Beloir, *Yes, yes! The South of France. I'll do it. Give me an hour to pack.*

"I know La Maison Fournaise," Cécile-Louise said, gliding up to them. *Sacrebleu!* Ears to match her mouth.

"It's a pretty setting by the river," Cécile-Louise said. "I insist on being there too. Marguerite, don't you agree that I should be?"

Madame Charpentier drew in her double chin. "It would be nice if you consented, Auguste."

He felt the room spinning. Or was it his brain? "This isn't a group portrait. It's a scene, a moment in modern life."

"All the better. I am, I must say, a modern woman."

Ellen rolled her eyes. "I'll be happy to help you," she said, "just so you don't paint me as an absinthe-sotted waif like Edgar Degas did."

"No, Ellen. I'm not a *flâneur* making harsh observations on society. It will just be a joyful moment in a beautiful day."

"My mother saw Degas' painting and hasn't trusted me since. I said I was acting. 'All the worse,' she said, 'elevating make-believe depravity to art.'"

"This one she will love, I promise you."

"When would you like us?"

"Sunday, at noon, for luncheon on the terrace. Several Sundays."

"Oh." Ellen's face clouded. "I'll have to leave by five or six. I have performances on Sunday nights."

"We'll have you off in good time. If you'd like to go boating before lunch, I'll make sure there are rowing yoles saved for you."

"I'll sail there from Argenteuil," the baron said, "and take you out for a boating party. My new sloop, *Le Capitaine,* flies faster than wind."

Auguste felt a sinking in his chest at this threat to Gustave at the helm of his *Iris.* "A thoroughbred of the river, I'm sure."

"Or maybe I'll use *Nana* and keep you in suspense about *Le Capitaine.*"

"It will be a privilege to be in on a painting of yours from the start," Jules said.

Auguste gave his thanks and Madame Charpentier drew him aside behind an enormous dahlia plant in a Chinese jardiniere and whispered, "You've made your decision, then."

"Yes."

"And you're going to leave it for me to tell them?"

"No. I'll tell them."

"You must ask Jeanne to be in it. Her cachet will smooth the way into the Salon."

"I already have, though I doubt that she'll pose. She hated my full-length portrait of her."

In a flash of memory he saw the shimmering white gown with a train, the white satin slipper peeking out from her hemline, her white-gloved hands holding a handkerchief, her lips parted sensuously—every detail an injury to him now.

"How could she hate it? It's a masterpiece."

"She said it would do nothing for her reputation."

"She would have liked it well enough if it had been hung where Sarah Bernhardt's was."

"The truth is, she's left me for more academic painters. They'll present her identifiably in her theatrical roles to advance her career, something I wouldn't do. I'm not an advertiser."

"Left you? Completely? In all ways?"

"I thought you, all-wise and all-knowing woman of society, would already know." Auguste brushed his left palm down his pant leg as though smoothing a wrinkle. "When a lady and I go our separate ways, it's been my custom to paint her one last time, and give it to her as a *souvenir d'amour.* She condescended to let me, but then she didn't even want it."

Madame's quiet, sudden intake of breath gave him a fleeting consolation.

She patted his cast. "Perhaps a word from me might bring her around—to model for you, I mean. This Sunday, you say?"

Renoir nodded. "I'd be much obliged."

"That means, of course, that you will take Cécile-Louise too."

His head snapped up to see her eyes, hard as the diamonds at her throat.

"No."

"You're rejecting two of my offerings? Auguste, you're middle-aged now."

"Sounds like you're talking about a cheese."

"You've been labeled as a philanderer, running with one model after another. If you persist in this profligate life, you'll be called worse things. Marriage is the most crucial social institution in France today, to re-people the Republic—"

He guffawed at the leap in her conversation.

"And if you're seen much longer in your perverse denial of the call of the Republic, no amount of beautiful paintings will touch the walls of the Salon or the drawing rooms in the better quarters. Find someone, Auguste. Fall in love and marry."

"It's not that I don't want to be in love, but marriage is something else completely."

He saw himself in Madame Charpentier's eyes, nearing forty and already brittle in his bones, his forehead as high as the grand boulevards were wide, still trying to charm women a decade or two younger. Pathetic, maybe. But a philanderer? He refused to accept that.

"I'm urging unmarried women to marry also, so they won't fall to the province of the *demi-monde*. If Jeanne has truly left you, then consider Cécile-Louise. She is full of money, and owns a mansion on Île Saint-Louis."

"Hm. Inherited?"

Madame pursed her lips. "Acquired. Not by marriage. By social contract."

Wasn't that the *demi-monde,* living off a man? "The man still lurking?"

"Conveniently dead. A duel. Auguste, such a match would leave you free to paint whatever and however you want."

"I don't even know her."

"Ah, but you will, *n'est-ce pas,* when she poses for you?"

"You forget. One of my rules is never to do anything out of any impulse other than pleasure."

She laughed outright at that. "Then take your pleasure in her."

He wanted to be stubborn, to show her that he had some self-respect, and that she didn't have him in her pocket. She looked at him with the stern expectation of a mother. He pulled his shoulders back. The right one twinged.

"*D'accord.* I'll let her pose. That's all I promise."

"And shall I give Monsieur and Madame Beloir your regrets?"

"Please."

A yellow glow poured out the windows of the Café Nouvelle-Athènes, the triangular-shaped building jutting like a white nose into place Pigalle at the foot of Montmartre. Pigalle, center for nightlife, for rendezvous at the fountain, for a vibrant mix of high and low culture. With any luck, Angèle would be in the café, one more model, one of the best.

The etched glass door scraped against the sand on the floor as he entered. The place smelled like cigarettes, garlic, and cognac. Auguste nodded to Edgar Degas, who did the same from his own table behind the glass partition surrounded by his ducklings who never challenged him, Forain, Raffaëlli, and Bracquemond. Paul Lhôte was hunched over a sheaf of papers at his regular table forward of the glass partition near the front windows.

"Clean your glasses, Paul, and you'll see better," Auguste said.

Paul shook his head. "You just can't stay off that *engin de catastrophe,* can you? At least this time you didn't break your other arm."

Auguste sat down next to him. "I need your help."

"Fine, but right now I'm writing a story," Paul said.

"Ah. In the heart of every Paris clerk lurks a fiction writer."

"It's called 'Mademoiselle Zélia.'"

Auguste sat down. *"La belle Zélia. Une Montmartroise?"*

Paul nodded, dipping his pointed nose down to his paper and writing.

"She's got to be beautiful, right? And pale, though capable of feverish gaiety. Just the way we like them. Is she someone I know?"

"No."

"How about this?" Auguste breathed in loudly, pulling together his nostrils, and gazed up at the ceiling, water-stained in familiar shapes— a cumulus cloud, a violin, a breast. "She was waltzing in a delicious yellow gown, in the arms of a dark-haired stranger with the air of an oarsman."

"You dunce. It's about you. But the character's name is Resmer, a painter who paints in the overgrown garden of a run-down house on the Butte."

"Ah, the rue Cortot, my old street."

"And he's feeding her wine-soaked *galettes* and trying to convince her to model for him."

"Nude, I hope. There's nothing as delectable as a dimpled buttock, unless it's a dimpled breast."

"It takes place at Le Moulin de la Galette."

"What I have in mind takes place at La Maison Fournaise. Sunday. How many sentences do I have to contribute to equal you posing for a painting?"

Paul scratched something out. "Don't talk. I'm trying to write."

"Trying, that's what we do in Montmartre. We try to write, like Duret, or we try to compose, like Cabaner, or we try to paint, like Cordey. To be a Montmartrois is to be a trier. And if we fail, we mope in a café or rage or drown ourselves in absinthe, and then we try again. We're a village of triers."

Paul took a long draught of his amber bock. Auguste rolled a cigarette, lit it, and doodled on the marble table with the burnt-out match.

"Give me two pieces of paper, will you?" Auguste asked. He leaned forward and wrote to a rich collector who had become a friend.

Cher Monsieur Bérard,

    I trust that you are in the best of health in those fresh sea breezes of Normandy. As for me, I have taken upon myself the task to answer Zola's criticism of the latest Impressionist show, particularly the charge that no masterpiece of complexity and thoughtful preparation has been painted in the Impressionist vein. I'm going to paint boaters on the terrace of La Maison Fournaise in Chatou, which I've been itching to do for years. I'm getting on, and I don't want to postpone this little celebration of *la vie moderne* for which I might not be able to meet the expenses later. Even if the cost prevents me from finishing, it will teach me something.

    You know that I'm grateful for the commissions you have given me in the past, but I may find myself in need of money for this new, uncommissioned endeavor. I thought it best to alert you ahead of any prospective point of desperation. From time to time, a man has to attempt things that are beyond his capacities.

    Please give my regards to Madame Bérard and the children.

Ever yours,

A. Renoir

He wrote a similar note to Charles Deudon. He hated this kind of letter-writing, laying the groundwork to hit them up for money later. He had some misgivings. Bérard had bought seventeen paintings from him last year and only three this year. If he had said yes to the Beloirs at Madame Charpentier's salon, he wouldn't have to write such letters.

"Have you read Zola's review of the last Impressionist show?" Auguste asked. "He blasts us for not producing a masterpiece. He who championed us from the start."

"You've got it in your head that he approves of the Impressionist style. He doesn't give a flap about style. He supported you just because you're insurrectionists, and because your subject matter is proletariat."

"I swear, this painting will make his head spin. Will you be there or not? Every Sunday for a while. No wild doings to interfere. No stowing away to Africa until I'm finished. No disappearing down in the catacombs."

Paul ran his hand through his hair and leaned back. "Are you going to ask that Valadon girl to pose too? Marie Clémentine?"

Auguste spoke in a low voice. "And bring down Degas' wrath? He thinks he owns her because he put a brush in her hand after she left the circus."

"I thought that was Puvis de Chavannes," Paul said.

"Maybe he did too, after he put his pubis there. Pubis de Chavannes, painter of stiffs. No doubt they both exercised themselves on her. No, I'm not dawdling after her. She's only a girl. What do you take me for, a philanderer?" Paul chortled. "Will you be there anyway?"

"Yes." Paul peered at his pages. "Just leave me alone now. It's coming."

"Then let it come and come again." Renoir snickered and snapped his finger against Paul's shoulder as he stood up. "Come early if you want to take out a girl in a yole. Bring Pierre Lestringuèz, to keep you in line. There'll be plenty of boats."

He stood to leave and Edgar Degas hailed him. My God. He couldn't have heard him. Auguste went over to his table.

"Look here, Renoir," Degas said without a smile, his mustache and his shoulders drooping, permanently tired. "I'm starting a new magazine, *Le Jour et la Nuit,* entirely made up of lithographs depicting society in the style of Realism. Lithography is the new way to advertise your work. Forain and Bracquemond here have already submitted. You're welcome to submit too."

The false ring to Degas' invitation made him sense a trap being laid.

"All in the style of Realism, mind you. Nothing false. You embellish your models because you can't stand ugliness, and it's a deception, an offense against reality. If a woman has a horsey jaw, give it to us that way."

"Or if a man has a bloody cheek," Forain said, looking him over curiously.

"What we're after is the truth of life," Degas said.

"Prettiness is truth too. You've painted plenty of pretty dancers."

"This is a journal of modern life," Raffaëlli said with the smug assurance that he was Degas' favorite. "So the subjects are café scenes of solitary down-and-outs, beggars at train stations, ragpickers in the Maquis, old men crippled in the war. That's modern life."

"If you want to preach, young man, you ought to wear some kind of clerical costume so people would be warned. In my mind, there are too many unpleasant things in life as it is without creating still more of them. I hate *le misérabilisme*. I'm in the shining business, not the darkening business."

"Still doing commissioned portraits, then," Degas said, taking charge again. "Prettying up your sitters so their husbands will throw their money at you. Renoir, you have no character at all to continue churning them out."

"There's character in paying my own way and in painting my own way. I won't have my motifs assigned. I'm not some student, if you haven't noticed."

"We certainly didn't notice you at the last Impressionist show."

"I would have been noticed there as well as at the Salon if it weren't for your arbitrary rules."

"Raffaëlli here made an astonishing showing," Degas said.

"So I've heard." He gave him a nod as recognition.

Degas smoothed his grizzled beard the way he always did before pontificating. "Thirty-six works to your two that the Salon allows. Not that your two weren't good paintings, but hung so badly among thousands that they were wasted. You're making a mistake casting your net there."

"Several hundred thousand people come to the Salon compared to our three thousand in a good year. I go where I'm likely to be more noticed."

"And betray the group with your selfishness in the process."

A hot brand in his gut, that accusation.

"Fine, fine. Think whatever way you will. Good evening."

He went out into the warm night. Two prostitutes on the café terrace looked like Degas' marvelous pastel come to life. Inadvertently, he caught the eye of one of them in the yellow light from the window. A pitifully hopeful expression played across her lips. She was trying too. He passed her by.

No, it wasn't a hot brand. It was a setup. Degas knew he wouldn't want to submit to the magazine under those terms. The prickly bastard just wanted an argument. The group was in trouble.

Fatigue suddenly weighed him down. He dragged himself the four blocks to his studio and lay down on his narrow bed. His whole body throbbed. He had six, nine if Charles Ephrussi, Pierre Lestringuèz, and Jeanne would come. He needed a few more. He thought how good the day had been, on the whole, how different he was this night compared to the night before. Something miraculous *had* happened. He closed his eyes. It had been a long day.

Chapter Four

Reflections on the Seine

Alphonsine finished the week's accounting in her father's office and slapped the ledger closed. Normally she was content doing this task as she'd done in the hat shop in Paris, but today she thought, I have more appealing things to do—preparation for the painting-that-is-to-be.

She would not be just the hostess of the restaurant, as usual, but hostess to the birth of a painting. A midwife. She wanted everything perfect—the weather, the light on the water, the fruit on the table, the dessert. If she picked pears today, by Sunday they would be golden streaked with bronze, with a pleasant tang. Auguste might want to paint them. She had river errands to do. She went to the oar shed for her paddle, basket, and collecting can, and lowered them into a *périssoire* at the dock.

She pushed off. It happened to be her favorite *périssoire,* not because of anything about the boat. All their *périssoires* were nearly the same—long, wooden, needle-nosed boats with open hulls for one person using a doubled-bladed paddle. Their narrowness made them precarious for first-timers, but she had navigated the river in them for twenty years. It was her favorite because of its name. *Aurore.* Dawn. Full of promise.

The painting-that-is-to-be was full of promise too. All the models to get to know. A chance to make real friends, not just day-trippers out for an afternoon affair in the country with any *grenouille,* any of the easy country girls of La Grenouillère who lifted their skirts and spread their knees like a frog to attract hungry young men eager to lie on the bank with them.

She paddled out beyond Restaurant Lemaire on the northern point of the narrow island. Here commercial traffic wasn't separated from pleasure boating. If she kept paddling up the big north loop, rounded it, and turned south along the Bois de Boulogne, then rounded the south loop, she'd eventually be in Paris, but she doubted if anyone had done that in a *périssoire*.

Once, when she was a little girl, her brother had lifted a stone and pointed to a worm curved into three loops. "Look, it's the Seine," Alphonse had said.

"No, *imbécile*. It's a worm," she'd insisted.

"It's the river. The river's a worm."

That a worm could be a worm and a river, or that a single word could signify a worm as well as a river, was devious trickery. Her eyes told her it was only a worm, and she'd stubbornly held to that, stamping her feet, until he made their father show them a map. It was as Alphonse had said. For calling him names, Papa had given her the task of memorizing the river towns from the two that their island straddled, Chatou on the west bank and Rueil on the east bank, all the way to Paris. But knowing their names was less momentous than realizing that a person could look at one thing and see another or call it another. That was something truly thrilling. From then on, she'd felt justified in thinking of boats as wooden shoes, lily pads as frogs' beds, and white fungi on trees as nature's meringues.

Now she conjured an image of the river as a blue-green ribbon tying the Maison Fournaise to Paris, not in a direct line as the train would go from Rueil-Malmaison, but meandering through loops of memory beginning with childhood here, school in Paris, and Louis, then through the time of peril to the eventual and permanent locking of the shop door behind her.

Or the river was a cord plaited of many strands, as when slivers of islands like theirs divide the water for a time to reunite with its remembered self downstream, as friends separated for many years finally reuniting, flowing calmly, evaporating into fog, clouds, rain that would make puddles, rivulets, brooks, streams, the Marne, the Aube, the Oise, all joining the mighty Seine, until Le Havre and the sea, where the water evaporated again into fog, clouds, rain. Rain that could fall in other streams going to other rivers, the Loire, the Rhône, the Rhine. The Rhine, the river of the land of the Prussian. She trailed her hand in the water that might go anywhere, like a thought.

She stayed close to the bank where there was hardly any current moving against her and the midsummer foliage overhead gave her shade and turned the water green. Under the sycamore boughs, she looked for marsh peppermint to make a wreath for Auguste's luncheon on Sunday. When it was dry, it had a piquant, minty fragrance that might mask the occasional smell from the sewage plant upriver in Asnières. She wanted their day to be lovely in all ways so their pleasure would show on their faces for him to paint.

Not that the Seine in Paris didn't have its own pleasures. For six years, she and Louis had enjoyed them when they lived there as a young married couple ambling along the quays watching sunlight dance on water, or cooling themselves in the shade of the towers of Notre Dame stretching to the opposite bank in the afternoons. She loved the flower sellers on the Île de la Cité, the Sunday bird market with hundreds of beaks twittering at once, the floating bathhouses, the café-concert barges sending intoxicating music across the water, the roasted chestnut sellers standing over their braziers in front of Notre Dame in winter, the *bouquinistes* tending their green metal display boxes attached to the quay walls where she had bought used books—Hugo, Flaubert, Zola, Guy de Maupassant, George Sand. Life was full then, with theater, opera, the Universal Exposition, the annual painting Salon, the Salon des Refusés of new painters, scores of journals and fashion magazines, and Louis.

One day along the Quai du Louvre, she had pinched off a three-pointed leaf from a plane tree. "It's an amphibian's foot," she had said, and walked it up Louis's arm. On Pont Neuf, she had leaned over a rounded parapet and dropped it. She darted across to the other wall of the bridge to watch it appear and float downstream.

"How long do you think it will take to float the loops and crawl up on the bank at Maison Fournaise?" she had asked.

Louis had laughed at her notion, and drew her tight against him, and said, prophetically, it seemed to her now, "There's no guarantee, Alphonsine. One can never be sure of arriving home again."

She'd kept her fantasies to herself the rest of the afternoon. They were the stuff of books, not to be shared. Darkness came over her as it came over the city and the river. The light of the gas lamps quivered double, once on their street posts on the Quai des Tuileries, and again in the water, more violently, flame-colored strips of silk blazing the river. Or giant golden fish angrily lashing their long tails, she'd thought, but didn't say.

She *had* arrived home again, to the island of Chatou, after the Prussian Siege of Paris, after the Commune, after she had sold the shop. She'd had enough of looking across the dinner table at an empty chair. On the bank in front of the Maison Fournaise, she had put her hands in the river, hands that had sewn flesh, washing them.

And the day before yesterday, she had washed Auguste's raw flesh. A woman couldn't do that for a man without feeling an intimacy. His was the same inside, oozing red, and when she daubed it, for a second that fish-white raw skin was clean, and then the pinpricks of red came again, and spread until they joined. Auguste had a touch of that same helplessness too, the same endearing surrender. She had felt the possibility of being close to him then, close and needed, just as she had felt during the Siege before she knew him. She would do all she could to feel that again.

Now, alongside the *périssoire,* she spotted a spread of peppermint with pale lilac flowers just out of reach. She took off her canvas boating shoes and tied up her skirt. As she stepped onto the cool mud, a tug pulling a coal barge tooted. The sound vibrated through her chest, startling her. She slipped on the gooey mud and righted herself with a splash that dirtied her skirt. "Idiot! Now look what you've done!" she yelled. She could see the pilot laughing. He'd done it on purpose, just to let her know he was watching her.

She picked her way to the peppermint clumps and yanked. Two small green frogs jumped away. Several plants came out, roots and all. Plenty for a wreath.

On the far bank beyond a sawmill, asparagus fields alternated with chalk quarries cut into the hillside in yellow squares like a patchwork quilt. And there, just what she was hoping for, the orchardist's little boy was playing by the landing. She paddled diagonally across the river and got out.

"*Bonjour,* Benoît. What are you doing this morning?"

He knelt alongside a gurgling rill, his small hands and pant legs muddy. He stood back and pointed. "I'm making a dam and a lock."

"Aha. You are an engineer! And when you finish, what will you make?"

He pointed to a cleared patch near the rill. "The locksman's house."

"Then you are an architect. What will it be made of?"

He gave her a look as though he couldn't imagine that anyone could be so dumb. "Mud." He packed some into a square to show her.

Here was a child who could surely look at a leaf and see the foot of a frog. "And then what will you make?"

"A factory."

"Ah, you are a man of the modern age."

He scratched the side of his face in perplexity, leaving a muddy smear.

She showed him three twenty-centime pieces. "May I pick some pears? Will you give these to your papa? Here, let me put them in your pocket."

He thrust out his little chest. She picked according to beauty as well as ripeness, filling her basket.

"Don't forget to give your papa the money."

"I have to finish the dam first."

"Don't go too close to the river. It goes faster than it looks."

"Only on the top, my papa said."

She paddled on past the laundry barge at Bezons toward Argenteuil, where the sailing regattas were held. A dark blue sailboat with a red horizontal stripe cut through the water at a tremendous speed. *Le Capitaine,* she read on the stern. She didn't recognize it, but the marina at Argenteuil had two hundred boats. This one would be a tough rival for

Gustave. She kept a sharp lookout for his boats, the *Iris* and the *Inès*. It would be a stroke of luck if she saw him.

The clanking and screeching of the tall steam dredge disturbed her. It was an ugly machine, looking like an enormous, relentless praying mantis. The chain crawled up the framework, hauling up rectangular buckets of sand and depositing them onto heaps on the bank in order to deepen the channel. She looked away from what that mechanical monster might be dredging up.

She passed the rubber factory that looked like her school in Paris if it weren't for the smokestack, and the Joly iron foundry that made parts of railroad bridges and their own decorative half arches that held up the terrace of Maison Fournaise. Alexander, the Russian engineer, had asked her to go with him and her father to see the first one being made here. His excited eyes had looked at her for approval as much as at her father. And now Auguste was going to paint on that terrace. Strange how a dead man was part of the painting.

Up ahead, the *Iris* was sailing her way. She raised her paddle above her head with both hands to hail him. Gustave saw her and let the sails luff.

"Did you see that dark blue sailboat with a red stripe? *Le Capitaine?*"

"Yes, I saw it," he said.

"Will you be able to beat it in the regatta?"

"Depends."

His boat was passing her. She turned. "On what?"

"On whom you'll be cheering for."

"You, of course!"

Gustave grinned. "Then that settles it."

He sheeted in, his sail filled, and he was gone. Surely he'd be in the painting.

Her arms were tired now so she tied the boat to a tree and walked, looking for the weeping willow that marked the way to the secret place where there would still be raspberries to pick. They grew over the ruins of the convent where Héloïse was taken by her secret lover, Peter Abelard, seven centuries ago.

She had bought an old book of Héloïse's letters at a *bouquiniste* along the Seine. Héloïse addressed him as *my only love.* What an inconceivable promise was contained in that. Fifteen years without a word from him and she still affirmed her devotion, her need for his affection, and even for sexual intimacy despite the vows she'd taken at this very convent. *To him who is specially hers, from she who is singularly his,* Héloïse had written. When she was younger, she had thought Héloïse's fidelity honorable, but was fidelity to a memory as important for a widow now as it used to be? This was *la vie moderne.*

There was the willow with its reverse image in the water. Behind the green veil of its trailing branches, mallards quacked at the intrusion, a loud hoarse quack, followed by softer sounds diminishing into a muttered "qua," as if grudgingly resigned to her presence. She walked up the incline. Hidden behind a thicket of hedge nettles, the ruin wasn't known by Sunday crowds. The raspberry vines had threaded themselves like a net over the remains of a stone wall she imagined to be the wall of the refectory where Héloïse and Peter had stolen away between the offices of compline and vigils for their mad, happy feast of love.

She plucked a raspberry. Sweet juice, sweet pleasure. Within that tangle of tendrils, inside a blossom, a tiny bead was kissed and blessed by the sun, from which it took in light and warmth and heaven's rain imbued with the richness of the soil of France. All of the elements of the river world helped that bead to expand and multiply into sheer casings for sweet pulp, wedged together in a knobby globe until it released its juice in her mouth.

The urge to gorge herself flooded her. She plucked and ate until her fingers were red from juice and the backs of her hands were scratched with a web of red threads. Plenty for two *feuilletés aux framboises,* one pie for each table on Sunday. When the models would eat them, they would be blessed with all of the elements of earth and sky and water, all the goodness of this river world. The sweet, sharp taste would kiss their tongues, and that would be Héloïse's blessing on them, but it would be her own blessing on the painting.

Chapter Five

Colors, Credos, and Cracks

La Crémerie de Camille was crowded with young women chatting over their *café au lait* before heading to work at milliners' shops or dressmakers' lofts or laundries. Auguste greeted Aline, a seamstress with a Burgundian accent and a creamy complexion, and Géraldine, a pork butcher's assistant with a meaty fragrance but with a silk rosebud pinned to her gray frock. There was no room at their table, so he sat with a plasterer downing a *mazagran,* cold black coffee and seltzer water, remedy for a hangover. His painting still hung on the wall. He drank his *café* slowly, planning. Colors, canvas, and Gustave.

If he had to pay for his paints he wouldn't be able to pay for his models. If he paid his models, how would he pay for Mère Fournaise's luncheon and the wine that would make them relaxed and convivial, the mood he wanted to paint? If he paid them this Sunday, he couldn't pay them the next Sunday. What would it cost to feed a dozen people and let the wine flow? Eighty francs? Ninety? He had seven weeks to do the painting, if he counted the Saturday before the Fêtes. Six hundred francs for their meals, eight hundred more in models' fees, maybe three hundred in supplies. Impossible! He'd have to go to Tanguy for his colors even though Mullard's colors were truer, but Mullard wouldn't let him buy on credit.

Aline giggled. "You look like a gander worrying after his goose."

"Better that than a porcupine cozying up to his porcupinette," he said. Outside, he fell into step with Aline and Géraldine.

"Where are you going this fine morning?" Aline asked.

"To Père Tanguy's on rue Clauzel."

"That funny little man in the painters' store?" Géraldine asked.

"Funny only on the surface. Julien Tanguy is the patron saint of every poor artist in Montmartre. You're too young to know this, but Julien was on sentry duty up on the Butte during the Commune when a squadron of Versaillais descended on his post. He dropped his musket and held up his hands in surrender. He just couldn't fire on another human being. He was imprisoned for treason for three years. That's what gave him sad eyes and a soft heart."

"Who would have thought?" Without a hint of interest, Géraldine turned into the butcher's narrow courtyard overgrown with Virginia creeper. A pig, still dripping, hung by its hind legs. Géraldine picked a sprig of yellow blossoms and poked it in the creature's anus before she went into the butcher shop. Now, that was something Gustave would paint—an oddity of Parisian life.

"It must have been awful, being in prison," Aline said. "He's always nice to us." She dodged a troop of girls coming out of the school across from Julien Tanguy's shop.

Auguste said goodbye to her and opened the door. A bell jingled merrily. Tanguy turned toward him, buttons straining, and screwed up his puffy face. "Auguste! Whatever happened to you?"

"I fell off my steam-cycle." Auguste looked around the walls above the shelves hung with paintings edge to edge all the way to the ceiling. "I see Cézanne sent you some new paintings."

Julien pulled him deep into the narrow shop. "Look at this one! Montagne Sainte-Victoire on a spring morning. Magnificent. Cézanne's a genius."

"How many of his Sainte-Victoires do you have now?"

"Four. One for each season of the year." Tanguy spread his arms wide, and the furrows stretching down from his round nostrils curved into a euphoric smile above his stubby yellowish beard. "I have the best job in the world. How else would a poor man be able to live with paintings like these?"

"Seven!" Madame Tanguy said, pushing aside the curtain of the back room. She yanked her crocheted shawl across her ample figure. "The man's crazy."

"Who? Cézanne or Julien?"

"Both of them. *Grâce à Dieu,* I only have to live with one of them."

"And a very fine man he is," Auguste added, winking at Julien.

"So there!" Tanguy gave a sharp nod to his wife and turned back to Auguste. "What can I do for you today?"

"I need a roll of fine-weave linen, primed. As wide as you've got."

"One hundred thirty-five centimeters. Widest standard."

"Give me a hundred ninety centimeters of it. And stretchers."

"The largest I have is a number one-twenty."

"For one painting?" Madame asked. "That's nearly as tall as you are."

True. He could hardly believe what he'd said. "That'll be the width."

"You'll need cross braces for a painting that size," Tanguy said. He took off his straw farmer's hat and scratched his head, motioning to the cast. "How can you paint?"

"I can paint. I'm ambidextrous."

"Never heard of a painter who could paint with both hands. Show me." He pushed paper and pencil across the counter where Auguste sat on a tall stool.

"Anyone who writes with his left hand is the devil's accomplice," Madame said. "What's your hurry? Why don't you wait until you get that thing off?"

"The light. It's a painting of *canotiers* on a riverside terrace. In two months the good light on the Seine will be gone by four o'clock."

The bell jingled and a young woman came in with three girls trailing behind her. Auguste jerked to attention. Blond hair hung loose from her chignon, and her slender neck had a patrician quality. Using his left hand, he drew her in profile as she looked at a display of colored chalk.

Madame Tanguy pursed her lips as he worked.

"It's amusing to draw left-handed. My strokes go the opposite way. Hm. This might even be better than what I could do with my right."

"Sign it," Madame commanded, tapping the paper with her fingernail stained green from grinding pigments. "Someday, when you're famous and we're on our deathbeds, we'll sell it, and get back a fraction of what you owe us."

He signed it, "The Devil and A. Renoir."

He held the roll of canvas taut for Julien as the big shears opened and closed, advancing toward him with a rasping noise like a mechanical fish about to bite his fingers.

"That's twenty francs fifteen," Madame said. "You're going to need a lot of paint for a canvas that size. I don't see your pocket bulging."

"Never mind, Fionie. He'll die if he doesn't paint," Tanguy said as he rolled the canvas around the stretchers and tied it with a cord.

The young woman chose her chalk and a colored pencil for each of the girls, and approached the counter.

"You're a teacher at the girls' school, aren't you? Here, look at this." Madame showed her the drawing. "Monsieur Renoir is a very famous painter. Everyone in Paris knows him. Wouldn't you like this?"

The girls crowded around to look. "Buy it. Buy it," they chorused.

The young woman couldn't keep back a modest smile.

"Ten francs," Madame said.

"Oh." She shook her head. "Just the chalk and the pencils, please."

"Five," Julien said.

The girls hopped up and down.

"Three," Julien said.

She blushed modestly, looking at her image. "I suppose."

One girl tugged at her arm and whispered something to her.

"Would Monsieur draw the girls too?" she asked. "One franc each?"

"Yes, he will," Madame snapped, and laid out three pieces of paper.

Amused, he said, "There's nothing I'd like better," and went to work.

"Please, if you would just sign them 'A. Renoir,' that would be lovely," the young lady said.

When he finished, the teacher slid the coins across the counter and Madame scooped them up, dropped them in the cash box and slammed the lid. "Come in again, dear. Bring in your other pupils."

Julien smiled with his wide blue eyes, wide nostrils, and wide lips, a face in harmony with itself, elfish and pleased that he knew enough to set a tube of cobalt blue on the counter. "What other colors do you need?"

"A far sight more than six francs' worth, I'm afraid."

"Name them."

"Flake white, large."

"That's six francs fifty already," Madame said.

"Two tubes?" Tanguy asked.

"One for now. Chrome yellow, vermilion, rose madder, Veronese green, emerald, cobalt, ultramarine blue large, Prussian blue."

"No. I will not sell you Prussian blue."

"Julien, it's only a name. You don't have to prove your principles."

"I spit on anything Prussian. Arrogant brutes, commandeering Pissarro's house during the war. Walking on his paintings so they wouldn't muddy their boots." His face tightened with pain. "Only forty canvases saved of fifteen hundred. And squeezing our national treasury for war reparations. Inhuman."

"France paid every last franc. Five billion! And ahead of time too!" Madame said, beady-eyed, her chin thrust in Auguste's direction. "How's that for principles?"

"No Prussian blue," Tanguy said. "To foreigners, I sell it. To amateurs too. But I will not have Prussian blue in the Louvre!"

Auguste chortled. "You're sure of where this is going, then, are you?"

"*Bien sûr!*" He folded his arms across his chest. "You know what it's made of? Blood, flesh, bone-black, soot. I won't have those disgusting things on your French painting! Use *French* ultramarine."

"I will, for some things, but I also need that inky quality of Prussian blue. The *canotières* will be in dark blue dresses."

"You never had it in your palette before," Julien said.

"I never had so many *canotières* in one painting before. You wouldn't want them undressed, would you?"

"Use cobalt."

"Too transparent. It has a greenish undertone. I need the finest grade of Prussian blue, well washed to keep it from fading."

"Non!" He put his hands on his hips. *"C'est final!"*

Tanguy picked the other tubes off the shelf, holding them all against his chest. "You don't need burnt sienna or burnt umber?"

"I can make them with these."

"These won't last for a painting that large. Come back when you need more," Tanguy said.

Madame Tanguy blew out a breath that lifted the lank brown bangs on her forehead. "Don't glop it on like Claude does and you won't need so much."

"What's the condition of your brushes?" Tanguy asked.

"He likes his old ones," Madame said, thrusting out her jaw.

The perfect Xantippe, Auguste thought. As commanding as Socrates' wife.

"You can't paint a masterpiece with brushes worn down to the nubs. You need to start fresh, with no residual color."

"They won't feel like mine."

"You'll make them your own in no time. Don't scrimp on this."

"You remind me of my father's friend, the assistant of Sanson, the state executioner during the Revolution. When I was a boy the old man and my father liked to say that one of them cut out cloth, the other cut off heads. One needed sharp scissors, the other a sharp guillotine blade. Their nonchalance shocked me then, but they agreed on the vital importance of a workman's tools."

"So, there you have it. What do you need? A filbert?"

"Yes, in marten hair, number oh-two, and two hog's hair, wide and medium."

"I give you the best, two Isabeys, made with great care by Bretons, my countrymen."

While Tanguy was getting them, Madame darted behind the curtain a moment and then turned her back to wrap the tubes in newspaper and tie them with string. "If you can't pay, at least you can bring us a buyer for these Cézannes, another one like Monsieur Chocquet."

Julien patted her arm. "Don't worry, Fionie. The amateurs who will disappear in ten years, I make them pay up front."

Auguste placed two ten-franc coins on the counter, only a fraction of the cost. Fionie slapped her hand on top of them.

"Thanks for trusting me for the rest. You have a big heart."

"Ah, yes, he does. We're going to have roast trust for dinner tonight, and *terrine de patience Montmartrois* tomorrow. The next night"—she thrust her chin toward Julien in an exaggerated glare—"brochette of heart à la Communard." She stuck a brush behind each of Auguste's ears, the filbert under his cast, and looped the cord of the rolled canvas over his shoulder so he could carry it. "There. Now stay off that silly engine!"

Auguste dropped off the supplies at his studio and walked the half dozen blocks to Gustave's apartment on boulevard Haussmann. Lined with elegant cafés and smart shops, the boulevard was clearly a different neighborhood than his own. He entered beneath the gilt ironwork, went up two flights, and pulled the bell cord. Piano music stopped. Gustave's brother, a composer, let him in.

"He's painting on the balcony," Martial said.

"Then I won't interrupt him."

Auguste lingered in the foyer to look at Gustave's painting collection, one reason why he came. There were several by Claude, a luncheon in his garden, a regatta at Argenteuil, and Gare Saint-Lazare. Both Sisley's and Pissarro's versions of the street in Louveciennes showing his mother's ocher cottage and her prized trumpet vines always moved him. Degas' pastel of the Café Nouvelle-Athènes with four faded prostitutes made him wonder what one of them meant by that gesture of flicking her thumbnail against her top front tooth. Maybe it meant, *Not even a sou tonight.*

None of these were what he'd come to see, the two paintings he knew would open the wound of remorse. He had a phantom model to consider. Margot. Panic gripped him. She wasn't in her usual place. Gustave owned so many that he rotated them. Auguste strode into the drawing room. His own *Bal au Moulin de la Galette* was there, and Margot, dancing. Her gaiety vibrated in the mottled light of the outdoor dance hall under the acacias. He loved the freshness and innocence of the place, so he didn't think it hubris to love his painting of it. He studied it. Yes, he could surpass it. He would surpass it. He had to.

But where was *La balançoire?*

He checked the dining room. Not there. The study. Ah, there. Margot. She had a place all to herself. Margot in her pink dress with blue bows down the front standing on a swing talking to two men in the leafy garden of the studio he'd rented on the Butte, Montmartre *d'en haut.* Three people snatching a few hours of pleasure to last them the whole week.

He stepped close and stroked her cheek. She wasn't a raving beauty. Her face was a bit too chubby and her hair was thin and lifeless, but oh, her spirit. He remembered the sweltering summer day when she had jumped into the fountain of place Pigalle, fully dressed, and splashed him. Her zest would have been perfect for his new painting. She had done some good things with him, *Cup of Chocolate, Lovers and Confidences,* and *Woman with a Cat.*

But the one good thing he could have done for her in return, he hadn't done. The one thing any responsible lover would have done. Regret made him unable to stand still in front of her now. A year and a half ago. He had allowed the worst to happen.

He searched her eyes for forgiveness, but her gaze was slightly to the side, so it offered him no answers. He didn't even know whether she had forgiveness in her nature. He'd never asked her the important things. He just used her the way Monet used the Seine and Pissarro used the boulevards, as a pretext to study light flickering through the trees onto her face and dress.

He had painted a study of her from memory, the one time he'd forsaken his rule of working only from the live model. If she were here, she would be in his new painting. She would bring out the best in him, out of his love for her, out of her love for him, and this painting at this critical time in his life had to be his best.

He could ignore his credo once more and put her in. He could study the paintings he still had of her, and ask Gustave to lend him *The Swing.*

It could be a means of making amends.' The thought lifted him momentarily, but two lost women might tinge the painting with sadness.
And if he broke his credo the second time, it might crumble to bits. He
could not risk that.

Inès, the orange cat, rubbed up against his leg and interrupted his
deliberations. He went back into the drawing room and looked at Gustave's self-portrait showing him at work in this very room, with a man
sitting on the flowered sofa, legs crossed, reading, and above the painted
sofa hung his own *Bal au Moulin de la Galette*. It always gave him a
start, his painting within Gustave's painting, a tribute to their mutual
regard. Now he could return the recognition and give Gustave a favorable position in the foreground of his new painting.

He made his way between potted plants and enormous bouquets,
walking around Gustave's pointer dog, Mame, asleep on the Oriental
carpet, past a replica of Houdon's sculpture of a lanky male nude. On
the balcony he found Gustave painting in his cream-colored artisan's
blouse, blue cotton cap, and linen shoes. Amusing. This son of a textile
magnate who had supplied the French army, this self-effacing son who
had inherited a fortune, dressing like a common laborer, while laborers
who used to wear their workmen's clothes with pride even on Sundays
now pretend they're gentlemen in ready-mades.

They were two painters, though opposites in a way, highborn and
low, but occasions allowed or required them to dress in the clothes of
their unnatural selves. Two selves for both of them. What devilishness
of nature to toss such ambiguities of identity at them.

Two men posed looking down on boulevard Haussmann. Auguste
nodded to one of them, Marcellin Desboutin, an engraver who frequented the Café Nouvelle-Athènes, a writer of verse tragedies. What
an impossible thing to sell. No wonder he was also working as a model.
He slouched back against the building in a bowler hat with his hands
stuffed in his casual jacket pockets. Auguste didn't know the top-hatted
gentleman posing in black frock coat leaning forward on the railing.
Now, there's a difference between us, Auguste thought. I would have a
man *and a woman* on this balcony.

Gustave turned toward him. "Ah, Auguste." He told the men they could take a break and ring for a *café* in the dining room. By the fluid way the two models glided across the drawing room, Auguste could tell they'd been here often, and not just as models. He envied Gustave always being able to paint out of love, and doing his best work because of it, painting after painting.

"How very democratic of you," Auguste said. "*Grand bourgeois* with *petit bourgeois,* yet together in a private space. People are going to wonder."

"Some *flâneurs* will know. Those snide observers strolling the boulevards and picking apart society in the weekly journals." He dipped his brush in turpentine and cleaned it with a rag. "The morals brigade will skewer me."

"You're courageous."

"Only by proxy."

Auguste studied the plunging perspective on the unfinished canvas, and the difference in size of the figures as a way to give the illusion of depth on the balcony. He came inside to look at Gustave's overpowering painting of a Paris street on a rainy day. Same achievement of perspective. And again on *Pont de l'Europe* displaying Gustave himself as a wealthy *flâneur* glancing toward a laborer leaning on the bridge railing, with his dog connecting them.

"Your unusual perspectives draw a person right in. There aren't any boundaries between the scene and where I'm standing. You eclipse us all in inventiveness."

"Zola called it my 'curious artistic personality.'" Gustave stepped over Mame and sat on the sofa. Instantly Inès curled up on his lap.

"Zola be hanged. You know who you are. Me, on some days I'm sorry I wasn't Ingres. Other days I'm sorry I'm not Monet. You make Impressionism and academic painting work together, modern subjects but conservative brushwork. You thumb your nose at the critics."

"So could you, you know." Gustave rubbed the cat under her chin.

"Easy for you to say. You who can tell the Salon jury to suck eggs and you'll still eat at Café Riche and spread out in ten rooms without ever having to sell a square meter of canvas for your rent."

"Eight rooms." Gustave offered him a cigarette and lit it for him. "I thought you were staying at Louveciennes for the summer."

"I was, until I read Zola's review."

"He's a two-headed bull," Gustave declared. "Next year he'll say the opposite of what he says this year. He said my *Floor Scrapers* was too tight. Too tidy. Too . . . too . . . too. He called me anti-artistic, said I paint with pedestrian exactitude. Later he said I'm courageous. Don't pay him any attention."

"You don't mean that. When other critics read Zola, they'll repeat his opinion like lemmings and will predict the failure of Impressionism too."

Gustave scowled. "And then the group won't hold."

"So I want to make him eat his words. For all our sakes. And I have a subject that can make him do that. The terrace of Maison Fournaise."

"Finally! Bravo!"

Auguste traced the pattern of the brocade on the arm of his chair. "Not that I'm ready, mind you."

"We're never as ready as we'd like to be. Time forces our hand."

"But this one has to be my *chef-d'oeuvre*. My sales are slipping. I have to get out of a rut. Will you help me stretch the canvas?" He held up his cast. "I'll get this off soon, but I have to start Sunday."

"You've been working on sketches with your left hand?"

"No time for sketches. I have to finish it by the regatta in September to catch the best light." He could see practical concerns swimming in Gustave's eyes.

"How big?"

"The same as *Moulin de la Galette*."

"A Salon painting, then, that size?"

"Don't think it gives me any pleasure to be hung between Mary Magdalene and some togas."

Gustave looked troubled. "If it's for the Salon, that'll deplete our ranks again. Degas is as stubborn as an ox about his prohibition. Of course, you have every right to submit where you want."

Auguste saw agitation tighten his mouth. "What's the matter?"

"Degas and I had it out."

"You too?"

"I told him a person's work should be the only criterion for exhibiting with us, regardless of whether he showed in the Salon that year, and that he's a zealot to think otherwise. He was once my mentor, yet I called him that."

"Mutual exclusiveness is his sacred principle."

"But that will crack us down the middle!" Gustave snapped. "He can't see that it's a matter of financial need. He called me an obstinate turncoat."

"Ha! You have to admit—the first is true."

"He's determined to replace you and Monet and Sisley with his cronies. Raffaëlli, Zandomeneghi, Lepic, Legros, and others. They're rank amateurs, though Forain has possibilities."

"And Pissarro?" Auguste asked.

"Pissarro has no use for Degas because Edgar's an anti-Semite. It's Degas' haughty attitude that infuriates me. He said to me, 'You mean to say you let Monet and Renoir in your house?' He's gone sour. He bears the whole world a grudge. He doesn't deliver on his promises either. God knows we only have a certain number of years to work, and he's wasting them. Squandering his talent."

"You can't shoulder the fate of our whole group, Gustave."

"But what's to become of us? I get so miserable thinking about it that I get a pain right here." He touched his chest. "If Bazille were here, he'd keep us together."

"If Bazille were here, it would still be the same," Auguste said.

"You're wrong. Frédéric would be smart enough to maneuver Degas into a corner and skewer him, and then he'd be forced to concede."

"Frédéric was a brilliant painter," Auguste said.

"Do you remember his painting of two nude fishermen with a net?" Gustave asked. "Classical male nudes, but not gods, just fishermen in the woods."

"Of course."

"It had such a profound effect on me I'll never forget it. It plugged the academy right between the eyes. I could kick myself for not buying it when they rejected it." A tremolo threaded Gustave's voice.

"Don't regret what's past. You've done what you could. You still are."

"But if we're not careful, we're going to lose something precious."

That was it, of course. Not just the staunch camaraderie that had supported them for a dozen years, but the force of their combined work. If they split, they'd be viewed as individual crackpots, not the harbingers of a bold new art. That possibility gnawed at him when he considered abandoning the Impressionist stroke, but that was too much to say to Gustave at the moment.

"You'd think it would be unbreakable by now," Auguste said, "but it's more fragile than ever. And if I desert our next show—"

"If you don't show with us, you have a good reason. Claude too. I really don't think he will. I had to hunt down his canvases and frame them myself for this year's show, and it's not going to be any easier next year. He gets discouraged in a way that scares me."

"*You* get discouraged in a way that scares *me,*" Auguste said.

"It's not for me that I'm grumbling. I know I'm second-rate. That doesn't bother me. It's for you and the others who've been together from the start. We can't allow it to fall apart."

Gustave rubbed Mame with his foot. "But I have a plan, and when it's carried out, you'll be in the Louvre," he said in a low voice.

Auguste howled with sardonic laughter. "You're dreaming."

Gustave gave him a steely look. "I've written out my will. I'm leaving my entire collection to the Musées Nationaux, with the stipulation that it will be displayed in the Musée du Luxembourg's contemporary galleries for twenty years, and then moved to the Louvre. You're going to arrange it."

"Ha! Assuming I haven't starved first." Auguste chortled, but the seriousness on Gustave's face made him stop. In the last few years, Gustave's parents and his younger brother had died. He'd hardly touched a brush all last year. "What does this mean, making out a will at your age?"

Gustave lowered his voice. "I just don't feel my generation of the family can expect a long life."

"Nonsense. You're younger than I am."

"Will you or will you not be my executor?"

"Only if you stretch my canvas."

"Tomorrow. At Maison Fournaise," Gustave said. "You can't take a thing that size on the train already stretched."

"You're right. But there's one more thing. You're in the painting."

Gustave sputtered out a breath.

"A painting of the pleasure of a Sunday afternoon on the Seine. A boating party. See? You belong there."

"Which me? Dressed as . . . ?

"A *canotier,* of course."

Gustave grinned at that.

Auguste patted his shoulder. "Buck up and get back to work now. Come to my studio when you can tomorrow. I need help getting my easel there."

CHAPTER SIX

Looking for
Mademoiselle Angèle

In his studio Auguste had scraped and sanded his palette and was rubbing linseed oil into it when Paul Lhôte knocked twice and came in, his custom around five o'clock.

He jerked to his feet. "You didn't tell anyone else I'm here, did you?"

"No. I didn't see anyone. What's the matter?"

"I just don't want to talk about the painting to anyone not in it." He slipped out of his mules and put on street shoes. "Let's go."

It was the green hour at the Café Nouvelle-Athènes, and the anise fragrance of absinthe permeated the room. Glasses of the beautiful green liqueur decorated many of the tables. They ordered mutton ragout for two francs twenty each, and a bock. The beer was thirty centimes.

"Has Angèle been in?" Auguste asked the waiter.

"If she's the model with the raspy laugh, no."

"A model for your new painting?" Paul asked. "Can't you go to her flat?"

"I don't know where she lives these days. Neither does she half the time, street-bred as she is."

"Then why don't you just go to the model market?" Paul motioned with his thumb toward the gravel *rond point* in the middle of place Pigalle where hopeful young laundresses, dressmakers' apprentices, and *grisettes* in gray muslin dresses living off students in the Latin quarter lined up around the circular fountain, hoping to be picked by painters looking them over.

"That cattle auction? It's where academicians choose their Venuses. Nobody I want would be there."

"Models hang around Le Rat Mort in the mornings."

"Trash. I don't want some chippy I don't even know and don't care about. Imagine, two months saddled with some Jezebel. I do have some standards. No cowface with dirty armpits is going to inspire me."

"Why are you so set on Angèle?"

Because she's the only one who could take the place of Margot, he thought.

"Because I only want to paint women I love, or imagine I could love."

"That leaves a wide field, then, doesn't it?"

"I never experience anything joyfully unless I can touch it. Even with commissioned portraits, if I don't feel something for the woman, it comes out stiff and lifeless. I can touch Angèle all I want."

"Hm."

"She revels in it. I need her *joie de vivre*. She's entertaining. She'll loosen up the group so they'll enjoy each other right away. They need a reason to keep coming back every Sunday. Nobody else can do that like she can. Angèle is Angèle."

"Then why have you been hiding her?"

"I haven't. She drifts. She's the type for your story too. A pretty girl who uses her charms to her advantage, monetary and otherwise. How's this for a line? *The painter set up his easel under a windmill to watch the women spin in a fast mazurka. Their simple muslin skirts whirled out behind them. A saucy one with teasing in her eyes laughed in sweet abandon knowing she'd go back to her one-room flat flushed and satisfied.* See? She's the perfect emblem of *la vie moderne*."

"Then you write it," Paul muttered. "I have a commission to do, a *fait divers* for *Le Petit Journal*."

"On what?"

Paul took off his glasses, narrow rimless lenses on thin metal bows, and rubbed his temples. "Any diverse event that shows Montmartre as the envy of lesser capitals of culture." Hunched over his plate, Paul forked boiled potato wedges into his mouth one after another. "Montmartre, where men made windmills and women make hats and waiters make art and grocers make poems and junk dealers make songs. But I need a premise."

"And somewhere, the elusive model, Angèle, is making eyes at a man in a café or cabaret as distinct and full of character as any on the grand boulevards." Auguste found himself eating as fast as Paul. "You need a story. I need a model. So. Two problems, one solution. A *fait divers* about searching for a particular model. Call it 'Looking for Mademoiselle Angèle.'"

Paul lifted his head in interest. "The diversity will be the spectacles in the cabarets of Montmartre which we, the *flâneurs,* observe with a purpose."

"We tell the doormen that you're going to write about their cabaret for *Le Petit Journal* and they'll let us in free."

Paul gobbled the rest of his meal and stood up. "Where first?"

"Across the square. Le Rat Mort. But only to look for Angèle." ·

Place Pigalle on a summer night sizzled like rancid butter in a hot pan. He loved the yellow gaslight, the blare of a trumpet spilling out of a cabaret, the piano tripping up the scale, the jugglers entertaining at the fountain. The odor of grease and whores spewed out as they entered the café.

Inside, the dead rat was still hanging from the ceiling, reminding patrons that this was one of the oldest cafés in Montmartre, and caricatures of the adventures of Le Rat were plastered on the walls to satisfy the Montmartrois' taste for the bizarre. A ragged intellectual was haranguing a group at Gambetta's table about the bourgeois imitating the aristocracy. Manet reigned politely at table eight as usual, overdressed in his top hat. Models lounged on benches to attract painters. They spotted Auguste and backed him against the wall. His shoulder knocked down a picture of Rat painting at an easel.

"I posed for Degas," a stringy-haired blonde said. "We can start early. Morning light." As if she knew something about art.

"Puh! I modeled for Balzac," another one bragged.

Paul stifled a guffaw.

A third one spat on the floor. "I *slept* with Baudelaire!"

"Ah, nice. Very nice." Auguste peeled her fingers off his cast while Paul just stood there and laughed. Auguste surveyed the room, didn't see Angèle, and tipped his head toward the door.

Outside, Paul wrote feverishly in his notebook. "Oh, isn't that rich. Modeled for Balzac."

"And the other one. She must have been twelve."

He steered Paul inside the Brasserie des Martyrs. Under gas lamps multiplied in the gilt-edged mirrors, the impresario blew on a trumpet. "Ladies and gentlemen. Ladies of the night and ladies of the day, ladies of the washtub and ladies of the satin drawing room. Gentlemen of the boulevards and gentlemen of the Butte, gentlemen of the stock exchange and gentlemen of the junk exchange, you are welcome all, true heirs of Gallic culture."

"Blowing smoke in their faces, those top hats who deigned to come to a common man's entertainment," Paul murmured.

The impresario sang out the first line of "La Marseillaise," urging on the children of the fatherland for whom the day of glory had arrived. At this the small orchestra fired off a salvo of the anthem.

"Welcome to what?" The impresario pranced across the stage in patent leather shoes. "To our little hill of ragpickers? No!" He flung his red scarf over his shoulder. "To the seat of culture, the glory of the city, Montmartre! Welcome to what our honored statesmen Léon Gambetta so nobly named our salon of democracy, where, tonight, our native sons will delight you with poetry and our native daughters with song."

"He's too full of himself," Auguste said. "Let's go. She isn't here."

"Charming women of various prices," Paul muttered as he wrote.

At Chez Père Laplace, a rustic cabaret-gallery, used palettes smeared with paint hung on the wooden paneling.

"Whose are they?" Paul asked.

"Were they. Every hopeful in the quarter. It started when Manet gave Laplace the palette he'd used for *Olympia,* and when Pissarro heard of it, he painted a couple of peasants on a palette and offered to sell it to Laplace. They bickered over the price until Laplace grudgingly paid him fifty francs. Then Claude Monet needed rent money and did the same. Now every two-bit amateur about to be kicked out of his garret has been hitting up Laplace for money. It makes Madame Tanguy happy, my colorman's wife, this constant need for new palettes."

"Are you tempted to offer yours?"

"And be labeled a tinhorn?"

While they were walking the periphery looking for Angèle, Thérèsa, still popular after fifteen years on the cabaret circuit, took the stage with a flourish and opened her large red mouth to sing, *"J'ai tué mon capitaine,"* accompanied by lewd gestures. Out poured the coarsest female voice he had ever heard, but after the refrain, her voice slid into something as delicate and tender as a choir of wood nymphs.

"Just when I think I'm getting too old for Montmartre, she sweetens a middle-aged man's fancy," Auguste said.

"Then why not her instead of Angèle?"

"That old cockroach?"

Paul guffawed. "Is Angèle here?"

"No luck. Onward."

"I want a drink," Paul said.

"Outside the *octroi.*"

They headed toward boulevard Rochechouart, which marked the old city walls and tax district. Beyond it, establishments were permitted to charge less for wine. These days the *octroi* was taken over by streetwalkers and *hôtels de passe* where cheap rooms were rented by the hour. One in flounced violet sidled up to them, but they ducked into the closest doorway, La Roche, a shabby café where La Macarona, a belly dancer from Algiers, was jiggling everything that would jiggle. An odd foursome was playing dominoes within spitting distance of her. Père Léonard, a violinist; Dupray, the military painter; the editor Lemoine; and a knacker from a slaughterhouse in La Villette, a notoriously clever man, hunched over their games, oblivious to the dancing.

"Perverse powers of concentration, those fellows," Paul said, taking down some notes, his face close to the page.

"She's not here." He thumped Paul on the chest. "You got an eyeful?"

"Aw." Paul put on an exaggerated pout.

In front of Auberge d'Audace, Paul said, "You go in. I'll stay out here." He moved away from the light of the gas lamp.

"Why?"

"Someone I don't want to see might be in there."

"How do you know?"

"He's a habitué. You go in, but come back quickly."

It was Paul's own business, but Auguste was concerned. Inside, a shadow theater was being performed. He had to wait until the lamps flickered and brightened. When he didn't find her, he hurried out.

Near Cirque Fernando, Offenbach's *La Vie Parisienne* poured out of Cabaret Elysée-Montmartre. The chorus line of dancers onstage was doing a wild cancan, hopping, knees up to their chins, kicking, flinging up their skirts to show white ruffles and black stockings.

"How about one of them?" Paul asked.

"I told you. I don't want anyone I can't imagine loving."

Shouts from the audience urged the dancers to kick higher and show more skin. The dancers shouted back, working up to a frenzy of kicking, pivoting in one-legged hops while holding their ankles above their shoulders, impossibly straight-legged, falling in exact formation into the splits, to a thunderous roar from the audience.

"'Bread! Bread!' they demanded a century ago. 'Spectacles and hussies' is what they cry today," Paul said in an overloud voice. Heads turned.

The police inspector Père la Pudeur leapt onto the low stage and fined two dancers for revealing too much underwear. The crowd jeered.

"Père le Prude," Auguste said.

"A fine job you have, Monsieur le Prude," Paul shouted, "being forced to look at that indecency."

Everyone laughed, including the chorus line. One of the dancers who was fined tossed the inspector a ten-franc coin that had been heating up between her breasts. "Let that burn your pocket," she bellowed.

The other protested that she had no money. "Please let it pass this time, monsieur. I'll be more careful."

"You should have been more careful this time," the inspector barked.

Paul dug into his pocket and smacked a ten-franc coin into the inspector's hand. "Now lay off the poor girl. She busted her corset stays on that one and now she has to go out and buy more."

Laughter exploded from the audience again.

"Bravo, Paul!" shouted a blond at a front table. "Aren't you a prince!"

Paul squinted to see who she was and a burly man sitting next to her sprang up and climbed over other people to grab Paul by the lapels. He fought to free himself, but the man got him in an armlock behind his back and pushed him out the door. Auguste followed, shouting, "Lay off him!"

The man slammed Paul against the building, nose first. "Stay out of my sight, you bastard."

Auguste tried to pull him away, but the man shook him off, and said, "Butt out. This isn't your affair."

Paul turned to get away and the man grabbed him by his coat and slammed him against the wall again. "Stay away from Gabrielle, or something worse will happen." He stormed back inside.

"Jesus Christ, Paul. What was that about?"

"Don't take a step! Do you see my glasses?"

Auguste picked them up and they hurried away. "A wonder they're not broken. Are you going to tell me, or do _I_ have to fight you to find out?

Paul rubbed the back of his neck. "He thinks I'm after his tart."

"Are you?"

"No. She just uses me to make him jealous. Let's get out of here."

"So he roughs you up whenever he sees you?"

"I don't want to talk about it. Where are we going next?"

They walked to the corner before Auguste said, "There's one more place Angèle might be, but it's a climb. Cabaret des Assassins."

Paul groaned. It was nearly on top of the Butte. "Nice name."

Before leaving Montmartre _d'en bas,_ Paul wanted to stop for a brandy at Brasserie Liberté, one of the cafés that had ignited the Commune. The place reeked of cigarette smoke and sauerkraut. Only steady, sodden, near-silent tippling here, elbows on black-lacquered tables, waitresses sitting and drinking with the clientele. It was little more than a dramshop selling *petits verres* of brandy and rum.

"How about that one?" Paul tipped his head sideways to a woman alone.

"Good God, no. She looks like she's thinking."

He was glad Angèle wasn't here. He had found Margot drunk here with some rogues when he had gone looking for her because she didn't show up on time to model. He didn't want to relive that with Angèle.

Paul was absorbed in his own thoughts while they climbed to Montmartre *d'en haut,* and Auguste was too, wondering why Margot had drunk herself into a stupor so many times when she'd known he was waiting for her with a half-finished canvas. Why had she purposely disappeared whenever he needed her most? The complexities of love baffled him. He had known she wasn't dependable, but he'd kept asking her to pose anyway.

So many things about her he didn't know, yet they had been lovers for three years. He hadn't thought to ask why she was attracted to disreputable men, or whether her family was still living, or what was on her mind when she was posing. He hadn't asked her if her soul was at ease with God, but wouldn't asking that have been selfish? He would have wanted a yes answer so *he* could be at ease. Maybe that was the highest form of love, one soul easing another. But it wasn't him. He wasn't sure if it ever could be him. Yet even now he wanted that from her.

He knew even less about Lise, his first love, so shy he'd had to coax her to model nude. He remembered less about her too, though he should remember more. Seven years with her, and a child, maybe his, maybe not, probably ten years old by now. Then she married well and stopped modeling, and he'd lost track of her. After Lise, there had been Nini and Henriette and Anna. And the earlier Jeanne and her sister Isabelle, both of whom he'd used in *Moulin.* Where were they all now?

A painter of women was what he wanted to be known as, but that meant having a steady stream of models to inspire him, to make his pulse pound with the urgency to paint what he saw, what he felt in his body, what he wanted to touch. Madame Charpentier's comment had stung. Couldn't she see that it wasn't philandery? It was compulsion. To adore what he painted. To do brilliant work not out of technique but out of desire, and to feel that desire, hot and full in his loins, not just his fingertips. He cared for each one in his own way because they had helped him to make beautiful paintings. But people were slippery in Montmartre, and he'd lost touch with them.

Too much of life was vanishing. Having the paintings helped him to remember, but when he was lucky the paintings were sold, and all that was left was fleeting sensation. He may have achieved the Impressionist ideal, to record sensation, but it always kept him hungry for more.

Climbing rue Lepic beyond the plaster quarries near the top of the Butte, they both stopped at the same instant. Building stones and girders had been laid out for walls, a floor, and a roof over Moulin de la Galette, the dance hall under the windmills.

"Enclosed?" Auguste sputtered. "The whole place will be enclosed, not just the mill shed?"

"I suppose to stay open in winter. To compete with the cabarets on the boulevards," Paul said.

Auguste shook his head. "People don't care a bean if the place has a roof. They should leave it be, its innocent self. We can dance just fine on the bricks and stamped-down dirt. We like it. Everyone feels welcome, even children. Even dogs. People can come in their artisan's smocks. It's all right with me for the bourgeois to dress down and come up here to mingle with the people of Montmartre, but enclosing it turns it into something commercial. Not ours anymore. A spectacle for somebody else."

"Would that they'd come to your benefit for Le Pouponnat," Paul said.

"Ha! What a jolly catastrophe that was," Auguste said, remembering his grand project of an amateur vaudeville at le Moul' to fund an orphanage and *pouponnière,* a day nursery, for the illegitimate babes of Montmartre abandoned and dying in the streets. It wrenched him that the lives of the street waifs orphaned during the Prussian War were so wretched compared to the lives of the little darlings whose bourgeois fathers wanted them painted in their stylish frocks. The project was the one thing he did the summer he painted *Moulin* that his mother approved of, she who washed and fed every urchin who ever came to her door.

All his friends had taken part, composing songs, poems, skits, painting scenery and posters, practicing their dances and acts, and writing articles in the local journals. Margot worked side by side with him on everything. She hand-printed tickets and strung paper garlands tree to tree. All of Montmartre was giddy with anticipation. Front-rank seats went for ten francs, two francs in the rear, and fifty centimes to stand. No one outside Montmartre came, and no Montmartrois could afford the ten-franc seats, but the rear seats and standing room were packed, and his idea of a nursery for foundlings had to wait until Madame Charpentier funded it herself later.

"It was one of my happiest times. That spirit Margot had with me that summer, that's what I need now in my painting. The spirit of Montmartre. It will die if this place turns commercial."

"This is going into my story, you know."

"Fine! Tell them Pierre-Auguste Renoir who immortalized the place without a roof is outraged!" He raised his fist high. "Infuriated!"

The yowl of a cat in heat tore through the air. He yowled back, feeling the same wild need as they trudged uphill on rue des Saules. If Angèle wasn't there, he knew no other place to look. There wasn't anyone else. The painting would be diminished from the start.

A person could pass by Cabaret des Assassins without noticing. It looked like any other cottage. In the dark they'd have to be careful not to miss it.

"Look for a donkey tied to a tree," he told Paul. "The owner rents it to painters to carry their equipment down the backside plunge to the Maquis."

"Any way to make a franc, I guess. Who would want to paint that rat-infested shantytown?"

Auguste had gone to look once and found the wasteland behind Montmartre dotted with quarrymen's cottages, scraggly kitchen gardens, and hovels of ragpickers and cutthroats. He never painted there. The poverty tore at him too deeply.

"Raffaëlli, for one. Or any of the other Realists in love with misery."

Out of an opened door spilled music and yellow light onto the small hillside vineyard. Above it, he could just make out the trees in the garden where he had painted Margot standing on the swing. He listened. Canéla, a painter by day and a tenor by night, was singing the melancholy song from Offenbach's *La Vie Parisienne* about a man writing to a prostitute asking her to give his friend the same pleasure she had once given him. Just the kind of song Angèle would request. They ducked under the low doorframe.

There she was. Angèle, resting her bosoms on the table next to a man leaning toward her, his intentness almost palpable. Now, wouldn't that be a sight to paint? In the light from the oil lamp, he saw the glint in her frolicsome blue-black eyes gobbling up the man with a hunger that her former struggles as a Maquis dweller had put in them. A *raconteuse* she was, captivating the man with a story. A few strands of her light auburn chignon had come undone in the ardor of her telling.

She turned to see who had come in.

"Well, if it isn't the lanky bon vivant of rue Saint-Georges. What happened to you?"

It was embarrassing to explain. "Oh, I was in a duel, that's all." He thought he was being amusing until he caught Paul's glare.

"Plumpy you down and let's have a squint at you. Hm, your face got in the way of a right hook, looks like. You should have come to me. My own true love is a stand-in. Rapiers only. No pistols. He saved a baron from certain death once, and got paid handsomely."

"I thought your true love was a police spy."

"That too. And a forger and a snatcher." She laughed a throaty, deep-voiced laugh. "He's disappeared of late." She lifted her shoulders. "I suppose I was only fancy-sick about him after all."

That's the insouciance and spirit he wanted, but not just for his painting. He wanted to drink it in so his worries and regrets would be pushed away. He sat next to her and caught a whiff of the murky, animal scent of ambergris.

"This is Antonio Maggiolo. An Italian to the bone," she said as though she knew him well, which was her way with everyone. "He's a journalist."

Auguste glanced at Paul and then scrutinized the man. His tousled brown hair, slender neck, and tanned face, smooth except for wisps of a light brown beard at his chin, gave him the air of Ganymede, the beautiful youth of Greek legend carried off by Zeus. Truth to say, he *was* on the pretty side of handsome, with that angular jaw and narrow nose.

"A journalist," Auguste said. "Everybody's a journalist. Every week new journals. New critics. Anybody can call himself an art critic if he has two eyes and owns a pen. Soon the only new thing they'll have to write about is each other." He gestured to Paul. "Meet Paul Lhôte. He's a journalist. You can write about him writing about you."

Paul shook Antonio's hand, pulled up a chair, and sat down.

"Antonio is interviewing me, and introducing me to grappa. Upsee down." She tipped her head back and poured in the potent clear drink as if it were white wine. "Ah, that'll drive away my toothache." She licked her lips and introduced Auguste. "I'm going to pose nude for him someday." She took obvious delight in saying this, tantalizing all of them in one fell swoop.

"So much the luckier man." Maggiolo turned to Auguste. "Will she pose for Vice or Virtue, for a goddess or just for her beauty?"

"For Beauty," Auguste said. He appreciated the man's cleverness in contrasting academic art that needed a classical goddess as pretext for a nude with modern painting in which a nude could be merely a beautiful woman at the bath or in the boudoir or waiting for a client. "Angèle needs no trappings of Roman ruins or Mount Olympus to justify her. She is what she is." He touched her under her chin. "An embodiment of beauty."

Angèle beamed flirtatiously and blew him a kiss.

"Are you an art critic?" Paul asked.

"Not at the moment. Just now, I'm a social observer. I'm writing a piece on the ladies of Montmartre for *Le Triboulet*." With slender fingers, Maggiolo whipped out a card from a silver case in his breast pocket.

"Ah, les Montmartroises. Are you going to include the singers and dancers and circus performers?" Paul asked. "And the ladies of the evening?"

"Especially the ladies of the evening."

"Then you can take your pick," Paul said. "The fresh buds of girlhood newly arrived from the country or the trollops of the gutters. The Montmartroises are more Parisian than the Parisiennes."

Maggiolo tipped his head curiously at Paul. "I can see I have much to research. I may send the results to a journal in Milano as well. I'm somewhat of a roving correspondent."

"Where have you been roving lately?" Paul asked.

"The spas at Baden-Baden."

"Been there," Paul said.

"The casino di Locarno."

"The casino of Lugano pays out higher."

"The Wagner opera season at Bayreuth."

"Ah, you've got me there," Paul conceded.

"Antonio's made of piles of money. He's got brains too." Angèle gave him a teasing glance. "And something else, I do believe."

"Brain enough to hear stories of Paris from Montmartre's most accomplished *raconteuse*," Auguste said. "What were you telling him just now?"

"About my life," she said blithely, wagging her head.

"Ah, then he must have charmed you more than I ever have, since I've never heard the tale."

"Don't let us stop you," Paul said.

"I was telling how as a girl, being that I had no mother to speak of, I lived in an attic space in the Maquis and slept on hare skins. Oh, a regular ragtag was I, in the clutches of a flower broker from rue du Temple, what some call rue du Crime. Every day, just after dawn, the Beadle, as she was called, met me at the flower market on Île de la Cité, and if I was late, I'd get a smack on my cheek. She would hang an empty coin pouch around my neck and send me off with a bundle of roses in both arms to Pont Neuf where the jugglers perform, or to l'Opéra, or La

Madeleine, and I couldn't come back to her flat until I'd sold them all. She would empty the pouch and give me a few sous, enough for bread and soup. If she thought I was hiding a coin, she'd strip me down to the skin to see if there were any between my cheeks."

"I don't believe it," Maggiolo said.

"Why, aren't you a white goose! Hang me if it isn't true. Once, outside l'Opéra, I got shoved by the crowd, and fell into the street, and a carriage wheel rolled over the flowers. *Là,* she beat the tick right out of me.

"Such things went on until I sprouted breasts. *Mon Dieu,* was I happy when those titties swelled, because I had a plan. I knew I could survive beatings aplenty, so I made up stories about being robbed by snatchers. It broke my heart to do it, but I tore my dress to convince her I'd fought back. Time and again she walloped me, but I'd already emptied what I collected under a loose cobble in that stub of a street of women's cribs off rue du Temple.

"Seeing as how I was so itchy to get out of her clutches, I put up with it only enough to go to Madame Hortense who rents dresses to *femmes publiques,* me being in rags, you see, but now with a collection of coins. I begged her to rent me one for just one hour. She took pity on me because I was plucky and scrubbed me down good before she let me so much as touch the fabric. 'Why, your hair's near to golden,' she said. 'Who would have thought? You bring this dress back with one stain of a man's comings, and I'll flay that beautiful face right off your cheek-bones,' she croaked. You can imagine, I felt like a queen in such a dress as was clean and respectable, which I guess showed on my face, because I only had to stand in the models' market on place Pigalle for half an hour before I got picked up. I knew right then I wasn't a throwaway, and I didn't deserve to be beaten."

Angèle swelled as though a prince had just given her a box of choco-late creams. "After that I moved up a notch and could buy from the used clothing stalls of the Marché du Temple."

"Bravo!" Her spunk was one more reason why he wanted her in the painting. She was climbing out of penury just like he was. They shared the same hope, that security was just around the corner.

With the perfect timing of a born actress, she slid forward her glass for more grappa, and quaffed it down. "Now my friends have come here—"

"For a particular reason," Auguste said. "I have a painting in mind in which you could figure prominently, and your roving correspondent as well."

As he explained, her sly eyes shot sparks to Antonio and then to him. "You can bet your brushes we'll be there."

"Every Sunday for a while. Wear a blue boating dress, if you have one."

"I know blessed well where to get one. I'll be traipsing through the Marché du Temple come nine in the morning."

CHAPTER SEVEN

Dans l'Avenue Frochot

Sunday morning. Yes, it had to be. The roar of applause last night as she took her bow, the hot carriage ride with the shades drawn leaving the theater, the slick feel of the leather seat under her damp palms, the heat of his body underneath his frock coat, and his low voice breathing words in rhythm with the clop clop of hooves on cobbles— this man, this Joseph-Paul Lagarde, last night, had murmured in the carriage, "Marry me, Jeanne. Marry me tomorrow. No, not tomorrow. Marry me at Christmas and we'll have a *fête* that will set Paris abuzz for the season." And she had said, "Whenever you'd like."

She had used the formal *vous* to show she knew he didn't consider the daughter of a music professor from the edge of Montmartre, an actress playing ladies' maids, equal to the son of the Most Honorable Michel Lagarde, *agent supérieur* of the stock exchange, and *châtelain* of Château Saint-Clair in Compiègne.

And early this morning Joseph-Paul had come to call upon her father, very properly, mustering respect, asking for her hand in marriage, and Papa was pleased, knowing that Joseph-Paul had a sound future, and Maman was happy because her daughter was happy, and Joseph-Paul had made them promise not to tell anyone until he told his parents, and he kissed her mother on the cheek, and now the two of them were promenading back and forth along avenue Frochot, astonished at what they'd just done.

Avenue Frochot, her little oasis of a street, a one-block crescent, calm and leafy. Not a monstrous block of apartments on a busy boulevard, nor the oddly shaped cottages of Montmartre, but an avenue secreted between the two, each *maison particulière* separate the other and with a distinct character, her home since girlhood. She would hate so very much to leave it.

She looped her hand around his arm and told him where the painter Eva Gonzalès lived, and showed him Madame Galantière's cast-iron bench where her life had taken a turn, Madame who was like an aunt to her and never missed her opening nights. She told him Victor Hugo had once lived at number five, and she described the grand day of her childhood when crowds followed him home when he returned to Paris after the Siege, and how he spoke to them from his balcony above the tier of arches, the great world coming to her little street.

"Let's go to the Bois now," Joseph-Paul said.

She was miffed. Was he even listening? She had so much more to tell.

"To do what?"

"Stroll to the cascade, take a gondola ride, meet my parents at the Kiosque de l'Empereur on the island. Let's get your parasol and we'll be off."

"I don't need it." She knew what he liked to hear. "All I need is you."

"Yes, but I must promenade you in all your splendor. Come now, Jeanne, let's go back and get it." He kissed her on her temple, a quick assurance of affection. "We have a bit of work to do."

She stopped in the cobbled street. "Work?" She squeaked out the word so he would laugh. "You've just described pleasure."

"Work that will be pleasure. We have to convince my parents. It's a delicate issue. Father is very old-fashioned."

He paused. Was she supposed to guess his meaning?

"When I mentioned you to them"—he stroked her hand as if smoothing the nap on a velvet glove—"Father said, 'Once upon the boards, no matter how irreproachable their character may be, actresses can never be received by people of character and condition except in their professional capacity.'"

A slam. It was like tripping and falling flat on the stage, not knowing how she'd gotten there.

She planted herself on Madame Galantière's bench. The playwright in the Flemish house was tap-tapping on his writing machine. When he stopped for a few moments, she held her breath for him, willing him to go on, and didn't look up at Joseph-Paul until the man was tapping regularly again.

"I know it's terribly conservative of them, but they'll come around. Let's go."

"No."

"No?" He stretched out the word into two rising syllables.

"I'm not going with you to the Bois."

"But you need to meet my parents. They need to see that you are—"

"Refined. Yes, you may show me off, and I shall charm them, I promise you, but not today."

"Why not?"

"I have a rendezvous. I did not expect today to be taken up with this. I'm going to pose."

"On a Sunday? You can't be serious. You couldn't have arranged that any day but Sunday?"

"No. It has to be Sunday. Sundays. For Auguste Renoir."

He raised both arms, an overly dramatic gesture, and gave her a stern look. "You said that was over."

She could not suppress a giggle. "Stern looks don't play well on men who have just asked one's father for one's hand in marriage. It is over, but this is a favor."

"Posing nude is a favor?"

"It's not for a nude. I've never posed nude, but what if it were?"

"You wouldn't do it, that's what. And you're not doing it today, regardless. I forbid you—"

"Sh."

He lowered his voice. "Darling."

Those words, *I forbid you,* sent an icy tingle through her, head to toe. That a man would command her like that. Heaven and earth! It gave her a shock. She had never been told such a thing by Auguste. He was so blithe, letting her go her own way after an evening together, she to the theater, the shops, a friend's flat, while he went to some *hôtel particulier* to paint a portrait, or out to his river. Auguste never questioned her. Was it titillating or merely inconvenient to love a man she was a jot afraid of?

"It's only a favor done out of good will. A pleasant thing to do." She reached into her drawstring bag and pulled out the note. "See?" A touch of jealousy would do him good.

He read it, and in a broad gesture, tore it in two.

She grabbed for it. "You have no right—"

"Remember the sight of this." He tore it into smaller pieces, and still smaller, and dropped them in the gutter.

She watched all those bits of male adoration float down like stage snowflakes. She hadn't known that he was capable of so theatrical a gesture. It would play well at the Opéra, better there than at the Comédie-Française, where it wouldn't convey genuine sadness.

Such a difference in men. The joy Auguste took in her had been purely visual, sensual, and spontaneous. It wasn't founded on possession, which was all right for a lover, but not for a husband. Joseph's love was based on notions new to her, seriousness and permanence.

"I've made a promise," she said.

"To him?"

"No. I haven't seen him for half a year. To Madame Charpentier. She said if this painting gets in the Salon and I'm not in it—"

"You have your new painter to get you into the Salon."

"She doesn't have his reputation."

"Precisely."

"I *meant* as a painter."

He loomed above her as though that alone would convince her. Was his manhood at stake? A woman had to be clever in order to cherish a man's manliness without letting it get the better of her. She'd have to find subtle ways of getting what she needed without him ever suspecting that he'd been manipulated. Then his manhood would remain intact. Men were happier that way. God knows she wanted a happy man.

"We're expected at eleven. A matter of honor," he said, looking at her steadily, taking her elbow, guiding her home to get her parasol.

Hm. A happy woman married to a happy man needed to choose her battles shrewdly.

CHAPTER EIGHT

Glorious Insanity

Auguste sat on the upper terrace of Maison Fournaise, his feet on a wooden chair, knees up to his chin, waiting. He surveyed the sky. A few high wispy clouds. Weaklings unable to keep out the sun. Good.

He hadn't slept well in his room above the restaurant. Worries had tumbled as he thrashed. It would be overcast. It would rain. He couldn't work left-handed. The terrace would float in midair. Not enough people would come to convey the right atmosphere. The composition would be jumbled. Zola would be proven right. He wouldn't be able to handle a complex painting *based on long and thoughtful preparation.* How long did Zola want? A decade? He'd been working up to this that long. All those portraits, every painting done *en plein air,* they were all exercises. Even the Marie Antoinette plates were exercises leading to this terrace. A village of triers, and he was one of them.

He stood up, sat down, stood up again. On the Rueil bank a hundred meters away, Parisians poured out of trains with picnic baskets. From the station, some took the double-decker horse-drawn omnibus downriver to be ferried across to La Grenouillère to swim and dance at The Frog Pond. Others crossed on the Chatou bridge, and were already promenading on the island they claimed as theirs one day a week. Already Alphonse was renting out yoles and the river was sliced with racing sculls. Already the lower terrace was filled with exuberant people without a worry on their minds.

"Don't forget to save some *canots* for us," Auguste called down.

"Plenty. Don't worry."

Well, that was one thing he *didn't* have to worry about. He cranked the awning out. Not enough light. He rolled it in again.

Alphonsine came up to the terrace with two white tablecloths and a stack of napkins. "Every time I come up here, you've changed the awning," she said.

"The light keeps changing."

"And you're upstairs, downstairs, upstairs. Relax. They'll come." She shook out a tablecloth and smoothed it. "Oh, no! I'm sorry about these folds."

"But I love to paint folds."

She snickered.

"It's true. See how the white changes to pale blue along the ripples?"

"I'm going to play waitress for you today, just for the pleasure of it. And Maman insists on preparing all the models' meals so my aunt will cook for the restaurant. How many shall I set the table for?"

"A dozen. Set the tables six and six."

"Twelve people in one painting?"

"Fourteen. Counting you. You're the darling of this place."

He liked watching her try to hide her pleasure.

"Who's the fourteenth?"

"Your brother."

"Do you know what the picture will be like? Where everyone will be?"

"I don't even know who will come."

"Who might come?"

"Some friends of mine. Writers. Models. Actresses. Ellen Andrée and maybe Jeanne Samary."

"Jeanne Samary! I saw her in *School for Husbands.* You *know* her?"

He tried to be expressionless but he knew he wasn't succeeding. Her eyes opened wider. She pinched her lips together with her index finger and thumb, a pretty little action, which claimed she knew a secret.

"Will you do one thing for me?" he asked. "Go put on your straw *canotier* and a boating dress. In this painting, you are a *canotière,* not a hostess."

"Gladly." She disappeared into the corridor.

In a few minutes he heard Pierre and Paul singing as they came across the bridge. *"Oh-ho! les canotiers, C'est aujourd'hui dimanche."* Boaters, today is Sunday, the song began. Paul, in a red-and-white-striped boating jersey, waved his *canotier,* apparently recovered from being roughed up when they made the rounds of cabarets, and Pierre waved his bowler.

Auguste hailed them. "Pierre, I haven't seen you for a couple of months, long enough for you to fall in love. Did you?"

"Twice!"

"You lucky devil."

Pierre lifted a basket with two bottles of wine. "In case we drink the restaurant dry."

"Do we have time for a row?" Paul asked.

"Before it rains," Pierre added.

"These aren't rain clouds, you worrywart," Auguste said. "They're just puffs of decoration. Alphonse is saving a pair of sculls if you want to race."

Paul turned to Pierre. "Then, to La Grenouillère for a bock."

"That's the wrong way," Alphonse said. "Upstream first, to the boatworks at Bezons, and back with the current when you're tired."

"Good," Pierre said. "That'll keep Paul from getting into woman trouble at La Grenouillère. It's my duty."

"And you'll be improving the nation's moral fiber two ways!" Auguste said.

Alphonse joined in with, "Exercise for the sake of the Republic!"

"Revitalizing France," Paul said, beating his breast with his fists.

Laughing at themselves, they settled into the two boats, maneuvered into the current, and Alphonse shouted, *"Allez!"* to start them off.

Louise Fournaise in a blue-gray dress and long white apron came up to the terrace carrying a tray of wine glasses clinking against each other.

"Louise, my sweet," Auguste said, summoning his most charming smile, which cracked his scabs. "Do you think you could use your glasses made at Bar-sur-Seine instead of these?"

"My, you are a picky one. Whatever for?"

"They're made by hand, so they're irregular and have tinges of color. It's important to see in a thing the person who made it."

"I would think you'd want the best we've got."

"Machine-made glasses are sham. The imperfections of handmade glass give each one a personality, a soul."

"If my glasses had a soul they'd wash themselves," she muttered.

"Good taste is disappearing with all this trashy sameness. If there were a Society of Irregularists, I'd drop everything and join it."

"You're crazy, you know. Crazy." She tapped her temple. *"Un fou."*

He knew he was on safe ground now. "And don't cut the bread. Let them tear it. It makes more interesting shapes. And don't let anyone bring out that silly little tray and brush to sweep up crumbs. It's pretentious. Leave them lie."

"Fussbudget." She clinked down the stairway.

"Merci, ma chérie."

The *Iris* sped by on a broad reach. Gustave was showing off. He tacked quickly and came back. No one was as smooth a sailor as Gustave. Auguste hurried downstairs to help bring in the boat.

As he stepped onto the dock Gustave tugged at his sleeveless singlet. "Is this all right?"

"Perfect. It's naturalness I want."

They watched a stream of people come across the bridge—bourgeois couples under parasols and top hats, young lovers arm in arm, shopgirls chattering gaily, young men on the prowl.

"Doesn't it remind you of Watteau's paintings of Cythera?" Auguste asked.

"Ah, the isle of Venus. A day of love in some secluded glen."

"Willing *grenouilles* waiting on the bank in bathing costumes or summer dresses ready to jump into action."

Gustave shook his head. "Cythera's only a myth."

"It's a hope for some. The bushes will be moving in a few hours."

They both chuckled, somewhat wistfully, Auguste thought.

"You know what Guy de Maupassant named his new barque?" Gustave asked. *"L'Envers des Feuilles."*

"The undersides of leaves?"

"What couples see when they're on the ground."

"Ah, yes. Frenchmen appreciate *la nature.*" Auguste sat at a table under the maples and drummed his fingers, watching the footbridge.

"Relax. They'll come."

The next train arrived and chugged off to the west, belching black smoke. Soon Angèle stepped off the bridge with Antonio Maggiolo, the Italian journalist, jaunty in pin-striped jacket. She looked delicious with a white velvet toque perched on her auburn curls and a red carnation tucked between her breasts. Right behind her, petite Ellen Andrée, wearing a *canotier* with a flower pinned to the side, came with a man she introduced as Émile.

"One more is always welcome," Auguste said.

Now if Charles and Jeanne didn't come, he would still have a dozen. But what if only one of them came? Thirteen. Not knowing was making him sweat.

"I'll have you know I had a crushing performance last night," Angèle said, her eyes glinting at Auguste. "I usually sleep till noon after the likes of such a one."

Antonio made no effort to hide his lusty smile.

"I appreciate you being here. You both look splendid."

He wondered if Jeanne had given an actual performance last night.

"Would you like a *café?*" Auguste asked.

Angèle sized up Gustave in his singlet. "We'd like a boat ride."

"I'll take you for a sail to Bezons and back," Gustave offered.

They pushed off. He turned back and saw Alphonsine in a dark blue boating skirt and white middy blouse trimmed in red.

"Oh. I wish I'd seen you in time. You could have gone with them."

"That's all right. Is Mademoiselle Samary here yet?" she whispered.

Auguste made a show of looking under the tables, in the arbor, up on the side balcony, in the trees, in the water.

"No, but here comes Jules Laforgue, natty in country tweed and mariner's cap." He introduced her as *la belle Alphonsine,* the soul of La Maison Fournaise. "You ought to appreciate that, Jules. You write poems about soul, don't you?"

"Among other things equally elusive." Jules chuckled. "Equally impossible to express."

"Right, so I'm glad you've come down to earth for a day. You'll have to excuse him, Alphonsine, if he spouts Shakespeare now and then. Jules may be quiet, he may be looking off in the distance, but he's always thinking."

"I hear, yet say not much, but think the more," Jules said with a self-mocking grin. *"This breast of mine hath worthy cogitations."*

"Then cogitate on that a moment." Auguste gestured toward the river.

Baron Raoul Barbier was arriving under sail at a dangerous speed, just as he'd said at Madame Charpentier's salon. A brave fellow. Alphonse leapt down from the bank and cushioned the hull from crashing into the dock. Raoul tossed him the bowline, lurching sideways on his stiff leg. *"Nana* is as frisky as a filly in her first race," he said apologetically. "Are the ladies here yet?"

Right at that moment, Auguste saw her. Not Jeanne. Cécile-Louise, the woman with too much name. On the top step of the bridge. Her dress! Shimmery blue and white stripes. He didn't know if he could love *her,* but he could love the dress. Composed, expectant, twirling a coral-colored parasol with ruffled edge, packaged and sent by Madame Charpentier. A porcelain figurine of a Watteau lady already posing so that at any moment a nobleman would bow and escort her to Cythera.

He felt himself moving toward her, unconscious of the grass and gravel beneath his feet, the luminous skin of her face and décolletage unmistakably coming closer, and he arriving somehow, in time to take her hand as she stepped daintily onto the ground. Her hand was warm—this was no myth.

"I've been breathless, waiting for this day," she purred through a dazzling smile and the overpowering scent of cheap perfume.

"You look ravishing. A striped dress is every painter's dream."

Her nose poked at the sky. "A bird told me so."

"One who answers to the name of Madame Charpentier, no doubt."

A calculated coup. He forgave Madame her manipulation in anticipation of what he could do with those stripes falling in folds.

The *canotiers* climbed out of the boats and Alphonse declared Paul the victor. Paul did a celebratory dance step on the slanted dock, an oar on his shoulder.

"You won't feel like dancing if this dock collapses," Pierre said.

Paul grinned at a young girl on the promenade, turned to follow her, and whacked Pierre on the back of the head with the oar.

"*Zut!*" Pierre cried and chased him up the bank. "Give me that before you brain someone prettier than me."

"Who are they?" Cécile-Louise asked.

"The one in the bowler with the bushy red beard is Pierre Lestringuèz. He works for the Department of the Interior. A good sort, but ever since he began studying the occult, he's become a bit of a calamity howler, always foreseeing the worst."

"And the winner?" Alphonsine asked.

"Paul Lhôte. A loose screw. Hungry for experiences. Reckless. A writer of articles and an amateur painter. He escapes his deadly conventional post at a shipping company by collecting unconventional adventures."

"Such as?"

"Stowing away to South America on a packet ship. He lost his post for that escapade, so he immediately stowed away to Asia. On the isle of Jersey once he dared me to dive from a high cliff out over the rocks into furious waves. I thought he was crazy, but he did it, bare-assed, and came up laughing."

"He would make a good *canotier,*" Alphonsine said. "He's not afraid of getting wet."

"What Paul lacks in caution, Pierre supplies in fretfulness."

When Gustave's boatload arrived they were singing a *canotier* song about feeling good on Sundays:

> *Mais le dimanche, mais le dimanche,*
> *Moi, je me sens bien, bien, bien,*
> *Car je ne fais rien, rien, rien.*

As they went upstairs, Auguste sang loudest.

Louise came up to set out the uncut bread. A pretext only. He knew she couldn't contain her curiosity. "Why, Auguste, I never knew you could sing."

"When I was a boy, Gounod said I should be an opera singer. I can dance too." He grabbed her around the waist and twirled her under his left arm.

"*Oh, là là,*" she cried, took one look at the models, and hurried downstairs.

The moment lacked only Jeanne and Charles to make it perfect. Not one, but both of them.

Auguste made sure that Cécile-Louise sat so that she'd be in the foreground of the painting and her dress would spill over the side of her chair in a cascade of stripes. She was as decorative as a lady-in-waiting to Marie Antoinette on one of his china plates. He was dying to start painting right then, but there was the meal to get through.

Fournaise brought up a bottle of white wine and another of *crème de cassis* to combine as an *apéritif.* He held the cassis up to the light. The black currant liqueur would be a gorgeous deep red in the glasses.

Angèle tapped her cordial glass. "Be a good man and pour me a schnick."

"Did you know this was invented by monks in the sixteenth century?" Fournaise asked. "As a cure for snakebite, jaundice, and wretchedness."

Angèle winked at Antonio. "*Alors,* I do believe a snake bit me just last night, come to think of it, so don't be afraid to be generous."

Paul raised his glass. "A toast honoring Auguste's painting-to-come. A toast to *la vie moderne,* which allows us the freedom to row where we please and eat at the table of life. Let us spend our wealth and time gaily, preserve our liberty, and enjoy life whatever happens. *À votre santé!*"

Whatever happens, Auguste thought. It sounded ominous.

The itch under his cast was tormenting him. He needed to get started painting so he could be absorbed, body, mind, and instinct, so the itch would disappear.

"*Liberté, egalité, fraternité, et gaîté,*" Raoul said.

Pierre sang a Béranger drinking song urging people to avoid drunkenness by taking small sips, but plenty of them.

"*Vive la bohème!*" Angèle sang out, and all chorused the toast.

Louise and Alphonsine served the entrées. "A family effort," Louise said. "Alphonse caught the eels in Marly, Alphonsine caught the artichokes at the market last month, and I conserved them in jars."

Someone downstairs at the piano was playing a medley of Béranger's ballads of Lisette, the *grisette* from the country living on bread and diluted wine, as faithful as her poverty allowed. Pierre sang some lines and Jules made up a verse about Lisette as a *canotière*. People were getting to know each other. The toast was working. Or maybe it was the cassis-and-wine.

The main course was *canard à la paysanne,* braised duck garnished with carrots, turnips, onions, celery, bacon, and fried potatoes. Auguste didn't know how he could sit still and eat. He was conscious only of the painting moving before his eyes. Conversations separated, blended, jumped from one topic to another. He didn't follow them.

Alphonsine brought out two large raspberry tarts. The light on her raised cheeks issued from within. She cut generous pieces, and lingered by the railing watching intently as each person took a bite.

"Did you make these?" Auguste asked.

"With a little help from the sun and rain."

When Père Fournaise set out a small wooden cask of brandy, all Auguste could think about was how much everything was going to cost.

"You have no Menuet Hors d'Age?" the baron asked.

"This is the brandy *de la maison.*"

Raoul gave Fournaise a condescending look. "What I like about Menuet Hors d'Age is that the quality is always the same. You can depend on it."

"What a good definition of nothingness," Fournaise said. "Isn't variety one of the pleasures of life?"

"With ladies, yes," Raoul said with a silly grin.

"With brandy too. You have country brandy once in a while, woody and nutty in flavor, and when you return to your expensive cognacs, they're downright boring. You'll see."

Fournaise pressed the spigot over a glass and held it aloft to show its deep copper color, then held it to Raoul's nose. "Rich, *non?*"

Raoul sniffed twice and then sipped. "Earthy."

"That's the roasted sugar and spices." He filled glasses all around.

Auguste set his aside. The time was approaching. Anne, one of the servers, removed the plates and delivered a compote of figs and golden pears and purple grapes with burnished grape leaves still on the stems. Perfect.

Alphonse *fils* came upstairs. "Where do you want me?"

"Over here by the railing. Lean up against it. Look at Ellen."

Ellen raised her hand and wiggled her fingers. "Me."

Alphonse held out his arms awkwardly, not knowing what to do with them.

"Put your hands on the railing."

Maggiolo stood up to stretch, leaned over Angèle to speak to her, and tried to take advantage of a bird's-eye view down the front of her dress. He couldn't see much. For all her raucous talk, Angèle was a modest dresser.

Jules stepped back from the table at the far end with Paul and Pierre and lit his small white pipe. *"All the world's a terrace, and all the men and women merely models,"* he said, obviously amusing himself. He turned to Pierre and Paul and pointed back and forth to each one. "And so, *my excellent good friends, Rosencrantz and gentle Guildenstern, or is it Guildenstern and gentle Rosencrantz?* Let us pose with panache."

Pierre chuckled, got in one last gulp of wine and one good scratch of his beard, and then stood still. Gustave lit a cigarette. Raoul stood next to Alphonsine who was bending forward with her elbow on the railing. It was a natural pose for her, but standing so long might be hard on Raoul's leg.

"Raoul, please, sit."

Veronese situated his figures symmetrically at a U-shaped table in *The Marriage Feast at Cana.* Today, the models themselves made an asymmetrical U around an array of bottles, glasses, a heel of bread, the fruit compote, Angèle's heaped-up napkin. A still life worthy of Cézanne. The composition was close to perfect, but close wouldn't do.

"Stop, please. Don't move."

He almost wished he didn't have to stop them, they were so joyful.

"Silence," Alphonse boomed.

Was he impatient to get back to the boats already?

It was the moment.

"Do—not—move," Auguste said.

"But I'm looking down at my plate," Cécile-Louise whined. "Can't I—"

"Look at Antonio. No, at Gustave."

"Can't I look at you? You know how I hate profiles."

She gazed at him so adoringly, making a purring sound, that he agreed just so he could start.

He liked the way Angèle was leaning toward Gustave, as if she were flirting, which she was, always was, with everybody, young or old, rich or poor, just for the pleasure of it.

"Angèle, drape your arm over the back of Antonio's empty chair. Good. Now, Antonio, slide your hand down so that it almost touches hers."

Auguste stepped into his picture and tipped Angèle's head more to the side and adjusted her white velvet toque. He lifted her chin and felt the bone under the skin. Touching the hollow behind it seemed an intimate thing. He stroked her neck.

"You said I wouldn't have to pose like a drunkard," Ellen said into her wine glass tipped up to her lips.

"You aren't. It's a coquettish gesture, ignoring a man gazing at you," Auguste said.

"Degas made me look lonely."

"You don't look lonely in the least," Gustave said. "Émile is adoring you."

"In that painting, Degas was presenting modern life as he saw it, being alone in a city of strangers," Auguste said. "I have a different view, conviviality, so you don't need to worry."

"Can you see my face?"

"Yes. Through the glass. Sparkling."

A challenge to paint. He wasn't sure if any painter had attempted it since Vermeer. Was he a fool to try?

"My mother's going to have a fit."

"Stop complaining, dollface," Angèle said without moving. "Think of the rest of us, sitting here parched and dry all afternoon, dying while wine is untouchable right in front of us, and you can sneak little sips."

Gustave was sitting too formally considering his sleeveless singlet. "Gustave, turn your chair around, please."

Gustave straddled it and leaned back. It would be a torturous position to hold without a back support. He wouldn't ask anyone else to do it, but Gustave knew instinctively what leaning back would convey, an instant of movement in time, an Impressionist ideal. God love him for offering that pose.

"Good. Hold on to the chair to help you."

Gustave pushed back his flat-topped *canotier* rakishly and held on.

"Perfect."

"Auguste," Cécile-Louise said. "Pardon me, but looking this way at you, I can't see anybody else."

"Then turn to Gustave like I asked you to." He positioned her elbow on the table closer to her body so it would be a better support. He drew his hand over her wrist hinged by thin bones, and stretched out her fingers, one by one, which made her look up at him and bat her eyes. He turned her chin toward Gustave, but she turned back to face him. Did *she* even know what she wanted?

Behind her, Alphonsine watched this little interplay with a look of amusement or judgment, he didn't know which. Alphonsine, the Mona Lisa of the Maison Fournaise. He stepped toward her and stroked her forearm in order to connect with her. The pads of his fingers tingled as they passed over the downy hair. The minute movement of her mouth told him she enjoyed it.

Moving among them to make slight adjustments was an exquisite pleasure. By God, those jurists would stand in line to walk around in this painting, touch the women's cheeks, and sit down to join the party for a brandy. He would paint so prettily the pleasures and beauties of this age that the painting would topple the stodgy bastion that sat under that dark, gold-ribbed dome.

Light bathed the models and the table with warmth and brilliance. He admired each one, and had to blink back his joy so it wouldn't spill over. Alphonsine blinked too. She knew.

"I'll say one thing, and then let's be quiet for a while." He paused to swallow. "You're all beautiful. Thank you."

"I have the urge—" Cécile-Louise said.

"Here I am," Pierre said, flinging his arms wide.

"To go to the toilet."

Angèle rolled her eyes. "Squeeze it, princess, just like you know how to do. I'm sure you're an expert."

People laughed, which changed the angle of some heads. That was all right for now. He didn't need to be precise until a later sitting. But then what? How could he keep them all still? What had he gotten himself into? Some glorious insanity? The number of people was unmanageable. How could he expect them to be quiet, patient, cooperative, and immobile, when people come out to the river to be just the opposite?

He nodded to Fournaise. Together they wheeled out the easel and clamped on the canvas, nearly two meters wide. Jules whistled at its size.

"Why did you need one so blasted big?" Père Fournaise asked.

"Because he thinks big," Paul said.

"Because it's going to make a big splash at the Salon," Auguste said. "Because it's going to put to shame those monumental dead history paintings by Meissonier because this one will be live history, history in the making. What happens right here every Sunday on *your* terrace."

He tried out several angles for the easel, settling on an orientation in line with the table edges. He chalked the position on the floor, and the positions of those standing as well.

Alphonse was having a hard time not turning to look whenever he heard a boat bumping the dock, but soon the talking and shifting of feet stopped. Auguste could feel a recognition descending on them, the enormity of the project, the length of time it would take, the effort it would demand from all of them. Shouts of boaters across the water and an outburst of laughter from the arbor below rattled him. The models were surrounded by people who had no task before them except enjoyment of the day. What was he asking?

He didn't know where to put his palette and Bazille's color box.

"Papa, bring my bedside table," Alphonsine said.

Fournaise pulled back his chin at being commanded by his daughter in public, but hurried off and came back with a table of just the right height.

Auguste opened the packet that Fionie Tanguy had wrapped and arranged the tubes by color. There, unmistakably, was Prussian blue, so strong in its effect it only came in very small tubes. It astonished him, seeing it there in his palm. Fionie, the sly Xantippe of Montmartre.

"What's wrong?" Père Fournaise asked.

He cleared his throat. "Nothing. Everything is right."

He squeezed out paint onto the palette, small, lovely dollops shining in the sun. The shock of pure color worming out of the tubes made him feel flushed. He placed the lightest at the thumbhole and progressed to the darks around the perimeter of the rectangle. Very small amounts. To waste some at the end of the day would be a sin against Tanguy's good will. The position of his arm in the cast did not allow him to hold the palette flat. Linseed oil would spill out from the tin cup attached. He'd have to use it from the table, an awkward movement to reach across his cast.

"Can you move this to my left?"

"Certainly, my friend." Fournaise jumped to move the table. "May I stay here to watch the first stroke? This painting will make my restaurant famous."

Auguste nodded. "Time will tell." His arms, legs, chest all felt tight, as though his veins suddenly had twice as much blood to pump.

He bent the hog's hair of his new broad flat to break the sizing and tried out the balance of it. Where to make the first stroke? How large to make the three foreground figures—Alphonse, Cécile, and Gustave? How small the grouping in back—Jules, Pierre, Paul? It was better not to think. Let instinct take over. Still, a dozen figures and no sketches to go by. No certainty that he had them positioned in the best way. No word from Charles or Jeanne. Should he leave space for them? Alphonse had to get back to the dock. The light might change. A dozen people waited for him to make the first stroke. People good enough to give up their Sundays for him.

The blossomy, weedy smell of the oil, the solidity of the paint on the palette giving way to plasticity with his brand-new brush as tight and springy as a virgin, as lively as a whore. His pulse raced as though he were a raw novice.

All were silent, all still. He breathed.

Start.

He slashed a diagonal for the railing with the palest, most watery ultramarine and rose madder diluted with linseed and turpentine. An upward stroke. Awkward with his left hand.

"Bravo!" Fournaise shouted, and ducked downstairs. No one laughed.

He laid down the awning supports, as transparent as watercolors in case he didn't want them later. For now, they were good guidelines. He took a clean brush for the lightest areas, the front table edge. He couldn't have the railing running parallel to the retreating table edge and achieve the foreshortened plunge. He'd have to fudge. There was nothing wrong with irregularity. Working foreground to background and left to right as usual felt awkward with his left hand. He set the lightest values, the sunlight on Alphonse's back, Raoul's shirt collar, Gustave's singlet at his shoulder. Hm, an interesting gesture stroke. He wouldn't have done that with his right hand.

He worked in a mite of chrome yellow for a creamier white across Alphonsine's back. She must be luxuriating in the sun's warmth along her spine, enjoying it like a cat. She *was* catlike. Adorable. The same tint on Maggiolo's jacket, Angèle's hat. Positioning the straw hats with pure chrome yellow but still transparent. Pure joy to touch down here and there.

"My elbow's tingling," Cécile-Louise said.

His normal method of working on all parts of a painting simultaneously would try their patience, but he needed to set the positions and
values over the whole canvas in this session. For *Moulin* he'd worked up
two studies first. He had nothing to go by here except what was before
his eyes. He'd like to see Zola try this!

"You don't need to hold your positions stiffly if you need to move.
Just stay more or less in place. When I want to make sure of something,
I'll ask you individually to hold the pose."

He picked up vermilion and a pinch of ultramarine to tone it down,
mixing them on the canvas for the chairs and Alphonse's beard, adding
a tinge of Veronese green for Jules's jacket, just flecks to build color
harmonies. The browns, a trace of rose madder for Pierre's curly reddish beard, like a poodle's coat, Raoul's jacket and bowler, so juicy it
ran. The sheer magic of alchemy took his breath away, as if he'd never
seen or performed it before.

Back to his cool tone brush with ultramarine for Cécile's torso, Alphonsine's skirt, Angèle's bodice and sleeve, Ellen's left shoulder, the
grapes, the wine. Mere gesture strokes. No more than gauzy suggestions for a later time when he'd mix opaque blues on the canvas to create the shapes. Darker, but still transparent, that triangle of Gustave's
pant leg, Pierre's bowler, Antonio's cravat. Oh, he was loving this. His
arm moved as if in a dream.

"My elbow's gone to sleep," Cécile-Louise said. "How can a part of
you go to sleep and the rest stay awake? Do we tingle like this when all
parts of us are asleep only we don't notice?"

"A little longer, *s'il vous plaît.*"

He wiped his light brush clean for the skin tones. Keep it going. No
shapes, just dabs with the edge of his brush. The lightest first, Cécile's,
like ivory. Adding pale soft yellow for the brightest area of Angèle's
throat. Adding rose madder for Émile, more for Ellen and Pierre. Gustave, Angèle, and Paul still wore the sun on their cheeks from a morning on the river. Alphonse's cheek and temple too. More tawny for the
Italian. Eventually an infinitude of hues depending on what surrounded
the face or arm or hand. No two places alike.

The vanishing point. Upper right. Right about here.

He added white to Veronese green and ultramarine, pale and watery, and flicked on suggestions of the foliage, but stopped. They were left-handed strokes, curved the wrong way. How much of this would be wrong when he could paint right-handed again?

He heard footsteps on the stairs. Alphonsine's expression changed. He turned to look.

Jeanne!

CHAPTER NINE

Models, Friends, Lovers

J eanne.

Her glittering, triumphant green eyes met his. *If you have any feeling left for me, if only the fond remembrance of things past, come.* She came. Wearing the hat he had drawn, with a chestnut curl dropping over her forehead. *My little quail,* he used to call her when she wore her hair like that.

He said with his eyes, *Je t'adore.* With his mouth he said, "Thank you for coming." The tic in his cheek went wild.

In an instant he turned to ice. Thirteen. She was a blessing and a curse. This was more serious than a bad omen. Positioning thirteen figures around a dining table spelled carelessness, not *long and thoughtful preparation.* Zola would be right.

How artfully her gaze slid over any mouths that might ask why she was so late. Her presence commanded, as though she were onstage, and he was in her thrall, she who found she could not love unless she was immortalized on canvas as the roles she played. If he had acquiesced, would she be loving him tonight? He tried to send his thought to her: Can you glimpse, even for a moment, that what we do here might immortalize you as well?

She aimed a guarded smile at him, then looked back at the stairwell.

More footsteps. A top hat emerged, then a black frock coat, white silk cravat, and ivory-tipped walking stick. The dandy he'd seen in her dressing room. Condescension oozed from his face like grease. Auguste's hand cramped, resisting a handshake. How dare she rub salt into the wound! A sour taste rose in his mouth. Was she insinuating that he should put his own replacement in the painting? He'd rather heave the thing in the river.

Jeanne glided toward the far table. Pierre thrust a glass of wine in her hand. A pictorial instant. A possibility.

Auguste went to work whitewashing the position marks for Pierre and Paul in order to move them to the right and have them face Jeanne. Paul assumed his characteristic stance bending forward to see better. My God, was he going to lick her? That left Jules leaning against the back railing alone. Now he needed Charles all the more, to fill the space, to have Jules engaged, and to be the fourteenth. Ephrussi's top hat right there would show the group to be a mix of classes. Here was a substitute, top-hatted and tall. Her companion, lover, gigolo, whatever he was, placed his hand on her waist and smirked in his direction, claiming her for all to see.

No, he would not use this cocksure fop. Not in the center of his painting. That would be a bad omen too. He'd hold out for Charles.

"Ah," Paul said, squinting at the man. "So this is the lucky Monsieur Joseph-Paul Lagarde whom *Le Temps* reports as frequenting the Samary house on avenue Frochot. *Un habitué?* Let me tell you what people are saying."

"Oh, no, I refuse to listen." She covered her ears with her fingers.

"Are you wearing a ring beneath those pert black gloves?" Pierre asked. "A ring from this gentleman, perhaps?"

"Take them off and let us see whether we must go drown ourselves out of despair," Paul said.

She let loose her shrill, infectious laugh climbing up the harmonic scale. Audiences loved it, but it had always grated on his ears. She touched her gloved index finger to Paul's nose. "Drown yourself in wine?"

"No. In the river."

"Oh! *Mon Dieu!*" she cried in that exaggerated, high-pitched comic way of hers and set down her glass to take them off.

"Leave them on," Auguste commanded. He didn't want to see a

shattering truth at this crucial moment. "I want your white sleeve next to the black."

"It won't even be seen way back here," she said petulantly.

"It will if you put your hands to your ears like you just did."

Her haughty bourgeois lover kept shifting his weight, probably ambivalent about being in a painting with men in undershirts. Ha! Let him think he would be. Let him stand still for an hour hovering over her for nothing. Then he'd know what Pierre-Auguste Renoir thought of him. Or he might use his hand and a slice of his hat to suggest a person cut off at the edge like Manet and Degas sometimes did. A faceless, anonymous nothing of a person. A cipher. A nonentity. Not even enough of him to count as a fourteenth.

Cécile-Louise had turned in order to look at Jeanne. It was closer to what he really wanted, her interacting with the others, but she'd turned too far. "Your chin a little to the right, please, Cécile."

She turned back toward him too far now. "I insist on you calling me Circe. If you don't I shall have to box your ears. Gently, of course." The tip of her rosy tongue came out and made a dainty circuit of her lips.

He pretended he hadn't noticed.

Just when everyone had settled, Jeanne said, "Don't paint me with those patchy dabs. You made my skin look like fish scales in that portrait." Ellen tittered. "You laugh now, Ellen, but fishy arms won't do your reputation any good."

Gustave cleared his throat as if to make a point. "Are you referring to Auguste's half-figure portrait of you that hung in the *place of honor* at our *Impressionist* show three years ago? The one in a green dress that critics praised? The very one Zola called the success of the show?"

"Then why was Auguste's full-length portrait of me hung above the toilet in the next Salon?"

"Because the graybeard jurors are subject to influence," Auguste said. "Because Sarah Bernhardt—"

"Filled the place of honor. It isn't enough that she gets all the best roles at the Comédie-Française. She has to get the best spots in the Salon too. Anyone wanting to look at me got a crick in his neck."

"I've got a crick in my neck *now,*" Circe whined.

Ah, was that jealousy speaking? He could play that game too.

"Such a beautiful neck," he said. "It's made of white satin, isn't it?"

"How much longer?" Circe asked.

"Soon. Just a little more."

"Just a little more," she mimicked. "A little more, and a little more. Usually I want a little more, but—"

"If you don't button up that pretty mouth of yours, I'll be forced to—"

"Kiss it?" Circe puckered up her lips.

"Now, there's a tempting pose," Jules said. Alphonsine snickered and the angles of some heads changed slightly.

He was losing them. "Give me half an hour more."

"But I'm sooo tired. Haven't you done enough to imagine the rest?"

"Out of the question."

"Some painters do that. Madame Charpentier told me."

"I'm not one of them. It's one of my personal principles which I've rarely broken. Paint only from the motif."

"I commend any man who sticks to his principles," Jules said.

"Can't you make an exception just this once? My arm hurts." Circe's voice was tinged with a childish whine.

"Pain passes, but beauty lasts. Think of that and you'll forget the pain. Any beautiful thought will do."

"You'll have a devil of a time getting him to bend his rule," Gustave said.

"But think of me. I'll have a devil of a time getting my elbow to *unbend.*"

He tried not to listen and just let his instinct take over. Mentally, he walked around the table to remind himself of what he wanted out of each person. Circe, the porcelain doll. Alphonse, the lordly observer. Alphonsine, enchanting, alert, her eyes roving, not missing a thing as she lounged on the rail. Raoul facing Alphonsine, murmuring to her, calling her *lady,* the English way. In the right foreground, Gustave in his flat-topped boater looking younger than he really was. Angèle provocative, with her arm familiarly behind Gustave. Antonio Maggiolo looking down at Angèle. A good model. Antonio adoring Angèle who was adoring Gustave—the three of them could be substance enough for a painting all their own. Ellen, elusive behind her glass, piquant and charming. Maybe it was a bit unkind to hide her face, but the painting needed someone in the act of drinking. Émile facing her, captivated. Paul and Pierre talking to Jeanne.

Jeanne. The hot glistening skin of her cheek, her throat, her inner thigh flew through his mind. Her lips moist against his. If it weren't for Lagarde touching her, he could indulge himself by imagining a mutual love, for the sake of the painting, to give it his best.

He went around again letting his brush extend the comma strokes into sweeps to suggest the placement of large areas of color, like the strong dark triangle of Gustave's thigh, Angèle's skirt repeating the triangle set upright, and now a slimmer triangle of Jeanne's skirt. He held the spread of bristles vertically and rotated it to make a widening swath as he went down the bottom right of the canvas, ignoring his worries in the act of painting.

"You're not using green for our skin, are you? We're not lizards," Jeanne said, always the entertainer. "Don't forget what that critic Albert Wolff said in *Le Figaro* about your *Nude in the Sunlight. A pile of flesh in the process of decomposition and needing immediate burial.*"

"Ugh." Circe stretched out the sound in a funny way. Competing.

"There's hardly any skin showing," Auguste said.

"Would that it were otherwise," Pierre said.

"But not green. We don't want green faces," Jeanne said.

"No, darling. Your lovely face is a secret mixture of chrome yellow, rose madder, white, and ultramarine."

He took great satisfaction when Joseph-Paul shot him a sharp look at the word *darling.*

"What's ultramarine?" Circe asked. "Deep sea sludge?"

"Blue."

"I don't want blue circles under my eyes."

Circe sensing a rival was amusing. Jeanne knew that he'd do whatever he wanted. Circe's demands were made out of ignorance, but because she was so beautiful, because her dress had those luscious, Prussian blue stripes, he paid her no mind. If he'd been forced to use ultramarine, in a few years the sulfur in it would yellow the edges of the white stripes. At least that was one disaster he avoided, thanks to Fionie.

"But you want red lips, don't you? When the time comes to paint them, I'm going to use vermilion. Don't worry. It's not like the carmine you use on your lips, which is made from dead bugs from South America. Red ones. Females."

Circe pretended to faint.

Everyone laughed.

"All right. Remember your positions. We can take a break."

"Finally!" Circe sprang up and shook out her shoulders which made her breasts jiggle. "I thought I was going to turn to stone."

"Like Lot's wife?" came a voice from the far table. Aha! The quiet poet had noticed her.

"No, like Venus," Auguste said.

"I played Venus once in *Orpheus and the Underworld,*" Angèle said to Antonio.

"And she's been playing it ever since," Jeanne said in a husky stage voice.

Pierre poured another round of wine. "Then let's drink to Venus!"

Angèle sliced a pear into wedges and speared one wedge on the end of her knife. "One for you," she said, her wet mouth opening, her tongue flicking as she aimed the pear wedge at Gustave's opening lips. "And one for you," she said to Antonio. "Don't move or I might stab you."

Auguste drank a glass of seltzer water and inserted his longest brush handle up his cast, trying to scratch an itch. The light would change soon. He couldn't give them too much of a break. He hadn't finished setting the values. He didn't want to go over and talk to Jeanne, not with this Joseph-Paul standing there smug and proprietary. Let Pierre and Paul entertain her.

Piano music came up from downstairs, "Le Toréador" from *Carmen*. Pierre sang a few lines in his rich baritone until Auguste stood up, a signal. He'd lose them on the chorus if he didn't call them back into position. "Two minutes," he said above their talk. Antonio rolled his shoulders and stretched. His forward lean was an excruciating position. Ellen faced forward and waited before raising her glass. Alphonse smiled at her. Was he smitten already? "One minute." Gustave assumed his position. The talking stopped.

"A little more to the left," Auguste said to Pierre.

He lost himself to his unconscious instincts of composition. Circe hummed loudly, dancing her fingernails on the table, then on the edge of a plate so the tink, tink drew attention to her. Jules stood alone now, drifting in his own mental world, probably composing lines of verse. Pierre swayed, struggling to hold his position. He'd had too much to drink. Gustave was as still as a statue. He knew what was necessary and, by example, was trying to teach the others.

Auguste made another circuit of the canvas, positioning smaller areas of color. Circe let out a long, loud sigh. He'd lost track of how much time had passed. The light had changed. He'd gotten the bones of the painting.

"Enough for today."

Alphonse bolted downstairs to relieve his father at the dock.

Auguste raised his shoulders to stretch and began to clean his brushes. With only a nod to him, Jeanne and her new man slipped out. He'd pay her privately the next time she posed—without her beau, he hoped. Jeanne, the most famous, would demand the most, even though she was only a smaller figure in the rear. He paid Ellen first, so she could be off. Dance music lured some of them downstairs.

Alphonsine seemed reluctant to leave. She stood on tiptoe to whisper in his ear, "This is one of the loveliest things that has ever happened to me."

He dipped a brush in turpentine and worked out the pigment onto a rag. Loveliest? For him it was the riskiest.

Jules lit his pipe and came around to the front of the canvas. "Painted with a feather on a sunbeam. Intriguing before one even knows what it is. I can't wait to see what tints you'll show us vibrating against each other."

"Vibrating? That would make me swoon," Circe said.

"Then you'll have to retrain your eye," Jules said. "Normally we recognize objects by outline, but we'd see more if we noticed the vibrations between contrasting colors."

Circe squinted at the painting. "We suffered aching muscles all afternoon and we're only smears. Is it because of your broken arm?"

"He has intentions for those smears," Jules said. "It's a rare thing to see a painting so complex emerge step by step. You ought to feel privileged."

"Step by step sounds like dancing." She did a waltz step, thrusting her hip forward, holding her skirt out, and turned her head slowly from Auguste to Jules to Gustave to Pierre and back again. In a measured way, she waltzed to the stairs, gave them a backward glance, and descended.

Pierre blew air out his mouth. "Quite the dish. Where in the world did you find her?"

"Madame Charpentier thrust her on me."

Jules cleared his throat. *"She the primrose path of dalliance treads."*

"Conscious of her every move," Gustave said. "Calculated to entice."

Auguste wondered if she'd be that calculating horizontal as well as vertical.

Jules relit his pipe and looked at the canvas. "You see the whole, don't you? We see only marks."

"In a haze I see it. I know that what I'll see later is there now, but I don't see it yet. I'll keep making discoveries until the very end. Sometimes the most important things come out last."

Jules nodded. "You sound like a writer."

He tossed his paint rag onto the table. "Now I remember how hard *Moulin* was. You'd think I would have learned. What I'm trying to do is absurd."

Gustave gave him a censuring look.

"Don't mention that I said that. They've got to have faith that I'll finish the thing or I'll lose them. It'll be a long ordeal for all of us."

"Why is it absurd?" Jules asked.

"To capture a fleeting instant with so many figures? My brush can't move across the canvas that fast. I need to be an octopus with eight brushes going at once to paint all these people and bottles and glasses, the tablecloth and fruit, the foliage, the river, the boats, the opposite bank. Separate perceptible touches of the brush to give the impression that all million of them were laid on in one instant."

"An intriguing approach, one that lies at the core of Impressionism, the attempt to catch an instant in time. Would you mind if I used that in an essay I'm writing?"

"Just so long as you don't make me out as a theorist. I detest painters prattling about theories. They should paint, not talk it to death."

Jules gave him a teasing look, and he realized he'd come close to theoretical babble himself. He tipped his head for them to go downstairs.

"Wait a moment," Pierre said, scratching his beard. "Am I right that there were fourteen people today?"

"Yes, but I'm not going to use Jeanne's beau."

"Then you're on dangerous ground. Thirteen figures around a dining table makes reference to the Last Supper."

"I know. It's impossible for a painter not to know that."

"The thirteenth is Judas. The number brings ill to one of them. He'll die within the year."

"A superstition, Pierre. You fret too much."

"Don't be so quick to dismiss it. There's truth to omens and this one goes back to ancient times. The number is deadly. There are thirteen witches in a coven."

Auguste laughed. "I'm not painting witches. I'm painting goddesses."

"There's a reason no house in Paris bears the number thirteen. And why prudent hostesses, having invited fourteen, always arrange for a last-minute substitute, a *quatorzième,* in case a guest does not arrive. It's a hex."

"No, it's a hoax perpetrated by cranks and fanatics," Auguste said. But he knew the gravity of the issue. He would appeal to Charles Ephrussi.

Downstairs, Auguste drew Raoul aside to pay him.

"Don't be stupid, Renoir. Don't you think I had a fine time?"

The pianist was playing a quadrille. Without the required eight dancers, Paul and Pierre shared Angèle as a partner in the *chahut,* a prelude to the cancan with bent knees, lower kicks, and animal imitations. "Shaking out the kinks," Raoul said, joining them despite his bad leg. Circe, too highbrow for such displays, stood off to the side under her opened parasol. At the end of the dance, Raoul headed for the nearest chair and a glass of seltzer water.

Angèle tugged on Auguste's cast and he followed her. She spoke in a low voice, out of breath. "I hate to ask, but I'm in trouble for fifty francs for my rent. I must pay it by nine in the morning and I only have eight. If you could advance me my earnings, I'd turn a spin or two in your honor, else, you know, I'll have to . . . And modeling is more respectable, you have to agree."

Her veins ran with bohemian blood, equal parts insouciance, vitality, and risk. Auguste dug into his wallet and produced forty in addition to her ten for posing.

Angèle asked the pianist for "Habanera" from *Carmen,* and raised one arm over her head like a Spanish dancer, snapped her fingers, and slid into Carmen's bewitching dance, the rage at cabarets. She swung her skirt to the pulsing rhythm and sang, building intensity in her sultry voice:

> *When will I love you?*
> *In faith, I do not know,*
> *Maybe never, maybe tomorrow,*
> *But not today, that's certain.*
> *Love is a rebellious bird*
> *That nothing can tame.*

All eyes were on the temptress, even the crowd of regulars under the arbor, as she sashayed among the men, grabbing her skirt in her fists and raising it to her knees, flirting voluptuously—a sensuous touch under Raoul's chin, lingering strokes along Paul's shoulders, snaking down his spine and around his waist. She pulled the carnation from between her breasts and drew it along Pierre's throat. She lifted her skirt and straddled a chair in front of Gustave just like his pose in the painting, and tickled his ear with the flower. Oozing sensuality, she backed up against Antonio, swiveling her shoulder into his chest, then whirled away, leaving him gaping. With her eyes fixed seductively on Antonio, she stood on a chair and went on singing:

> *Love is the child of the bohemian.*
> *It has never, never known any law.*
> *If you don't love me, I love you;*
> *If I love you, keep guard on yourself!*

She hopped down and flung the carnation at Antonio's chest. Bewitched and speechless, he picked it up and everyone on the lower terrace clapped.

"Beware, Antonio," Pierre teased. "Stay on guard."

"Bizet is applauding from his grave," Père Fournaise said. "You know, he lived just downstream near Bougival. Is that where you found this brazen gypsy, Auguste?"

"No. Montmartre, the Bohemia of *la vie moderne.*"

Circe was standing by herself with one arm around the maple trunk, a position of petulance. Auguste walked over to her.

"Madame Charpentier said I mustn't ask you for more than you paid the others, these Montmartre *gypsies.*"

"Then you shall have ten francs, the same to a centime." He placed a coin into her palm. Her fingers folded over his.

"Do you ever go out in a yole?" she asked.

"Not as much as I'd like to. I love boats, every kind. I've never been able to afford one, so I have to take my pleasure by watching others."

"You're dreadfully honest."

"I don't know how to be any other way."

He did own a boat once, not one that would count in her eyes. When he was a little boy his father took him to see the pretty toy sailboats in a pond in the Tuileries Garden. The next week, he tried to make one out of a carpenter's scrap, scraping it against a stone wall to make a prow, but when he set it in the pond, a breeze blew it out of reach and the fountain in the center pelted it with water and it got trapped there, looking only like a stray piece of wood.

"Might you like to go rowing, after a day of painting?" she asked.

He held up his cast. "It will be a little while yet before I row any-thing but a brush across a canvas."

"How long before that comes off?"

"A week more."

"I can wait a week."

But after another session like the one today, he knew he'd be too exhausted to row. "Will a short promenade suffice?"

"Nicely."

They ambled down the lane. It was something to promenade along-side a rustling dress. They remarked about the people lounging on the banks, eating, drinking, playing cards, yawning, content to do little more than breathe the languor in the air. The eyes of the men and women in boats close to the bank subtly taunted the picnickers on the grass, and the picnickers eyed the boaters with envy. He understood that look, but doubted that she did.

Circe launched a tedious account of a soirée, describing every count and countess in attendance as if they were intimate friends. He wished she'd be more like Ellen when she performed her mimes at the Folies. Silent. Holding up his half of the conversation required more energy than he had left. Finally, they turned back and he walked her across the bridge to the station.

He came back feeling elated until he remembered the problem of thirteen. And the perspective. And anchoring the terrace. He shook out his shoulders to release the tension of the day. Even if they were avail-able to pose day after day, managing so many people would be too much. How did Veronese do it with forty figures around the table, plus the ones on the upper level? He must have posed small groups at a time. He would ask a few to come on weekdays. Only now did he realize the complexity of positioning so many interacting figures, and it made him weak in the knees as he stepped off the bridge.

He went inside to find Fournaise in the dining room and took out his wallet, depleted now by the francs he'd given to Angèle. "I won't be able to pay you the whole bill now, but take this and keep a record."

Alphonsine stood behind her father next to a sideboard, watching.

Fournaise raised his hand against the money. "It's been taken care of."

"By whom?"

"You don't need to know."

Alphonsine picked up a bowl and held it over her head upside down. Trying to keep a straight face, she took a few lurching steps.

A lump formed in his throat. He fumbled putting his money away.

From the kitchen doorway, Louise asked, "Did the glasses have soul enough for you?"

He kissed her on the forehead. "Everything did."

CHAPTER TEN

Cork in the Stream

In the morning, Alphonsine slipped through the upstairs corridor that led from the family's rooms to the three rental rooms on that floor and to the terrace. The painting was there just as she'd hoped. Dabs, patches, curves like crescent moons produced a scattered calligraphy of colors. What would they become? she wondered. What has he glimpsed in us to lay over that vast white land? Us. *Nous.* She said the word aloud, dropping off the *s,* a kind of lowing. The exhilaration she had felt yesterday surged again. She was part of something.

"Nous?" she heard and turned around. Auguste was coming up the top step. "What do you mean, *nous?*"

She wanted him to know her, but this might make her seem lonely.

"Just something silly."

He sat and tipped back the chair. "What do you see on the canvas?"

"I can't imagine it as a picture yet the way you probably can, but I know it will become a fine painting."

"Either that or a colossal failure."

"It's not good to start out thinking that way." She couldn't resist asking, "Is this smear me?" She pointed above the brown diagonal.

"Yes. The beautiful one. Light salmon pink beneath the yellow. Exquisite, the color of your skin. Like the inside of a shell."

She didn't speak for a moment in order to prolong his thinking.

"It's a brave thing to start such a big canvas. Is it the largest size?"

"The largest width. It was given to me by a man who could ill afford to. A good man, Père Tanguy. I'll pay him for it someday."

"I'm sure you will, in one way or another."

Right then, to her this good man, this Père Tanguy, became part of *nous*.

"How many people were in the painting yesterday?" she asked.

"Thirteen. That's a big problem. Jesus was betrayed by the thirteenth person at the Last Supper. The painting's cursed until I find a fourteenth."

"It's a curse only if you count the face dabs. You can count Monsieur Tanguy too."

A shallow spurt of a laugh came from his throat, but she'd meant it half seriously.

"I wonder what will happen to the rest of the cloth from that roll."

"Another painter with big dreams will buy it for another monstrous painting. That size, probably some classical or historic subject."

"The same origin yet entirely different, like brothers separated at birth."

"You have an interesting way of looking at things."

"You're the one who can look at a grease spot and see a face."

Between them she sensed a growing accord, a *rapprochement,* the possibility of partnership in the painting. When he was painting, she felt that some things were understood between them, tacit in a look or a gesture. She wondered if he felt it too. What was he made of, this man who came and went so blithely? What made him banter with everyone and say funny, ironic things sometimes, and other times sit all balled up in himself?

"But I can't do anything with those grease spots without models."

"What about the tablecloth and bottles?"

"Not without more built up around them." He stood up and leaned on the railing. "If I had another canvas I'd go down to the piling of the railroad bridge. Some tamarisk trees are in bloom there. I hate being idle."

"Do you want to go for a row?"

He held up his cast as an answer.

"I can row a yole. You can work the rudder cords, can't you?"

He extended his arm as far forward as the bent-arm cast would allow.

"Good enough," she said. "I'll show you some places I know upriver."

When they got in the boat, his long legs tangled with hers. She had to put hers between his in order to row, so he spread his wide. She was embarrassed, but he wasn't. She liked that about him. She caught him looking at her ankles, which amused her. They were only ankles.

"Do you have a favorite place on the river?" she asked.

"All the spots I ever painted."

"I mean one place."

He was quiet for the length of two strokes. "La Grenouillère."

"I wouldn't have guessed that. It's so noisy and crowded."

"That was the spot where we started Impressionism."

"You can say that for certain?"

"Yes. I can name the day. The first Sunday in July 1869, when Claude Monet and I set up our easels next to each other and experimented to learn how broken strokes show light dancing on the water. Like now. Do you see the yellow?"

"I see where the sun catches the ripples."

"They have color. Right now it's yellow ocher even though the water's dominant color is blue, but there's lavender and green too. We knew we were discovering something revolutionary. We couldn't wait to get back to Paris and tell Bazille. We were living in his studio in the Batignolles. It's his color box I broke."

He seemed to drift away from her. She wanted to call him back, wanted to know all the steps that brought him here, to this painting and to her in this boat.

"Who is Bazille?"

"Frédéric. The three of us lived in two rooms—one that overheated when the stove decided to work, where we slept in the buff, and the other unheated where we painted and ate with our overcoats on in winter. Poor Lise, the model for my nude of *Diana the Huntress*. Every half hour Frédéric ran down the six flights of stairs to buy her a *café* while Claude and I wrapped her in blankets. When she stopped shivering, we went to work again."

"That sounds awful."

"It was wonderful! We were in our twenties and doing what we wanted. When we had no money for models, we painted each other. Or we painted bridges and boulevards. We always went to Le Moulin de la Galette on Sundays because it was free, long before I thought to paint it. But whenever Bazille got some money from his parents, he insisted on taking us on a round of theaters and cabarets and circuses and dance halls, the Folies-Bergère, the café concerts on barges, the horse races at Longchamp, until the money ran out. Then we would have to start the fire in the stove with our watercolors and drawings again. We were brash beyond our means, but Paris, sublime and sordid, was there for the taking, if not in those days then in the future. We were drunk on possibility, intoxicated by the thousand delights yet to be tasted.

"At night, to keep warm, we went to the Café Guerbois nearby and played dominoes or checkers, sometimes with the writers Duret, Zola, or Durant. They educated us. We met Manet there, and Cézanne and Pissarro and Degas. Every Thursday night without fail there were spirited discussions about a revolution in painting. Before the press labeled us Impressionists, we called ourselves the Batignolles group. Then the war came."

"Go back all the way."

"More? You want more?"

"Can you name the day you decided to become a painter?"

He smiled on one side only.

"It crept up on me. When I was a child I drew a dog with my father's tailor's chalk on the tenement floor, drew a frame around it, and told my family not to walk on it. It was surprising that they respected it enough not to. It made me feel important, so I did more—my sister, my mother, the houses on our street, the Roman well. I ventured farther, to the Fountain of the Innocents in a maze of market stalls, which held me spellbound even then with its sculptures of women. Soon my parents, three brothers, and my sister were all tiptoeing between my pictures of Paris done from memory on the floor."

He paused as though he were enjoying the memory.

"My mother had to do something to keep peace in the house so I was taken out of school and apprenticed to a porcelain manufacturer on rue du Temple when I was thirteen. I loved it, and was able to help my parents buy a house in Louveciennes. It was piecework and I was fast. The older workers called me Monsieur Rubens. I had high hopes to earn six francs a day, which would have provided me a good living eventually."

"Does that mean you quit?"

"When I was seventeen, the workshop was shut down by companies that printed designs on ware by machines. Hundreds of them exactly the same. Progress and science killed off the kind of slow handwork that had made me happy. It was my first disillusionment. I had thought I would be content painting Venuses and Marie Antoinettes forever, but I was born a century too late for that."

She kept rowing slowly so he would keep talking.

"I set up a cooperative and painted my own designs faster than the machines, thinking I could outwit progress, but by that time shopkeepers didn't want anything made by hand. They wanted uniformity. To me it signaled a decline in taste."

"Your second disillusionment? What did you do then?"

"I got a job copying eighteenth-century paintings on ladies' fans. It was easy to obtain a card allowing me to paint the Old Masters in the Louvre as a study during my lunchtime. I painted murals in cafés too. Imagine how thrilling it was to cover a whole wall after years of working in miniature. I felt liberated by bigness, by the chance to swing my arm and leave a trail of color. It paid a pittance and wasn't steady work so I switched to painting window shades. Lucrative, but so repetitious it nearly killed me. Twenty years old and I'd come to a point of decision."

"What decision?"

"My parents agreed to call in someone they thought was an 'expert' to determine if I had any talent. The only person we knew was a student at a second-rate drawing school. The whole family was nervous, one moment hoping they wouldn't be made to feel foolish if the 'expert' laughed, the next moment hoping that he would say I was a pathetic dreamer so that I would forget painting and turn to a more dependable trade."

"And the expert said you had talent."

Without a hint of a smile, he nodded. What a pitiful look—his eyes dark, his cheeks hollowed.

"The man said I must get a proper art education. There was only somber silence around the dinner table that night. Even my younger brother stared at his plate and wouldn't eat. My parents were plunged into despair as wrenching as if they'd lost a son."

"Weren't they pleased at all?"

"It meant giving up steady work and taking on a monstrous risk. It meant the end of my contributions to the family's well-being."

"But what did *you* feel?"

"Wronged. Tricked by my own talent. I'll never forget my mother sobbing into a dish towel. It made me feel as though I'd committed a crime. But the next morning she managed a motherly look as she bravely sent me off to apply at l'École des Beaux-Arts. That was my third disillusionment."

"Oh, no. Why?"

"I got next to nothing out of it. But I met Bazille, Sisley, and Monet there. They were disgusted too, so we left the academy and painted outdoors in the Forest of Fontainebleau. I painted a rustic inn in Marlotte, Mère Anthony's, with Monet, Sisley, and Le Coeur posing around a table. The waitress and Mère Anthony too. That was my first step here, to this painting of people around *two* tables."

That's what she'd been waiting for. It placed her, somehow, in his life. She realized she had stopped rowing, and began again.

After a few minutes he pulled himself out of the past and said, "There's a beautiful maple behind you with an overhanging branch. Just think. There's no other tree exactly like it."

"No two leaves exactly alike either."

"Some say a tree is only made of chemicals, but I believe that God created it." A glint came into his eyes. "And that it's inhabited by a nymph."

She liked that he could be playful. Edgar Degas would never say that.

"Then I'll tell you a fairy tale when we get to a place," she said.

"Do you have a favorite place?"

"Two of them." She looked behind her, and saw the farthest of the Elizabethan cottages of Rueil spreading its garden toward the water. "We're close to one of them." She rowed past the rotting trunk that lay diagonally in the river, the hawthorn with berries beginning to redden, the rill that ran down to the river. And there were the two sycamores with their branches intertwined and leaning over the water. She stopped rowing.

"Do you remember the fairy tale of the yellow dwarf? Two lovers, a prince and a princess, were separated by an evil dwarf who killed the prince?"

"Vaguely," he replied.

"The princess was so grief-stricken that she died too. A wise siren buried their bodies next to each other and they became trees. Their branches became intertwined. She knew they needed that in order to remain faithful. These two big sycamores, this is it."

"Because of the tale?"

"Partly. Louis asked me to marry him here." She reached up to grab a branch to keep them from drifting. "I was eighteen. He wanted to carve our names into them, but I wouldn't let him hurt the trees. Now I wish I had."

"Why?"

"Why are you painting this painting? It's for the same reason. To let the world know after our time that we were here, and that we loved."

"How do you know that for me?"

"By the way your face came alive when Jeanne Samary came up the stairs."

"It's only that I wanted her in the painting."

"Then why didn't you welcome the man with her like you welcomed Émile?"

Several minutes passed before he said, "You're pretty sure of yourself."

She started rowing again, sorry she'd made him feel exposed.

"What's your other favorite place?"

"We're going there."

A cork bobbed alongside the boat and Auguste leaned out to grab it, but it eluded him and was drawn into a whorl of grasses.

"I took the cork of the bottle of cassis yesterday," she said.

He tipped his head. "What for?"

"It was the first bottle of the first day painting the first luncheon of your boating party."

A soft look came into his eyes. "No one else there thought to do that. What a petite bundle of big feeling you are."

Now it was her turn to feel exposed. "Sometimes more than what's good for me."

For amusement, she rowed toward the cork and tried to wave it within reach with her oar. It plunged and popped up, going this way and that, riding the ripples downstream until it became lost in the glare on the water.

"There I go," Auguste said, "just drifting with the current. Not deciding anything for myself. My friend Paul—"

"The one who smacked his friend with the oar?"

"Yes. He thinks that in order to have good memories at the end of your life, you have to behave like a cork in a stream, letting yourself go. Who's to say whether letting things be what they will isn't the better way?"

"It's what brought you here, letting that expert decide."

"But it goes beyond that. Some painters think they are creating a world in each painting. I don't. I think the world is creating my motifs for me. In that way, it's creating me too, carrying me along like that cork."

"What's wrong with that?" she asked.

"It could lead me down several paths at once, false starts all of them. That's the way I feel with my painting styles—a little of this, a little of that. Experimentation is all right for a painter when he's twenty, even thirty, but I'm almost forty."

"I hadn't noticed."

A brief, wry smile came across his face. "Forty and still merely setting down what I see."

"Is that an issue of faith?"

"One might see it that way. You can say it's an issue of responsiveness and appreciation. The world is ravishing, Alphonsine. Just look. The distinct colors of the water quivering like moiré silk, the lattice of shadows made by branches shifting, that mallard with the iridescent head, posing for me so the light catches his white neck ring. You with your hair peeking out from your hat. Life. Ravishing life! If I were to paint what I see right now, it wouldn't be my invention. It's just what has been given me—by God, if you will, or by the current of life. Why not think it was made so gorgeous for me?"

She rowed slowly, relishing the moment. He was different than other painters. Claude spoke of the beauties of nature, but Auguste included her in them.

"Other times, I wonder what I'm missing. Not in the visual world, but with people. What I don't think to ask. So much slips away. Just drifting can lead a person to a dead end, and he's stuck going around and around endlessly. How long am I going to keep on not knowing something important?"

"Like what?"

"Like finding my way as a painter."

He was honest. She appreciated that.

"Or as a human being," she said, wondering how long that would take *her.*

He gazed across the water. "That too."

"I believe you're less of a cork than you realize," she said. "Don't you see that you make decisions every day? Small ones, practically imperceptible, but plaited together they make a cord running through your life?"

"That doesn't make me feel any more anchored. I think I'll still be unsure of myself on my deathbed."

"Only zealots aren't."

She had nearly passed the row of willows trailing their green curtain of branches in the water. Behind them was the bed of grasses and sweet alyssum.

"Turn in," she said. "This is it. Do you remember the flood of '74? The water overflowed these banks. When it retreated, Alphonse and I were out in the steam launch towing runaway boats back to their own-ers. On that slope we saw two bodies tangled together with a rope, all purple and bloated, a man and a woman. Alphonse thought they'd been using the rope to haul something from the flood and had gotten swept away. I thought they were lovers who were denied each other and had twined themselves together and leapt off Pont Saint-Louis, the suicide bridge, and the flood had brought them here. They lay with their heads turned toward one another, as if they'd gone down with a kiss."

"You have a big imagination."

"Do you think their kiss could have been a kind of blessing?"

"It could have been. Kisses can be blessings. Should we find out?"

She hadn't expected that. Really she hadn't.

"When was the last time you were kissed?" he asked.

She hesitated and looked down at the oars. "Ten years."

"Too long," he whispered.

He leaned toward her, and if she did too, they would touch. He had that same sweet look now that he'd had when she picked out the grit from his face.

The old knot of restraint squeezed. He didn't know the one thing about her that defined her. She couldn't let him kiss her without him knowing that. He'd been honest with her. She wanted to be honest with him, but if he knew the truth, he might condemn her, and then there would be two months of the painting to live through with him at the Maison every day.

He came closer, awkwardly, kneeling in the boat, wobbling it. She wobbled too, between wanting and waiting, present and past, knowing that she was repeating her calamitous hesitation. Heat rose up her throat to the top of her head. Slowly she raised the heavy oars in front of her, crossing them, a barricade. His expression darkened. The boat drifted back downstream. She let the moment float away like the cork in the river.

He sat back, and she turned the boat around by rowing each oar in opposite directions. A bird trilled in the trees. "That's a wood thrush," she said. "I love their song. They sing even when they're hungry."

"How about when they're sad?"

"Maybe then too."

It was important to let him know that a kiss might be possible someday.

"The word I was saying when you came up the stairs was *nous*. Everyone in the painting. My little salmon pink smear on the canvas means I am one of Us. That's something, for now."

CHAPTER ELEVEN

Cycle of Pleasure

On Wednesday, Auguste drank his morning *café* on the lower terrace with Alphonsine and Alphonse. The sun heated the top of his head right through his cycling cap. "It's going to be a scorcher today and I've got models coming."

"I'll make some lemonade, then. Who's coming?"

"Antonio, the Italian, and Angèle, the cheeky one who speaks in argot."

"Carmen," Alphonse murmured.

"She only speaks her own slang for play," Alphonsine said. "She can speak properly when she wants to."

"Do you have a saw in the boathouse?" he asked Alphonse.

Alphonse gave him an incredulous look. "What's a boatyard without a saw?"

Auguste held up his right arm. "This thing's got to come off."

Alphonse's look turned wary. "No. I don't want to be responsible." He finished his *café* and went off toward the floating boat garage.

When he was out of earshot Alphonsine asked, "Why haven't you gone to the doctor if it's ready?"

Auguste studied the color of his *café*. "He's in Paris."

"So? You don't have the money to pay him, do you?"

He turned away from her.

"You don't need to be ashamed. It's only me. I'll saw it off, if you want me to."

"I believe you would."

The *Iris* sailed by. Auguste enjoyed Alphonsine's little intake of breath. When the boat came about and headed for the dock, she tucked some loose strands into her chignon. "You didn't say *he* was coming."

"Since when do I need to get Mademoiselle's permission?"

She ran to the dock to receive the bowline. Her skirt billowed behind her and showed her ankles. Gustave's dog, Mame, nearly knocked her over.

"Mame, mind," Gustave commanded.

"It's all right. I love dogs."

Gustave swaggered onto the bank swinging his arms. "I bought a painting yesterday. It's not even dry. *Crysanthèmes rouges,* by Claude. I went out to Vétheuil to convince him to commit to the next group show."

"Unusual for you, a still life," Auguste said.

He sat down. "Not really. I love flowers as much as Monet does. A flower is an idea."

"What a nice thought," Alphonsine said, petting his dog.

"Someday I'm going to own a greenhouse." Gustave sat down.

"So you can raise ideas?" Alphonsine quipped. "Where will it be?"

"I'm looking at a house upriver in Petit Gennevilliers."

"*C'est merveilleux!* That's not far at all."

"Depends on the wind. And I'm going to buy another painting today."

"Whose?" Auguste asked.

"Yours. *Sunset at Montmartre.* Will you let me have it for two hundred fifty francs?"

Alphonsine cleared her throat to get Auguste's attention, and bent her right arm back and forth, grinning.

"That's overgenerous of you. It's not worth that, but yes."

Gustave stacked a tower of two napoléons and seven louis and a ten on the table. "I want it to be in the Louvre someday."

Auguste puffed out a loud breath. "I'd be content for it to hang anyplace where Delacroix once hung."

"You mean Durand-Ruel's gallery. It'll hang in a better place than that. The Louvre can't turn down the collection I'm building. It's too important."

"Why all this sudden buying?" Auguste asked.

"Because the work of the group has to be shown together as a solid movement long enough to outlast the ridicule heaped on it. Long enough so Impressionism won't be a blink of an eye in the history of art. That means everyone has to cooperate, and someone with the best interests of the group has to build a collection that will never be sold off piecemeal."

"You mean you," Auguste said.

"Of course I mean me."

Auguste looked up. "Well, now, look at the happy couple."

Stepping off the bridge, Angèle plucked a white wildflower from the bank and twirled it. *"There was a young maiden as I have heard tell . . ."* she began singing, tilting her head toward Antonio.

"And the language of flowers she knew passing well," Auguste sang back.

Together they finished the ditty,

"She would finger and fondle her sweet Shepherd's Purse—

"You can all take my meaning for better or worse."

Angèle laughed in an earthy way at Antonio's slack-jawed surprise.

Auguste stood to go up to the terrace. "Shall we begin?"

"Do you want Alphonse and me too?" Alphonsine asked.

"You definitely, and Alphonse if he's free."

She hurried away to tell her brother and reappeared a few minutes later in her boating costume and *canotier* hat.

"Mame could be in the painting too," Alphonsine said.

"You won't catch me painting another dog after I suffered through a society lady's snoring bitch."

With them in position now, he wasn't sure how much he'd be able to do on the painting today because he couldn't harmonize the edges of these five figures against the others. He'd have to keep his paint thin in case he would have to make changes later, and paint only the relation of their figures to one another.

Holding her pose facing Gustave, Angèle asked, "What is Hercules staring at behind me?"

Alphonse was caught off guard. He'd been staring right at her. "Trees. I—I'm going to have to trim them soon."

A slow smile of satisfaction crept over Angèle's face. She knew it was a lie.

Auguste picked up chrome yellow from his palette for Gustave's hat. Light falling on Gustave's forehead made it reflective. Fine. Sweat would convey summer. One wide stroke of a paler yellow there and on the sunward edge of his shoulder and upper arm.

"And what am I staring at?" Antonio said, looking down over Angèle. "A beautiful woman. That makes my pose the best."

Angèle leaned toward Gustave, ignoring Antonio. "You must be special to have the front position in the painting. What's your secret?"

"I'm just a friend," Gustave said.

"A fine friend," Auguste said. "All of us in the group owe much to Gustave."

"You mean he's a *souteneur?*" she asked with mock shock. "One of those nasty pimpersnappers hounding the *femmes publiques* on the boulevards for his share? Auguste! You pay him to sell your wares?"

"*Bien au contraire.* He keeps *us* solvent. And on top of that, he's a fine painter."

"Aha." Her eyes gleamed. "In case you ever need a model of my type, come to eight rue Gabrielle in Montmartre."

"I rarely paint women. Auguste here beats the lot of us in that regard."

"That's true as gold. I've posed for him myself. Remember, Auguste?"

He remembered, all right. Their one and only wild night together a few years ago. In the morning she had fallen asleep in his armchair with the neighbor's cat on her lap, a happy accident suggesting the reason for her dishevelment.

"I remember your blue-and-white-striped stockings which you wore when I painted you asleep. Where in the world did you get such outlandish things?" He pictured her going without lunch for a week in order to buy them. That they had been so clearly for her own delight made that painting all the more delectable. "Do you have them on today? I'm sure Antonio would give a tooth to see them."

"What would I want with a rotten old tooth? I have enough of my own already."

"Well, are you wearing them? The stockings?" Antonio asked.

She blatantly lifted her skirt to check, far more than she needed to, flutter-kicked her legs back and forth, and quickly covered them up. "No. I guess I'm not. Only pinks," she chirped.

Always the opportunist, Auguste thought. He wiped his narrow brush clean, whitened some Naples yellow and licked up a dab of ocher already mixed, then blotted it on a rag. The sun reflected off Antonio's cream-colored jacket in pale yellow highlights. He dry-brushed them in on his shoulder, his collar, down his arm. The same color warmed Alphonsine's back. He made long, gentle strokes, imagining that he was stroking her bare back. Ingres loved to paint women's backs. He understood why.

"Will it be a long session today? I had another performance last night." Angèle winked at Auguste.

"Where?" Antonio asked. "I would have liked to see it."

"Not exactly in a theater. My mother says I mustn't tire myself out."

He remembered her telling him about the pleasure she took in making love to a virgin. She had claimed she was actually doing the chap a favor by guiding him through that perilous passage to manhood. "'Pon my soul, what a frisky colt that one was," were the words she'd said. "Don't pretend you're shocked, Auguste." And he'd replied, "I'm only shocked that you found one!" They'd had a good laugh.

"I thought you were an orphan," Antonio said.

"Oh, no! I have a mother, legitimate enough, only she ran off to Provence with a sergeant after the war and left me with her cousin, but she couldn't stand the mistral, so she came back after some years only I didn't know it. One day, as I was going in to pose for some cheapjack dabbler in his studio on rue Foyatier, the street that's all steps, I recognized her coming out dressed up like a peacock, oozing *fla-fla* in feathers and bows. She had to own up it was me again. She was his full-time mott, I was just his *modèle d'occasion,* so we ended up living together, the three of us, in a one-room studio where only a curtain separated me from them taking their pleasure."

Auguste noticed Alphonsine listening with every nerve.

"That devil's stoker came on to me with a hankering hot as fire one night when she was out parading, but I brushed him off with a whack across his familiars. 'If you're hungry, eat your fist,' I said. After that he was a proper gentleman to me, but when it happened the second time, I knew I had to get a place of my own. Pity that my own *mère* had gone to the bad. Now, we've got to be quiet awhile or we'll be here till doomsday."

"I don't mind you talking," Auguste said. "Bend forward a bit more, Antonio. I want the brim of Gustave's hat to rest at the edge of your cravat."

He loved the way Angèle kept Antonio engaged and admiring her. All the impulses of her being were aware of it even though he stood behind her and she was looking at Gustave. He wouldn't be surprised if Antonio and Angèle asked to use his room right after this session. She was like an insect sensing heat, buzzing in anticipation, in complete complicity with Antonio while engaged with Gustave, aware of Alphonse looking at her too. Flirtatious command, that attitude, just that instant.

"Angèle, don't move a muscle. Don't blink. Hold it. That look on your face belongs to me."

He worked quickly, coloring her cheeks with a flush of sensuality, positioning her blue-black eyes for a pinpoint highlight of creamy white later. Everyone was silent until he said, "All right. I've got it."

Angèle sent Gustave a kiss through the air.

"Where do Frenchwomen learn such coquetry? Do they take lessons?" Antonio asked.

"We suck it from our mothers' tits as babes," Angèle said. "All of Paris is a lesson in love, even the puppet shows of medieval knights and ladies on the Champs-Élysées."

"Just from watching them you learned it?" Antonio asked.

"Not just that. When I was no taller than a man's cock-a-doodle, I was an orange-girl selling fruit among the tables at the Jardin Mabille, a dancing and pleasure garden. I watched how the ladies got the men to buy them oranges."

"You probably watched how women danced too," Alphonsine said.

"*Bien sûr!* A woman's body is as fine an instrument as our Heavenly Father ever created."

"I agree to that," Antonio was quick to say. "Auguste, isn't that why you dedicate yourself to painting it?"

"Just so."

"Will you tell me your theory of painting?" Antonio asked. "Maybe I'll do an article on you next."

"I have no theory. Painting is a craft. If you come to nature with a theory, she'll knock it flat."

"Hm," Antonio murmured. In a few moments he asked, "Are you religious about nature?"

"Religion's everywhere." He painted a few strokes. "In the mind." He loaded his brush. "The heart." A few more strokes, and then he stopped. "And in the love you put into what you do."

What was to the left and above Angèle's hat? He needed to know because the color of her hat would be affected. He couldn't remember and his marks on the canvas didn't tell him. Frustration seized him. Even if he knew whatever shoulder or face or sleeve was above her hat, he would need what was beyond that, and beyond that too. And how high was Circe's head against Alphonse's chest? He couldn't paint his singlet too far down. Working only from brushstrokes, it was impossible to keep all the relations in his mind.

"Surely you have some techniques, some aesthetic principles."

"I see something beautiful, I paint it. Just like a child does."

Like Alphonsine's short, solid arms, which he was painting now, pale peach with a dusting of pale yellow where the light fell, warming them. He imagined them sawing off his cast. She had none of the practiced flirtations of Angèle, just her genuinely helpful actions. Sometimes, while she was posing, or when he caught her alone a moment lost in her thoughts, her face had an air of gravity. It had come over her in the boat the other day, unexpectedly, and made her unreachable. He shouldn't have asked when she'd been kissed last. He should have just kissed her.

"I'll be quiet again soon, but I want to tell you," Angèle said. "I saw a newfangled kind of velocipede with three wheels in Jardin du Luxembourg."

"Auguste owns one," Alphonse said eagerly. "It's right here."

"You've been holding out on me? I'll pose free today for a ride."

Had she forgotten that he'd given her forty francs? "It's broken," he said to close the matter.

"A crying shame, that," she said.

"Besides," Auguste said, "women shouldn't muddle around doing mechanical things."

"You think I care a fig?"

"I can give it a temporary fix," Alphonse offered.

"I understand it can give a woman quite a tickle."

"You won't be able to ride it in a dress," said Auguste.

Alphonsine piped up, "I'll lend you my swimming costume."

Angèle tempted him in a singsong voice. "I'll pose free on Sunday too."

"Watch out, Auguste," Gustave said. "She knows right where to get a man."

Angèle tipped up her chin. "Hang me if I don't."

"All right. You'll get your ride."

During their break for lunch, Alphonse went into the boathouse. They heard clanking on metal, some wrestling and banging, and then swearing.

Alphonse came back wiping grease from his hands. "It'll do for a trial run."

"Not until I have my fill of you today," Auguste said, and started painting Angèle's dress. A nest of tulle bordered her neckline like froth spilling over her blue flannel. If only he could take her dress all the way today, even to the red edging on the tulle.

"I'll have you know, Angèle, that I'm using one of the most expensive and cherished pigments for your dress. Ultramarine blue made from the precious stone lapis lazuli. In the Renaissance, it was used exclusively for the Virgin."

"And it's had a coming down ever since," she said.

"I wouldn't say that," Antonio said.

"Nor I. Mixed with cobalt and rose madder, it makes a gorgeous violet shadow on your skirt."

He was doing too much guessing of hues and sizes in the areas where today's figures touched the models not present, but eventually he got Angèle's right hand close to Gustave's, and her left curling around the empty chair barely touching Antonio's thumb. He liked the way she encircled Gustave, and Antonio encircled both of them.

A large cloud rolled overhead, darkening the terrace. He had to quit.

"You can have your ride now, but for God's sake be careful," Auguste said.

Alphonse thumped down the stairs, and Alphonsine crooked her finger, signaling Angèle to follow her down the hallway to her room.

Auguste saw in his mind's eye the painting of Angèle as it would be when he'd be finished. "The glint in her eyes, the tilt of her head, and the lean of her body tell you all you need to know about her to love her."

"I can't keep my eyes off her," Antonio murmured.

"Ha! You must be becoming an Impressionist!"

"Why do you say that?"

"Because you must have had some enjoyable impressions during the posing." Trying for a deadpan look, he mimicked Antonio's pose gazing down.

"As any Frenchman would," Antonio said.

Auguste worked at cleaning his brushes—even that a joy—until he heard the women chattering in the hallway.

Angèle leapt onto the terrace, arms out, in Alphonsine's red-and-white-striped blouse and blue bloomers. Bare arms, bare calves, bare feet.

Antonio let out a long whistle. *"Madre di Dio! Che bella!"*

Auguste chuckled as much at Antonio as at Angèle.

"Skimpy enough to make me cut capers, *oui?*" She kicked her heel out to the side as in the *chahut.*

"You need shoes," Auguste said. "I won't let you go without shoes."

"Voilà!" Alphonsine held up her canvas espadrilles she used for boating.

Downstairs, Alphonse wheeled out the cycle, steam hissing already.

Angèle turned to Alphonsine. "Will you stand me some redfire before I mount that thing?"

Alphonsine retreated to the kitchen.

Alphonse and Auguste told her the parts of the steam-cycle she shouldn't touch, where to put her hands and feet and where to sit.

"How do I get up there?"

Alphonse lifted her onto the seat as if she were as light as a cat. She squealed in delight. Alphonsine handed her a glass of brandy.

"Upsee down." She threw back her head and quaffed it in one gulp. "How do I make it go?"

Alphonse released the brake lever and the cycle lurched forward. "Ooh, it vibrates!" She kicked her legs out, shapely legs tapering to dainty ankles.

"If anything goes wrong, pull this lever as hard as you can. Ready?"

She blew noisy kisses over her shoulder. "In case I never come back."

Alphonse cracked open the valve and trotted alongside with his arms out ready to catch her.

"Don't let her stand up," Auguste called after them.

Mame barked at the sendoff, and Gustave had to restrain her.

Alphonsine brought out a platter of sliced sausages, Roquefort, a baguette, and red wine. Angèle and Alphonse were gone a long time, longer than it would take to ride to the upstream tip of the island and back.

Antonio ground his heel into the gravel. "I should have gone with them."

"Don't worry," Alphonsine said. "My brother will take care of her."

"Gustave, will you sail up to the point and see if they need help?" Antonio asked.

"No. Leave them be," Gustave said.

Eventually they heard the rhythmic scraping of a front wheel against the frame and Angèle's whoop of triumph. Mame barked at their approach.

"What a bone-rattler that thing is! It shook the eggs right out of me." Alphonse helped her down. She winked at him, flushed, her hair unpinned and loose. "Not to worry. There's plenty more berries in the basket."

"She did fine," Alphonse said, out of breath. "She took to it like a jockey. I had to run to keep up."

"I'll bet you did." Auguste folded his left arm over his cast.

"Natural balance, she has."

"Hm, no doubt."

"And so quick to respond."

"Indeed, very responsive."

Alphonse was more talkative than he'd ever seen him. Alphonsine stared at her brother in disbelief. As for Antonio, he was notably silent, his eyebrows pinched together.

"A few more adjustments and it will be as good as new," Alphonse said.

Auguste would never have guessed that Alphonse could wear an expression of rapture, but he definitely did now. Good for him, then.

CHAPTER TWELVE

Paris Encore

Auguste stepped out of Dr. Guilbert's office on rue Notre Dame de Lorette and swung both his arms. By God, that felt fine and free. He straightened and bent his elbow to get rid of the stiffness. Having his arm again was like a chance meeting with an old friend after a long absence, both of them so happy in the encounter that they couldn't stop looking at each other. An urge to work pulsed down his arm to his fingertips. He would take some small canvases back to Chatou.

What should he do next? Walk around Paris waving at people with his right arm like a perfect idiot? Hail a hackney cab just so he could show off how he could stretch out his arm? Take a train to Louveciennes to show his mother? No. He would do that tomorrow. Today he needed to get Charles Ephrussi.

He passed the church where so many young working girls lived. *Lorettes,* they were called, as if the proximity of Notre Dame de Lorette lent them a dose of morality. The truth was that the church was named after the *lorettes* of the last century, women kept by wealthy aristocrats in the quarter. One *lorette* was coming toward him now, her saucy rose-colored hat and veil lending its color to her cheeks. She was carrying two hatboxes as though she were delivering them for a milliner. It was only a ruse. The blithe way she swung the empty paper drums gave her away. So did her deft, practiced motion of lifting her skirt higher than necessary to step onto the curb. A middling prostitute. He could put his right arm around her waist as she passed. Was that philandering? No.

He chuckled to himself. It was only celebrating the use of his arm again.

He turned onto rue Lafitte, street of the big banks, and the view changed as he headed toward boulevard Haussmann—from the nubile *petits rats* of the Opéra slinging their ribboned toe shoes over their thin shoulders, to illiterate *lorettes* hurrying to dressmakers' lofts to earn their three francs a day, to their tailor-made clients in silk shantung, cinched-in women careful how they stepped out of carriages, the backs of their skirts layered with flounces, their rings flashing on their way to the private jewelry salons on rue de la Paix. Heavens, how he loved the women of Paris!

It was partially his parents' doing. If his father hadn't been a tailor and his mother a dressmaker, he wouldn't have learned to pay as much attention to fashion and fabric. His earliest memory was sitting on the floor of the parlor, which served as the fitting room, and learning the names of colors from the dresses that women had his mother make. It would have been a shame if he hadn't had that start. A man unconscious of such things was depriving himself of the erotic force of color, texture, and even the sound of taffeta rustling—all those delights a man must content himself with until the fabric falls to the floor in a heap around two bare legs. He felt incapable of ever satisfying himself with enough beautiful women—both painting them and touching them. It wasn't lechery. It was devotion. How could he squeeze his broad appreciation into one woman acceptable to Madame Charpentier and her portrait-buying friends?

On rue Favart alongside the Opéra Comique, a woman in an emerald green dress coming toward him cast a quick look backward at Ephrussi's window across the courtyard and turned in at the stage door. Now, wasn't that curious?

He slowed his pace as he approached the gray-shuttered building that housed the *Gazette des Beaux-Arts*. A seed of doubt lodged in his throat. Charles hadn't bought anything from him for more than a year and it wasn't because his bank was doing poorly. It was symptomatic of what he knew to be true, namely that his buyers were seeking him out less. As yet, the slide was publicly imperceptible, but he feared it would soon be talked about in the cafés. Charles had been good about introducing him to upper-class buyers like the banker Louis Cahen d'Anvers, who had commissioned a portrait of his wife, the Comtesse Cahen d'Anvers, who also happened to be Ephrussi's mistress. Charles had a gift for convincing men that they would make a handsome profit by investing in Impressionist paintings. His aesthetic preferences were always governed by an eye to profit. If Charles thought the financial gain might shrink, would his willingness to put him in touch with wealthy clients dry up?

The Chatou painting had to reverse the slide. It was for that reason exactly that he needed Charles in top hat standing in the center rear— Charles, the Renaissance scholar, art collector, financier, man of fashion, *flâneur* of high culture, and above all, principal contributor to the *Gazette des Beaux-Arts.* Then Paris would have to take notice.

Even Ephrussi's outer office was redolent with sandalwood incense, the exotic aroma of his past as the heir of a corn-exporting dynasty in Odessa. Although Japanese prints adorned the anteroom, Auguste knew he'd find paintings by his friends in Ephrussi's private office. Some by Degas, at least. Whether Edgar was still a friend remained in doubt.

Jules Laforgue in his shirtsleeves was sitting at the desk behind stacks of manuscript pages puffing on his Dutch porcelain pipe. "No cast?"

"I've cast it in the rubbish." He made a flamboyant gesture of tossing it aside.

"*Formidable!* If you want to see Charles, he's working at home today."

"*Ah, bien.* What are you working on?"

"An index to his book on Dürer."

"As his personal secretary?"

"As his disciple, or so he fancies me. If it weren't me, it would be someone else. His sense of identity needs that."

"Indeed. I won't interrupt. Rue Monceau, is it?"

"Yes, number seventeen. One more thing. I want you to know that you're doing me a favor by letting me see the process."

"The struggle to come, you mean."

. . .

A manservant in knee breeches and white hose answered Ephrussi's door and ushered him past Monet's *La Grenouillère* to Monsieur's study. Thank God Gustave didn't go in for such costuming of hired help.

Charles, in a red silk Chinese kimono, stood up behind his desk. "Auguste! Welcome! Jules said you were staying out in the country."

"I am. At Chatou. For my new painting, which is why I've come to see you."

"And I've wanted to see you too, to advise you to be cautious."

"About my arm? It's fine. See?" He picked up a pen from the marble stand on the desk, stretched out his arm, and pretended to write in the air.

Charles's cheeks lifted in a brief, indulgent smile. "Impressive, but that's not what I meant."

Auguste replaced the pen next to a paperweight of an iridescent blue-winged insect caught in amber. The human condition, Pierre would call it.

"Tea?" Charles asked. "It's Petrushka. Steeped and ready."

Auguste nodded and Charles poured two glasses from the spigot of a silver samovar on a carved rosewood table. Behind it was an awful mythological fantasy framed in heavy gold baroque. By Moreau, no doubt. On the opposite wall, a series of pastels, Degas' ballerinas exercising at the barre.

And between two windows, his own painting of Lise Tréhot. Seeing it after so long sucked the breath out of him. How much coaxing she'd needed to pose nude. He'd kept the painting for years as a remembrance of joyous love until need had forced him to sell it. Everywhere he went lately he ran smack up against his past. Such a tumble of remembrances. Pierre would call them portents.

Charles held up a sugar cube in silver tongs. "One cube or two?"

"Two."

He dropped them into the glasses in silver filigree holders and brought one on a tray. Auguste took it in his right hand. The glass chattered in the holder. He moved it to his left. It still chattered. He set it down.

"Kousmichoff is the purveyor, by appointment to the Tzars. I have it sent from St. Petersburg. It's Ceylon tea with cardamon, cloves, almonds, and rose. You'll find it quite delightful."

Auguste managed to get it to his lips without catastrophe, but it burned his tongue.

Charles gestured toward two armchairs upholstered in pale yellow brocade, and they sat. Auguste crossed his legs.

"You know, don't you, that Degas has no patience with you and Claude and Alfred Sisley returning to the Salon?"

"Ah, the self-proclaimed spokesman declaims in holier-than-thou tones."

"Such a large painting as your *Déjeuner des canotiers* is surely a signal that it's intended as a Salon work."

"Jules told you about it?"

Charles nodded. "A dozen people?"

"Thirteen at the moment. That's why I came to see you."

Ephrussi's face turned serious. "Thirteen won't stand a chance with the Catholics on the Salon jury."

"What's worse, they're around a table after a meal," Auguste said. "It will probably be unsalable anywhere unless I get a *quatorzième*."

"It will be mocked in a cartoon. The press will be licking their chops."

"I know, I know. *Again,* I'm telling you that's why I'm here, to ask you to be in it."

"Me?" Charles put up his hand in front of his face. "No, not me. You need another, though, or otherwise scrub one person out."

"It would be better to have you. You'll lend authority to it."

"Jules says it's as large as your *Bal au Moulin de la Galette*."

"It's intended as a tour de force. It's intended—"

"For the Salon, which you know I approve of, but—"

"Yes, for the Salon. And I don't want to just figure honorably, as they say in horse racing. I want to blow the whole stuffy Salon apart with an assimilation of styles they won't dare deny is genius." He had raised his voice. Now he held up his index finger and spoke slowly and deliberately. "I want to prove that one can exhibit there *and* produce original paintings of *la vie moderne*." He crossed his legs the other way.

"But you must be aware that if you do a painting this large, word will get around. It signals another Salon entry just when Edgar is on the verge of saying good riddance to you and to Claude and Alfred if you submit there."

"So *they'll* be excluded by Degas because *I'm* submitting to the Salon? That's monstrous! Diabolical!" He shifted in his chair. "He's bluffing."

"Not so. He intends to fill your spots with his young Realists."

"Like Raffaëlli, in love with ugliness. Under his brush, even the grass is sordid."

"At the moment Degas is getting more favorable critical press than the rest of you combined, so it would behoove you to be cautious about any break with him. You could be criticized all the more."

"Are you trying to talk me out of this painting altogether?"

"No. I just want—"

"If I were criticized for selling out to easy portraits, I'd deserve the censure. But I only want to do what seems to me good work, regardless of its destiny, and a large painting is what I can do now, when the light is right and I have no commissions in Paris."

"No one is questioning your art." Charles flicked off a shred of tobacco on a lacquered Russian cigarette box on the table between them. "It's your politics, I mean the group's politics, that concern me."

Auguste waved his hand dismissively. "I have no politics. The world is big enough for all of us. I didn't come here to debate about Raffaëlli. I came to ask you to be in my painting. You'll have a spot center back, next to Jules, your top hat silhouetted against open air. Or you and Madame Ephrussi together there. I know you like to spend Sundays with her, so spend them at Chatou."

"Out of the question. To have her exposed to the riffraff of La Grenouillère? *That's* monstrous."

"It's not at La Grenouillère. It's at Maison Fournaise."

"Not to mention exposing her to the crass eyes of the public scrutinizing your painting. No. I prefer to keep Madame for my own eyes. You're from a different world, Auguste. You don't understand the niceties required of people in our position."

"You mean *you* are from a different world."

Charles raised an eyebrow at that. "To sit for a portrait in one's own home is one thing, but to be painted in that raucous environment, in a *genre* painting—"

"All right, all right. Not Madame, then, but you." He leaned forward again and tapped his fingernail on Charles's desk, once for each word—"I want you in the painting. It's only right, after all you've done for me."

"You've done studies already? An underdrawing to restrain your colors?"

"No studies. I'm painting it directly on a blank canvas."

"That may be enough to lure me out there, just to see what you're up to. For your own sake, don't let any critic see you do that, or see it at all until it's finished. You'll be labeled a sensualist seduced by color, a chaotic painter."

"I don't care what they call me."

"You care acutely." He sipped his tea. "What's your stand on Raffaëlli?"

"Is your posing contingent on my stance?"

"To a degree."

"That's unfair of you, but I'll tell you anyway." Auguste tried his tea again, making him wait. Still too hot. "He wants us to expose misery. He spouts lists of character types we should paint, with ragpickers at the top. He even mandates locations. Let him paint what he wants, but we left the academy because subject matter was imposed on us there."

"He considers artists as social educators, and I commend him for that."

"Fine. Fine. So will this painting contribute to a social education, by showing that we're enjoying our lives again. At least most of us. His concern for tramps and ragpickers is all well and good, if he likes to wallow, but birds sing even when they're hungry."

"Meaning?"

"Meaning that there's a purpose for prettiness—to give joy. Besides, Raffaëlli is not an Impressionist."

"Degas is committed to him."

"Enough to risk the breakup of the group? I think not."

"I think so."

He could see by Charles's pinched mouth that he meant it.

"Will you come to pose or are you afraid you'll be seduced by color? I might as well cut up the canvas to reuse the pieces if you don't come."

"I can't say."

"Gustave will be there. You can talk to *him* about Degas and Raffaëlli."

Outside, Auguste passed two women without even a glance.

Prissy foreigner, protecting his good wife from wholesome riverside society, Auguste thought. No doubt he also protects her from the *comtesse,* or the likes of the actress in green who looked back at his office window. And to hang that dog of a Moreau painting! Charles was taken in because it has the color of gold in it. Moreau can't even draw a foot.

But if Charles didn't show up, he might have to consider Jeanne's dandy, if he dared to come again. Auguste hawked and spat in the gutter. No, he wouldn't. He would pose some ragpicker first.

He dashed out in front of a carriage and was cursed by the driver. Auguste cursed him back.

He knew where he had to go next, but Gustave's two hundred and fifty francs for *Sunset at Montmartre* was already depleted by yesterday's posing fees, the doctor, his rent at Chatou. The rest ought to go to Père Tanguy.

When the bell jingled, Madame Tanguy teetered on a chair reaching for a box on an upper shelf. Auguste rushed to her.

"You shouldn't be doing that. Here, let me."

He offered her his right hand. She took it with a momentary look of distrust, and stepped down.

"That box of palette knives marked *trowel*," she said, pointing.

He reached it easily without the chair, helped her reach a few more things, and carried them to the counter.

"Where's Julien?"

"At the café around the corner, but he's shorter than I am. I have to fill this order and take it to the *bureau de poste* by two."

"What do you notice about me?" He stood with his arms out, palms up.

"That you have no money in your hands to give me."

"Aha, but I do!" He made a broad circular gesture with his right arm and patted his breast pocket conspicuously. Grinning, he said, "That's why I came."

She gave him a squinty-eyed look.

"Now, don't pretend that you loathe me. I know it's an act. I know it was you who slipped in that tube of Prussian blue."

She pressed her lips together, trying to appear stern.

"And I want another one, quick, before he comes in. And flake white, ultramarine, and cobalt." He snapped a fifty-franc napoléon on the counter.

"*Oh, là!*"

"How much do I owe?"

She thumbed through a stack of papers tied with string. "If you see that Cézanne, tell him he owes us two thousand one hundred seventy-four francs."

"Minus the paintings of his you have."

"You owe a hundred and forty-one francs, eighty-eight centimes, plus twenty-one francs forty now." She dropped a slim tube into his chest pocket.

He felt his shoulders drop. He had intended to stock up on colors he knew he would deplete soon, but that would have to wait. He had his models to pay again in three days.

"Will you take eighty for now, until I get more?" He laid out three ten-franc coins next to the napoléon. She slapped her hand down on them, stubby fingers splayed.

"I guess that means yes."

"I guess I'll take what I can."

He blew her a kiss. "You know, that blue dress looks lovely on you. It brings out the color of your eyes."

She shook her head, hands on her hips. *"Monsieur le Flatteur."*

"Have you enjoyed your *pâté de foie* Julien?"

He patted the contraband tube, then backed to the door waving both outstretched arms to his sides like a bird, trying not to smile.

"Ah! Your arm. No cast!"

"Bonne journée, Madame l'Observatrice."

Down to thirty francs again. He headed toward Camille's *crémerie*. Maybe she had some luck with the painting of the girls juggling oranges.

He opened the door and saw the wall bare. "Ha!"

Camille's plump face spread wider in a doughy grin.

"Sold?"

She didn't say yes or no. She just ladled out some *potage crème de légumes,* set it on a round table in front of him, and sat down opposite him.

"Eat." She pointed to the bare wall with her thumb. "You have my daughter, Annette, to thank for that. The shoe shop girl. She ran into that clown Sagot outside the Cirque Fernando and told him she had a painting she knew he'd want. 'By Renoir,' she said with awe in her voice. 'It's of two circus performers.' She dragged him here right then. He offered thirty francs. *'C'est ridicule!'* she said. 'Won't you be sorry when I tell you I sold it to a man for fifty!' 'Then why is it still here?' the man asked. 'The buyer's coming for it tomorrow,' she said. She was lying through her teeth, but I let her operate and just watched. She was so pretty with her dark brown hair piled up, and he was looking at her as much as at the painting. In the end, they settled on thirty-five."

"Bravo!"

Camille sauntered behind the counter in a rolling motion, opened the cash drawer, and clicked the coins together in the air like a Spanish dancer.

"That's the wife you ought to have. Annette did it once, she can do it again."

Just this once, he'd promised himself, as a leg up for his Chatou painting. Never again.

Titters came from the next table—Géraldine and Aline, the girls of the quarter, regulars at the *crémerie*.

"She's got you under her thumb now, *pardi!*" Aline said with her pert little nose in the air.

Pardi. Interesting that she didn't say *by God. Pardi* was archaic and countrified. A country girl by choice. He liked that about her. She had a freshness that neither the *lorettes* with the hatboxes nor the *femmes de la grande bourgeoisie* on the boulevards nor even the actress in emerald green possessed.

"Next thing you know, she'll want you to paint her daughter," Aline went on with a lilt to her voice. "That's how it starts. Then she'll have Annette deliver *cuisine de campagne* to your studio every night, and that will keep you from going to the Café Nouvelle-Athènes . . ."

". . . So you won't meet other women," Géraldine added.

"And soon you'll give in, leastways out of gratitude as much as out of the itch of the flesh, and *hélas!* You'll find yourself married, and all your bachelor *soirées* will go up in a puff of smoke."

"How do you know that I'm not married already?"

At this, it was Géraldine who laughed, while Aline flushed a deep rose.

"Oh, she knows," Géraldine said brightly. "We have our ways."

CHAPTER THIRTEEN

Hats on Sunday

Alphonsine took special care winding her chignon. In the glass, her face was rounder than she wished it, but joyous with the expectation of the day, her face never revealing on Sundays what it sometimes showed on other days.

In the back garden, she clipped three roses, a pink, a dark red, and a floppy cream one, the color of fresh Brie. Flowers are ideas, Gustave had said. Ideas of what? She was going to ask him. She put them in a small vase, and brought them up to the terrace.

Anne, one of the waitresses, was about to whisk off the tablecloth.

"Stop. Don't do that."

"But the leaves and twigs—"

"I'll take care of it. Set all forty tables downstairs today."

How would she get fresh linen on without disturbing the position of the bottles of wine if he'd already begun to paint them? And the napkins too. Angèle's was bunched up tightly like a bouquet of lilies. Gustave's was hanging over the table like a tousled bedsheet after a night of love. She studied the arrangement, then set the bottles one by one in the same relationship on another table and scooped up Gustave's napkin as though it were something precious and alive. She lifted Angèle's napkin, changed the cloth, put everything back, and placed the roses in front of Gustave's seat.

Auguste came up the stairs. "You really think people aren't going to move those bottles?"

"I just wanted to have everything how you left it."

"There'll be new bottles, but we'll have to leave the old ones in place."

"They can use new napkins and leave the others just as they are."

Guy de Maupassant scurried down from his top floor room and ducked his head out the door to the terrace. He saw Auguste and they gave each other the briefest of greetings.

"I'll take my *café* downstairs, if you don't mind," Guy said.

"Anne's there. She can serve you," Alphonsine said. "But first, tell us which of your boats you are going to take out today."

"Before it gets too hot, a little exercise in the *as,* my smallest *périssoire, Frère Jan.* Then I have friends coming out for lunch and a promenade on the water. I'll use *L'Envers des Feuilles* for that because it's bigger. Later, I'll practice with my team in my *triplette.*"

"Why do you call it that, *The Undersides of Leaves?*" she asked. "It's a silly name."

Guy smoothed his bushy mustache, scrutinizing her. "Haven't you ever lain with a man on the bank under trees? What do you see when you look up?"

"It doesn't take lying with a man to see that," she said.

"But it might be more pleasant with a man," Auguste said. "I like the name. It's clever."

Guy turned to him. "I understand you're going to do another painting with blinders on, like you did at Moulin de la Galette. You're out of fashion, Renoir. It's realism, the grit, that's current now, *la vie moderne,* not *la vie en rose.* You're an escapist."

"Then society is too. How do you account for the whole working class of Paris escaping to every river town from Asnières to Bougival every Sunday, you included? Is that what you're writing these days, grit? Like Zola? He thinks he portrayed the people of Paris by saying that they smell."

"I'm not writing. I'm boating. When the weather turns bad I'll write."

"Well, there you have it. Escapism."

Guy smiled with a touch of chagrin. "Flaubert used to tell me, 'Young man, you must work more. You spend your life with too much exercise, too much *canotage,* too many prostitutes. You were made to write. The rest is vain.'"

"Too much gazing up at the undersides of leaves," Alphonsine said, and dodged Guy's arm which shot out to grab her.

After Guy left, she asked Auguste, "Why aren't you and Guy more friendly?"

"Oh, we like each other well enough, but we have nothing in common."

"Yes, you do. He loves the river just like you do."

"Every time I see him, he's in a different boat, or he's bragging about owning a small fleet, one of every kind. I'd consider myself fortunate to have just one."

They watched Guy maneuver the *as,* the narrowest, most precarious style of *canot* on the river.

"He's a better oarsman than I am," Auguste said.

"You're a better painter than he is."

He dismissed that with a jerk of his arm. "I told him once that he sees everything in black. It has to do with the size of his mustache. It's a veritable hedge. The weight of the thing pulls down his lower eyelids which affects his vision."

"You're being silly."

"He told me I see everything through rose-tinted spectacles. He keeps it up every time we run into each other, the same as Degas does. They have a conspiracy, *le misérabilisme.* Guy thinks I'm mad. I think he is. We've reached an equilibrium."

"Well, I don't like *le misérabilisme* either. Who wants to be in a room with Victor Hugo's wretches and scoundrels?"

Two short whistles announced the train from Paris at the Rueil station. Soon working girls in pairs or on the arms of their beaus, picnicking families with baskets and quilts, fishermen with poles, children with butterfly nets paraded across the bridge.

So many things she loved about summer Sundays on the Île de Chatou—the red and yellow omnibuses from Rueil taking people to ferry docks, the flat-bottomed *bachots* with their tinny bells ferrying them to the large *guinguettes* of La Grenouillère, where they could eat and swim and rent *canots,* or Le Bal des Canotiers at Bougival, where they could dance. Women in hats decorated with flowers and feathers, men in top hats, the wee ones in cotton bonnets toddling after ducks, their sunburned arms outstretched, dogs frolicking, even a monkey once. Guitar and accordion music at the small *guinguettes* under the trees, the river dotted with swimmers' heads, the flapping of sails and rattle of rigging against the masts of the sailboats, the water in the channel cut by *canots* of all types—racing sculls, *périssoires,* rowing yoles, even an *as* occasionally—bringing songs from one bankside café to another—she loved it all, loved her part in it. She, the hostess, mingling with the guests as though she had invited each one to her own party, loved to say: "Look what we've got. Enjoy, taste, bask, and go back to Paris refreshed."

"None of the people arriving know what an important thing is happening here today," she said.

"What important thing?"

She put her hands on her hips. "Sometimes you act like your head is made of wood."

"Weathered wood, you mean."

Ellen arrived, the one who had posed with a glass to her mouth. Auguste had said she was a mime from the Folies. "Her beau isn't with her."

"Maybe it was a mistake to include him. He has no loyalty to me."

"So now it's only twelve. Poof. Your problem just vanished."

She watched her brother move right in and offer to take Ellen out in a yole. How careful he was, one foot anchoring the boat to the dock, extending both of his hands as she stepped in. He was giving up time when he could be renting boats.

Angèle came with Antonio and sat at a table under a maple tree. The two men who had been in the back of the painting were busy trying to attract the attention of some young women on the promenade.

"Which is which?" she asked.

"The one doffing his hat to that lady is Pierre Prophet-of-doom Lestringuèz. A regular at Café Nouvelle-Athènes suppers along with Paul. Pierre's mad about that bowler, thinks he looks dashing."

"A bowler isn't dashing. A bowler is merely respectable. A yachtsman's boater like Gustave's is dashing."

"Paul Lhôte is the one wearing glasses. Blind as a bat. He always whispers to Pierre, 'Which one is prettiest?' and then goes to work on her. Of course, Pierre never tells him the truth."

"You shouldn't have told me. What am I to think now if Paul compliments me?"

Auguste chuckled. She loved it when she could get him to laugh. It wasn't often enough.

A tall man in a black frock coat and top hat came across the footbridge in a clipped, impatient manner, and paused at the steps down to the bank, as though he wanted to assess the firmness of the ground before he placed his foot down. He looked toward the Maison curiously.

"Are you expecting someone new?"

"Aha! I've got him!" Auguste said in a low voice.

"Monsieur Urbanité? Who is he?"

"Charles Ephrussi, only son in a line of wealthy Russian bankers. Self-taught art connoisseur who buys and sells profitably. He's tapped his ebony walking stick on the marble floors of every bank on rue Lafitte."

"Hm. Interesting. And nice-looking too."

"Always razor-sharp creases in his trousers. Always dignified, the true *flâneur* strolling the boulevards, observing, then retreating to his plush study to write esoteric articles about his observations while snacking on caviar on toasted rye. But here, ha! A fish out of water. Wait till he discovers that he'll be posing with two sweaty men in singlets, undergarments to him, one with the air of a carefree sailor, the other as brawny as a pirate."

"Now it's back to thirteen," she said.

"Did you think that fact escaped me?"

"Do you want him for his top hat?"

"For his cachet. For what he's done for painters, this gallant of the rue Monceau."

"Rue Monceau? In the seventeenth? We had our hat shop in the seventeenth before the war. We lived above it."

She felt proud because it was in a good neighborhood, until a stabbing memory caught her off guard. Auguste's eyes seemed deeper at that moment, and the corners of his mouth drooped. Could that be on her behalf?

"Someone else owns it now. I wonder if he bought his top hat there."

"We can ask," Auguste offered.

"I'd rather not."

"See how the sheen on it catches the light and makes a column of deep blue?" Auguste said. "It's a streak of the river reflected."

"Clipped beaver fur makes that sheen. It's the highest quality."

The top hats had sat in a row on the mahogany shelves, with the price tags she'd written tucked into the hatbands. Louis had always been so genuine in his desire to bestow just the right hat on each gentleman. Better that the memory come back on a summer Sunday when even the air sparkled with gaiety than on a winter Monday when the dull quietness made her feel her widowhood more sharply. She must not think of that now. She made her mind leap a decade and land in the present.

"Charles," Auguste called. "Up here."

Just then, Circe stepped off the bridge, swaying her stripes and twirling her parasol like a windmill. She wore a dainty, narrow-brimmed *chapeau* of white felt trimmed with silk violets, tipped rakishly forward. Auguste hurled himself downstairs to greet her. Circe laughed in a rising melody not entirely pleasant. Alphonsine watched him offer her his arm and guide her to the table under the maple, as though she couldn't arrive there on her own. She took small, slow steps, to make their time together longer. She was playing the coquette, and making full use of every minute of opportunity.

Jeanne Samary was missing. Would Auguste be crushed if she didn't come? She would watch to see if his joy in Circe's company sufficed.

Jules arrived, took off his mariner's cap, and spread both arms wide toward the river. *"Fair Seine, nursery of arts."*

"You borrowed that!"

He spun around, took hold of the iron terrace support under her, and looked up. "I admit I did. It was actually fair Padua, but speaking to a lady on a balcony reminds me more of fair Verona."

Just then, the *Iris* and then *Nana,* Baron Raoul Barbier's sailboat, came to opposite sides of the dock. Everyone piled into them. They were both going out! She rushed downstairs, but the *Iris* floated away from the dock just as she got there, so she boarded *Nana* with Jules and Angèle and Antonio. Angèle insisted on a position in the bow. Fine for a figurehead like Angèle, but she took a spot next to the tiller, where the action happens in a sailing craft. Raoul lurched to one side on his bad leg to trim the sail and the boat shot out to the middle of the channel. Alphonsine asked if she could steer.

"Let's hold the tiller together," Raoul said. She grasped it some distance behind his hand. He moved hers next to his, toward the end. "It's easier here," he said. Their hands were touching side by side, and then his was covering hers, warm and firm. She could tell he was nervous about letting her take control completely, but when she stayed on course, his grip relaxed and he let go, though he still kept his eye on the sail and on the *Iris*.

"You wanted to make it a race, not a lesson, didn't you?" she said.

"Competition is in my blood, lady, with horses and boats."

"In that case . . ." she murmured and drew in the tiller to bring the boat closer to the wind. It scudded faster. She loved that tiny tremble of the wooden tiller under her grip that she could control by pulling in or letting off the wind. She wanted Gustave in the other boat to see that she was steering and gaining on him, the boat heeling, slicing sharply through the water which fell away in wavelets.

Antonio and Jules looked at her in astonishment. Raoul merely said, "*Nana* is as fast as a bullet, isn't she?"

Nothing about her skill. Not a word about her steady course. Just smugness about his boat.

She knew she had to tack soon. Raoul reached for the tiller.

"Let me," she said. "You can stand close if you want to, and manage the sheets."

With Raoul controlling the sails, she worked the tiller, and *Nana* came about neatly. He gave her an approving look and let her handle each tack until the *Iris* reversed directions near Bezons. Gustave was faithful to Auguste who wanted to get started painting earlier today than last week. She brought *Nana* about to windward of the *Iris,* stole his wind, and shot ahead.

Approaching the Maison, she relinquished the tiller to Raoul, stepped onto the dock first, greeted guests in the restaurant, and made sure all was in order. She wanted to be everywhere at once, unmistakably present. The models came up in high spirits.

"You're quite the skilled *matelote,*" Gustave said to her as he sat down. "I've never seen a woman handle a sailboat with such finesse. The baron will have to take a lesson or two from you before the regatta."

"Impossible," she said. "I told you I'll be cheering for *you.*"

"It's you who should worry," Raoul said to Gustave. "Although my *Nana* is a dream to handle, I can trounce you with *Le Capitaine.*"

All right. Diminish my contribution, she thought. The slight did not escape Gustave, who tipped his head toward her while looking at Raoul.

Raoul turned to her with a slight bow, hand over his heart. "How gauche of me, lady. I welcome you in any of my boats anytime, day or night," he said with a gleam in his eye.

"Thank you, Baron. I love all types of boating."

Gustave noticed the roses, turned the vase, admired each one.

"You said flowers are ideas," she said. "What ideas are these?"

He pointed to the pink one. "Sweetness." He pointed to a thorn on the deep red one. "Fragility protected. Providence in nature's plan." He touched the creamy one and an outer petal fell. "Brevity."

"There's a poet's mind under that yachtsman's boater," Jules said.

It was like a door opening, what Gustave got out of three roses.

She was amused by her mother announcing the entrées as she and Maman set the platters on the table. "*Pâté maison* and *asperges d'Argenteuil en conserve.* The best quality in France, grown less than five kilometers from here."

"Pretty as a picture, madame," Charles said and helped himself to quite a few spears. "I love asparagus so much I had Manet paint them for my dining room, as a hint to my cook to prepare them more often."

Maman flicked her hand against his shoulder. "You're teasing me."

"It's true. I agreed to pay eight hundred francs for it."

Maman let out a whistle through her teeth. "Unbelievable."

"I liked it so well I sent him a thousand. A week later I received a delivery of a small painting of a single stalk of asparagus with a note: *Your bunch was one short.*"

With a flinty look in her eye, Maman forked one stalk from the platter and placed it ceremoniously on his plate. She was obviously pleased with herself when everybody laughed, especially Charles. His delight at Maman's joke was surprising. She'd taken him for an aristocrat unlikely to condescend to gaiety brought on by a country cook.

Later, when she and Anne brought up the roast chicken smelling of Madeira, Auguste and Charles and Gustave were in a heated conversation about some painter named Raffaëlli.

"He's content with the old academic style," Gustave said. "All he's changed is subject matter."

Circe leaned toward Auguste and asked, "What does he paint?"

"The underside of life. Tramps, thieves, the denizens of the Maquis."

"How disgusting!" Circe screwed up her nose.

"Careful, that's touching on territory dear to my heart," Angèle said.

"They're sentimental caricatures," Gustave said. "It's not just his subjects. It's that he hasn't embraced the Impressionist aim of recording fleeting moments."

"He's a fine draftsman and observer of character, in the same way that Degas is," Charles said.

"He's a Beaux-Arts painter. He doesn't belong in an Impressionist show," Gustave retorted. "If we include him and the others then we're diluting our identity just when it's beginning to be recognized."

"Not quite," Charles said. "True, the Realists don't translate scrupulously and sincerely the sensations of changeable light or the spontaneous, unedited moment. Then, won't your work appear more fresh? You ought not to fear the comparisons. You ought to welcome them."

"If we don't include Raffaëlli, Degas will pull out, and that's fine with me," Gustave blurted.

She had never seen him so agitated.

Auguste was scowling. "No. That's not fine with me. I know Edgar can be contrary, but he's an astonishing painter."

"No one's arguing that," Gustave said with an exaggerated sigh.

Auguste continued, "Think what Impressionism would be without him. Only *plein-air* painting and the juxtaposition of distinct patches of color. But we're more than that. With Degas, our exhibits show a wider range of subjects and more innovation in composition of near and far, of cropped figures, and of oblique, even eccentric angles of vision. You, of all of us, Gustave, ought to appreciate that. I admit without reservation that his work has influenced me. He's influenced you, Gustave. You've influenced him."

"But that doesn't resolve the problem," Gustave said.

The conversation died out as they ate. At the end of the meal Angèle rang her glass with her fork. "Since this is to be a painting of *la vie moderne,* I propose that after a week of *flânerie* on the boulevards or in Montmartre, or in the Bois or the cafés, we, the *flâneurs* and *flâneuses* of the Maison Fournaise, each come back with a report of the most outrageously modern thing we saw."

They raised their glasses in agreement. Then Auguste said it was time to start.

"No! One more toast," Pierre said. "Here's to Auguste's right arm!"

They drank again and made him raise his right arm as though he were a boxing champion.

She cleared the table carefully so it was just as it had been last week, called Alphonse upstairs, and Auguste began to work.

From her position she couldn't see the front of the painting, but she could see his hands. He held three brushes between the fingers of his left hand, which held the palette too. Despite his enlarged knuckles, his narrow hands had a delicacy to them, and the many ways he held the brush were elegant.

He didn't do much mixing on the palette. He just squeezed colors out of the tubes, lapped them up with his brush, sometimes more than one color at a time, one edge of the bristles filled from one smear on his palette, the other edge from another smear, moving like he was danc-ing. He held the palette so naturally, like a tray of colored wafers, so sticky that they didn't slide if he tilted the tray. Sometimes his tongue poked out of his mouth, as though he were going to lick the paint he loved so much. His hand flew from the canvas to the little tin of linseed oil, to his palette, then to the canvas, back to the oil, canvas, palette. There was something wild about it, like a swallow darting to catch insects.

He turned his wrist often to change the way of applying paint. Some-times the brush handle was perpendicular to the painting to use the ends of the bristles, sometimes almost parallel to it, dragging the flat side along the canvas. He was like a violinist constantly changing the angle of his bow. She imagined the music he was making, imagined dancing with him, his arm firm on her waist, waltzing together to the music, two as one, two as one, two as one.

He paused and the muscles around his eyes tightened. He took off his bicycle cap and scratched his head. It must have been unconscious because he was never without his cap on. His receding hairline was like the letter M, the two outward triangles just skin, and the middle section coming downward in a point filled with a dark brown shock of hair. She felt she was seeing something private.

Her thoughts of Auguste were interrupted by Circe expelling a melo-dramatic sigh. Without moving, she could see Circe flutter her eyelashes caked with blue kohl whenever Auguste looked toward her. She was definitely in the methodical process of snagging his affection. He'd be a fool if he fancied that he was her first even though she was young. What else was she fit to do, fashioned as she was for love? She was a courtesan on the hunt for a prosperous keeper. A misplaced aim for her. Circe would drop him like a hot iron if she knew he could ill afford to pay for the meal. Better that she aim for Monsieur Urbanité, but since she'd wanted to face forward she wasn't positioned so that she could make eyes at him. How shortsighted of her. Charles must have a wife, of course, if for no other reason than for appearance's sake, but that wouldn't discourage Circe. Paul and Pierre were too Parisian to settle down so young, but even together, they couldn't afford her.

Auguste asked Raoul, "Would you mind turning around to face Alphonsine at the railing?"

"Whatever you want," he said. "For me to look at Lady Alphonsine is no torture, except, of course, I cannot touch."

A small mustache perched itself on his upper lip which he twitched back and forth, trying to make her break her pose and laugh. She took him to be a few years older than Auguste.

"What do you think about, lady? *L'amour, oui? Je t'adore,*" he said as though he were speaking French with a husky foreign accent. "Your thoughts are full of longings, *oui?*"

"No, they're full of the dishes I have to wash after everyone leaves."

It wasn't true, but it made a few people laugh. Circe didn't laugh. She twittered.

"Listen to me, lady. I come from zee East. No dish to wash. Only fruit to pluck from zee trees. A land of mystery. I tell you stories of caravans and bazaars, rubies, melons beeg as the sun."

"As beeg as your hat?" she mimicked. "In this country, it's called a *melon.*"

"Beegger. A lady who can bring my boat about can bring my heart about too. You come with me to the river. We go in a, what you call it, a yole, with sticks to make go. We get out where no people are. We rest under big tree."

She could be irritated that he would think her a *grenouille,* but his voice was so droll, his eyebrows popping up, his antics so entertaining.

He broke his pose to pick up a fig from the fruit compote. "I feed you figs. I peel for you grapes, each one, like they do in Samarkand. Juice drips down your pretty chin. I lick it off. What then? I tell you, lady. We lie down like Persians on rugs of silk."

"Not on your life, you fancy pants," Angèle said without moving a muscle. "She gives you a right crook hard enough to rattle your bones, jumps in the boat, and leaves you there."

CHAPTER FOURTEEN

En Canot with the Baron

Alphonsine did go with Raoul in a yole after the light dimmed and Auguste stopped working, but not to lie with him on the bank. She went with him because she felt young, her oldness put away in a hatbox for the afternoon. She went with him because the day, the painting coming along, the exhilaration of steering the sailboat made her inexpressibly happy.

And she went so she could tease him as he'd teased her. Since the lady sitting on the cane-back bench in a yole has the steering cords that operate the rudder, and the man facing her has the oars, she had control of where they went. She pulled one cord so that the boat went in circles as they left the dock. On the bank, Auguste and Alphonse and Gustave laughed uproariously.

"All right, you coquette of *canots,* I'll tell you something that happened to me on this river that won't make you so sure of yourself."

"Speak on, Baron." She let him go straight but kept him away from the bank.

"I took out a skiff to fish one afternoon in a pretty little spot where the river bends, not far from Bougival."

"Your first mistake."

"Why, lady?"

"No one ever catches a fish there."

He shrugged. "It was a beautiful sunny afternoon when I started, just like this. The river flowing calmly, a light breeze, just enough to rustle the leaves, birds chirping in the branches. I had no luck in fishing—"

"*Naturellement.*"

"But I was content to wait and enjoy the river, so I lowered an anchor. I lay down and dozed, lulled by the motion of the boat."

"It's nice to do that," she said.

"A cool breeze made me wake and I discovered shadows stretched like arms across the boat. Since I had no luck, I reached to pull up the anchor. It wouldn't budge. I yanked harder, but that only served to dig it in deeper to whatever it had hooked itself upon, perhaps a submerged branch. I rowed upstream to try to loosen it, to no avail."

"Why didn't you cut the anchor line?"

"It was a chain. Soon fog crept in, and as twilight came, it changed from gray to murky purple. I hallooed for help, but there were no pleasure boats foolhardy enough to venture out in the fog. All I could do was lie down and wait until morning."

"Weren't you afraid?"

"I didn't sleep. Every sound mocked me."

Why was he telling her this? To impress her with his bravery?

"Damp and cold crept into my bones, and in the morning, I was stiff. I couldn't move one of my legs at all. It pained me from hip to ankle as acutely as if it had been shattered by mortar fire. I feared paralysis."

This struck a false note. It didn't belong in the telling.

"With the dawn warming the river by degrees, it became numb. I was able to move my arms, so I tugged at the anchor line but it was still caught. I thought I might be able to drag the thing to shore, so I set the boat crosswise to the river and pulled on the oars as hard as I could. After an hour or more of strenuous rowing, I'd made no progress. No one, not even your brother, could have."

"So what did you do?"

"Eventually a steam tug came by and I hallooed until I was hoarse, and it came athwart, tied itself to me and dragged me and the thing ashore." He leaned forward here, raised both eyebrows, and spoke in a low, unctuous voice. "Lady, the thing was a body. I'd been tied to a corpse all night."

He waited for a sympathetic response.

"That's an awful thing to tell me."

He sat back. "I'm sorry, lady. I should have known it might be too raw for your tender sensibilities."

"That's not why. It didn't really happen. That's why. At least not to you."

"*Ma chérie,* but it did."

"*Mon cher* Baron, but it did not. It's a story by Guy de Maupassant. It's called '*En canot.*' And it didn't have anything in it about an aching leg."

It irritated her that he assumed she didn't read literature.

His shoulders sagged, and his face reddened. "I'm sorry, lady. I misreported myself." His whole demeanor became troubled.

She guessed then why he had told a borrowed story as his own. Not to impress her. It was a substitute for his own. The mortar shell. The truth still too sharp and too personal to reveal, but the need to tell still aching. She understood all about needing to tell something. She felt a wave of empathy for him.

"That's all right," she said.

"You've got to admit that it's a good story," he said.

"Not as good as some of his others. I read everything he writes, and everything else he tells me to."

"Do you know him?"

"Of course. He stays here sometimes. Alphonse takes care of his boats."

"So do I know him. We go about together in Paris."

They passed the place where she'd found the two bodies after the flood. She had made Alphonse promise not to tell Guy because she feared he would use it in a story and make the couple appear foolish and shallow. She wouldn't tell Raoul because he might tell Guy. Telling him would be triumphant of her, but it was such a private thing.

"That's not to say there aren't bodies in the river," she said. "You know the big dredger that shoots up sand through a chute onto a hill to be carted away? All sorts of things are flung out too. I've watched carriage wheels, trunks, rudders, goats thrown up. Once I saw what looked like a mud-covered dog, but it wasn't. It was a boy."

He looked abashed, as if he knew that hers was the true story, which it was, and his had been plundered cheaply. But hers of the boy was a substitute too.

"I'm sorry I lied," he murmured.

This man at the oars, sorry. This man who limped, wearing a fine bowler, who had tried to entertain her, had been trying all afternoon, in good humor, calling her "lady," this man who had cheerfully turned the way Auguste wanted even though that meant no one would be able to identify him in the painting.

"That's all right. I like the way you told it. In your personal way."

He wore his *melon* just right, not on the back of his head. There had been that man who came into the shop wanting a *melon* and she advised him how to wear it. And just before him, that moment of cold horror when, after the Siege, the surrender, the Commune, they told her—the two army officers with serious faces, their eyes darting to the display of umbrellas on that gray day, and she had asked if she could help them find something, though she knew all along. Otherwise Louis would have been home by then. He would have wasted no time coming back to her. It rained that afternoon—better if they had come for umbrellas—not a hard rain, just the slow, fine, interminable drip of tears.

As the officers left, their message delivered, the door still open, that customer had come in wanting not just any bowler, but a French *melon*. Thousands of Communards in Montmartre not even buried yet, and he wanted a *melon*. He must have been a Versaillais official. They're frightfully dear now, she had said. All English imports. She spent a long time advising him the way she remembered Louis doing with customers. It was so dreadfully important to her that he would be satisfied. And he was, and left the shop smiling, and then she was alone.

"Shall we go back now, and have a brandy with the others?" Raoul asked.

"My father does have some Menuet Hors d'Age. I know where he keeps it in the cellar. He won't miss a glass." She pulled the right steering cord so that the boat made a wide loop.

"It *is* a beautiful afternoon, isn't it?" All the oiliness had left his voice.

"The river flowing calmly, a light breeze, just enough to rustle the leaves, birds chirping in the branches."

She hoped he would take her smile to be one of understanding. "But we *did* have luck in fishing," she said softly.

After everyone left, she and Auguste went up to the narrow balcony that wrapped around the building, and watched the sky on both sides of the island play out its tribute to the day. Turquoise spread with wisps of rosy chiffon blushed the river with a lighter rose.

"*La vie en rose,*" she murmured.

Auguste kept tapping the railing with his fingernails.

"What's the matter?"

"Gustave paid for everyone's meal today."

"That's because he saw the day as an idea."

"What idea?"

"Friendship. Collaboration. *Nous.*"

One corner of his mouth turned up. He was never one for big smiles.

"Did you enjoy the company of our titled buccaneer?" he asked.

"Yes. He tried to impress me with a story, and he did, but not in the way he had intended."

"Did he tell you about himself?"

"Not directly. Would you mind if I asked how he got his limp?"

"He was wounded in battle twice," Auguste said. "As a young recruit in the Crimea and again at the Battle of Reichshoffen. He was a cavalry officer by then. He dragged himself on his elbows through Prussian lines. At a field hospital in Alsace, some army surgeon threatened to amputate, but he screamed bloody murder and walked out with only a cane, shouting, 'I have more life to live.'"

"Does it still pain him?"

"He won't talk about it."

That might mean that it did. And yet he danced the *chahut* last Sunday, overcoming pain with joy.

Too moved to speak, she could only watch the rose sky deepening.

Chapter Fifteen

School for Wives

Sunday morning *again*. The applause last night. The slippery satin sheet under her. Hers at home were cotton. These had the monogram of l'Hôtel Crillon. Still feeling the delicious lassitude of having been loved nearly to death, tumbling on a high cloud, she didn't want to move, didn't want to breathe except in time to the rise and fall of his chest with the black curls so close to her. She ran her hand over his arm. He rolled onto his side toward her and she threaded her fingers through the springy hair.

He leapt out of bed. "We have to decide on a date."

He reached into his coat pocket and found his small engagement calendar. She steered him clear of her rehearsals and costume fittings. They settled on the second Friday in August, less than two weeks away, at a village outside Pontoise where they were unknown. They could get there and back to Paris in a day and no one would be the wiser, and Joseph-Paul would tell his father at the right moment that it was a *fait accompli,* and Monsieur Lagarde would just have to get over it in time for a grand winter wedding in Paris. After all, Joseph was doing what the old man wanted, taking his place on the Exchange even though he loathed it, so he could live out his father's obsession of wearing a diamond lapel pin and salting away cash.

"I've been creeping up on the subject with my father," Joseph-Paul said. "He still carries on about actresses."

"What does he say?"

"'*Comédiennes* have been excommunicated for appearing in certain roles. You know what that means, don't you? If they die without absolution, their children are condemned to hell.'"

The way he told her was as though it were his opinion too.

"That was in 1815!"

"What happened to Mademoiselle de Raucour could happen again."

"You can't be serious, Joseph."

"She was refused absolution—"

"Until all the players in Paris threatened to become Protestants."

She had to do something quickly to get him to shake off his father's declaration.

"Just imagine," she said. "Actors and actresses going from theater to theater, gathering more members until the troupe became a mob, spouting lines from *Tartuffe*. From *Phèdre*. Imagine the mob singing arias in the streets, shouting, 'We will never play again, or sing again unless Mademoiselle de Raucour is granted absolution! This will be the last time the streets of Paris will ring with lines from Racine or Corneille!'" She was shouting now. "'*Le Cid* will become unknown. The French stage will die!'"

Joseph-Paul was laughing, so she pushed her advantage, stood up on the bed, arms pumping, and sang, *"Marchons, marchons!"* to spur on the mob. She thumbed her nose at the archbishop and shouted, "No more Molière! No more Racine!" She bounced to the chant until they had wrung themselves out laughing at the absurdity, laughing down the powers of social control and outmoded institutions, and declaring the reign of *la vie moderne*.

Out of breath, she said, "I wish I could have been one of them."

She had won him over, and had done so in the spirit of Molière himself. He'd said to his king that the duty of comedy was to correct men by entertaining them, and she had. The issue was closed, at least for today. She bounced down onto the bed, breathing hard.

After some time of silence, he brushed her hair back from her face and took her hand in his. With only a touch of sadness but with gravity, he said, "Someday, you just might have to give up theater."

Stunned. Her lungs empty, yet she couldn't inhale.

. . .

Monday morning she opened her upstairs window and leaned out over Avenue Frochot. She hadn't slept well. She had lost her edge yesterday. Lost the chance to pose for Auguste. She had been victorious once, but at a cost too great to pay each Sunday.

Some little bird sang its four-note tune over and over—tum, ta-ta, twee—the two middle notes low and quick and the last one high and long. Poor thing, that's all he knew.

Joseph-Paul hadn't said she had to stop performing now. It was only a warning of things to come. She picked up her script. She could memorize her lines outside as well as in. Downstairs she passed her father working out a composition on the piano, the same three bars over and over, and then a bit more, and then more, making something out of silence. She opened the wrought-iron gate to the avenue, and passed Madame Galantière's ornamental pear tree. Molière could wait. A little walk would clear her mind from yesterday.

The shutters were open in number eight, Gustave Moreau's reddish stone house. Peering through one of the pointed arched windows, she saw him standing before an enormous canvas on his easel.

There was Eva Gonzalès in her garden at number four, painting to Papa's rhythm. She was surrounded by orange puffs of marigolds, and behind her, yellow honeysuckle trailed down the garden wall like a veil. "You look like a painting yourself," Jeanne said.

"A glory of a day. I couldn't stand to work inside."

At the base of the crescent, near the iron gate separating avenue Frochot from rue Laval, she listened awhile to a soprano voice pouring out of Victor Massé's window at number one, auditioning, perhaps, for a new opera. She thought how she had grown up singing the "Song of the Nightingale" from his opera *The Marriage of Jeannette*.

The tapping of the playwright's writing machine made her go back to Madame Galantière's bench in front of her ivy-covered cottage and open the script, Molière's *Le bourgeois gentilhomme*. She underlined all of Nicole's lines. Papa played the same three bars, adding the bird's tum, ta-ta, twee, tripping deftly up the scale. Then he switched instruments and tried it out on the violin. How dear he was, working so methodically. Avenue Frochot beat with creative life more passionately, it seemed, knowing it would soon lose its actress. By Christmas, she would be gone.

That made her grip the bench where she'd fallen in love for the first time, with Molière when she'd read her first play, and had said some of the lines aloud. It was his *School for Wives,* a silly play, she'd thought at the time, yet she'd loved how that old fool, Arnolfe, had gotten his just deserts for imprisoning his would-be wife, body and soul, and the girl, Agnès, had outwitted him in spite of his attempts to keep her ignorant. A simple comedy targeted at the stuffy, rigid bourgeoisie. She was only fifteen when she'd read it, and Madame had said in astonishment, "My dear, you ought to be an actress." And three years later, she played Dorine in *Tartuffe* at the Comédie-Française. Audacious for one so young, the reviewers said.

She felt a pang, thinking that on this bench Madame had opened to her a future. She would have to leave this street she loved in order to live in an apartment above a grand boulevard and go to parties with stockbrokers and bankers and their boring wives.

And leave theater too? Unthinkable. Unspeakable. This would require all the artfulness of Agnès. To Joseph-Paul, esteem was the higher aim. To her, it was admiration for creation. He had to assert himself over a woman more popular and better known than he was, for the sake of esteem. She had to find a way to work around his assertions.

There was that bird again, peeping out his four notes. She tried to whistle it. It came out too breathy, but identifiable. She could whistle it in her new role at inappropriate moments. Better yet, she could try to whistle it and just blow air, even blow air in a coarse way, but concentrate so hard on it, so innocently, and screw up her face so comically. She practiced it now until she burst out laughing at herself. Yes, it did sound like a particular, unfeminine thing. She hoped no one heard it. She could get a laugh that way as Nicole, earnestly trying, only to have it sound like something unmentionable. Amusing, that one little bird could have an influence on music and theater.

"A wife in our social position needs to exhibit a certain level of decorum," Joseph-Paul had said, sounding for all the world like the character Arnolfe delivering one of his pedantic maxims for good wives. "She should have Wednesday afternoon salons, not Wednesday afternoon rehearsals."

And certainly not Monday morning practices of unmentionable sounds.

What about modeling? Would he try to curtail that too?

She had to plant her feet in what she knew to be her being, and learn to say no, cleverly, firmly. *I love you, Joseph, I can't live separate from you, but no.* She had set a bad precedent yesterday by bending to his demands and not showing up for Auguste. She practiced a line. *In all other ways I will honor you, Joseph, but not in this. I must have theater and I must have art.*

She went inside, changed into her dark blue dress, and took the script to memorize on the train. In the foyer, Maman waved her arms to Papa's music. "He hasn't told me, but I think that will be your wedding waltz."

Jeanne went into the music room and circled around Papa with his bow raised, waited an instant so she wouldn't be impaled by it, and aimed a kiss on his temple. "I love it, Papa. It's lovelier than birdsong."

"I'm going out," she told her mother, putting on her gloves.

"Black gloves on a summer day? To the theater or to lunch with Joseph-Paul?"

"To pose." Looking in the hall mirror, she positioned her felt bonnet with the maroon feathers. "For Auguste."

Maman's hands flew up. "Ah, wait a minute." She hurried into the kitchen and cut an enormous piece of cake. "Chocolate, just like he likes." Maman grasped her wrist. "If it had been him instead of Joseph-Paul, I would have been just as happy."

CHAPTER SIXTEEN

Remembrance of Times Past

T he still life was coming along, the bottles, the footed white compote of grapes, figs, and pears, the glasses with a sip of cassis left in some, wine in others. His table would be as rich and sparkling as the one in *The Marriage Feast at Cana*. Prussian blue with rose madder for the wine in bottles. A touch of cobalt with white for the lit side of the bottles and the grapes. The last of the season, Louise had said, so he had to finish them today. A change of brushes, a thick daub of white at the bottom of the empty glasses. He reveled in the gooeyness of it. Only a preliminary laying in of the whites. When these were dry and the painting was finished, he would build up another layer of them so they would protrude and catch the light and send it back brilliantly. Let them see in that the workings of his hand. If viewers saw only the things depicted and not the act of painting, they were missing half the pleasure.

Feet stomped up the stairs, fast as a drumroll.

"Auguste," Alphonsine said. "She's here. Mademoiselle Samary."

He shot up and his chair tipped backward with a clatter.

She came up the stairs and Alphonsine disappeared down the hallway.

The slight opening of her lips announced, *I'm here*. Simply that. An expectant curtain call on a stage.

"You are dazzling."

He took a moment to suck pleasure from the sight of her. Her skin translucent, like mother-of-pearl in the light, a few curls of chestnut hair peeking out from under her hat, the crisp white cuffs, the black gloves with the pearl buttons—all these elements together released a tumble of feelings.

"When you didn't show up yesterday, I thought you were trying to tell me something I didn't need to be told."

"Not at all."

"I put you in the painting, repositioned two men to adore you, and then you didn't show up."

"I was hoping to be able to."

"No letter. No telegram. I would have understood. A fit of pique because you're in the back?"

She glared down that notion.

"I would have positioned you more prominently if you had come on time."

"It couldn't be helped." She placed the packet on the table. "From my mother."

A calculated change of subject. He peeked inside the paper wrapper and felt his mood softening. "*Chocolat*. She remembers well. Tell her *merci*."

Jeanne studied Angèle and Antonio, the only faces painted so far. She tipped her head at the vague shapes of Pierre and Paul, and examined the few dabs he had made for the colors of her dress and hat and gloves.

"It was mighty hard for them to pose with no one to look at."

She ignored that. Her hand went up to her mouth, tapping it, pointing to Circe blocked in with no detail. "What's her name?"

"Cécile-Louise Valtesse . . . de la Bigne." A flush of embarrassment swept over him at so pompous a name.

"From the loges at the Opéra or the *promenoir* at the Folies?" The fall in her voice charged him with the latter, less respectable possibility.

"From Madame Charpentier's salon," he said, clipping off each word separately. "I was hoping I'd find you there."

"I've been occupied lately."

"So I hear. Shall we begin? You did come to pose, didn't you?"

"Yes, but I have a fitting at four," she said.

He felt awkward and formal with her, directing her where to stand, as though she were chaste, every muscle taut, and it was her first time, their first time, on the divan in his studio. He positioned her shoulders, lifted her chin, and felt that delicate hollow behind the bone. "Impossible to know the correct angle of your head without Paul and Pierre here."

"I wasn't looking at them."

"Then where were you looking?"

"At that woman leaning on the railing as if she owned the place."

"Be careful. She has every right."

"Oh, my! Such protectiveness. Your new muse?"

He turned away from her and stepped back to the canvas. How was he to answer that? He didn't have to. "Now your hands, to your ears."

She tucked her hair behind her ear as she always did, even in bed after they had taken raucous fill of each other. With that common little gesture, she still had the power to overwhelm him.

He took time to clean his brushes in order to get control of his voice. "Who is painting you now?" he asked.

"No one at the moment. Did you know that Louise Abbéma's painting of me as a soubrette was hung in the same room as Bastien-Lepage's Sarah Bernhardt?"

"Yes. I saw it. The bow was too big."

"It was my costume. For Lisette in *Jeux de l'amour,*" she said, a defensive edge to her voice.

"No one will know that when they look at it years from now. It looked ridiculous, stretching shoulder to shoulder like a clown."

Her lips tightened. He had hurt her feelings.

"She did a nice job on your face, though."

In order to get as much done as possible in case she didn't come back, he mixed ultramarine, cobalt, and rose madder right on the canvas for the gradations in the fabric of her dress. He added vermilion to brown it for shadows. At one angle the iridescent feathers on her hat were maroon. At another they were a brown-black, like serrated obsidian, with the fluff a deep red-orange. How richly they gave back the light.

"What have you been painting?"

He noticed she didn't ask whom he was painting. "In Normandy. I've been painting in Normandy. I was curtailed awhile with a broken arm."

"I didn't know." She let a long moment pass before she asked, "Whatever happened to your painting of me? The full-length one in the white gown?"

"Durand-Ruel bought it for eighteen hundred francs. And that was at a time when he was buying very little from anyone."

She murmured approval.

"You have to admit, we enhanced each other's reputation," he said.

It was awkward, and he hated it. Their hesitation was as though they were speaking in a foreign language and had to work out each sentence first before stammering it.

"You rarely came to see me perform. You don't come at all now."

"I appreciated the real woman more. The one I could touch."

"I went to your exhibits," she said, a countermove.

He pretended absorption in his painting for a few minutes. "What have you been doing since I saw you last?"

"I've been to London with the company." Moments later she said, "They don't laugh as easily there."

They were the necessary questions, to ascertain how each of them had gotten along without the other, asked and answered in a guarded way.

Her creamy skin glowed from within, like a lit candle in a dim church, and her green eyes flashed with specks of gold. Alight with what? Love? Perhaps, but not for him. For that sullen-faced dandy. His hand tensed. No, he must have no ill feeling. Not a dot. It would bleed through the opalescence of her face.

He loaded one brush with light tones for her skin, another dark for her gloves—those gloves revealing that little opening of naked skin, the calculated allure of what is partly hidden. And those buttons announcing that they can be undone to get at her, that she could be undone. He painted the pearl rounds, the sliver of wrist below them, painted the memory of the smoothness of her skin, and of his love for her.

Not that he had ever expected them to have the conventional culmination of marriage. No, he couldn't quite have conceived of himself as married, even to her. He just wanted it to go on as it had been. What was wrong with that?

"You know, it was a supreme folly to sacrifice love because you didn't like a painting." Reducing it to that might make it seem to her not only damned foolish but dead wrong.

A small sound came out of her mouth as if from a baby bird.

He was vaguely, then acutely conscious of his hand hurting. Maybe he'd been holding the brush too tensely. For a cold instant he couldn't release the position, couldn't voluntarily arch his fingers to pick up paint from his palette. The ache was different than a twinge of fatigue he sometimes felt at the end of a full day of work. He'd only been painting a couple of hours. He could not let that spoil this brief pleasure.

"Such skin," he murmured.

"You're not doing dabby strokes, are you? Remember the critic. 'Putrefaction.'"

She'd been hurt, poor thing, and now it hurt him that she saw so clearly what was taking him anguished months to recognize, that visible Impressionist strokes didn't allow him to do what he wanted with figures, what Ingres had done with invisible strokes early in the century. A shock ran through him. Carried to the extreme, choppy strokes and feathery touches could destroy figure painting. Where did that leave him?

"*Non, chérie.* I'm leaving no record of my brush on your face. You'll love it."

If he had painted her a year ago *not* as an Impressionist, without visible, discrete trailings of his brush, and without the green tinge to her skin that truly was reflected from her surroundings, if he had painted her as Ingres would have, with subtle shadings to model her form without the slightest demarcation of a stroke, as he had painted Lise as *Diana the Huntress* a dozen years ago—if he had done so with Jeanne, would she still be his? A hard price for artistic experiment, for a style that may vanish someday, a style that may have already reached its apogee, at least with him. If he had painted her in her white ball gown as he had painted Marie Antoinette on thousands of plates . . .

He didn't ask her. She might not know any more than he did, and it would spoil this intimacy of silence, the oneness of their endeavor.

He had to satisfy himself in knowing that he would always have that, the act of painting her in that white gown. He would always have the remembrance of her standing there in perfect accord with him as he laid his doomed love on the canvas. He would refuse to let that slip from him. He could continue to love her and it would be none of her business.

Her quietness while modeling was unusual. Maybe she was doing the same thing he was, taking moments off a shelf, playing out the roles again, a reprise before the final curtain. It was the prerogative of former lovers, a sort of morbid delight. Words, moments, their laughter at forgotten little things, her kindness to adorers when he met her at the stage door after a performance, his impatience when she signed every program that was thrust at her, the smooth firmness of her inner thigh.

That one time she introduced him at a party of theater people, "This is Auguste Renoir, my painter," as if to say, *my wallpaper hanger, my shoeblack boy*. "How about saying next time, this is Pierre-Auguste Renoir, my good friend? Or Pierre-Auguste Renoir, my lover?" he'd suggested later. She had flown into a rage. "I thought I was helping your career," she'd said. And he'd said, "How would you like it if I said, 'This is Jeanne Samary, my model'?" That was the beginning of the end. His words had been prophetic. Here she was, his model.

He tried to locate the source of the little pain that announced itself again, traveling the length of his finger. With horror, he realized it was where that hard lump was beginning to grow on his middle finger where the brush rested. At least he could say the pain had nothing to do with her, nothing to do with anything except himself.

"That small painting you did of me at the last? The very last. The small one of just my face, done like the ball gown painting?"

"The painting of remembrance of times past? The one you didn't want?"

"Yes. Do you still have it?"

He could tell her no, and she would be hurt, if he wanted to hurt her.

He paused long enough for her to have a pang of anxiety. He set down his brush and rubbed the hard, swollen joint.

"Yes. It's in my studio."

"Could I . . . I mean, would you?"

"Give it to you?"

She could only nod. A change had come over her, something of which she was unwilling to speak, but nonetheless palpable between them.

"You would like it *now*?"

She nodded again, not looking at him, keeping her pose.

"More than a nod, and it's yours."

"I would like it, as a remembrance of the happy hours in your studio on the rue Saint-Georges."

"The rue Saint-Georges is only a few blocks from avenue Frochot."

"Yes," she said, her eyes moistening. "L'avenue Frochot."

The happy hours in your studio. The way she said that lifted him and placed him down in an afternoon more than a year ago when, painting her in his studio, he'd had such an urge, the exquisite, torturous conflict of two pleasures, that he had set down his brush and had rushed to her and she'd laughed in a wonderfully abandoned way. Open your dress, he'd said in a husky whisper as he was unbuttoning his trousers. They had just enough time before Paul or Pierre would burst into his studio at five o'clock as happened more days than not. We have time, he'd said, and indeed they had, and were buttoned up and at work when his friends came in, only both of them were giddy and flushed, and she laughed softly at little nothings until she went home to avenue Frochot and he caught up with his friends at Café Nouvelle-Athènes, buoyant.

"Why did you come today?"

"Because I care for you." Her voice came out in a lower register, that voice that could mold an audience to her will. "I care about your painting."

Well, now, that was something else entirely. Or was it?

She blinked a few times in rapid succession, holding her pose. "You were always so good to me, so liberal."

"Liberal in my affection for you? Of course."

He knew she had broken the pose even though he was looking at his painting. When he turned to her, she quickly resumed the position and gazed over the railing to the river. In that split second turning toward him, what had been in her eyes?

"I meant in not constraining me. You took an interest to show me you cared for me, and that was all."

"Constraining you?"

Turning from the painted image to the woman, he saw a tear grow on her bottom lid and tumble. The feathers on her hat trembled. A consummate professional, she kept her pose.

He ignored the great solid shift their relationship had taken, set down his brush and stepped toward her. Holding her by both hands, he backed into a chair and pulled her onto his lap, the feathers tickling his ear. She went limp, her body melding familiarly to his, as he hardened. There might be a chance. He burned to carry her into his room, not twenty footsteps away, and on the bed remind her of the happiness they had enjoyed.

He whispered, "My little quail." A new tear swelled when she heard that endearment. Then the earlier tear had not been for him. His urge slackened even while he held her to his chest, crooning to her, *"Ne pleure pas Jeannette."*

"Is that a song?"

"A very old ballad."

He sang in a hushed voice the words, *"Don't cry, Jeannette. We will marry you to the son of a prince or a baron. I don't want a prince or a baron. I want my friend, Pierre, who is in prison."*

She shifted in his arms. "What's the rest of it?"

"It's silly."

"Tell me."

"You will not have your Pierre because we will hang him. If you hang Pierre, hang me with him," he sang softly.

"And? Sing the rest."

"Et l'on pendouilla Pierre, et sa Jeannette avec lui."

"And they hanged Pierre and his Jeannette with him? No!"

"It's only a song."

She looked down at his hands and touched an enlarged knuckle as though she remembered it. He felt a sharp grain rubbing between bones.

"Do you want to keep working?" she asked.

"No. That's all I can do today. It would be helpful to have you here sometime with Paul and Pierre, though."

"I'll try."

It was a long moment before she stood up. He offered her thirty francs, fifteen for each session, the amount she would have required if she'd been a major figure.

"To keep it professional," she said, "but only today's." She took fifteen francs and left fifteen in his palm.

The final curtain.

"Don't forget to eat the cake," she said, dropping the coins into her drawstring bag.

He walked her to the middle of the bridge. "Think of me," she said. Two brief kisses at each cheek, in the air really, and then she walked away, down the path leading to the station in Rueil, stretching the thread of love until it broke as she went around the corner of the *boulangerie*.

Think of her. What a thing to say. A parting shot. She wanted everything. She was in love with mere adoration.

The river glistened with silver highlights riding on the ripples between blue-green furrows, the colors distinct, then blending, then separating as the water moved relentlessly under the bridge. He realized he'd let her go without explaining to her the Impressionist vision of broken strokes, perfectly visible from here. She had eluded him.

Chapter Seventeen

The Convocation of *Flâneurs*

Looking down the length of the terrace on the third Sunday, seeing the dozen people posing before him, Auguste was filled with joy. They had gone boating, eaten Louise's delicious rabbit stew, had drunk Pierre's favorite *petit vin* made at a small château that didn't produce much, but what it did was very fine. They'd sung a few songs while eating the Charlotte Malakoff, a mold of strawberries, ladyfingers soaked in rum, and almond cream, and now they were ready to take their poses. He squeezed luscious, shiny smears of color onto his palette, and filled his nose with their sweet oily smells.

This Circe had perfect posture, too perfect. But the dress and the jewel hanging from her blue velvet ribbon like a shard of pale blue ice were exquisite. Her skin was too white. Easy enough to rosy her up a bit. Pale coloring was a sign of a nervous temperament, and he didn't want to suggest that.

"Circe, I need you to face the table. Not so stiff, so posed."

"Isn't that what we're doing, posing?"

He caught Alphonsine rolling her eyes.

"Pretend we're not." He bent her hand back and forth at the wrist. It went limp. There was hope. "Pretend we're just sitting here talking." He put a glass of wine in her hand. The sheer white ruffle draped down over her blue sleeve like a veil. "Take a drink now and then. See how Angèle is leaning toward Gustave? Look at Alphonsine standing there like she does any other day, relaxed and natural."

Circe looked and then leaned forward, hinged like the lid of a wooden color box, still rigid. Alphonsine couldn't stifle her giggle.

"What she needs is a good rambunctious lay," Angèle said. "That'll get her to loosen up."

Pierre scratched his beard. "I'm sure someone can accommodate her. For the sake of art."

"And there are plenty of secluded sites on the island," Paul added.

"It's too hot," Circe said. "My shoulders hurt."

"Let me be the first to offer my services as a masseur," Pierre said.

Auguste ignored their banter. If he were in love with her, he would find a way to work with her, but he wasn't. Yet. Maybe if he gave her something to do, she would cooperate.

"Didn't you agree to be *flâneurs* last week and make observations on *la vie moderne?*" he asked. "Well, what did you observe? Circe, you preside."

If she would turn her head to look at someone once in a while, he might catch her then.

"Moi? Oh, là là."

She cleared her throat and sat up straighter, if that was possible. Maybe this wouldn't work after all. He hurried to mix colors and have a brush ready with her skin tone, another for the blue stripe, another for the white.

She turned to look at the group and struck her fork lightly against a glass. Three pings. "As Sovereign of the Convocation of *Flâneurs,* our gentlemen social observers, and *Flâneuses,* our lady observers, of the Maison Fournaise, I declare the first session open to undertake an examination of *la vie moderne.*"

He got in a few strokes on her bodice before she remembered she didn't want a profile and turned back to face forward. He indulged himself by working on the stripes of her dress falling in folds.

"I call on Monsieur Ephrussi," she said.

The staid and proper Charles Ephrussi tipped his head, the gesture of *un homme galant.* "With pleasure, mademoiselle."

Auguste had noticed him eyeing her. Maybe because of her this painting would hang in his rue de Monceau mansion. *After* the Salon, of course.

"On Thursday, the air was so heavy I thought it might be pleasant to take a ride on the upper level of an omnibus, just to feel a breeze."

"That's it? Just that omnibuses are part of *la vie moderne?*" Circe turned to look at Charles. Too far.

"Patience, mademoiselle," Charles said.

"Circe, keep your pose." Poor, nervous wisp of a thing, unwilling to yield the center of attention. Her need to interact battled so prettily with her determination to be painted full face.

"I took a seat on the roof. We stopped at Rond Point and the paperboys lifted their poles with newspapers attached to the clips. I put my coin in the cup on one pole and took *Le Temps.* My eye fell on this curious notice."

Charles pulled a clipping from his breast pocket and read.

"An old man nearing life's end wishes to ask forgiveness from one known as Le Balafré, a frequenter of Montmartre cabarets. The lie about him told to Madame Marie-Pauline under the gas lamp on the corner of rue de Roche-chouart and avenue Trudaine on the night of June 13, 1864, has never ceased to haunt the mind of him who now confesses it and who wishes to die with a clean soul. Monsieur Le Balafré, pardon it, and give peace to a troubled man."

"Le Balafré. The Scarred One. Scarface! I know him!" Angèle said.

"You can't be serious," Charles said.

"He's got a gash from his mouth to the top of his ear. Give me that clipping when we're finished. He's blind now, and just sits under the acacia trees in place du Tertre on the Butte telling stories for a sou. I'll have someone read it to him. It might make a world of difference to both of them."

"No comments after each one," Circe said primly. "When we're finished we'll have a vote for whose observation is the best." She tapped her chin. "Hm. Whom shall I call on next? Ah, you. Gustave."

She looked at Gustave a moment. Time enough for only one rushed stroke for her throat.

"Mine is a Left Bank story," Gustave said. "I found a crowd gath-

ered in place de la Sorbonne listening to a woman on a makeshift platform. 'No duties without rights, no rights without duties,' she was
saying. 'Perfect equality of the sexes before the law and in customs and
moral codes. We must not timidly beg for a little more education, a little
more bread, a little less humiliation in marriage. No. We must firmly
declare our natural rights.'"

"Hubertine Auclert, most likely. A radical Amazon on crusade,"
Charles said.

"She went on and on about universal suffrage, legal separation of
wealth in marriage, the right to run for public office."

"The right to scrub the floor," Auguste put in. "If women did that
domestic exercise, they'd make better lovers. The generations to come
won't know how to make love worth a damn, and that would be very
unfortunate for those who don't have painting."

"Don't be beastly, Auguste. It's not a scrub job that makes a woman
cut capers, and you know it," Angèle said.

He snickered. "Well, I can't see myself getting into bed with a lawyer,
if there are such female monsters. I like women best when they don't know
how to read, and when they wipe their babies' bottoms themselves."

"You can't mean that," Ellen said. "Words, language, they're as important to women as to men."

"For a man who paints *la vie moderne,* you're a century behind the
times," Angèle said.

"But why teach women such a boring occupation as law when they
are so perfectly suited to do what men can never dream of attempting—
that is, to make life bearable?"

"Let Gustave finish," said Circe, turning to face forward.

A will of her own. It was maddening.

"One man in the crowd shouted, 'Women don't know how to vote.'
The speaker gestured to the Sorbonne behind her and said, 'Then open
the university to us.'" Gustave shook his head. "She had an answer to
everything."

"Because she's no clod-knocker," Angèle said. "She's smart and she's
plucky and she's right."

Paul nudged Pierre. "Ho-ho! Angèle's an Amazon herself."

"Who would have known it under that pretty face?" Pierre said.

Alphonsine said to Alphonse, "It looks like Papa is going to take out the steam launch. You'd better go down."

Alphonse looked over his shoulder.

Circe turned around completely and touched the muscle of his forearm.

"Circe, hold your pose, please."

"First Alphonse has to give us his contribution."

"Just this." He gestured with his thumb toward the promenade. "These office clerks in new striped shirts trying to act like oarsmen, strutting around here with an oar on their shoulder—they're only weekend pretenders. They buy their *canotier* in Paris instead of on the river, wear a cravat by la Coline, and smoke their fancy Chacom pipes from Saint-Claude. Take a look at the ones in frock coats tapping silver-tipped canes on the dirt of the promenade. They steal glances at how other men dress. They're afraid of getting their white trousers dirty, afraid of sunburn, afraid of blisters, afraid for their liver. They don't really care about the river. They care about putting on a show."

"Then you think leisure is turning into a performance?" Jules asked. *"That all the island's a stage and all the men and women merely posers?"*

"Something like that. I'm sorry, Auguste. I have to go," Alphonse said.

Auguste nodded and Alphonse went downstairs.

Looking right at Circe, Jules said, "People pose in order to make spectacles of themselves. Thanks to Haussmann's public places, we've become a nation of stage players, and the play we're performing is class."

She of the articulated wrists flapped and fluttered to make Jules stop. "It's not your turn. Right now it's Antonio's turn, our foreign correspondent."

She turned to flirt with Antonio, but Auguste missed his chance. Damned infuriating.

"Con piacere, signorina," Antonio said. "The women of Paris, that's the subject of my little report. Everyone from laundresses at two francs a day to Mademoiselle Zénobie, star of the Folies-Bergère who had the soles of her dancing shoes paved with diamonds."

"Glass," Ellen said. "Just glass. She's trying to imitate Cora Pearl in *Orpheus and the Underworld*. Hers were real, but that was during the Second Empire."

"You didn't start low enough," Angèle said. "Two francs a day is too high. You've left out the wakers-up. Ragpickers' daughters in the Maquis who work from midnight to four in the morning making the rounds of the merchants of Les Halles vegetable stalls and the poor devils who fold newspapers. Five centimes a wake-up. Millionaires of the profession have as many as thirty clients. That gives them one measly franc fifty by dawn."

"How is it that you know so much about the riffraff?" Circe demanded.

"Because I was one, princess." Softly at first, Angèle sang Rosa Bordas' rousing song, "La Canaille," famously sung at the Hôtel de Ville the night that ignited the Commune.

"*J'en suis! J'en suis,*" Angèle sang in Rosa's raspy voice, declaring she was also *canaille,* riffraff.

Pierre joined on the mesmerizing, mounting refrain. Promenaders stopped to listen and the *Palais* sailboat crowd came out from under the arbor. Paul stamped his feet, and Angèle, her arm raised aggressively, belted out the last victorious note. Applause came up from below.

Paul raised his glass. "*Vive le peuple!*"

"Bravo, Angèle!" Ellen cried. "You do Rosa proud!"

"You'll have the stinking *mouchards* reporting us," Alphonse called out from the dock.

"And the Maison will be shut down!" Alphonsine wailed, which made everyone laugh, especially Paul with his deep-toned horse laugh.

Circe had lost control of the group. Or Auguste had. Bewilderment flushed her cheeks. Finally some color to them. A few strokes on her face.

"Antonio, are you finished?" Circe asked.

"No. I've hardly begun."

That brought on the laughter again. How could he paint with all this going on?

"I've been studying your social classes as they pertain to that oldest of female professions. As a foreigner, I find the nuances fascinating. At the bottom, you have the ladies of the pavement, hatless Montmartroises posing as milliners' delivery girls with the most piercing, desperate eyes that chide you for not buying what they're selling." Antonio shuddered, which made Alphonsine snicker.

"The next lowest, I believe, is the dancer of the *chahut* in Montmartre dance halls. Not professional performers, just women who come to be picked from the *promenoirs.*"

"Girls who have an intimate acquaintance with a washtub during the day," Jules added, then took a puff on his pipe.

"Unbelievable, their kicks and contortions. We have nothing like it in Italy. Their catcalls advertise wild frenzied sex."

"Among the French," Charles said, "it rarely happens that a taste for anything is not carried to such an extent as to become folly. The *chahut* began as an orderly *quadrille des lanciers.* In its extreme, it's the cancan of the finale at the Folies-Bergère ending in a row of chorus girls falling forward in the splits, like dominoes each knocking the next one down. That too is *la vie moderne,* splintering women's bodies for entertainment."

Looking into her wine glass, Ellen said, "You surprise me, Monsieur Ephrussi, that you would attend an entertainment of *le peuple.*"

"As a foreigner myself, I must learn all aspects of my adopted culture."

Auguste chortled, and Charles tried to recover himself. "In my opinion, the elasticity of the leg in the *chahut* and cancan leads one to suspect an equal flexibility of morals. So continue, Antonio."

"Then there's the shockingly young amateur, the *trottin,* flowers of the rues hiking up their skirts while sizing up their potential customers."

"Mere buds," Pierre cut in. "They're a gamble of inexperience."

"Take a closer look, Antonio," Paul said. "There's a difference between how the women lift their skirts on the Right Bank and the Left."

"I see I'll have to continue my study," Antonio said.

"Use caution in your investigations," Raoul said. "There are dangers."

"I understand. A step above, if I'm not mistaken, is what I believe you call the *demi-mondaine,* older than a *trottin,* and more expert.

Dressed in finery that would admit her to a higher-class café, or a theater loge."

"Or the Jockey Club or the Hippodrome at Longchamp," Raoul
put in.

"Or the Château Rouge or the Valentino," Charles added.

"And finally," Antonio said, "the courtesans."

"Deriving their name from serving the royal court," Charles inter-
jected. "They participate in the arts and the finer things."

Amusing how Charles was taking part with such enthusiasm.

"The most exquisitely dressed," Antonio continued, "the most jew-
eled, the most intelligent, the most—"

"Expensive," Pierre said.

Circe raised her chin. *Zut!* A mind of her own. He gave up on her
for the time being and mixed darker shades for the shoulders of Raoul,
Jules, and Charles, positioning them in relation to one another, breadth
and height.

"You've certainly been busy this week, Antonio," Circe said.

"Oh, no, mademoiselle. These are the results of a month of observations."

"Don't think you have it all wrapped up," Angèle said. "It takes a
keener eye than yours to cut respectable from loose. Take a squint at the
size of her bows, dear boy, not her bosoms. See where she places her
chignon—high like a crown or low like a bunny's ass. Watch how she
lifts her skirt at a curb, how long she holds it up, whether she lowers it
gracefully or drops it with a flump, whether she looks you in the face—
them's the things will tell you she is or isn't a *femme de la rue*. Back to
the streets you go, and do better, or you'll make a blunder that will land
you in the cells of Rochefort."

"And your conclusion?" Jules asked. "So far, that is."

"That Montmartre is indeed the seat of democracy. The poor are
offered the same treats as the rich, only the dressing is different."

"Caution, my friend," Jules said. "Dumas *fils* said to go to Chevet's
and look at the peaches at twenty sous. Perfect, fresh, juicy. Then look
at those for fifteen. Each one has a flaw, hidden until you take a bite."

Auguste cast a glance at Gustave. He had said nothing during all of Antonio's report, the only man not contributing. His expression was inscrutable, his pose leaning away from the table was exact. He must have shooting pains in his back. They'd been posing for nearly two hours.

"Time for a break," he said.

"But we haven't gone around to everyone," Circe said.

Ellen shook out her arm. "And you haven't called on any women."

Pierre gave his beard an energetic scratch and made good on his promise to massage Circe's neck and shoulders, then moved on to Ellen, and asked her about bringing Émile again. She gave him a guarded answer.

"I thought I was the *quatorzième*, brought in to save the day," Charles said. "Today we have a dozen. Why make it worse?"

"One woman not here today is already in the painting, which makes thirteen unless Émile comes back to fill his space," Auguste said.

"Then if I might say so, prevail on him to come, mademoiselle," Charles said to Ellen. "It is essential, for the sake of the painting's reception."

"Otherwise," Pierre said, "we're subject to dire consequences. Thirteen gathered in an upper room for the Last Supper. This is an upper terrace."

"I'll try."

"If Émile doesn't come back, your painting will suggest a different story than you intend, Auguste," Pierre said.

"I don't intend any story." He resolved not to think of it for a while, and just keep on painting. He couldn't allow one more worry to set in.

Circe patted her bosom. "Don't all paintings tell a story?"

"Not this one. If I had wanted to tell a story, I would have used a pen. Choose a history painting if you want a story. The important thing here is not *what's* going on, but how it *conveys* what's going on."

"You're trying to confuse me."

"Painting, the act of it, that's what's important. Let them see paint— thick, thin, smooth, rugged, one color brushed wet into another, or lying alongside another, distinct. That's what modernity is to me."

"This will be famous, won't it?" she purred.

Her eyes were alive with light like wet sapphires washed with lavender.

"Ask me in ten years."

She was perverse, yes, irritating, yes, but, confound it, he felt himself slipping into her aura.

"You've enjoyed leading the conversation, haven't you?" he said.

She dipped her head in a movement of bashful pride, the practiced gesture of a coquette. Over her shoulder he saw Alphonsine wag her head just enough for him to notice, as if to say, *La-di-dah*. Alphonsine, the hostess of the Maison Fournaise, was the true *flâneuse*, missing nothing.

Soon Circe clapped her hands like a schoolmarm. "It's time. Places, everyone."

At this, Alphonsine glared at her outright. He had to laugh at that.

A sick feeling came over him as he compared his friends to the painting. On the canvas, Circe was an ambiguous mess. Her torso and shoulders faced forward, her head was sketched in to face sideways like an Egyptian queen painted flatly on a wall, and the stripes of her bodice didn't connect with those on her skirt. And Charles was as stiff and out of place as Circe. Auguste drew his broad-bladed scraping knife across the canvas from Charles's top hat to his waist until he was only a ghost image.

Seeing him scrape, Jules cried, *"Out, damned spot! Out, I say."*

"The second session of the Convocation of *Flâneurs* and *Flâneuses* is about to begin," Circe said. "I call on Jules."

"*Oui,* mademoiselle. To me, modernity consists—"

"Just a minute," Auguste said. "Charles, I've changed my mind. I'm sorry, but I have to have you turn more toward Jules."

"Whatever you'd like. How far?"

"More. More. That's good."

Alphonsine's beady-eyed look bored into the back of Circe's head, as if to say, *That's how a model should behave!*

"Go ahead, Jules," he said.

"To me, modernity consists of new forms in all the arts. I went to Stéphane Mallarmé's house this week to hear and discuss the new poetry."

Alphonsine raised up slightly.

"Were the poems about love?" Circe arched her back and thrust forward her breasts. "All poems should be about love."

"I can't rightly say. These were *les Symbolistes.* A mood was more important than a clear meaning. But I can tell you the feeling they gave me. They made me keenly conscious of mystery in life."

"That's snobbish of you," Circe said. "You think we're not clever enough to understand. It's easier to say 'mystery' than to explain."

"Well then, I'll explain as well as I can. It has to do with a concrete thing suggesting an abstract idea to the writer personally. Think of x equals y and y equals z. Mallarmé only writes x and leaves us to discover the z. He said that to name something outright takes away much of the enjoyment of the poem, which comes from guessing the mystery."

"Give us an example," said Alphonsine.

"Suppose I'm writing a poem about us here today. Instead of Parisians out in the country, I might speak of animals of various stripes let out of cages, gorging themselves on meat and drink and then licking their paws in the mutual comfort of the pack."

"That's not very complimentary," Circe said.

"There's nothing wrong with it. Licking their paws suggests the mood of hunger satisfied. The poem would actually be about pleasure."

"Excuse me," Alphonsine said. "Can it be this? Those Sunday strollers on the promenade down there with their top hats, x, make me think of a hat shop, y, and that hat shop puts me in the mood of sadness, z?"

"Yes, even though for others it might suggest a happy occasion, buying a new hat. That's what makes *Symboliste* poets so difficult to follow in their personal associations, but the words and images you use to describe that hat shop will convey the feeling."

"Then a thing can suggest an idea." Alphonsine looked at Gustave. "A rose, brevity."

Circe let out a noisy breath. "I don't know where you're going. X, y, paws, roses. It's all gibberish."

Her throat tightened in panic, her muscles springing out like wires under her blanched skin. "Circe, turn your head toward Gustave."

She did for a few moments, and then turned back to face forward. Every time she did, the folds in her skirt moved, and that changed the stripes. It was driving him mad. "Circe, you must hold still!"

"It's the ladies' turn now," Circe said. "Ellen, what did you observe?"

"Auguste, may I lower my arm so I don't have to speak into the glass?"

"Yes. I won't paint you while you're talking."

"Since I work at the Folies, my story comes from there," Ellen said. "The impresario, Léon Sari, is trying out a new trapeze artist, a young Russian with inventive new tricks. Novelty is everything, and the regular act had become stale. Marcel and Marcelline just swing from two trapezes over the audience horseshoe, and Marcelline flies into Marcel's outstretched arms. To enliven it for the summer revue, they added a rubber baby. Marcelline swings it by its feet, Marcel by its arms. They're so high up it looks real, even from the balcony, and they fling that baby back and forth when their trapezes swing them toward each other.

"Last night they couldn't find the rubber baby. Accusations flew down the corridor that the Russian stole it to cripple their act. They searched his dressing room and the prop room. The prop master was frantic. The impresario said they couldn't go on without it. He'd advertised their act, The Flying Family. Their picture with their real baby was on the posters. The audience expected it. They'd be booed without it. He threatened to put the Russian in their place.

"Their real baby is nearly two. Last night Marcel grabbed him and ran down the hallway when the caller came for him. Marcelline ran after him, shouting, 'No, No!' All the performers crammed the wings to see. Marcel mounted the hanging ladder carrying that babe just like the rubber one, and the show went on. They flung their child in the air like he was stuffed with straw, his squeals silencing the audience, and at the end of the act, Marcel swung himself onto a rope and lowered himself down onto the stage, carrying the baby. When the child touched the boards, he toddled in circles, dazed, to thunderous applause. People whistled, stamped their feet, stood up and cheered. Monsieur Sari was wild with excitement. Now he demands that they forget the rubber baby and use the child from now on. Petit Marcel. 'Step right up. Two francs for the chance to see catastrophe. An extraordinary pleasure.' That's *la vie moderne* for you."

He had stopped painting. Everyone was silent, even Circe. Her game had fallen apart. Their lively expressions changed to sullen staring.

Circe said in a flat voice, "Angèle, it's your turn. I'm sure you have something to tell."

"Next week. I'll tell it next week."

Some meditative minutes went by before Jules said, "It seems to me that each of you is a prism through which the light of city life has passed."

"You mean we're dead?" Circe shot back.

"Quite the contrary," Jules said. "The mark of the true *flâneur* or *flâneuse* is detachment, the observer who disdains emotional involvement in reporting the shallowness and anonymity of city life. Ellen has given names and faces and feeling to her observations. That's different than being a *flâneuse*. It's being a poet."

That didn't make them any more animated. He couldn't paint a lifeless scene. "Enough for today," he said, rubbing the knuckle on his index finger.

He drew Ellen aside and paid her first. "You have a good heart," he said. She left immediately. He paid the others and they went downstairs.

Circe swiveled her hips getting out of the chair and stood before the painting. "I don't look like that," she shrieked. "I'm not a smudge!"

Auguste ground his teeth. "If you held your pose like all the other models for more than a few seconds at a time, I could get more done, and then you'd see yourself, which I know is all you care about."

Her eyes aimed daggers at him. "What are we on? A barge or a ship? Is that why Alphonsine is leaning over the railing? She's seasick?"

She was stretching his nerves like piano wire. "It—is—a—terrace. If you spoke less, you wouldn't show your ignorance."

He paid her but left her there and went downstairs to find Fournaise. At the base of the stairs, Jules was waiting for him. *"Trust her as you would adders fang'd,"* Jules whispered.

Auguste nodded.

The lower terrace was filled with people, but he found Fournaise on the bank.

"How is it going?" Fournaise asked.

"Never again, this many people. My next painting will be one person I love, in my studio, alone. Or a vase of flowers. They don't talk back."

He took out his wallet.

"Put that away. It's been taken care of."

"By whom?"

"The new fellow in the top hat."

"Hm. That's a surprise. I owe you for my room, and my own meals. I'm hoping for an advance from a collector, Paul Bérard, the man in Normandy—"

"Pay me with a painting."

"Again? It may never be worth anything."

"That makes no difference to me. Paint a pretty one of Alphonsine. She's the reason many people come here. I'll hang it in the dining room."

Auguste thanked him and noticed Circe taking Charles's arm to step onto the bridge. Now, didn't that beat all.

He went upstairs and looked at the painting. *Merde!* Even Circe could see the anchoring problem. He wrestled the thing into his room and flopped on the bed, exhausted. Zola equals gauntlet equals masterpiece. *Merde!* He had a long way to go.

CHAPTER EIGHTEEN

In the Time of Cherries

Auguste took his empty coffee cup into the kitchen, thinking of the relief and pleasure of painting a compliant model today. Alphonsine.

"You didn't have to bring that in here," Louise said. "Do you want something else?"

"No."

"You know, the one who calls herself Circe? She came flouncing in here on Sunday right when I was cooking for a full restaurant, asking for a bowl of ice water. Ice water! As though we have ice to spare."

"What for?"

Louise wiggled her fingers. "To dip her hands in to make them white."

He groaned. "Don't let her have any flour. She'll be flouring her face next. She'll see, though, when my painting is finished, how lovely she'd be with a little sun on her cheeks."

"Like Alphonsine's?" Louise's eyebrows lifted.

"Yes, like Alphonsine's."

Louise gave him a quizzical look. "Have you noticed? Alphonsine has been a different woman since you started this painting. So much happier. She sings in her bedroom in the morning."

"She's been a delight."

"She gives more than she takes. That's her way. A pure soul, she is."

"Yes."

She wiped her wet hands on her apron and stepped toward him, lowering her voice. "Can't you find someone for her, Auguste? One of your fine friends? The only men she meets out here are those looking for a lusty afternoon with an easy *grenouille*. She'll have none of that. She hangs on to the memory of Louis. It's honorable, yes, but so sad for her to be alone. She has to let go."

"True."

She folded down his shirt collar like his own mother often did.

"Have you ever thought of her tenderly? It seems at times you do. She's a faithful woman, Auguste, and she adores you. Can't you tell?"

He nodded, looking at the floor.

"She'd be furious if she knew I was talking like this. I shouldn't have said a word." She flicked her hands at him. "Go on about your business."

"My business today is to paint her."

Louise's eyes widened. "Oh! Then go, right this minute."

"May I have a table setting and a white linen napkin?"

"So that's what you came in here for." She gave him what he needed and hustled him out.

On the terrace, Alphonsine was having a *café* with her father. A bowl of cherries sat on the table. Perfect.

"Where do you want me?" she asked.

"Sitting next to the railing, facing me but showing some of the chair." Auguste set out a plate and tableware and handed her the napkin. "Will you fold this to make it stand up like a sail?"

She took great care and set it on the plate, adjusting it until she was satisfied. He positioned her with her left elbow bent and resting on the table, her left hand at her cheek.

"This won't hold you up on the big painting, will it?" Alphonse asked.

"No. I'd go mad if I didn't have something to do between Sundays."

"You'll finish it on time, won't you?"

"Close enough." He hoped Fournaise didn't detect doubt in his voice.

Auguste put a cherry in his mouth, licked its smooth skin, and bit down, the juice exploding, the sweetness. He placed the bowl closer to Alphonsine. "Eat one."

She lifted two by the joined stems and tried to catch one in her mouth. Her little mauve tongue curled like a cat's in search for it. She giggled, caught one, and pulled off the stem. He loved watching her roll it around in her mouth, and bite it to taste its succulence. He cupped his hand under her chin. She hesitated, making a soft purring sound as she chewed, then squeezed the pit out of her mouth and it dropped into his palm. Its wetness, where her tongue had been, an intimate thing.

"Keep that smile. Slightly openmouthed. Good. I'll call this *Alphonsine au temps des cerises*." The time of cherries, so brief.

He tugged on the red-orange bow at the back of her *canotier* so the streamers would show at the side and lifted her right arm to rest on the railing. Its weight in his hands told him she was relaxed and willing.

"A good model, *non?*" Fournaise said, patting her cheek. "We'll hang it in the dining room next to the one you did of me."

"I've got to paint the thing first."

"Then paint. Don't let me disturb you. Finish the cherries," he said on his way downstairs. "They're the last of the season."

She was quiet, letting him work, and very still. Her stillness issued from within as a deep contentment, at one with her river world.

A thin layer of high stratus clouds diffused the sunlight. The myriad of minute gradations of hues he saw in her dress he also saw in the river—her form in accord with the background.

"The sky is giving me a gift today," he murmured. "It's making lovely color harmonies, you against the river, the trees, alongside the tablecloth."

He laid in those delicate harmonies—pale lavender-blue for her dress, white for the tablecloth which he would overlay with tints of blue from her dress and yellow-gold from the sun shining softly through the clouds. Light brown for the wooden railing, lavender for the ironwork below it, olive and ocher foliage, deep ocher for her chair, pale ocher for her hat, paler still for the braid on her sleeve, near white where the sunlight lay over her outstretched arm. Every hue surrounding her was reflected in her image. Every shape softened by light. Feathering one shape into the other with small distinct touches would make the painting's harmony one of stroke and not just of color.

How much farther could he go using separate feathery strokes to diffuse edges? As far as to blur the figure into the background? Would that be so bad, having a female form emerge from a riverscape—the two things he loved? Or from a landscape? The idea excited him, but there was a danger in going too far. He wouldn't risk it for this painting of Alphonsine. He didn't want her to dissolve into a swirl of color.

"There's a sailboat near the railroad bridge the same shape as the napkin, and the curve of your chair back is in harmony with the curve of the bridge support. The bridge is nearly on the same diagonal as the railing."

"It will mean something to Papa to have the bridge and the railing in the painting. The same man worked on both of them." Her face lost its peace and her hand tightened its hold on the railing. "And to me."

A bird trilled a song in the trees. Her eyes moved, looking for it, but she kept her head still. "What would the river be without its sounds?" she said. "And smells too. Wet grass, mud, wild honeysuckle." Her hand relaxed and peace returned to her face.

"You are a river creature, aren't you? Maybe I'll call this *The River Goddess Sequana*."

"When you paint a portrait, do you try to see into the person's soul?"

"This isn't a portrait. It's a full genre scene with background. When I paint portraits I have to paint tighter. The men with the bankrolls have to recognize their daughters and wives. But your father understands Impressionism, so this will be softer."

"Still, do you? Try to see into a person's soul?"

"I leave that for lovers and priests. I just show that your face is an egg shape, your chin slightly narrower than your forehead."

"Oh, wonderful. You're going to paint me like an egghead. A person is more than color and shape, don't you think?"

"It's not my job to think. It's to feel and to see." He gave her a hint of a smile. "I paint women as I'd paint carrots."

"And I suppose Madame Morisot paints men like green beans? You're being obstinate and doltish."

"Ah, yes, that's what I'm after. A little fire in your eyes."

He worked on her face while that expression lasted.

"A person can love carrots, you know," he murmured.

He accented her narrow waist with a blue sash and lightened the pale blue of her bodice where sunlight rested on her breasts. He had the feeling, like a warm breeze coming from nowhere in the still air, that someday, seeing this painting in the dining room, he would be overcome.

"When I suggested that you paint up here, I didn't have in mind the kind of big painting you're making, with all those people," she said. "I was just thinking of the view."

"You don't like what I'm doing?"

"I love what you're doing! All your friends, all the talking and singing."

"How's that different from any other Sunday crowd?"

"We're doing something together. *Nous.*"

Ah, yes, that quaint concept of hers.

"Do you want to know what I think of them? The models?" she asked.

"If you wish to tell me."

"Antonio is his mother's precious darling. He doesn't walk. He glides. He's so far gone on Angèle that I'm worried for him."

"Ah. Our Carmen who sings of bohemian love. What do you think of our Monsieur Ephrussi?"

"I wouldn't be surprised if he never sat down out of fear of mussing himself. His accent reminds me of someone I knew."

"Who?"

She tapped the railing. "Alexander. The man who designed the ironwork under the terrace. He was Russian."

"So is Charles, but his wife is French."

"Why didn't he bring her?"

"Propriety. What about Paul Lhôte? He's my closest friend," Auguste said.

"He laughs like a barge hooting."

"At everything, even danger. On a bet he went down into the Paris sewers, claiming there were street signs down there and that he could find his way from Pigalle to the Hôtel de Ville in two hours. Pierre waited there four hours in a panic, but he finally climbed out, stinking and filthy. 'Like a walk in the park,' he said."

"Ugh! I think Pierre is funnier, the way he tries to get his hands on Circe."

"And Raoul?"

"I like the faces he makes. And I like him. His spirit. His leg makes him lurch, but he dances anyway."

Louise came up the stairs talking. "Auguste, what would you prefer on Sunday, *côtelettes d'agneau à la forestière* or *fritures de la Seine*?"

"Hmm. Lamb or fried fish. I'm sure that they'd both be delicious. Whatever you'd like to prepare. Both of them, one this week, one the next."

"Which one first?"

"The fried fish, I suppose, in keeping with the setting of the painting. I didn't think there were any fish left in the Seine."

"I order from Le Havre."

"We won't tell anyone, will we?"

Louise raised her shoulders and covered her mouth. "A secret. Will *pâté de canard* and *aubergines à la Russe* be all right for the entrées this Sunday? I'll bet that Russian fellow would like eggplant."

"I'm sure he would."

After she left, Alphonsine said, "She's been planning the menus weeks in advance."

"Then why is she asking me?"

"She likes you. She wants to feel part of it. That's why she comes upstairs and announces the dishes. She never does that for anyone else."

From his side, it was also true—he was feeling part of the family. Maybe too much for his own sense of independence.

He darkened the blue slightly and added a tint of violet for the shadows in the folds of her skirt. "And Jules, our anglophile poet with the irrepressible habit of quoting Shakespeare?"

"I like him doing that."

"He can't stop himself. It's the way he experiences life."

"I liked him from the first time I saw him gazing at the river with a far-off look on his face. Maybe he was composing a poem. It's fascinating, I think, to line up words in a way they've never been before to allow you to see something differently."

"Paintings allow you to see something differently too." He made a pale yellow ocher for the trim on her sleeves. While he had it on his brush, he added green and feathered in strokes for the foliage behind her bordering the river. It was coming along quickly.

"I have to tell you about the women too. Ellen has a serious streak even though she works at the Folies, but Angèle's frivolous. Angèle's so funny when she speaks roughly. She's not the type who would endure hardships for a loved one, man or woman. She'd just go where impulse takes her."

"She's a pleasure-seeker, all right. After that cycle ride, Alphonse had better be wary."

"He is. He's so wary I wonder if he'll ever fall in love."

"Does that run in the family?"

Her eyelids lowered. It took her a moment to answer.

"With me, it's not wariness. It's something else."

Louise came up the stairs again with a pitcher of lemonade and two glasses on a tray. "I forgot what I was going to say. Oh, yes. For dessert—"

"I'll make the dessert, Maman."

"You didn't tell me." She jabbed her fingernail into his shoulder. "I'm the cook and she didn't even tell me. So what do you *think* you're making?"

"Layered apple pastries drizzled with Chambord liqueur."

"And where do you think you're getting the Chambord?"

"Papa's cabinet, of course."

Auguste motioned for Alphonsine to take a drink and he did too.

"Have you noticed how these women drink?" Alphonsine asked. "Ellen takes careful little sips, a lot of them one right after the other, sip,

sip, sip, but Angèle drinks in a great, hearty gulp followed by a loud, throaty 'Ahh.'"

"And Circe?"

"Circe drinks with closed eyes, in order to see her inward pleasure. She'd probably want to watch herself making love too, careful to make every move precise. *Princesse* Circe, dressed by the Salon Clorinde or some other famous *maison de couture* on the rue de la Paix or rue St. Honoré at ten francs per stripe. Her voice is as sticky as the resin on a pine tree."

"Where did all that come from?" he asked.

"She's right," said Louise. "Don't be taken in, Auguste. Her fingernails are sharp as claws."

"That doesn't worry me as much as getting her to pose the way I want her to. She's amusing at times, but she's pigheaded."

"That she is, truly," Louise said, standing to go. "I tell you, if she comes into my kitchen again, I'm going to shoo her right out." She started down the stairs. "Right out the way she came in."

"You told Circe you don't want the painting to tell a story," Alphonsine said. "But you can't deny people's interpretations just because *you* say there's no story. When my brother gave his contribution, didn't you see how he was looking at Charles? He was almost laughing at him wearing that top hat. And what about Antonio leaning over Angèle as though he's going to lick her ear any second? You don't think there's a story there? Émile adores Ellen, but she won't let him near her, and now he hasn't come back. Something's going on between them. Something's going on everywhere in the painting too. There will be mysteries to people looking at your painting, but they'll bring their own feelings to it, and will imagine they know something. Like Jules said, how things are connected, one thing and then another and another."

"Ah, the promenaders reminding you of the hat shop. Will you tell me about it?"

"You're brave to ask."

He worked on the tablecloth. He loved to paint white, which was never pure white. The pastel tints would tie all the other colors together.

"We lived above it. *Papillon et fils, Chapelier,* our sign said. It was in the shape of a top hat. We had all kinds of hats, *chapeaux hauts de forme* like Monsieur Ephrussi's, *feutres, chapeaux de paille, chapeaux mous,* English bowlers, French *melons* a little shallower in shape, like Raoul's, *bérets,* mariners' caps, *canotiers,* flat-topped boaters for members of the yacht clubs, like Gustave's. I had a counter for ladies' hats. We bought the forms wholesale and I decorated them with ribbon, net veils, and silk flowers that I bought in the stalls of Les Halles. It felt like I was a bird building a nest with feathers and tulle. Sometimes I put a little feather bird in the folds."

He let her tell whatever it was she wanted to at her own pace while he painted her hand on the railing, the high curving arch under her fingers and palm, her thumb relaxed.

"Do you know, it's ten years almost exactly since the war began?" she said.

Her eyes glistened. He wanted to catch them just that way in his painting, like polished river stones of lapis. The peachy hues of her face made her seem much younger than she was, but behind her eyes, right this minute, lay a realm he had not seen.

Madame Charpentier had told him to find a wife. It would be easy to move right in with the family—he liked them all, and he felt tenderness for her. He hadn't realized it until she'd picked the grit out of his face. He could see now that Louise was right—Alphonsine was beginning to care for him. It would be satisfying, but that would end sowing his wild oats in Montmartre. Madame Charpentier's point precisely. No. Put it out of mind.

"Louis was called up."

The abruptness brought him back to the moment at hand. "So was I."

"Where were you sent?"

"To the South. I never saw any combat, but I treated myself to a vile case of dysentery. One day my comrade and I were at a wine merchant's, and the next day, he stopped speaking. The day after, he was delirious and couldn't stop laughing. A horrible, deranged cackle. Then he was gone. I would have died too if my uncle hadn't come to rescue me."

"I'm glad he did."

A pink blush washed her cheeks. She looked away.

"Did Gustave fight?" she asked.

"He was in the Garde Mobile de la Seine. I didn't know him then, but I knew Paul. Pierre and I were crazy with worry because he's such a risk-taker. After the war he told us he'd been taken prisoner east of Metz and interned in a Prussian barracks. He tried to escape and failed the first time, but Christmas night the cell guard was sleeping and he took his clothes and walked right out of the barracks and into a town in the midst of a holiday celebration. Of course, he couldn't resist having some German beer in a brasserie. He was discovered there in the morning, asleep, and was taken back to the barracks under tight watch. Somehow, he escaped again, and hightailed it back to France."

That peace in her face dissolved as her lips closed.

"Another Jean Valjean, escaping more than once, Victor Hugo fashion," she murmured. "Louis died of cholera in a Prussian prison camp outside Trier."

He stopped painting. It seemed insensitive to go on.

"I lived through the Siege without knowing," she went on. "Lived on birds and broth and rationed horsemeat."

To say he was sorry was to say words not normally used when a person learns of a death, but he did feel them. He set down his brush. That was all he could do.

He wished he hadn't described his comrade's death in the South.

He imagined her desperate for a letter from her husband while the Siege held Paris in an iron grip. Nothing in, and nothing out. Not a single piece of mail. Not a scrap of food. Alphonsine trapping a thrush on a window ledge, weeping as she broke its neck, plucked it, gutted it, boiled it, drank the broth. If she got word that Louis was dying of disease, he imagined her rushing into the street begging camion drivers to take her across the lines to his field hospital.

He imagined her dazed and silent when she realized Louis would be buried in a mass grave across the Rhine. He imagined her watching Paris burn during the Commune and not knowing whether to cry for the living or the dead. He wanted to hold her and whisper something that would make the memories go away. Words never came easily to him at such times. Touch did, but he remembered her raising the oars in the boat. No touch could erase her loss anyway.

He felt an urgency to dispel the tense silence. "You've heard me mention my good friend, Frédéric Bazille, who shared his studio with Claude and me when we didn't have a sou?"

She was still and quiet, waiting.

"He volunteered for a Zouave regiment from Algiers, the fool, just like Paul. Zouaves were put in the most danger. He felt no political compulsion to enlist. He did it just to demonstrate his manhood that was suspect. I wrote him a note. 'Triple shit. You've no right to do this, you stark-raving bastard.' The last word he had from me and I called him a bastard. He was killed at Beaune-la-Rolande. A puny little skirmish absolutely without consequence to the outcome of the war." The words came out pitched high with the effort.

"France lost more than the war. It lost his unpainted pictures," she said.

"He was a strong talent. I wish you could have known him. We all looked to him. Gustave thinks he could have held the Impressionists together. I can still see his gray carpet slippers with the red straps. Sometimes when I'm alone in my studio, I think I hear him humming Offenbach."

She sat there blinking away moisture. "Sometimes I think I hear Louis humming Schumann. A piano piece called 'Papillons.' Butterflies. So droll. Louis's last name was Papillon."

He was stricken. He had just tramped roughshod over her memory, discredited her loss by speaking of his own. This was supposed to be a joyous occasion, painting her, and they'd stumbled together into sadness. Yet he had wanted to lay his grief on her lap like a wrapped stone. To lay his head on her lap too. It might comfort both of them. When words stopped, something deeper took hold. He felt the eggshell fragility of a new intimacy, as though he had already made slow, careful love to her.

Every woman in the painting made his pulse race, his heat rise. Every woman, that is, except Alphonsine. Until now. He wouldn't say it would never happen, but until now, she had seemed too much like a sister. She had never played the coquette with him. What were they to each other? Something swirling, changing direction, lovely and unpredictable, like an eddy in the river. He ought to be careful. He ought to be very careful.

"When we're finished today, will you let me take you out in a yole?" she asked.

"If you row."

"Your hands ache sometimes, don't they?"

"How do you know?"

"The way you rub your fingers. And sometimes you squeeze your right hand in your left."

"Nothing slips by you, does it?"

"I wish mine ached instead of yours. I wish I could take it from you."

"Why?"

"The world doesn't need my hands. It needs yours."

Chapter Nineteen

Confession *en Canot*

Alphonsine stayed close to the bank where the current was slow but would still take her words downstream and pour them into the sea. She rested the oars across the gunwales and let the boat drift.

"I want to tell you about the hat shop. I couldn't tell you with Maman coming upstairs all the time. She doesn't know this. No one does."

"Are you sure you want to tell me?"

"I have to."

She had to know whether he was a man who could see beneath her actions to her reasons. She started with the easy things.

"The shop was near the barricade and the Arc de Triomphe. A musician lived in the flat opposite ours on the landing. He often played Schumann's 'Papillons' for Louis, but during the Siege he only played French composers like Berlioz and Bizet. When the Krupp guns thundered so close, he countered with 'La Marseillaise.' That dear old man pounding the keys as hard as he could, sending *l'esprit de corps* to our men on the barricades. Everyone doing what he could. Everyone a soldier. *Aux armes, citoyens!*"

Auguste's patient look made her trust him. But if he condemned her, she would never have the courage to tell anyone else, which meant she would never be known for what she was.

"Everyone a loyal soldier. Except me," she said, holding on to the oars lying across her knees. His face hardened and made her worry.

"One morning I heard a scraping noise outside. It sounded like a cat, and a cat meant food. I crouched and flung open the door. A man fell onto my feet. He held his shoulder with one hand, his thigh with the other. Blood oozed between his fingers and soaked his uniform. A French uniform. His eyes pleaded. *'S'il vous plaît, mademoiselle.'* Hardly louder than a breath, please. I told him I'd go get help and he burst out, *'Nein! Non, s'il vous plaît. Non.'*" This time I heard the German accent.

"A spy," Auguste said. "Amazing that he came through the barrier. Maybe some Prussian comrade shot him by mistake trying to go back out."

"I didn't think about that. I only saw a human soul in pain. I only thought about whether Louis knew how to say *s'il vous plaît* in German. Was he at some woman's doorstep in Trier or Sarrebruck?"

"Your way of looking at it, I suppose."

"The man's hand trembled and reached for mine. I said slowly, 'You will not kill me, because you need me.' He shoved a knife across the floor toward me and dragged himself into the shop, leaving a trail of blood on the entry. I was powerless to resist."

"You didn't call a gendarme?"

His voice carried a tone of judgment, already, and she'd hardly begun.

"I locked the door. He was bleeding onto the floor. I tied strips of a sheet above and below each wound and poured water into his mouth. I made a pallet for him in the stockroom and dragged him behind the door."

Auguste scowled.

"Well? What if Louis lay injured beyond the Rhine? Wouldn't I want some man's wife to do the same for him? I was taught by the nuns at school to love my neighbor as myself. Breaking Christ's command seemed a greater sin than helping the enemy."

"Why are you telling me?"

"I couldn't have you kiss me if you didn't know me. When you told me about losing your friend, I thought you might understand. Maybe I was wrong."

There. A huge disclosure. They were both waiting.

"Please. Go on."

"Gendarmes could come around the corner any minute. I scrubbed the stoop and rubbed ashes from the fireplace into the stain. The man slipped into unconsciousness. If he died, what would I do with him? I had to keep him alive. I poured brandy down his throat and cut away his clothes."

"All of them?" He gave her a steely-eyed glare.

She gave it right back. "Without any army's uniform, he was just a man in pain. His shoulder was only grazed, but his thigh . . . Whatever it was went right through. The opening at the back of his thigh . . ." She shook her head, remembering, and made a circle of her hands to show the size. "I cleaned the wounds as well as I could."

"No wonder you knew how."

How did he mean that? She had to go on.

"I sewed them with silk hatter's thread."

He winced. Good. She wanted him to imagine what doing that was like before she asked the big question.

"Do you condemn me?"

Every second of silence in the boat alarmed her more.

"How can I? I wish there had been an Alphonsine for Bazille."

She couldn't say that when she was preparing to burn the man's uniform, she'd noticed a round hole ringed by dried blood in the left chest piece of the jacket. The Prussian had no chest wound. She couldn't tell Auguste how, on her knees in front of the fireplace, she had wept over the French soldier killed for a suit of clothes. He would think she was a hypocrite.

"Did he talk to you?" Auguste asked.

"He only said, 'Merci. Merci.'"

As the boat drifted in the current, she saw Auguste glance at La Grenouillère. She didn't want him to think of the time he painted there with Claude. She needed his full attention. There was so much more. She waited until they had floated past it, then dug an oar into the bank to stop the boat.

"When he was able, I helped him up the stairs. It would be safer there."

"Did you feed him?"

"Of course I fed him. Was I just going to watch him die? I shared equally my sixty grams of horsemeat per day. There were rat hunts. The shooting of cab horses. The zoo in the Jardin des Plantes was depleted of everything that breathed. On the ninety-ninth day of the Siege, an advertisement for Christmas dinner at Café Tortoni listed consommé of elephant, stuffed donkey head, terrine of giraffe, roast haunch of wolf au vin rouge, bear cutlets in pepper sauce, and flanked tiger garnished with baby peas. I wondered where they got the peas."

"And you?" he asked. "How were you doing?"

"I avoided looking in the mirror."

"You were beginning to care for him?"

She didn't tell him that when the explosions rattled the windows, her arm shot out for his hand, and his ready grasp on her wrist stopped her trembling. Nor did she say that all the tender caring she would have given to Louis, if he had come home wounded, she lavished on this man. In some moments, she had pretended he *was* Louis.

"There were times of closeness." The only answer she wanted to give.

"He tried to walk a few steps. I could tell he wanted to be gone. I put a set of Louis's clothes and a pair of his old shoes by the man's bed. His soldier's boots would have given him away."

"Didn't you think of how you would explain when Louis noticed them missing?"

Of course she had, even in nightmares. "One risk led to another."

Just like now, a risk. But she had to know if Auguste could give her what she needed, not just forgiveness for betraying France, but understanding.

"I asked him to teach me a word in German. I held up a book and pointed to one word and then another. 'Word. *Allemand. Deutsch.*' He shook his head. I held up one finger. 'One. *Ein* word.'

" '*Nein gutt . . . Deutsch . . . vous,*' he said.

"I boiled a beaver top hat and we drank the broth together. The fine ones were rubbed with mutton suet for firmness. Then he whispered, '*Liebe.*'

" '*Liebe,*' I repeated, not romantically as we would say *amour,* or *Je t'adore,* but as a recognition of a universal need."

Her dry lips stuck together a fraction of a second when she made the *b* sound in the German word for love.

"Once, as I bent over him to rinse his shoulder wound and put on a clean bandage, he struggled to raise up in bed on his elbows, even with his injured shoulder. His mouth was so close I could feel his breath. His eyes took on the look I'd come to recognize as gratitude and yearning. Just think of what he might have been feeling, with his life so precarious."

Here was the moment, whether to tell all, or crumple. The stone of anxiety that had lodged in her chest for ten years swelled into something roused and frightful. If he wanted to, Auguste could make it melt. One word could free her, or crush her.

"I said I've kissed no one for a decade. I did not say I've kissed no one since Louis."

"Did you kiss him?"

He waited without moving, rare for him.

"What was a kiss since I'd already saved him? Already betrayed Louis, and France. Yes, Auguste. I breathed my life into him. I allowed him to thank me in that way."

Auguste's cheek twitched violently. It made her think that he needed her to say that nothing else happened between them.

"He was gone in the morning. He had straightened the daybed, military style, and had left a medal on the pillow. *Heiliger Christophorus,* it said. Saint Christopher, I assumed."

How quickly, that morning, she had hurried down rue du Faubourg Saint-Honoré to the church of La Madeleine. Bodies of French soldiers and citizens had been piled four deep in the portico. She covered her nose with her handkerchief and went inside. Amid the din of screams and moans, the nuns calling for more bandages, the stench of rotting flesh and feces, she squeezed her way past rows of wounded men on cots, to get to the small painting and offertory of Sainte Rita, Advocate of Desperate Causes, and said the prayer. *You, the saint of the impossible, give me the courage to hope. Tell me how to love more.* She'd lit two candles. Neither one was for her.

"I knew that Louis would know, but I could not, would not take back what I'd done. And Louis didn't come home."

"Leaving the man to die would not have brought Louis home."

"I know." She put her hand in the water, washing it cool and clean. The awkwardness of the silence made her say, "See? *X* equals *y* equals *z*. Hat shop, soldier, sadness."

"You are a poet. *Une Symboliste.*"

Was that all he would give her? That she was a poet? Not that she was a humanitarian or even a compassionate person? Not that he understood? He was as silent as a dumb brute.

She yanked one steering cord out of his hand to turn the boat around, and dug in the oars. Her rage exploded in each hard stroke.

"So, Alsace and Lorraine were to be joined to Bavaria." Words tumbled out in a hot flood. "Did they have to learn to breathe differently as Bavarians? Weep differently? Die differently? Did Bavarians make love differently? Does it make a difference whether we say *amour* or *liebe*? Every French person would say yes, including you, Auguste, but when Bismarck's legions marched triumphantly under our Arc de Triomphe and down the Champs-Élysées a month after the surrender, what was I doing while Parisians all around me were hissing? Looking for my Prussian in the ranks."

She was practically yelling at him. "And then the Communards. We hadn't had enough dying, we had to kill each other. That's *la vie moderne.* Your painting is celebrating modern life? Just think what we're doing in our modern life. Tossing live babies in trapeze acts to make us forget."

"Take a breath, Alphonsine."

She gave him a chance to say something, but he didn't.

"Isn't there anything more to you than a brush? You don't see me, do you? You with the vision to see hundreds of colors, you see only a carrot. Maybe Guy and Edgar are right about you and your pretty rose-colored world."

CHAPTER TWENTY

A Ride in the Country

Jeanne raised the pale green dress over her head and let it fall billowing over her shoulders and down to her ankles, feeling a cool swoosh of air bathing her. She read the script for *Le bourgeois gentilhomme* on the bed while she did up her hair. Nicole's lines were short, but they still had potential. How many ways could she say, "I won't"? She practiced it with a pretty pout. "I won't." A glare. A dash of spunk. A husky, unladylike outburst. A syrupy sweetness but fire in her eyes. She put on a touch of rouge, chose her cream-colored hat, and brought the script with her.

Downstairs, her father was already at work in the music room. How would she get by without music in the house?

"A Sunday dress on a Friday?" her mother said in the hallway, not frowning, but with an eyebrow raised. "Are you posing again?"

"No. Just going on an outing with Joseph-Paul." She turned her back to have her mother do up her row of hooks. "A ride in the country, then to the theater. I won't be home for dinner."

"Sit down. Don't rush through life. Have your *café*."

She sipped her *café au lait* with her eyes on the script. Maman always had her *café* ready when she came downstairs, and they talked a bit. Now how would it be? She and Joseph-Paul together speaking of the day ahead over their *café* and croissant? But who would make it?

"We have to live above a café. I'm going to demand it."

Maman's mouth formed an uncertain smile. "Just make sure . . ."

Jeanne's cup rattled as she replaced it in the saucer.

"Make sure you know what you're doing."

Jeanne took her last sip, and placed her hand over her mother's for a moment. "I will." She tucked the script into her drawstring bag.

Outside, she plucked off a sprig of honeysuckle at Eva's house and held it to her nose. A bride's flower. At the foot of the crescent she opened the iron gate and, with Joseph-Paul extending his hand, stepped into the waiting carriage.

"You had me worried. You're ten minutes late," Joseph said.

"I had to have a *café* with Maman."

The carriage lurched ahead and his kiss landed on her ear.

"You're especially beautiful this morning. It's a shame we don't have time to stop at Nadar's studio for your portrait."

"Can't we get married the proper way? Telling your parents too? I feel like a thief robbing them of happy moments."

He gave her an understanding look. "It won't be happy if my father thinks he can stop us."

"He's not God."

"No, but he has powerful connections on this earth. He and my grandfather spent their lifetimes acquiring an estate and a reputation which I will inherit and you will enjoy. I'm sorry to say it will be a come-down to him at first, until he comes to love you, which he will, I'm sure. So in the meantime, please pay him the respect to give him time to adjust and to put on a public face."

"He's only a financial middleman. My father's a creator, an artist. That should make him at least equal in the scheme of things."

"All artists are only playthings of a fickle public."

"That's unkind of you."

"I'm only telling you the way my father will see it."

She thought of Molière's line for Madame Jourdain: *Marriages between people not of the same rank are subject to the most serious inconveniences.* This deception, then, was a mere inconvenience? Molière had the lovers marry through deception, but each couple married within their class. Not a good sign, but that was in the seventeenth century.

She looked out the window. They were heading north through Porte de Clichy. Beyond the town, they turned to the northwest through rolling hills. Wheat fields were beginning to turn golden, almost ready for harvest, and pickers were on ladders in the plum orchards. In every fold of land a stream flowed, and at every crossing there was a village.

"You must promise me one thing. Two things. That we will have a proper wedding in Paris, for Maman and Papa and our friends."

"Don't you think I want to show off my bride to all of Paris?"

"Do your parents love each other?" she asked.

"I've never thought about it." He kissed her hand. "All that matters is that we do."

"It's not as simple as that. Where will we live?"

"I found a large suite not too far from the Bourse. You'll be pleased." He smiled as if knowing that he was going to drop her a plum. "It's on rue Molière."

"Rue Molière! That's near the theater!" There were two good cafés on that one-block street where actors ate. More important than the cafés, he wouldn't have chosen that street if he were going to deny her the theater, would he?

"Now, what was the second promise?"

"The dowry. Our parents will come together to discuss that."

"Our fathers only, when the time is right."

"When the papers are drawn up, I want the dowry to be designated as falling under the *régime dotal.*"

He puffed out a breath. "You surprise me. What's wrong with the *régime d'acquêts,* sharing everything equally?"

"Under the *régime dotal,* the capital, or principal of the dowry, is inviolable. The husband can use the income from the dowry, but not the dowry itself. It's a protection for the woman. Otherwise, if you go bankrupt, the whole dowry could be seized."

"*Mon Dieu!* Where did you learn all those big words, my little worrier?"

"From Hubertine Auclert. I attended a talk she gave."

"That virago! I'm not planning to go bankrupt, so you don't need to fill your pretty head with numbers and laws." He knocked his knuckle on her forehead.

She turned her head away and said with real pique in her voice, "I don't want my father's money, which he earned note by note, as a *lowly* musician to be used to make good on your debts if the Bourse turns fickle. I want the *régime dotal.*"

He let out a huge, false sigh. "We'll see. Let's not have that spoil this lovely ride, the only such ride we'll ever take."

She gave him a sharp nod, to tell him she considered it settled.

The carriage stopped. She poked her head out the window and breathed the smells of clover and earth and manure. A narrow bridge ahead was occupied by a boy and his goats. A bell on the lead goat rang out a cheerful sound. The bell would last longer than the goats, or the boy. A few stone houses, centuries old, were overgrown with vines. Right here, people had been born, were married, had children, and died. A timeless cycle. Here, no doubt, people all married within their class.

"These people, so close to Paris yet their lives are so different from ours, except for the broadest story lines," she said. "They may never have heard of Molière."

"Or the *régime dotal.*"

After an hour, the coachman stopped in front of a church.

"What village is this?" she asked.

"Saint Ouen-l'Aumône. The priest and mayor are expecting us."

Joseph-Paul leapt out and offered her his hand. Once, only once in her life would she step out of a carriage for so momentous an errand. When she would step back up, in only a few minutes, would avenue Frochot still exist?

The church was small, dark, and cool. Père Bellon, the round-cheeked priest with milky blue eyes extended both hands in welcome—thick hands like a peasant's, with age spots.

"The mayor will be here right away."

He rang the church bell and the mayor arrived and read the required sections of the Civil Code. Against his monotonous blur of words, the many ways of saying *I won't* kept creeping into her thoughts.

The emptiness of the sanctuary, its plaster crucifix, the dust motes floating in a ray of light coming through a window onto the altar made the moment solemn, timeless, and very private. Each time they stood for a recitation and then sat again, the pew creaked. The priest's words were a comfort, countering the satire of the playwrights. Finally he came to the crux, and she was ready. She looked directly at Joseph-Paul.

"Do you, Léontine-Pauline-Jeanne Samary, take Marie-Joseph-Paul Lagarde, to be your lawfully wedded husband, to honor and cherish for better or for worse, in sickness and in health, as long as you both shall live?"

"I do . . ."

Don't change that tenderest of expressions, she told him with her eyes. *Don't blink, don't twitch a muscle,* she told herself.

". . . on the condition that the dowry be contracted under the *régime dotal*," she said in the sweetest voice she had in her repertoire, but with fire in her eyes.

Joseph-Paul's smile vanished. The priest looked to him for a sign to continue. She kept her pose as though she were commanding a moment of drama on the stage. Joseph-Paul gave a slight nod and the priest continued, ending with, "I now pronounce you man and wife, with the stipulation that the dowry be contracted under the *régime dotal*."

The priest and mayor sent them on their way with benign smiles and a hand clasp for Joseph-Paul, and they climbed into the carriage to cross the Oise at Pontoise.

At an auberge festooned with ivy, she speculated about the apartment he had picked, the friends they would invite to the city wedding. She asked him about his favorite food, his favorite color, his favorite possession, what he kept in his pocket, when he got up in the morning, what he did at home in the evenings, those mysteries that surrounded him, and then she stopped. A certain mystique was essential for love, to anticipate touching the untouched. There were thresholds she didn't want to reach without imagining them first.

One more question nipped at her mind. "Will we have a cook and housemaid?" When he said yes, she nestled in his arms for the ride back to Paris. The house would not be the battlefield. Theater would.

After the last curtain call that evening, she hurried through the backstage corridors to her dressing loge. Red and white roses crowded her dressing table on both sides. Joseph-Paul sprang to his feet and pulled her to him. "Your performance was particularly brilliant tonight, Madame Lagarde," he said, whispering the last two words.

"Madame Samary," she corrected. "I honor you in all other matters, but it shall stay as Jeanne Samary. For sake of the stage."

Her parents had retired by the time she came in carrying a dozen of the roses. She opened the door to her room, and on her bed lay a flat package wrapped in brown paper with a delivery label. A wedding present? Did he dare send one before he told his father? She ripped off the paper and sank onto the bed holding Auguste's small portrait of her, his remembrance of times past.

CHAPTER TWENTY-ONE

Circe's Stripes

Auguste noticed that she of the ramrod back wore a haughty expression today sitting on the terrace as stiff as a figure in a wax museum, but he had a plan. He would flatter her vain self until she melted like Brie into something pliant.

Paul brought some peppermint liqueur of a gorgeous emerald green. It would be a good substitute for one of the bottles of wine in the painting.

"It's to mark the halfway point," Paul said.

That shocked him. He'd be far from half finished by the end of the day.

Angèle arrived with a note from Ellen. He opened it and read:

Dear Auguste,

I'm terribly sorry, but I can't come today. I'm forced to do the matinee because my substitute who has been doing them has gotten herself in trouble and went to one of those awful women in the Batignolles. Now she's abed. I'm sick with worry and feel awful for you. I don't know when I can come back on a Sunday. I'll try to come on a weekday although I have acting lessons in the mornings and rehearsals for a horrible new pantomime in the afternoons.

Ta bien dévouée,
Ellen

"Did you know about this?" he asked Angèle.

"I guessed as much. I knew she's had to pay her substitute to take her place every Sunday."

"I had no idea. I should have been paying."

He asked Alphonsine to take Ellen's chair and eat with them. "Let Anne serve from now on."

Louise came upstairs carrying a platter, one step behind Charles, the last to arrive. "Sit. Just taste this, monsieur. *Aubergines à la Russe.* Aren't they as fine as any eggplants in Russia?"

Charles tasted, his nose in the air, his eyes closed. "Hm! Nothing finer from Odessa to Moscow, madame."

"You ought to ask that fellow to paint eggplants for you," Louise said. "A companion to the asparagus painting. A thousand francs for three purple eggplants. *C'est ridicule!*"

Circe fluttered her filmy sleeve. "I agree, madame."

Auguste launched his plan. "That ruffle will be a delight to paint. See how pliant it is? That's how I want you to be."

Maybe her corset was the problem. He leaned toward her. "Circe, I'm wondering if you'd consider stepping into Alphonsine's room and removing your corset. That might make it easier for you to pose naturally."

She gave him a look a lady would give a street urchin who had just stepped on her hem, and turned to Antonio. "I understand you are a journalist?"

"I write for *Le Triboulet,* mademoiselle."

"That means you must be very funny."

"Not so. I am too limited in your language to produce the witticisms people expect in *Le Triboulet,* so I must write about the absurd."

"For example?"

"Oh, how to teach your pet frog to flirt, how to dress your poodle *à la mode,* how to express yourself by the manner in which you open your umbrella, how to piss on the street with style. Essential things."

"Disgusting." She made a face at Auguste as though that word was her answer to his request.

He had the rest of the meal to think of a different approach. Louise's fried fish was a big success, but he hardly tasted it.

"Perfect for a boating party by the river," Gustave told her.

"Why, thank you. Leave room for the dessert. Alphonsine made it."

"And what might that be?" Gustave asked.

"They're shaped like sails," Alphonsine said. "They're for boating champions, so you and the baron had better prove yourself worthy three weeks from today."

Did she have to remind him of the passage of time?

When Anne brought up the apple pastries, Alphonsine served Gustave a particularly large one. She went around the tables with a globe-shaped bottle banded in brass, drizzling the Chambord Royale on each person's sail, starting and ending with Gustave's, giving him a second pour while resting her hand on his shoulder. Gustave would be blind if he didn't recognize that something was happening. Auguste was worried, for her sake.

He was itching to get started. It seemed forever before Anne came up to clear the plates. He and Paul rolled out the easel, Pierre rolled back the awning, people took their poses. Then he just sat.

"We're breaking our bodies here. What are you waiting for?" Circe asked.

"The light, mademoiselle."

After a cloud blew by, he mixed a burnt sienna and added a touch of rose madder for Raoul's jacket, making it more ocher for some areas, and close to burnt umber for the shadows. He mixed in a touch of violet tint where the light landed on Raoul's shoulders and the wooden rail. With other brushes, he touched all parts of the canvas, bringing everyone out a little more, except for the vague spot in the middle, Ellen and Émile.

He laid in more of the folds on Circe's skirt and applied washes of pale pink and blue to the white stripes as he would do on the tablecloth, napkins, and Alphonse's shirt. Circe shifted in her chair and the stripes changed. He set down his brush and bent down to try to get them back the way they were.

"Don't touch my dress!" she cried. "Your hands have paint on them."

He looked at his fingers. Not a bit of paint that he could see. Alphonsine circled around the table and adjusted the stripes according to his instructions.

Circe faced straight ahead. "Turn to Gustave, please," he said. She moved her chin an inch to the left. "Ah, now your cheek is lit like a pear blossom at this angle." It was a strategy, yes, but it was also true.

"As round and white as an angel's arse is how he's painting it," Angèle said, baiting her.

"Turn a little more." Her frozen posture was a refusal. "As beautiful a profile as I've ever seen."

"What about my eyes?"

"Like the midnight sky studded with a star."

Alphonsine blew air out of her mouth.

"Then why don't I have eyes in the painting?" Circe demanded.

"You will, when you face Gustave and stay that way. Every time you move, your stripes change. Look. There he is, smiling at you. Talk to her, Gustave."

"You've posed for other artists, haven't you?" Gustave asked.

She turned to answer. "Yes."

Auguste hurried to paint her cheek.

"Then you know what he needs. Stillness and compliance. Did you ever pose for Henri Gervex in Café Nouvelle-Athènes?" Gustave asked.

"Yes." Her mouth tightened and she turned back to face forward.

Gustave glanced at him, as though trying to convey something.

Auguste remembered Gervex painting in the café once. The motif was three men at a table and one overdressed woman in pink silk and lace. My God! It must have been Circe. If he remembered rightly, she was painted from the back, with the nape of her neck, an ear, and a shapeless cheek visible, but not her whole face. The men were reading the paper, smoking, ignoring her. It was a café scene of people not connecting, like Manet's, suggesting the separateness of modern life. There was something pathetic about her in all her finery. Three men, and none with an admiring look for her. None like Maggiolo gazing at Angèle. She must have felt misused.

"Turn toward Gustave, please. See how he's adoring you?"

"*Je t'adore,*" Gustave said, but his voice cracked. He was trying.

"I insist on looking directly out. I insist on posing like Victorine

Meurent did in *Déjeuner sur l'herbe.* And in *Olympia* too. Manet let her face the people looking at the painting."

"The lady doth protest too much, methinks," muttered Jules.

Auguste set down his brush and palette. An annoying rivulet of sweat trickled down his chest. He rubbed the heel of his hand against it.

"I've been to Manet's salon," Circe went on. "I met Victorine there. She's famous now."

"Famous for being called a female gorilla by the press," Charles remarked.

Auguste took her hand in his. *"Chérie,* this is a different sort of painting. I want it to be a natural moment of friends enjoying each other at lunch. This isn't a portrait."

"So was Manet's painting a moment of friends enjoying each other at lunch, only it was on the grass. A picnic," she said petulantly.

"Then why don't you take your clothes off, like Manet's model did?" Pierre taunted. "Then you'd be sure to be the center of attention."

Paul cheered, *"Youpi!"* and Alphonse exploded in a belly laugh.

"Go ahead and help her, Alphonse. You're closest," Pierre said.

"No," Circe cried. "I don't mean that. I just mean her face."

"Circe, you are a beautiful woman," Auguste said. "As lovely from the side as from the front." His voice had a tone of pleading. He was reduced to that.

"I'm going to leave right now if you don't let me pose facing forward."

Auguste pressed her hot hand so she would think about what she just said. A pain shot up his middle finger. He peeled away his fingers slowly and held her by a look. Her eyes were glossy with moisture. Cautiously, he stepped back and pointed with his index finger to Gustave.

She rose halfway, wavered, her fingertips trembling against the tablecloth, then stood up completely and drew her shoulders back. "You know I can get you well hung at the Salon. Madame Charpentier can speak to—"

"He's already well hung, dolly," Angèle said.

Pierre and Raoul snickered. Paul and Alphonse were silent this time.

"Or I can get her to denounce you."

Their snickering stopped. Angèle and Gustave turned their heads toward him. Alphonsine raised up, looking grave. He avoided her eyes and studied Circe to see how determined she was. Her chin quivered, but her back was rigid. She picked up her parasol. Any second her porcelain face would crack, out of frustrated disappointment or bewilderment that it would come to this.

Jules lowered his pipe. Charles and Raoul turned to look. Antonio straightened up and scowled. Paul and Pierre glanced at each other.

Deliberately, Auguste wagged his index finger. "Look—at—Gustave."

The air was charged with her indecision. She opened her mouth. Only a high-pitched croak came out. She raised her chin and took one step. Then another, giving him a chance. He only had to lower his finger to keep her. He kept it pointing at Gustave. She crossed the terrace, in a melodramatic imitation of a queen in a procession. The sharp, slow tap of her heels on the stairs receded.

There would never be another striped dress so beautiful. He could have made that ruffle luminous, could have created a highlight on the jewel, a clear, hot crystal between her clavicles.

He picked up his scraping knife. The sooner he scraped, the cleaner he could get it.

"Wait!" Alphonsine cried. "Look there."

Circe was standing on the bridge facing the terrace.

"Do you want I should slap some sense into her?" Angèle asked.

"The Fêtes Nautiques is only three weeks away," Gustave murmured. "The sailing regatta four."

His knuckles cramped into position on the scraping knife. "Damn prima donna!"

"Go to her, Renoir," Charles urged.

"No."

"I'm sorry," Pierre said. "I brought it on. Shall I apologize to her and try to bring her back?"

"No. It was leading to this anyway."

Alphonse darted downstairs.

With one slow, deliberate stroke, he scraped a stripe from the top of her head to the bottom of his painting. Fionie Tanguy's purloined Prussian blue, eight francs a tube, now marbled with white in a mess on his scraping knife. Thirty francs for Circe's posing fees. A four-week setback.

"Look again," Jules said.

Alphonse was talking to Circe on the bridge, gesticulating broadly. She turned from him and strode stiffly to Rueil.

"She's a poor player who struts and frets her hour upon the stage and then is heard no more." Jules's quiet voice roared with contempt.

Auguste continued scraping. An ugly, raspy sound accompanied every swath. He scrubbed with turpentine, but the stripes remained a ghost image of what could have been exquisite. He noticed Alphonsine's cheeks glistening in the sunlight in wet crystal streaks. The sight left him short of breath.

Émile, Jeanne, Ellen, and now Circe. Who would be next to leave?

Gustave and Angèle resumed their poses. Jules and Pierre took their cue and did the same. Paul angled his head toward a missing Jeanne. Alphonsine leaned forward on the railing. Charles and Raoul turned their backs to him. They were telling him to go right on. He picked up his brush. Where to work? On Jules and Charles, Pierre and Paul, safe subjects high up on the painting, so he wouldn't have to look at the sickening vacancy.

Alphonse came upstairs. "I'm sorry. I couldn't convince her."

"You might as well go back to the boats. I can't work on you without—"

Alphonse cut him off with the flat of his hand, rested it on Auguste's shoulder a moment, and went back down.

Keeping her pose, Angèle began to sing softly, *"De ses vertus ne parlons pas."* It was one of the Béranger tunes about Lisette, the unfaithful lover. Of her virtues we nevermore speak. It was good advice.

He worked doggedly, trying to ignore and focus, but he couldn't get out of his head Zola's mocking voice chanting, *The Impressionists remain inferior to what they undertake, inferior to what they undertake, inferior . . .*

The burden of the chant, the fate of the movement, weighed on his shoulders. The whole endeavor was a mistake, a reckless, overambitious decision in Madame Charpentier's salon. All the same, he couldn't let the abyss of his doubt show. That would negate all of their efforts.

They refused a break and he kept working until the light faded. Downstairs, no one was inclined to stay to drink and dance.

Charles lay his hand on his shoulder. "Your painting is going to be too fine a thing to have any woman of her stripe in it."

Jules said, "Ulysses overcame Circe's enchantment by means of a magic herb. Maybe a glass of absinthe would do you some good tonight."

Auguste nodded. Jules followed Charles out the door. Gustave lingered at a table and talked quietly to Fournaise. Alphonsine and Raoul joined them.

Auguste drew Angèle aside. "How about a little walk?"

"I can't think of anything better."

They escaped up the path. "Will you trust me for your modeling fee today? I need to buy more paint if I'm to go on."

"If? *If?* You let that chit with a broomstick up her arse kick up a fuss and make you quit, then it will be you I'll have to slap some sense into. I should have cocked a snook at her, standing there on that bridge pitiful as a Maquis cat waiting for you to come crawling after her. She weren't no *fleur-de-Marie* pure as the Virgin's piss." She snapped her knuckles against his chest. "Now cheer up. You want I should do a boulevard for you?"

To Circe, that would mean walking down rue Saint Honoré on a binge of buying hats, gloves, dresses, jewelry, and mirrors. Then he realized.

"No, I could never ask you—"

"You're not asking. I'm telling. You'll have your money for paints sure as I'm standing here. And to keep things straight, I owe you my rent money back too."

"I can't let you do that."

"Oh, don't get your tit in a wringer. It's not like it would be my first time."

"Please, Angèle. Don't do this."

"You can't stop me. Don't worry you none. I have my scruples, and here they is. Fornication's a full-article sin when it's done to injure. It's half-half when done out of mere pleasure. It's only tinged with sin when it's done by necessity. It's no sin at all when it's done out of love. And this lands somewhere between a necessity and love. No tinges ever scared me off."

Here was the spirit of Montmartre, alive and beating, sensuality as a fully generous act.

"You saint of a hussy. Or should I say hussy of a saint?"

CHAPTER TWENTY-TWO

Moonlight and Dawn

It was too hot to sleep. Alphonsine kicked off the sheet. Moonlight cast a glow through the window. She turned away from it. Still, the ache of compassion kept her awake.

The strain of the day persisted even though she'd drunk an absinthe with Papa and Raoul. She had been desperate for Circe to stop whining and turn the way he wanted her to. All the same, she was glad when Circe took those first humiliating steps down the stairs. Auguste seemed dazed after Angèle left. Gustave brought him an absinthe and they had sat on the bank watching the river turn copper-colored as the sun set. She had wanted to be right there with them, but had left them alone. It was a man's moment with his friend.

She didn't know what he felt after her outburst in the boat. From the dock, she had just run into her room, and had kept her distance since. She'd been edgy, watching him. If she hadn't said that x equals y equals z, he would not have said that she was a poet. Instead, he might have given her what she needed. She'd ruined her own telling.

Someone stirred, a door opened, the hallway floor creaked.

She had told Auguste the facts, and that had relieved her somewhat, even though he didn't say he understood. But she hadn't told him her feelings. She hadn't said that in that crippled city where the cabaret singers belted out "La Marseillaise" while explosions torched the Left Bank, she was making her separate peace. She hadn't said that for a long time afterward she resented the Emperor and his ministers for starting a war that had taken her husband, had forced everyone on both sides of the Rhine to suffer, and had brought humiliation and trauma to the nation for a decade. And she hadn't said that the reason she had told him was that he was the first man after Alexander whom she wanted to know her deeply. That was still true.

She loosened her nightdress where it stuck to her damp skin.

She wondered if Paul or Gustave or Raoul would have understood. Maybe understanding was too much to ask of a man who fought. She wondered if the Prussian had a limp like Raoul's—that is, if he got through the barricades. She liked to think that he was saying *liebe* to someone, and that someday he would dance at a daughter's wedding. She could almost see him in a waistcoat and tails and top hat, like Papa at her wedding, like any *Frenchman* at a daughter's wedding.

She turned over her pillow to get its coolness. If anyone wasn't able to sleep tonight, it should be Auguste. She slung on her summer dressing gown, and stepped barefoot into the corridor and out to the terrace.

He was sitting by the railing looking out in his usual way with his knees pulled up, his heels on the chair. She approached and he jerked to his feet. He was bare to the waist. The surprise of his body made her tense.

In a low voice he asked, "Couldn't you sleep?"

"Too hot."

She held on tightly to herself, waiting for a sign.

He lifted her wide, filmy sleeves. "Angel's wings."

He looked like a marble statue—his shoulders, the subtle curvature of his chest, his ribs, his narrow waist—whitish in the moonlight.

"It's pleasurable to be the one looked at instead of the one looking."

The instant he said that, she felt flushed, and turned to look at the river. The moon cast a steady shimmer on the water, and a wide, frilled bar of silver reached down through its glassy surface. A nightingale sang. Crickets chirped their mating rituals. A bullfrog's moan made her giggle.

"He's lonely for someone," Auguste said. "Like me. When I'm awake in a place where everyone else is asleep, I feel all alone in the world."

"Even when it's so lovely out here?"

He threaded his fingers through her hair. "You've got moonlight in your hair. Your skin is creamy white like a gardenia. The moonlight makes everything insubstantial. What you bring to the river, the river transforms. Do you feel it?"

"Yes. I often do. It's something indescribable. The river has a soul, I think, and sometimes I can touch it with my thoughts, when I pause long enough to see the things of the river as ideas."

"Such as?"

She hesitated. This wasn't something she told to just anybody. "Birds in flight are aspirations soaring. Birds in nests tell of safety and family. A tree is stability. Leaves clapping together are the tree's appreciation for a breeze, and the breeze itself coming down the river is refreshment."

"See? You are a river spirit."

They spoke softly so as not to disturb anyone, and it lent an atmosphere of intimacy.

"What brought you out here?" she asked.

"I couldn't sleep so close to my wretched painting. The smell of the linseed oil kept reminding me of the hideous smear."

"Don't call it wretched."

"It is tonight. I wheeled it out here so I wouldn't smell it, but I still couldn't sleep, so I'm waiting for dawn. Not too long now. First light will tell me whether it's worth the canvas it's painted on."

"That's nonsense." Even though the figures were dim and ghostly, she could see the empty place. "Do you regret forcing the issue?"

"No. I regret losing the striped dress."

"Do you know how you're going to fill the space?"

"I don't know if I am."

"Don't even whisper that. Tell me, who do you want?"

Auguste looked away. A long moment passed.

"Margot."

She took a few breaths before she said, "I certainly hope she's modeled for you before."

One side of his face smiled, but his forehead wrinkled. "Many times. Once standing on a swing in a Montmartre garden."

"If she still lives there, you could ask her."

"She's dead."

The unexpectedness disoriented her. The dead were living with him too. She leaned toward him to encourage him to say more, if he wanted to.

"The winter before last. Smallpox. She was so young. I begged two doctors to go to her, friends of mine. One gave her something to ease her in the last days, but we knew there was no hope."

"Did she have family?"

A moment passed. "Did she have family. A simple question." He cleared his throat. "I don't know. I never asked." His voice wavered. "She sent me letters pleading for me to come to her. I was afraid."

"Of contagion?"

"Yes, that, but also I didn't want to remember forever what she must have looked like. I stood outside her building looking up at her window for two weeks. I didn't paint a brushstroke. What I did was inexcusable."

His chest heaved as though he was gathering all his strength.

"I loved her, but I let her die alone."

She struggled not to reel. What kind of man was he, that he could stay away from a dying lover?

One who puts himself first. Was that the kind of man for her?

He stood before her naked. Waiting. Remorse furrowed his face. His eyes asked for understanding. It had cost him much to tell her. She knew that anguish.

To hide her horror, as much as to dress his wound, she said, "I think she knew you were there. There are other ways of seeing than with your eyes, Auguste."

She was willing to say it was his passion for life that made him stay down on that sidewalk, the shuddering abhorrence of life stopping, his fervent, all-absorbing need to do more with it. The world needed him to do more with it. Would she have wished him to die in order to prove himself an ardent lover?

"I forgive you," she whispered.

How self-important that sounded. It wasn't a thing for *her* to forgive.

The contrition in his voice suggested that he had already been forgiven. He only needed to feel it. Whatever she thought was irrelevant.

"If you would have gone to her and caught smallpox, this painting would never come to be."

"You didn't let that Prussian die alone in the street," he said.

She caught her breath.

"And I forgive you," Auguste said softly. "You listened to your instinct, the best guide."

Out with her breath came a rush of relief. He had only needed time. She felt that hard knot in her chest, as familiar as her own knuckles, softening and shrinking.

"You must never regret it," he said.

"I don't. It's not guilt that I feel. I just regret the effect it's had on me."

"What effect?"

"How it's made me afraid that if I told someone I cared for, it would make him reject me. Once, I held myself back with a man because of it. That's what I regret."

"May I ask who it was?"

"Do you remember I mentioned a Russian, Alexander Demouy, the engineer who designed the repair of the railroad bridge after the war?" She swept her hand along the railing. "And the iron supports of the terrace, and this railing."

"Yes."

"We used to go rowing together, and to the Bal des Canotiers. He danced like a Cossack to the cancan. One day I showed him where I found the lovers tied together after the flood, and told him I thought there was some appalling beauty in what they had done out of love. I should never have said that.

"He began to love me, and I was beginning to feel the same for him. It was seven years after Louis died. I thought that was a respectable amount of time. We took a walk that evening to the point of the island and he tried to kiss me. Stupidly, I pushed him away."

"Like you did to me?"

"Worse. I actually pushed on his chest. I didn't want to let myself fall in love unless I told him what I had done during the Siege and was assured that he still loved me, that he wouldn't cast me away as unfaithful. But I couldn't bring myself to tell him right then. I went to bed determined to tell him the next day. Early in the morning, we heard a shot. On the bank, under the railroad bridge, he had killed himself."

He murmured a low sound, not words, stepped back to a chair and drew her onto his lap, rocking her, letting her nestle against him.

"Alphonse found him. Papa told me. Do you think it evens out? If I saved a life and caused a life to end?"

"It wasn't your fault. He must have been despondent about other things too. A man doesn't kill himself that easily."

He kept stroking her cheek as if he were painting it.

"All month, I've made you pose along the man's railing."

She felt his chest rise and fall in a soothing rhythm.

"Once when Alexander and I were in a yole under the west arch of the railroad bridge, the arch he had worked on, he asked me to imagine the bridge set on end, into the sky. He thought the same method to build a bridge with steel and bolts and rivets could be used to build a tower. Not solid like a stone tower, but airy and curved, the tallest in the world. What he had in his mind must have been a marvel because he became so excited that he began speaking in Russian by mistake. He and another bridge engineer, a Frenchman, were talking about it, drawing it. Now it will never happen."

"You don't know that. You're not responsible," he said louder, squeezing her arm. "A man needs a host of reasons to take his own life. Don't take it on yourself."

She nodded. Papa had said the same thing.

He rocked her until her breathing slowed. The weight of her curled against his chest and on his thighs was pleasant, one small breast pressing against him. The bullfrog kept up his hoarse, lovelorn moaning. *Sh,* he thought. She might fall asleep. As he felt her relax, he wished better things for her, and for himself, and felt his eyes close.

The frogs and crickets were silent when he opened his eyes some time later. The air had cooled. Violet vapor rose over the water and became mauve as dawn neared, and then dove gray. He remembered his wretched painting, her Alexander, his Margot. Moving would awaken her, so he just watched a pale yellow light rise above the rooftops of Rueil and turn the water olive green. His legs tingled with numbness. He shifted to relieve them, and she awoke with a little "Oh!" She looked around, unfolded herself, and darted down the corridor, a disappearing spirit.

His thighs creaked with the memory of hers. He tried to get up, thought better of it, massaged life back into his legs, raised his shoulders in circles hearing the crunching sounds in his neck, grasped the railing, and pulled himself up. He looked at his painting and felt himself wither. It wasn't just Circe. Several figures were angled incorrectly. The painting was slipping from him.

He hurried into his room, put on a shirt, and grabbed palette, turpentine, rag, and scraping knife. He scraped away Angèle's hat, her eyes, her chin and its shadow on her neck. He scraped off Alphonse's hat. He removed the tallest bottle of wine. It needed to be farther to the left so he could show the vertical support in Raoul's chair back.

The appalling sound went right through her, the raspy scrape ending in a higher ting when the wide blade sprang free. She raced back, buttoning her dress, horrified. *"Sacrebleu!"* He was attacking the canvas. Raw, shadowy parts defaced it. Wounds. One large one, Circe. Others smaller. Angèle's face mutilated. Alphonse, the top of his skull gone. Nightmarish.

She grabbed the wrist of his hand that held the knife. "Stop."

"I have to see what's left. Whether there's enough to salvage."

He yanked his arm out of her grasp and scraped her jaw and chin and nose off the canvas. The ruination sickened her. "Did I pose wrong?" she cried.

"No. It's my mistake."

"But it can be saved."

"Maybe. I need to have you face Raoul more. That means your hat and hand will have to change too."

"What's wrong with Angèle?"

"The angle of her head was wrong. Her eyes weren't looking directly at Gustave but somewhere between him and Antonio. I placed her hat too far on the left side of her head too. If she actually wore it in that position and straightened her head, it would fall off."

"But you loved her expression."

"Ellen has to be farther to the right, between Jules and Charles, not just in front of Jules." He kept scraping. "I may have to rework that in the studio when she's available again."

"Then it's all correctable." She made sure it didn't sound like a question.

"There's a bigger problem, what I feared from the beginning. The thing that made me postpone this painting for so long. It might be catastrophic."

"What is it? Tell me."

He stopped scraping. "Doesn't it look to you as though the people and the tables are floating out over the landscape without being anchored to a building?"

She tried to see what he saw. "No."

"Your mind is putting in the context because you know the setting, but others don't. There's no space to paint the edge of the building to attach it. No solution that I can see."

"Now. No solution that you can see right now."

"And the perception of depth. Gustave and Edgar are masters at it, at judging the sizes. I might have made the rear figures too small compared to those in front." He leaned forward, his hands and the palette hanging between his legs. "To toss it all might be the answer."

"You'll regret it if you do."

He raised up. "And if I don't but should have? I'll be crucified. After twenty years of effort and privation with only a few good years but no dependable assurance from the public, a man has the right to think it might be better to give up."

"Not when he's this close."

"Three weeks is all I have. The light will change. If I only come close to creating a masterpiece but fall short, it would prove that my talent has declined after *Moulin de la Galette*. A short career, one botched painting, foolishly ambitious, savaged by the press as a mishmash of styles, an indecipherable magic carpet of people floating in the sky, or on a barge, a thoughtlessly conceived subject between city and country with people of different social classes mixing together, a social threat which the government-sponsored Salon won't countenance, ridiculed by the caricaturists as a degenerate allusion to the Last Supper, a flagrant prophecy of doom to one of the models, a darkly ironic party designed by a wicked mind, one colossal failure, and then obscurity."

"Stop! You're arguing against yourself."

His palette clacked against the floor.

"Don't you want to prove Guy and Edgar wrong? Don't you want to present your vision of the world? In the end, it just might be your vision that we need most. To neutralize misery."

"I'm not a philosopher. I'm a painter."

"How many people are in the painting?"

He glared at her.

"Fourteen," she said. "You'll find someone else. For Circe and for Émile too. Besides the models, think of all the people who have contributed. Name some."

"You."

"Who else?"

"Your father."

"My mother too. She made the meals. Who started you?"

"Zola." He puffed out a breath. "Zola plus gauntlet does not equal masterpiece."

"That's seventeen. Where did you get the paints?"

"Père Tanguy. With some help from his wife."

"How about the doctor who fixed your arm? That's twenty. Add the people who don't know but still gave you something. Our grocer, Luc. The laundress who washes the table linens. The orchardist who grew the pears. The vintner. The butcher's delivery boy. Twenty-five."

"This means nothing to me."

"The train engineer who brings out the models."

"What are you getting at?"

"Even Alexander, who rebuilt the bridge, and built the terrace. Now, who taught you to paint?"

"No one. I don't know how."

"Be honest."

"Claude Monet. We taught each other at La Grenouillère."

"Before him. Start at the beginning."

"Charles Gleyre, a teacher at the Académie des Beaux-Arts. Once he said, 'No doubt it's only to amuse yourself that you're dabbling in painting?' I told him that if it didn't amuse me, I wouldn't be doing it, but right this minute it's not amusing me one bit."

She pressed on. "Who else?"

"Courbet urged us to paint outdoors. Delacroix taught me colors."

"And?"

"Rubens. I couldn't paint women without Rubens. And Fragonard. Boucher. Ingres. Watteau gave me the mood. Titian gave me the belief in human beauty. Veronese gave me a setting, and the courage to begin. So what was that all about?"

"This: To whom much is given, much is required."

"Are you my conscience?"

"All of us are. *Nous.* All of us are behind you, urging you or giving you direction. Dead or alive, all of us are living through this painting. If you have an ounce of gratitude, you have to go on."

"I don't paint out of obligation."

"No, you paint because you can't help but paint. Listen to your instinct. You said you're a cork in the current. All these people doing something for the painting are the current. You can't help but continue."

"Not if it's not salvageable. And not if it doesn't give me pleasure."

"What if you found another model? Someone with all the qualities you're looking for. Someone who would be a dizzy pleasure to paint. Forget about the stripes. Go to Paris today. Don't come back until you find someone."

"It will take too long."

"Don't be stubborn. Think about your friend who died in the war."

"Bazille." His voice cracked. "Frédéric."

"Don't you think he's here every day with you, still *living* through you? If you stop, he dies. Of all people, don't you dare let him down."

Or Alexander. Don't let Alexander down, she told herself. She would not let this marvel die.

She gentled the scraping knife out of his hand.

"Regret is a bitter knife, Auguste. You know all about it. Don't let it gouge your soul."

Frédéric. The purity of his generosity. The pleasure they took in painting together. Painting each other. Painting for each other.

All at once he saw what the painting could be. A painting to carry on the work of Watteau, of Rubens and Vermeer and Ingres and Veronese. To bring them live into this age. He turned from his painting to her. She knew art was collaboration, and standing on the shoulders of those who came before. He took her face in both his hands, pulled it toward him roughly before she could back away, and kissed her, not tenderly. Roughly. The kiss to end the drought of kisses. He heard his scraping knife clatter to the floor.

CHAPTER TWENTY-THREE

Repairing to Paris

He heard people stirring downstairs. Alphonsine backed away and went down. In his room, he found some letter paper, and wrote:

My dear Monsieur Bérard,

I'm at Chatou working on this cursed painting, the last big picture I will ever undertake. I'm struggling with the figures, the perspective, and other problems. I don't know if I have the courage to finish it. I suppose I'll sacrifice one more week on it and if it doesn't look as though it will ever come right, I'll pitch the damned thing into the river and go back to Paris to paint portraits.

I have some regrets, not the least of which is the trouble I've given them here, perhaps for nothing. It would spur me on to receive some funds from you. I'm in arrears here for food and rent, to my colorman, and now with the models, so if you can spare a little money, I'd be much obliged.

He wrote another letter to Deudon, who might be a more likely source, ending it the same way. Much obliged. He was always saying "much obliged" to someone. It made him feel like a charity case. He swore that there would come a time when other people, when Bérard and Deudon themselves would feel much obliged for the *chance* to buy a Renoir. On the bottom of his letter to Deudon, he drew a caricature of himself jumping out of bed with his cycling cap on to hug a postman bringing him a sack of coins.

He joined young Alphonse downstairs for a *café*.

"You seemed to have enjoyed your little excursion with Angèle on the steam-cycle."

Alphonse chuckled. "I did. If you permit me, I'd like to take it across the bridge to some smoother ground."

"What would it be worth to you to own the thing and take it wherever you please?"

"To buy it from you? You don't want it?"

"I want to pay my debts more."

Alphonse tipped his head and raised both eyebrows. "One hundred francs."

"It's yours for one hundred. Give fifty to your father and fifty to me."

Alphonse left and came back with fifty francs.

"I'm much obliged." *Zut!* There, he'd said it again. "Tell Alphonsine that I'm off to buy more paint."

He mailed the letters at Gare Saint-Lazare and stepped out of the cool marble station into the hot sun. If he didn't do the most difficult thing first today, it might not get done, and the loss might be inestimable. But on the way he might find a model.

In front of Au Printemps, he stopped. The big department store might provide just what he needed. What should he do if he found a woman he liked? Trot after her through the lingerie department? Say, *Excuse me, I think you're beautiful. Will you model for me?* How would he know if, after one Sunday, she would come back for the next two? Trusting a stranger was risky.

He walked down the glittering avenue de l'Opéra. Plenty of high-class shops. Plenty of beautiful women buying kid gloves from Argentina and silk scarves from Milan, living prosperously off someone. Why would any one of them be enticed to give up the last summer Sundays to a stranger for a mere ten francs a day?

He hurried past the Comédie-Française and crossed the Seine. The dark dome of the Institut on the Left Bank did not give him any comfort. It was the bastion of the Académie, the Salon, the jurists, all that could still decide his fate. All that made him put one foot before the other until he came to Madame Charpentier's *hôtel particulier.*

He ran through the reasons why he had to lift that lion's-head knocker. If his Salon success the year before was in fact due to Madame Charpentier's maneuvers for a good position for her own portrait, he owed her an apology. After she heard what he had to tell her, she might withdraw her influence. Circe was dead right about that. But if the Salon rejected it, he didn't want it to be exhibited with the Impressionists even though not exhibiting with them would crack Gustave's heart. It might be placed next to Degas' second-rate disciples, and he'd be seen as losing ground. It wasn't entirely Impressionist anyway. He needed the Salon to authenticate it as a masterpiece, and to prove that his *Madame Charpentier and Her Children* was the precursor of many successes. But getting it in the Salon among thousands wasn't enough. It had to be hung prominently. Even Circe was smart enough to know that. He sounded the knocker.

The butler ushered him to the Japonaise room with the carved lions as company. If stone could move, these beasts would be devouring him by now. Madame's commanding steps assaulted the parquet before he saw her round the corner, bosoms first, in a *robe d'intérieur,* her hair uncoiffed.

"Auguste, what a surprise." Those were her words. Her eyes said something different. She did not invite him to sit down.

"I came to talk to you about Circe."

"She already has. You've humiliated her."

"She brought it on herself."

"That may be, but you'll still have to apologize and let her pose full face."

"I came to apologize to you, not to her. I'm sorry it didn't work out. At first I thought she would be fine because she's always posing. All she does is pose. Her sweetness is a pose. She is nothing more than a pose. Life is a pose, on her terms."

"She told me you propositioned her to take off her corset."

He slapped his forehead and turned away from her a moment. "That was no proposition. I suggested that she pose without it *under* her dress. You can't tell a thing about a woman's body with such a contraption. She couldn't move inside that cage. She was as stiff and brittle as glass."

Madame smiled in a maternal way. "Yes, she does have a certain grace in her bearing."

"It's not grace. It's rigidity. As rigid in her body as in her mind. I couldn't get her to stay in the position I wanted for more than five minutes at a time. It was driving me crazy."

"Did you like her dress? I was with her at the couturier's."

"I have no complaints about the dress. It was gorgeous. She's gorgeous, but it's her mouth."

"I think she has a very pretty mouth."

"Yes, but pretty is as pretty does. And what she wants, she wants, no matter what I want. Her favorite words are, 'I insist.' "

Madame's heavy, shapeless eyebrows met in a scowl. She was not won over. If he went on, she might stop inviting him to her soirées, and there would go the portrait commissions of her friends. His words here would have consequences.

"Between painter and model there has to be a oneness to their endeavor. With Circe, that will never happen. She's all for herself. She's perverse in that way."

Madame Charpentier tapped her tooth with her fingernail. "What if I spoke to her? I think she'll listen to me."

"Too late. I've already scraped her off the canvas."

"You can scrape her back on, can't you?"

"She's already set me back four weeks. I'm out of time and out of patience. If you hadn't forced her on me, I'd be a far sight better off. You've done me no favor, Marguerite. Didn't you know she could be a pain in the ass? What were you thinking? Only your personal little morality campaign to get me safely married. I tell you, what you see as philandery, I see as inspiration."

Madame crossed her arms. "Using one woman after another."

"It's not using them. I really love them, each in a different way. I can't paint a beautiful painting if I don't have a beautiful feeling about the woman in front of me. How do you think your portraits would have turned out if I didn't care for you and your children? What I need is someone who feels at one with the endeavor and wants to do all she can to help. When a painter finds someone like that, and pretty too, he's so grateful for her, so thrilled by what they do together, that it's natural to want more, to ride his excitement farther by loving entry into the depths of her, and to bring her into his ecstasy. A shared passion. That's not philandery. It's sacrament. It's communion."

Her face was tight with disapproval. "If you never marry, you'll never belong to the bourgeoisie."

"I don't give a damn. I just want to live well enough and to love well enough to paint what I want the rest of my life. And that doesn't include whores in cafés like Degas' subjects. Talk to him about morality."

"Circe's rich, Auguste."

He snorted. "Rich in vanity. Stop feeding a dead mule, Marguerite." He raised his voice. "Cécile-Louise is not the answer to my life."

"Then find someone who is." Her voice rose to match his.

The spasm of twitching under his eye was maddening. He pressed his fingers against it and blew out a breath. "I'm sorry. I don't like to leave things raw. You can tell her I'm sorry, if it means anything."

"It might."

He moved toward the door. "One more thing. She wears Patchouli. Every tart in Montmartre wears it. Place Pigalle reeks of it. If she wants to carry out her pose as an aristocrat, she ought to refine her tastes."

"I'll be sure to tell her," she said with an edge.

"Take her to a proper *parfumerie* on avenue de l'Opéra. If I had money to throw around, I'd buy her a bottle myself, but I can't."

She stepped up to him. "It's the thought that counts." She patted his arm and noticed that the cast was gone. "Monsieur and Madame Beloir were extremely disappointed." When he didn't respond, she asked, "Did Jeanne come?"

"Twice. I doubt that she'll come a third time."

"Hm." Her eyebrows drew together again. "Émile Zola was here. He's curious. Charles told him about the painting. He wants to see it. Shall I tell him he can?"

"No! Let him chew on his curiosity. Let him see what it's like to live on that. I'm not some Sunday painter in the Bois painting for passersby to chatter about. Tell him to stay away."

With that he left, knowing that he may have just burned his most profitable and essential bridge. He crossed the street and kicked one of those soggy carpet rags directing the water coming out of the grating to flush the street. "Zola. *Maudit soit-il!*" he muttered and stormed toward the Seine, the curse vile on his tongue.

On the bridge, he looked down at the water moving. He would not be a cork pushed around in a current. A curse on pushy matrons who want to mold a man to their specifications! A curse on obstinate *arrivistes* with phony names longer than their diamond necklaces! A curse on ambitious actresses and their arrogant admirers! A curse on models from Île Saint-Louis to whom ten francs per sitting means only a *pâtisserie* at Café Riche!

It was a simple Montmartroise he wanted, like the girls who posed for *Moulin de la Galette*. Like Margot. Or Alphonsine. Someone with the physical qualities plus the insouciance fitting the mood of the painting. She'd have to be personable so the others would take to her quickly and that easy banter and enjoyment of each other would continue. He headed toward Montmartre.

Madame Charpentier hadn't offered him any food this time. Any other time when he was hungry he avoided the streets with high-priced sidewalk cafés, but now he was looking. This was urgent business. On the sidewalk terrace of the elegant Café de la Paix at place de l'Opéra, a waiter carried two plates of *tournedos chasseur* topped with discs of foie gras, trailing the smell of the Madeira sauce, but the women he served it to were homely beyond imagining.

Some *flâneurs* thought that the boulevard des Italiens was the center of the world, and on it, Café Tortoni *was* the boulevard, with the best tables in the city. Crowded, of course. No one wanted to be inside on such a warm end-of-summer day. Surely he'd find someone here. A long-necked blonde was a possibility until he glanced at her plate and imagined he saw what Alphonsine had described as the menu here during the Siege—an entrée of terrine of giraffe. The brunette opposite her raised a forkful of stuffed donkey head to her open red lips. He cringed in horror. After that, all the women he saw looked like donkeys or giraffes. Perhaps it was his mood.

He walked several blocks. Of course it was his mood! How could he even see straight when he was boiling with resentment? That was not like him. It was not *him*. Out of his past came the voice of Gounod, his choir director: *A singer can't delight you with his singing unless he himself delights to sing.* The same with painting. How far he had strayed from his principle of joy. He had to repair his mood before anything would come right.

He headed toward Tanguy's shop, for more than paint. It was in that northern part of the ninth arrondissement which caught whiffs of the ether of Montmartre in acts of creative genius and kindness. He needed to inhale deeply of both.

Julien bowed when he came in the door, taking off his greasy cap and bending low, in the manner of the old school. "An honor to see you here again, my friend." He pushed the curtain behind him aside and said into the back room, "Fionie, look who's here."

Madame Tanguy came out, chewing. He suspected that they were living in the back of the shop. She swallowed and said, "We thought we'd see you again soon." She gave him a genuine smile that made him feel wonderful.

"Look what I have for you, madame." He laid twenty-five francs on the counter, half of what he'd gotten from Alphonse.

Fionie's eyes darted to it like a small animal's. He could think of her as Fionie now that she'd slipped him the Prussian contraband twice, but he still used the formal *vous* when addressing her, to make her feel respected.

Fionie put her index finger on the louis and said, "You need more paint for that monster of a canvas, no?"

"How is it coming?" Julien asked.

"Fine if it weren't for a pigheaded model. Fine if I can get the perspective right. Fine if I can find a *quatorzième*. Fine if I can suggest the spatial context. Fine if I can find a model who will make me want to finish, but right now it's got half a dozen bare places where I've had to scrape."

"Oh, no, no, no," Julien crooned, as though speaking to a small boy who had just skinned his knee.

"Then you do need more paint," Fionie said.

Her assumption that he would finish the thing grabbed hold of him. She was as single-minded as Circe.

"True," he heard himself say. He named the colors, fewer this time, and Julien laid them out.

"Has Cézanne sent you any new paintings?" Auguste asked.

"Ah, he has indeed." Julien's mouth and wide nostrils spread wider. He waddled to the back of the shop where unframed canvases leaned against the wall. Auguste mouthed to Fionie, *Prussian blue,* and followed him.

"I think there are two kinds of Impressionists," Julien said. "I call one *les synthétistes,* those concerned with issues of form, like Cézanne, and the other, *les luministes,* those concerned with issues of light and color, like Monet and Pissarro. Am I right?"

"I suppose you can look at it that way. It's more like a continuum."

"But where do I put you?"

"I guess I'm floating back and forth in the middle."

"Look at this!" With all the adoration of a mother, Julien showed him a still life of apples and peaches. "It almost makes me cry, that peach among peaches, the shape of the crumpled napkin like Montagne Sainte-Victoire under snow. The angle of the table offering it to us." He looked over the top of his spectacles at him, rapt. "The man's a saint."

Something of Cézanne himself was here in this shop, more than just paint on canvas. His humble striving to reach the essence as well as the form of something humble like an apple no less than something grand like a mountain, and to express in matter the spiritual relationship between that apple or that mountain and himself. The man pressed on through solitude and howling criticism, finding his ecstasy in laying his individuality on canvas after canvas.

"With a saint's devotion," Auguste added.

Julien nodded thoughtfully.

"When my parents took me to Notre Dame for the first time as a little boy," Auguste said, "they showed me the saints in the stained-glass windows, and I thought that a saint must be a person with light shining through him. In a way, I still think that."

Today, Cézanne was shining his steady light on him. In their finest moments, that was what the members of the group did for each other.

He looked back and Fionie was wrapping the tubes. Her eyes revealed a spark of trickery. She totaled the bill and smacked it down in front of him. "You would almost be paid up now if you hadn't done that fool thing and scraped off."

He swallowed his anguish at having to say once again, to her especially, "I'd be much obliged if you trusted me again."

"We will. Of course we will," Julien said.

"It's a good thing I learned how to make a new dish," Fionie said before he could thank them. *"Fricassée de sot Julien."*

She had folded her hands as a nun would do, content.

"Delicious, I'm sure." Since *sot* could mean deceived as well as foolish, he knew a tube of Prussian blue was in the package. He picked it up and asked, "Do you remember that teacher I drew with my left hand? Do you know her name?"

"Marie, or Marguerite. No. Mélisse," Tanguy said, scratching his beard.

"It's Hélène," Fionie said. "Don't trust his memory. It's soft, just like his heart."

"Madeleine. That was it. Madeleine," Julien said.

Auguste stepped across the street and greeted the concierge of the girls' school through the iron gate. "I have an inquiry for *Monsieur le directeur, s'il vous plaît.*"

"Who are you?" the concierge asked through a bushy white mustache stained from tobacco.

"One of your teachers is my niece."

"Who?"

"Marie."

"No one works here by that name."

"I meant Madeleine. We sometimes call her Marie."

The concierge drew his mouth to one side.

"You know, Marie Madeleine, from the Bible. Her middle name is Hélène."

The concierge flung out his arm. "Move along. I'm not paid to admit any stray voyeur to ogle our girls."

Auguste walked away, but at the corner he turned back. "Look," he said to the concierge, "I'm sorry I tried that ruse. I'm a painter, and once a pretty young teacher came into Tanguy's shop across the street, and I drew a sketch of her. Medium height, dark blond hair, slim. I'd like to ask her to model. My intentions are honorable. You can ask Julien. I'll go get him."

He made a move to cross the street.

"No, no. Don't bother him." The man came to the gate with a key. "Main entrance, then turn left. The school's still closed for the summer, but you'll find the director in his office. Monsieur Lepage. I don't know which teacher you mean. Go directly, and know that I'll be keeping an eye on you."

"Merci."

It was stuffy inside. That girl would appreciate a few days on the river. He'd prefer to roam and see if he could find her, but he thought better of it and stepped into the office.

"Bonjour," he said to a lady at a desk. *"S'il vous plaît,* might I have a word with *Monsieur le directeur?*

"Your name?"

"Pierre-Auguste Renoir. He doesn't know me."

She poked her head through an open doorway, murmured a few words, and came back. "You may go in."

"Merci." He felt hopeful for the first time today.

Kindly-faced with deeply wrinkled cheeks, Lepage winced as he straightened up from his desk. Auguste delivered as polite a request as he could, explaining how he had met the woman at Tanguy's, how he'd drawn her, and how he would be much obliged if he could ask her to consider posing in a group painting.

"Absolutely not. Our teachers are ladies of honor and seriousness. It is not allowed." The old man flicked his hand at him and bent to his work.

Auguste left, ignoring the concierge on the way out. He was losing time. He was tired and hungry and frustrated with himself for not having someone he could call upon in a pinch. No one could help him do this. He had to do it himself. It felt cheap and unwholesome to be on the prowl like this. He wanted a wholesome girl, not some rummy who looked as though the ten-franc model's fee would keep her from needing a *hôtel de passe*. He didn't want to eat at Nouvelle-Athènes because he might find Degas or Manet there and they'd ask how he was doing and that would make him more miserable.

He went up rue des Martyrs and bought a paper cone of roasted beef from a cart in front of Cirque Fernando, an apple and two horse carrots at a greengrocer's, bread at a *boulangerie,* and went to his studio where there might be a bottle of wine. At the concierge's wicket, Victor handed him a letter.

Jeanne's handwriting.

He climbed the stairs and a dark question reared up in his mind. What if he had already had the perfect model in Jeanne, and would never find another as good? What would that do to his future? His life would shrink, like a balloon leaking air.

He laid out the food on a plate and the envelope on the table. He poured a glass of wine and stared at the precise, upright way she made the *R* in his name. The obligatory thank-you, or something more? He ate a little, to prolong the possibility, and then ripped it open.

> To my most ardent painter,
>
>   Thank you for my remembrance of times past, both what will hang on my wall and what will ever lodge in my heart. I must tell you that I cannot come to finish posing. Joseph-Paul won't permit it. And, as we have been married privately, I must make concessions. I wanted you to hear it from me.
>
>   You are brave in following your heart. I am trying to follow mine.
>
>   Ever your little quail,
>   Jeanne

He eased himself onto his bed, wanting only to surrender to sleep.

A commotion in the street below awakened him. Nine-twenty. Time enough to make the rounds of a few cafés and cabarets. He started at Le

Rat Mort. But after listening to Alphonsine talk about the Siege, the pictures of rats in frying pans and on plates with garnish sickened him.

He tried Chez Père Laplace, thinking that the palettes on the wall might attract a woman interested in painting. One brunette sitting alone was a possibility, though her hair looked like a weeping willow. In the flame of the small oil lamp on her table, her skin shone nicely, but would it in the sun? He invested a little time chatting her up. She seemed pleasant enough. He laid out the question and the rate.

"I'm not that kind of girl," she muttered through her teeth.

"It's a group painting. I assure you that my intentions are honorable."

"Ten francs!" she cried. "Get away from me, you disgusting old man!"

He couldn't get out of there fast enough.

Looking for Angèle with Paul a month ago had been a lark. This was desperation. He didn't want to search the shabby cafés and cabarets. He'd only find shabby women there. That cut out half the establishments in Montmartre. He'd try Cabaret des Assassins. Maybe Angèle was there. She might know of someone. Then he remembered. She'd said she would do a boulevard for him. God in heaven, he didn't want to find her in action.

He trudged up the Butte on the long stairway from rue Gabrielle to place du Tertre, the square atop Montmartre *d'en haut,* to check in Maison Catherine first. A respectable place. The moonlight lay in patches where it shone through the feathery leaves of the acacias. The warm air carried a mournful melody played on an accordion.

A couple was lying on the sparse grass under a tree. The blanket over them moved rhythmically, which made the patches of moonlight dance. He stood transfixed. How unfortunate that they had no other place, but how beautiful too. How absolutely necessary their loving was to them. It was bigger than that. How necessary, love.

Necessary to his painting too. How low he'd sunk, scouring the cabarets in a last-ditch effort to plug in a stranger to save his painting when he knew his best work was produced only when he loved his models as much as Cézanne loved his apples, when every brushstroke was a caress moving by the guidance of love from Alphonsine to Ellen to Angèle to Jeanne. Four reasons to finish it, but there were others, not the least of which was momentum.

He empathized with the couple under the blanket. They would suffer if they weren't together tonight, though probably not as badly as Alexander had suffered. He felt he had stolen the kiss from Alphonsine that rightly belonged to that Russian.

He sensed some movement behind him. A blow on the back of his neck stunned him. Shards of light flashed before his eyes. A few steps and a second man delivered a punch to his jaw. His stomach. He doubled over and sank to the ground. A kick in the ribs, another to his groin. He curled onto his side. His clothes rifled. His wallet leaving his pocket.

A voice. "Hold it, Jemmy! He's Angèle's painter friend."

The wallet falling on his thigh. Men running. Letting the pain subside, his breath jagged, the patches of moonlight dancing over the blanket.

CHAPTER TWENTY-FOUR

Peaches at Camille's *Crémerie*

Nine bells from Notre Dame de Lorette awakened him. His body remembered before his mind did. Gingerly, he rolled onto his side to find a position in which his neck, jaw, ribs, stomach didn't hurt. He wanted to stay that way all day, in oblivion. He dozed until eleven relentless bells clanged in his head. He opened his eyes to his dear old basket of paint rags on the floor. Safety. He was in his studio. He couldn't remember how he'd staggered home, what streets he'd taken. Down and down, every step jarring his ribs, leaning on the building, hand to his face, waiting for the concierge to come, dragging himself up six flights of stairs, opening his wallet, finding nothing.

He wished he'd given Fionie Tanguy all he had, but he'd thought he should hold out some for a new model. Now what? It was deceitful to ask a woman to pose when he knew he couldn't pay her.

Hunger forced him to rouse himself. Slowly, he swiveled to sit on the edge of the bed. He found a bruise on his ribs in the shape of a boot. He stared at it with a cold fascination. One Prussian blue boot. Nine francs forty remained in the jar. Not even one person's modeling fee. He took it and looked for his bicycle cap. Gone. The ultimate injury. He'd spent a good deal of time getting acquainted with that cap. If he ever saw it on a head in Montmartre, he would . . . he didn't know what he'd do. Montmartre was brash, raw, anarchic, and licentious. A young person's quarter. It was also charming, tender, and forgiving. He was on the cusp of being too old for it either way.

He crept down the stairs, holding his ribs, and crossed the street to Camille's *crémerie.* Opening the door required excruciating effort. Two girls from the quarter and three blue-smocked workmen with plaster dust on their sleeves were eating lunch. With just three tables, the only seat left was with Annette, Camille's daughter, who was turning the pages of *La Mode du Jour,* a fashion magazine. Carefully, he sat down opposite her.

"I'm much obliged to you for selling that painting. It helped me out when I was pinched." He was surprised his voice still worked.

"I was happy to do it," Annette said. "Maybe I have a future as a dealer, *oui?*" The look on her face was just a bit flirtatious.

He hated to disillusion the poor girl. "Who knows?"

Camille took a closer look at him and said, "You need an omelette."

He heard her crack three eggs and whip them for a long time, the same furious rhythm as his mother's, whipping in the same clockwise direction that was *de rigueur* in his mother's kitchen. Neither Camille nor his mother could be hurried in this sacred task. Another crack and more whipping delayed it further. That was like his mother too, always slipping him an extra wedge of cheese or spoonful of sauce or cream for his *café,* to try to put meat on his bones, even these days on his weekly visits. God love them both.

"Everything all right with you otherwise?" Camille asked, her back to him. "What's lurking beneath your beard? It looks swollen. So does your ear."

"Eh, good and bad. Like life."

"Another cycle accident?" She dropped butter into a pan. The homey sound of it frizzling comforted him.

"No. You'll be happy to know I sold it."

"Ah, you finally came to your senses."

"Don't say that, Maman," Annette said. "I was hoping for a ride."

"Too late," he said.

Something was slightly wrong with the proportions of Annette's face. Her eyes were too high. It made her chin pronounced, and that meant stubbornness. He couldn't risk another stubborn model.

He didn't remember if the other daughter had this defect. Camille would push one of them on him if he told her what was on his mind. At least they'd be reliable, but they weren't beautiful. He could make one beautiful, he supposed, lower her eyes, paint what he wanted to see rather than what he saw. It would be doing Camille a big favor, and she had always been good to him. But that would be painting from obligation again, not adoration.

It amused him in a distant sort of way, that he was just going ahead, flat broke, aching all over, his painting on the brink of disaster, four models short, without considering abandoning it. Alphonsine would be pleased.

He glanced at the two *lorettes*. One had a face that could stop a clock. Nose like a pear, lips like sausages. Hardly any lips at all on the other. Thin lips gave a suspicious look to a woman. Hair too dark anyway.

Camille served him the omelette with bread and butter, a voluptuous, rose-gold peach, and a *café crème*. "Tell me what happened."

He took three bites first.

"Two thugs worked me over on place du Tertre. The bastards cleaned out my wallet and left me half conscious in the gutter."

"Now you see," she whispered, tapping his forearm with her finger. "If you were married, you'd have been home with your wife and not out catting around all night." She tipped her head ever so slightly toward Annette.

"Maman, behave yourself." Annette lifted the magazine in front of her face.

He patted Camille on the cheek. "You're absolutely right."

The eggs slid down easily and he didn't have to chew much. She had chopped the mushrooms and ham and shallots in small pieces and the cheese had melted perfectly. He felt his shoulders beginning to relax. Soon he'd be able to think. He supposed he had Angèle to thank that they hadn't done permanent damage to his vital parts, all for a measly thirty-some francs. It served them right that it wasn't more.

With his knife, he peeled the peach methodically, watching the skin pull away from the succulent flesh, thinking of Cézanne. His peaches, and his dedication. Expensive vermilion mixed with chrome yellow. He wanted to rip the color out of nature and drink it, chew it, inhale it, make it part of his being, feel it in his viscera right under the Prussian blue boot, so he could take it out and use it whenever it pleased him. He ate the peach reverently, closing his eyes a moment, then finished his *café crème*.

"This peach is a lifesaver. *Merci*."

"Another *café*?" Camille asked.

"No. One is fine. I had intended to pay up some against my account."

"It can wait."

"*You're* the peach."

He shouldered the door open just as Aline was about to enter.

"Bonjour, Monsieur Renoir. Géraldine has been worried about you." Her eyes flashed with mischief. "Oh, *mon Dieu,* I can see why."

A jolt. A shiver. In the sunlight of the doorway her round, peach-tinted cheeks acted like a magnet. Hm, lively eyes. Rose-petal ears. Full, sensual lips. Part of the background of his quarter come to life. He swung around. "On second thought, Camille . . ."

She nodded. "Another cup."

Annette looked up over her magazine. "You can have this table. I've got to get back to the shoe shop."

It was a quick, calculated exit, full of grace. Annette knew when she was beaten.

Sitting down with him, Aline raised her hand as though she were going to touch his cheek but held it carefully away. "*Tch, tch*. At least no cast. What happened this time?"

"Last night," Camille said, "in place du Tertre, the poor man was violently attacked by notorious criminals of the worst sort, beaten near to death, and left to rot in the gutter." Camille brought them each a *café*. "Omelette?"

"*Petite, s'il vous plaît,*" Aline said.

Three eggs cracked in Camille's bowl.

"We haven't seen you for a while," Aline said. "Shall I tell Géraldine you're all right? She would want to know."

He could lose himself in her. A peach among peaches. Flecks of gold and green in her slate blue eyes splintered light and sent it back to him charged with an impish spirit. She had a kittenish face that made him want to tickle her under her chin. Reddish blond hair swept up into a chignon round as a country bun, an eggshell complexion, turned-up nose, almond-shaped eyes at the right position—the imagined face he'd painted on all those plates as a boy, telling Monsieur Lévy it was Marie Antoinette. And his Venus on a vase, it was Aline's face before she was born. How had he not noticed before? He'd found his shoe on his own foot. Timing. Timing was everything.

"How much time do you have for lunch?" he asked.

"Half an hour."

He had to get to the point quickly, and quietly.

"I'm sorry about your accident," she said. "I suppose I would call it an accident, being in the wrong place at the wrong time."

"Are you normally busy on Sundays?"

"My mother and I often go to the Jardin du Luxembourg. We like to walk among the pine trees and watch the wood pigeons. They remind us of home."

"Are you going this Sunday?"

"Or Géraldine and I go to La Grenouillère. She knows how to swim. Are you hurt badly? Did they punch you in the stomach?"

"Do you know the Maison Fournaise?"

"Oh, yes. Where did they hit you hardest?"

He couldn't tell her that, but he could play her little questioning game. "Do you like *le canotage*?"

"Yes, but did they kick you too?" She spurted out her questions more quickly that her usual slow, rolling way of speaking.

"Would you like to go there this Sunday?"

"Did they filch your money?" Her lips pushed out in a pretty little pout.

"Do you have a dark blue dress and a *canotier* for the sun?"

"Does your jaw give you a pain when you talk?"

"Only when you don't answer my questions."

"Oh." Her hand went up to her mouth to cover a giggle. "And all along I thought you weren't answering mine." Her scampish eyes sparked. Such a playful spirit would fit right in.

Camille clunked down a plate in front of Aline with an omelette nearly as big as his. "This is the craziest conversation I've ever eavesdropped on. Get to the point, Renoir. You want to take her boating."

"No! Well, maybe. I want her to pose in my painting. I've started this monstrous painting with fourteen people in it on the terrace of the Maison Fournaise. Well, it's supposed to have fourteen people in it, but one, *quelle peste!* I scraped her off so now I have a hole in my painting."

Aline attacked the omelette with vigor and her little cheeks bulged. "A real hole? That you can see air through? You want me to plug a hole?"

"No, just a big, scraped-off, smeared spot. She was one of the main figures. You would be perfect for it, and I'd be much obliged, but you've got to pose in profile and I need you to have a dark blue flannel boating dress so as to cover the shadows left from the other model."

Her dainty nose poked up. "*Tch, tch.* If you had asked me first, you wouldn't have this problem."

"I know, I know. Would to God I had." And while you're at it, God, please give her a cooperative nature.

"So you'll come?"

She tipped her head toward her raised shoulder. "May I bring Jacques Valentin Aristide?"

His hopes plummeted. Not another arrogant bourgeois bringing tension to his happy, harmonious group. "Who is this Jacques Valentin Aristide?"

"Truth to tell, his name is Jacques Valentin Aristide d'Essoyes sur l'Ource. You'll like him. He's very handsome with his hair in his eyes."

He felt himself tense up, and his ribs ached. A parvenu trailing a false name and needing a haircut. He didn't expect this simple girl, a laundress or seamstress with a Burgundian accent, to have such ambitions. He steeled himself. "Tell me who he is."

Aline blinked a few times, apparently enjoying his anguish.

"My new puppy."

"Puppy or puppy love? Human or canine?"

"He's a dog, monsieur. A little terrier. Oh, so sad. Sunday is the only day I can take him out for a good long walk. He'll be cross if I don't."

He let out a breath, then remembered Madame Charpentier's dog which had jolted him with surprise snorts. At least Aline didn't ask that the mutt be in the painting. He had sworn he would never paint another dog.

"And you, do you have a long name trailing behind Aline? Something Greek? Pandora, maybe?"

"No. Just me. Aline Charigot. I'm the one from Essoyes, in Champagne near the Burgundian border, not my dog. It's on a tributary of the Seine called the Ource." Her voice thickened and she rolled the *r* in Ource forever.

Camille barreled toward her and smothered her in a hug. "I just love to hear you say Ourrrce that way." She turned to Auguste. "I'm from Champagne too, from the Aube region, and hearing Aline brings it back to me."

Camille put one hand on her hip and wagged the index finger of her other hand at Aline. "Don't tell your mother, girl, if you're going to do this posing. When Auguste's painting of the two juggler girls was on the wall, she took one look and said, '*Eh, là,* he must have paid you handsome to hang that thing in your *crémerie.* Pity those poor innocent girls posing for lascivious painters' eyes. They're thick as thieves around here ogling the *lorettes,* and they're all the same, and none of them are honorable.' Oh, she has a monstrous dislike for painters."

Aline's happy expression drooped. "True enough."

"Respectability is everything to her," Camille said. "I know for a fact that she prays, 'Our Father who art in a respectable heaven, swept daily,' so you mind your manners, young man." She pulverized his shoulder with the bowl of a spoon, and stepped back to her stove.

He turned to Aline. "Will you still come?"

"I would have to tell my mother that I'm going with Géraldine to La Grenouillère."

Auguste chortled. "If she's set on protecting you from lascivious eyes, don't tell her that either. That's out of the frying pan into the fire."

"I could say Géraldine and I are going rowing. She knows I like that."

"So do I." His arm might be strong enough, but now his ribs would be the problem.

"I don't know if Jacques Valentin Aristide likes it."

All this time she was saying with her eyes, *Convince me.* He ought to tell her he would pay the modeling fee, but could he?

"If you pose for me, I'll make sure we'll take him for a ride."

Had he lost his mind? "If not this Sunday, then the next. I'll need you three Sundays, at least."

Her eyes widened. "Three Sundays? I don't know, Monsieur Renoir."

"Ten francs each sitting."

"Mm."

She'd finished her plate and was patting the napkin against her puckered mouth. He chuckled. "I can feed myself just by watching you eat."

"That's one thing. I do like to eat."

"Every Sunday we have one of Mère Fournaise's delicious meals. So far we've had *canard à la paysanne* with *artichauts à la vinaigrette, poulet forestière* with *asperges d'Argenteuil en conserve, lapin en gibelotte, friture d'ablettes, de gardons et de goujons.*"

"Mm. The duck must have been nice, but I'm sorry I missed the rabbit stew. It reminds me of home."

"And for dessert, raspberry tarts and apple pastry."

"Ooh, I would have loved that. What are you having this Sunday?"

What had Louise told him? *"Côtelettes d'agneau à la forestière."*

She rolled her eyes. He was making progress, thanks to Louise.

"Oh, I adore lamb, and mushrooms too."

He almost had her. He felt the room spin.

"You didn't answer me. May I bring Jacques Valentin Aristide d'Essoyes sur l'Ource?"

"Yes, but I must draw the line. No cutlets for him."

CHAPTER TWENTY-FIVE

The Blue Flannel Dress

After work in Madame Carnot's Atelier de Couture in Montmartre *d'en bas,* Aline Charigot climbed the steep streets toward the Moulin de la Galette until she found the cardboard sign for Chez Hortense, Ladies' Clothes to Let. She'd been curious about this place but had never gone in. A bell tinkled when she opened the door. In the narrow, dim interior, two racks of dresses hung from suspended iron rods. She walked through the aisle looking for a blue one, not touching anything.

A woman with a shadow of a mustache shuffled toward her in violet mules, Madame Hortense she assumed. *"Bonjour, madame,"* Aline said and smiled.

The woman returned the greeting but not the smile. "What might you be wanting?"

"I'd like to rent a dark blue dress, a pretty one."

"All my dresses are pretty, mademoiselle."

"Then I've come to the right place."

With that, a smile stretched across the woman's splotchy cheeks. "Blue, you say?"

The woman slipped into the familiar *tu* form. The informality struck her as false, but then this was Montmartre *d'en haut,* the Butte. Maybe she was being motherly.

"Why not this green one?" Madame pulled out an elegant dark green dress with draped side panniers trimmed in violet braid.

"No, it's got to be blue."

"This one?"

"No, dark blue."

"*Mon Dieu,* you're a picky one!"

"It doesn't have to be a fine fabric. Canton flannel will do."

"I've got this one, but it will hang on you like a sack. I can stitch it up for you, though."

It was the dark blue of boating dresses, and had dark red braid around a deep square neckline and down the front. A lace ruffle lay inward along the braid at the neckline. She felt pinpricks of excitement. "May I try it on?"

"*Bien sûr.* It's a good choice. A nice demi-polonaise drawn into a modest drape over the derrière. Not too bouffant, but enough to wag when you walk."

As it fell over her head in the back of the shop, it was like putting on a holiday spirit. She'd never had a dress with a polonaise drape.

Madame fastened the back hooks. "Such a clean one for a country girl. Your neck is as white as a swan's. Sometimes I have to give the girls a scrubbing they'll never forget before I let them have a try-on."

"How do you know I'm from the country?"

"You take a week to say anything. And your *r*'s."

With warty fingers, Madame Hortense went to work pinning the side seams. "This won't take but an hour. Then you can get started to-night."

"I won't be needing it until Sunday."

Madame Hortense shook her head, pins pinched in her mouth. "Sunday's the worst day to start. They're with their wives on Sunday."

Madame made basting stitches up the side bodice. "You'll be needing a place to take them, so you come back here tonight. The key for a tithe, by the hour. Two hours, two tithes. Discreet and clean. Mind you, bring this dress back as clean as I'm giving it to you. No grease spots from man or beast."

"You don't understand."

"Oh yes I do, certain enough. No need to be coy with Mère Hortense.

Eventually you'll be needing a *hôtel de passe*. It's good to keep up good relations with the proprietor. Bring him little cakes once in a while. Then, if you run over your hour by a few minutes, he won't charge you for two. Try Hôtel Maître Renard on boulevard Rouchechouart."

"I only want the dress, madame. Not a recommendation."

Madame Hortense scowled. "For how long do you want it?"

"Just three Sundays. Maybe more. You can have it back in between."

"Just Sundays! *C'est ridicule.* Raise your arm."

"Please, madame, I want the dress. It's perfect." She touched the narrow lace ruffle at the sleeve, coveting it.

"No. I can't be letting the dress on again, off again. As good a dress as this is? No, it's steady customers I need, night after night." Mère Hortense lifted Aline's arm, but Aline resisted until she saw a razor in her hand. Madame ripped out her stitches with one swipe of the blade. "Let go of the dress." Madame unhooked the back, but Aline held the bodice to her chest. "Let go."

"What if I paid you a little more?"

"*Impossible.*"

Aline let the dress fall in a billow around her, flattening sadly, like a deflating soufflé.

"Step out." Madame Hortense flicked her hand. "Out. Out."

"How much would the dress cost to buy?"

"A far sight more than what you've got in that string bag of yours. This dress is a prime moneymaker. It wouldn't do me any good to sell it. Out."

She stepped out and into her own gray muslin.

"You come back if you want it on my terms."

She nodded, picked up her drawstring bag, and left.

She couldn't afford a ready-made from Le Bon Marché or even La Samaritaine, the least expensive department store. It meant only one thing. She'd have to make one. Four days! She'd never made a whole dress start to finish, much less in four days. And she could only work on it in the evenings and Saturday after half-day work. Maman could do it with time to spare, but she would ask what it was for, and if she told her, there would be war. A fine pickle she'd gotten herself into. Géraldine would have to help.

She went to the *charcuterie* where Géraldine worked. Closed. She went to Camille's *crémerie*. Not there. She went to Aux Tissus de la rue Blanche, the *boutique de tissu* that Madame Carnot used when a fine lady like Madame Galantière of the avenue Frochot ordered a dress. Through aisles of bolts—*crêpe de Chine, mousseline de soie,* brocades, striped *satin du Barry*—her mind spun with fantasies of Monsieur Renoir being astonished at her beauty, but the plain dark blue he wanted was all she could afford.

The shopgirl recognized her from the times she'd been sent to pick up Madame Carnot's orders, and inquired what Madame needed. When she learned it was only cotton flannel for *her,* she brought out the right nautical blue and gazed out the window in complete disinterest.

Aline stroked the cotton nap. "I have no idea how much I need."

"What does your pattern say?"

"I don't have one. I was hoping to use one of Madame Carnot's." That would save some money. If she waited to find out for certain, she would lose a day. "Can we just make a good guess?" She described the dress with the demi-polonaise in back. "It only drapes from the sides, and the skirt is narrow."

"To be safe, you had better buy five meters."

"How much would that be?"

"One franc sixty-five per meter. That's eight francs twenty-five."

"That much?"

"If you want the polonaise."

Oh, she did. A polonaise was what separated the bourgeoisie from the working girl. She counted all her coins and watched the long metal blades of the scissors follow an invisible line across the flannel, cutting future from past. She waited until the piece was cut to say, "I'm short by two francs eighty-five. Would you trust me for that until tomorrow? You know I work for Madame Carnot."

"You should have counted before I cut." She went back to confer with someone and returned. "We'll save the piece if you pay what you can now."

"I'll come back midday tomorrow."

"We close from noon to two."

Now she had to find Géraldine. She'd be good for two francs eighty-five until Saturday noon when Madame Carnot paid her girls for the week. On rue Saint-Georges she asked the concierge at Géraldine's flat to buzz her. She waited ten minutes, perspiring into her dress. Géraldine didn't come down.

Why wasn't anything easy? Four nights, nearly three francs short, no pattern, and no money for red braid or lace. She went home discouraged until she heard Jacques Valentin Aristide bark as she opened the door.

"Oh, you poor thing, home alone all day." She scooped him up and cuddled him. *"Mon grand, mon grand,"* she cooed. He squirmed to lick her cheek with his small pink tongue.

"I took him out. He had already made a puddle," her mother said.

"I'm sorry."

She avoided her mother's glance, ate a slice of *terrine de campagne* and some fried potatoes, and slipped a morsel to Jacques Valentin.

"Where have you been?" her mother asked.

"With Géraldine. She's going to make a dress, and I went with her to choose the fabric." The wings of a trapped bird beat in her chest. "I might help her sew it too."

Maman's left eyebrow wormed up into an arch.

She didn't want to say more. She took Jacques to bed with her, feeling terrible for having lied when Maman had done nothing to deserve it. She fell asleep worrying where the lie would lead.

Wednesday already. At the *crémerie* in the morning she explained it all to Géraldine, who dumped out on the tin tabletop all she had and drew back enough to feed her for the day. Two francs thirty were left.

"What will you say when you bring the dress home and wear it on Sunday?" Géraldine asked.

"I didn't think of that."

"You'd better have your story rock solid," Camille said, "or your mother will call you a trollop traipsing after artists, and take after you with a broomstick." Camille snapped one franc onto the table and pushed the thirty centimes back toward Géraldine.

Aline flung her arms around her. "Oh, thank you for eavesdropping again. I'll pay you both back as soon as I can."

She arrived out of breath at Madame Carnot's atelier. It was an old-fashioned workshop with only one Hurtu-l'Abeille sewing machine, which only Madame's protégée, Clarisse, was permitted to use while she and Estelle worked by hand. Her mother worked in a better atelier that had three machines.

Madame took one look at her. "Early? That's not like you."

"I need to make a dress in four days."

"You know I don't allow my girls to take on private clients."

"It's for me. A boating dress. I'll have the fabric today, just cotton flannel, but I don't have a pattern. Is it possible . . . would you let me look through your pattern file? I want a square neck and a small drape in back. After work, would you let me use the cutting table? I'll pay for the thread."

"Slow down, Aline. I've never heard you talk so fast. What's this for?"

"You have to promise not to tell my mother. It's so that I can pose in a painting. She doesn't want me running with artists. I need it on Sunday."

"We have orders backed up, you know."

"Oh, I wouldn't think of putting mine first. I just need the cutting table today after the atelier is closed. Please, madame."

"You've never done a set-in sleeve. Or buttonholes."

"I know. But leastways I can try."

"Can't it be next Sunday?"

"No, I have to fill a hole in a painting this Sunday. Oh, I so want to help this man. I've been watching him at the *crémerie* where I take my meals. A nice, funny man. A good man, I think. This is my chance, madame."

"My chance to lose you, you mean." Madame smiled in a motherly way. "You're not usually so jittery. Take a look in the pattern file and show me what you choose. Only the commercial patterns, not my own designs, mind you."

"Yes, yes. *Merci,* madame."

The drawings on each envelope showed copies of dresses from chic shops on the boulevards. She found one with a square neck, but it didn't have a polonaise, and one with a polonaise, but it didn't have a square neck. She had her heart set on the square neckline. It was more nautical. She brought the two patterns to Madame. "Is it possible to use this bodice with that skirt?"

"Yes."

"How much fabric will I need?"

Madame read the two envelopes. "Five and a half meters."

"Oh, no!" Heat went to her throat. "I only have five."

"You should have asked me first. *Au travail!* Do Madame Galantière's hems now. Remember, she inspects them for any stitch showing through."

"One other thing. May I take my lunch early to get to the boutique before they close for midday?"

"You are a tumble of requests today, aren't you?"

"You won't get a stitch less out of me for your clients, I promise you."

The hours ticked by at a snail's pace, but she got the fabric, and hugged it to her chest while hurrying back to Montmartre *d'en bas,* giddy all the way despite the heavy humidity. She tried to be more agreeable than usual, more careful with her stitches, and six o'clock finally came. Estelle and Clarisse left, Madame cleared off the long cutting table, and Aline unfolded her fabric and began to place the tissue shapes.

"All the same direction," Madame warned. "See the arrows? Flannel has a nap. Double lines mean to place it on the fold."

She placed them the same way and had one tissue shape left over.

Madame was getting ready to leave.

"Wait!" Aline held up the piece.

Madame looked at her as though the answer was obvious to anyone with half a brain. "You'll have to buy more." She pressed a key in her palm. "Don't stay past seven-thirty. It will be too dark to work past then anyway. Be sure you clear off the table when you're finished."

She felt like a marionette whose legs were collapsing.

"You'll do fine. Just read the instructions before you do anything. *Bon courage!*"

The door closed. Buy some more. Read the instructions. She might as well have said, *Climb to the moon.* When had there been time to learn to read more than simple words in short strings? Fourteen she was when Maman had brought her here to launder and press. Three years of that before Madame ever put a needle in her hand. One year spent in doing only hems, another to learn seams, and now, *bon courage!* She needed more than good wishes to put this dress together. She needed an act of God!

Her hand trembled when she made the first cut. She made the second. The third. She stacked the cut shapes until there was only the left-over pattern piece without fabric. She took it with her and locked the door behind her.

The *boutique de tissu* was closed. That meant another night of worry. What would be missing from her dress if they'd sold the rest of the bolt?

The next day, Thursday, she asked Madame for two more favors— to adjust her lunchtime again so she could go to the *boutique de tissu,* and to be paid her two francs twenty-five each day this week instead of the total on Saturday noon. "I borrowed to buy the fabric and now I need to buy more and pay back my friends."

Madame agreed, and Aline took the pattern piece to the boutique at lunchtime. All afternoon, doing the hems on a three-tiered visiting dress for Madame Galantière who had never sewn a stitch, she thought only of the puzzle of the cut shapes.

At six o'clock Madame said, "Do a running stitch around the arm scyes and corners of the neckline first," and shut the door.

How did a person spell *scyes?* She laid out the shapes. Which pieces were they? She would die of humiliation if Madame found out that she couldn't read the instructions. She held up the pieces against her body to see where they fit. With no one in the atelier, she examined dresses partially assembled and guessed the order of things. She did the running stitch, the darts, basted the bodice seams, and stopped. What next?

On Friday, she skipped lunch to work on her dress, worked after everyone left, and at half after seven took the pieces to Géraldine's flat to work some more.

On Saturday morning, she arrived at work early and showed Madame what she'd done.

Madame shook her head. "I hope you're not dreaming of ever becoming a first hand in a good fashion house on the place Vendôme. It's as unrealistic for you as becoming a prima ballerina at the Opéra."

"I'm not hoping for anything like that. I'm just hoping to finish this dress."

"This must be very important for you. This posing, this man."

"Yes, madame."

"Just don't get it into your head to become a model. I don't want to have to go looking for a replacement."

"No, madame."

"You've sewn the side seams on the skirt before sewing the polonaise into them. You'll have to rip them out."

She felt like screaming. Silently she cursed her ignorance, and bent her head to hide her tears.

"Take today for your dress. You can make up the half-day next Saturday."

"Merci, madame." She choked on the words and started ripping. By eleven she'd reassembled the side seams. Madame gave her a bodice fitting before she shut down the shop for half-day. "Leave by six," Madame said.

She nodded and blubbered through her thanks.

If she had no blue dress, she couldn't model. Auguste was depending on her. If she failed, how could she ever face him in the *crémerie*? She eyed the sewing machine. With a machine, she could do the bodice seams and sleeve seams and maybe even attach bodice to skirt before six o'clock. It could save her. She studied the way the thread went through the loops. She could do it. She'd watched Clarisse. But then Madame would see machine stitching and chastise her. She might even lose her job. A worse disaster.

She threaded her needle and went to work by hand. At six she took the pieces to Géraldine.

"Whatever made me think I could make a dress like fine ladies wear for boating in four nights?"

"Do you want an honest answer?" Géraldine asked.

"No."

Géraldine reached for a sleeve and began putting in the seam. "You like him. More than like him. That's why. I can tell by your eyes whenever he comes in the *crémerie*."

"That skinny, fidgety, brittle-looking man twice my age? He could have any model in Montmartre he wanted. I have no dreams. He could never care about me. He only needed someone quick to plug a hole. I could tell he was desperate by the way his cheek twitched under his eye."

"Then why are you breaking your neck to make this dress?"

She shrugged. "I'm just doing a favor for someone. To be nice."

Géraldine wagged her head and hummed a popular romantic song, her smile a tease. Aline didn't look at her, but burst out laughing anyway.

She went home just after ten. The dress was unfinished, but she still had the morning. She'd get up at three. She'd go with it pinned if she had to.

"I was at Géraldine's. We were fitting her dress," she explained. Only one word was a lie.

Her mother put a bowl of cabbage soup on the table. "Why didn't she come here for a proper fitting? I know a far sight more than you do."

She was caught short for an answer, and kept her nose down to the bowl.

"Aline. Do you know what it feels like to be lied to?"

She raised her head. The grooves that ran from her mother's nostrils to the corners of her mouth seemed deeper than she remembered them.

"It makes a person feel no better than a mangy dog in the street."

Her eyes stung.

"The first night when you said you were with Géraldine, she came here."

"Why didn't you say so then?" she wailed.

"I wanted to see just how deceptive my daughter could be. It wasn't a happy lesson. First my husband, the biggest deceiver of all, and now my daughter. A small lie, granted, but lies grow. They require bigger deceptions."

Aline dove onto her mother's lap, and Jacques Valentin skittered away. "I'm sorry. I'm sorry."

Maman let her stay there but didn't offer a comforting touch.

"Can you tell me what you're doing?" Her voice softened. "Is it a man?"

She felt her mother stroke her hair. "No. It's a dress. It's for me, not Géraldine. I'm in an awful fix. I have to finish it by tomorrow noon."

"And you keep it a secret from your mother, a dressmaker?"

"I had to," she said into her mother's *robe d'intérieur.*

"What kind of a dress is it?"

"A boating dress with a polonaise. I had trouble because I couldn't read the instructions. I've made mistakes. I didn't want Madame Carnot to know I can barely read." She cried into her mother's lap. "I'm so stupid. When other girls were going to lycée in their pleated jumpers carrying their books on a strap, where was I? Bending over a washtub scalding my arms."

"Do you really think that's what I wanted for you? We do what we have to, the two of us. And if we let our twosome break apart, we'll have nothing."

"I know."

"And so you want a rowing dress like a proper bourgeoise to go promenading along the river. It's either with a man or to attract a man. Which is it? And where? At La Grenouillère where all the hussies go?"

"No."

"Why by tomorrow?

She backed away. "It's to pose in a painting at Chatou."

"*Eh, là!* After all I've said about painters, warning you." Maman shot up and began to pace. "They use one girl after another. It starts by painting her in a pretty dress, and before long she's posing nude, and then she's in a family way and the genius painter has dropped her because he doesn't want to paint her when she's lost her figure, and he can't support her, so he's gone on to another. One after another, a string of broken, used-up women behind him." She flung her arm backward. "Abandoned."

"Any man can abandon a woman, not just a painter. Even a man with roots in the soil of France." Maman froze. "A man with centuries-old grapevines."

Maman's hand covered her heart. "She's not only a liar. She's cruel too," she said to the wall, then turned back. "You might as well have slapped me in the face."

"A man with a daughter."

Her mother's eyes filled even as her own were filling. She was not going to be the first to look away. Their shared pain rose up like a great lumbering beast awakening from a cave, and she wept for the thoughts Maman would have to battle tonight.

"Who is this man?" All the anger had drained out of her voice.

"Auguste Renoir," she murmured. "He eats at the *crémerie.*"

"I've seen him. He wears overalls."

"He promised to pay ten francs a sitting. It would take me a week to earn that. And there'll be three sittings. Maybe more."

"Respectability is more important than money."

"Money can buy respectability."

Maman slumped on a chair and took out her hairpins.

"Show me the dress."

Aline unfolded the paper wrapping and showed her the skirt still separate from the bodice, the bodice without sleeves or buttonholes, the sleeves and skirt unhemmed.

"Ten hours, at least, if you can stitch as fast as I can."

"You know I can't."

"Then you'd better keep working. Attach the sleeves before you stitch the waistline seam. I'll show you how to make buttonholes in the morning."

Maman hadn't offered to help, but she would have said no if Maman had.

She watched her mother braid her hair for bed. She watched her chest rise as she sighed. She watched her carry the oil lamp into her bedroom and close the door. She heard her pour water into her washing bowl. In a few moments, the thin rod of light under the door went out with a *fitz*.

Maman's dazed look, the single braid down her back with sadness plaited in, the slowness of her steps, like a sleepwalker, defeated—she wished she hadn't seen her that way.

Around two o'clock she began to indulge herself by letting her eyes close as she pulled the thread, and wrenching them open again to take another stitch. It was hopeless. She would never make it. She turned the metal knob on the gas lamp and lay on the sofa and closed her eyes. She still saw the needle go down and up through the blue fabric, like the progress of a narrow silver boat over the waves and across an ocean—to America, where somewhere in that big land Papa lived, where Maman's thoughts would be forced to wander tonight, because of what she'd said.

CHAPTER TWENTY-SIX

Au Jardin Mabille

Angèle was scrubbed, dressed, perfumed, ready for business, and heading toward place Pigalle. The week had run past her, had rocked her footing with some sad news, and now there was only Saturday night to harvest the wheat she wanted to slap into Auguste's hand in the morning. She hadn't had to rub a *bon-bon* on a boulevard for years and didn't relish going back to her hardscrabble days, but she had the know-how now to enjoy doing this for Auguste and not get roughed up, body or soul. She had a better notion than the boulevards—the Jardin Mabille, where she could dance a fair jig and might not have to get down to commerce at all.

In place Pigalle, couples, prostitutes, children, and old men and women all vied to get a sitting spot on the edge of the large round fountain to cool off on this hot night and watch a gypsy dancing for coins to accordion music. Angèle caught an omnibus circling there and climbed the steps to the imperial even though the roof level was off limits to ladies. Dearie me, ladies might show some skin on the way up, carelessly or otherwise. What of it? If she was paying five centimes, she'd get the best view, right down through café windows on boulevard des Capucines. The chandeliers poured diamond light onto the dandies and princesses eating and drinking. Even though she couldn't afford a scrap there, nobody could keep her from looking. She'd been looking all her life. She felt the heart of Paris beat, and hers was keeping up the rhythm.

At Rond Point on the Champs-Élysées she got out and walked. All sorts of conveyances clogged the street in front of Jardin Mabille. The cream of the *demi-monde* who made their living off the haves of society arrived in their victorias and landaus with their clipped poodles and Afghan hounds. Wealthy men on the prowl came in their phaetons, and foreigners in their hired fiacres.

At the arched entrance, statues of some Greek specimens of manhood put her in the mood to squeeze. A piper was playing a nasal melody on a musette bag. Urchins who slept on the hay barges had climbed trees to peer over the wall at the gaiety and listen to songs they longed to memorize. She knew. When she was their size, she had done the same.

She hurried up to the ticket window ahead of three silly chits smothered in frippery, too gay for this hour, and was ushered in as lady number twenty-three. The first twenty-five didn't have to pay. That meant three francs saved for Auguste.

A young man wearing a boater beckoned to her and acted put out when she didn't recognize him. His friends guffawed and she saw it was a joke. He begged pardon, and in a few moments he repeated the trick with another girlie entering the gate. They would cut some fine capers, this group, but men in boaters didn't have any loose coin to drop.

In the pleasure garden she strolled among irises and fleurs-de-lis, hydrangea blooms the size of cabbages, and jasmine fragrant enough to make a weaker woman swoon. Curving paths lined with camellias led to secluded bowers, straight paths to the billiard tables, the ring toss, and bowling games. Lit with a hundred electric lights in the shape of fleurs-de-lis, Mabille was pure fantasy with rules of *politesse* all its own.

Edging the round wooden dance floor with the musicians' pavilion in the center, two semicircular *promenoirs* funneled each line of promenaders in opposite directions. The first birdlike notes of the flute announced Offenbach's Barcarole and the start of the promenade. She stepped into the outer *promenoir*. Two *chanteuses* sang the moony melody, "*Belle nuit, ô nuit d'amour.*" She swished her skirt to the measured rhythm, her slow steps accented by the ping of the triangle. Gliding along at the speed of a gondola was just right for coy greetings and comey-you-here looks.

She eyed the competition, the cost of the silk, the braid, the lace. Flounces, bustles, polonaises, bows, frills, here a glint of diamond or glass, there some roses nestled in tulle. This girlie ahead of her with the pushed-up titties wasn't a first-timer. That one hadn't sold her butter. The skin of another was plastered like an old cathedral. As for the men, shining top hats, waxed mustaches, pomades, and stickpins—a fashion parade with a purpose.

She had to be wary and not waste time on any cropper in borrowed clothes. No one in the peaked cap and sideburns of a pimp or the derby of a shopkeeper selling fabric or buttons without coin enough to buy Auguste a single tube. Top hats were the thing. In the pockets under them, the color of their money was gold.

The soft light of Chinese lanterns turned her rose linen dress into silk, her dress that some ragpicker hooked from a mound of refuse in one of the better quarters, sold to a stall holder in the maze of used clothing aisles of the Marché du Temple, who sold it to her last fall. It could have gone to the races at Longchamp or to the Kiosque de l'Empereur in the Bois de Boulogne on a Sunday afternoon. It could have heard Emélie Bécat sing at the Ambassadeurs. And it could carry her to some coin tonight, very like.

She had heard tales of princely bounties paid to clever women at Jardin Mabille, had seen it happen often enough when she was an orange girl here. Men coming by themselves to be entertained by pretty girls, a bit of strolling, a little talk, some dancing, some finger paddling under the arbors. Women pouring out tales of woe, and when the men get to squirming, they slip them a handful of napoléons, bow like courtiers, and bid them adieu. Tribute money, it was called in the society journals, but she suspected it was conscience money—paying a woman a man *didn't* use to square things right with God for the string of women he *had* used. Not so different from those pardons priests used to sell. And society was no worse for the exchange, just a mite more even.

That little maidie in pink ahead of her in the *promenoir* was trying too hard, laughing too loud. She'd be the first to get desperate and do the *chahut* too early and be branded a tart. *Give it time,* she felt like telling her. *It's easy, really. Enjoy it.*

The three teasers at the gate approached in the opposite *promenoir*. She mimicked the ruse, turning it back on them, and they doubled over laughing.

An older man's face coming toward her gave her a start. Père l'Epingle. It couldn't be, but the old chap had the same hook of a nose, the same kind gray eyes like stones plugging the mouths of caves under his forehead. She reeled and had to steady herself. Père l'Epingle. Impossible.

A top-hatted man with a gardenia in his buttonhole smiled as they passed in opposite directions. Not a flirtatious smile. Almost a forced one, as though it took effort. His jacket had a fine cut. Definitely a man of the *beau monde*. Too serious, but she could remedy that.

"*Bonsoir, mademoiselle,*" he said.

"*Bonsoir à vous,*" she said, waved her fan, and glided onward.

She gave a nod to everyone, a frolicsome eye to those who priced out. She imagined a few as lovers. No doubt the men were doing the same. Under the lights, the air was ashimmer with desire. People sucked it in, breathed it out. She wanted to pinch the women's cheeks, nibble the men's ears, press their heads to her bosom, all of them, the bright, lively people of Paris.

In case some duffer-wits didn't get the notion of the place, a *chanteuse* sang "Amanda," a ballad about a girl who tosses away her maidenhood in a dance hall.

On the next round, she took a closer look. No, of course it wasn't Père l'Epingle. She shook it off.

When the *promenoirs* were filled and going too slowly, the musicians began a waltz. She stepped out of the promenade and stood near the sprawling café under the trees. That fancy-ass Hyménée had staked out the prime spot. Angèle waved her fan in time to the one-two-three, one-two-three of the waltz. The violins, the clink of glasses, the chatter, the antics, her dress, her hair in a chignon with a cascade of curls at the back—this would surely be a grand night, for Auguste's sake, for the sake of the painting, maybe even for her. If a body expected good, then good was more likely to find you, was her notion.

She'd have to order something to show she was alone, but the drinks cost more at the outer tables where she would be noticed. It takes some to make some, she thought and sat down. The waiters made a practice of looking right through any woman sitting alone. They knew she would order something more expensive if a man joined her. There were no secrets about this place.

She beckoned to a waiter. *"Un petit vin d'Alsace."*

He gave her a hard stare. "Is that *all,* mademoiselle?"

"For now."

She let the waltz take her places in her mind. A little orange-seller came up to her and offered an orange in her grimy hand. Years flew backward.

"You have a sweet face," she said. "Squeeze every pleasure out of life, *minette.* Even from the rind."

"Monsieur told me to bring this to you." She thrust it at her.

"Who?"

"Le monsieur à la fleur."

She looked from the knobby shine on the orange, to the grease on the girl's nose, to a silk top hat gleaming under the lamplight. The man with the gardenia leaned against a lamppost. He gave her a half smile, one side only, Auguste Renoir style. Now, wasn't that a sign! She swept her open fan at her throat, as though the mere sight of him made her flush with heat. He wasn't in a hurry. She liked that. He took pleasure in watching from a distance.

She leaned toward the girl. "Did he pay you decent?"

"Bien sûr, mademoiselle! I can go home with the rest of the oranges."

"Good. He was an easy one, but others won't be. Nobody *needs* to buy an orange or a flower. Use your eyes to sell when the bloke doesn't know he wants to buy. You send him away happy, but always hold one back for yourself, because you're not a throwaway. Remember that when you're older and selling more than oranges."

She glanced up. Milord of the white gardenia was still watching. "You trot along quickly now. Don't dally. Wrap his coin tight in your underskirt."

He put out his cigarette, pushed himself away from the lamppost, deferred to people moving about in front of him, and came toward her.

"May I join you?"

"An orange can buy a seat any day, milord. Come. Take your ease."

The waiter descended on them instantly and said, "Bonsoir, monsieur." He had not yet brought her wine.

"Would you like something?" the man of the white gardenia asked her.

"I'd love a half plate of oysters. *Portugaises, s'il vous plaît.*" They were the inexpensive kind.

"I will bring you *marennes,*" the waiter said. "They are superior."

The *grand bourgeois* inclined his head toward her to be sure. She moved her index finger from side to side.

"The mademoiselle prefers *portugaises.*" He turned to her. "Only *une demie-douzaine?*"

"A little hunger is good for the soul."

"*Une demie-douzaine de portugaises pour la mademoiselle.*"

"And for you, monsieur?"

"*Blinis à la russe,* and champagne, a demi.*"

His very white collar and very white teeth and very white handkerchief edged in black poking up from his breast pocket were right fine.

"When I saw you sitting here so still, I thought you must be a model. And when you talked to the little girl, I thought you must be a teacher."

"A teacher! Oh, that's rich. You were right the first time. Some days."

A certain cachet in that. It would let him know someone considered her desirable. "In fact, I'm going to model tomorrow."

"For whom?"

"A talented man who doesn't deserve to be so poor. Auguste Renoir."

"Indeed. And other days?"

A calculated question, to determine if she was kept by a painter.

"Sometimes I work at the flower stall of the Marché de Saint Pierre in Montmartre." Specific in case he wanted to find her, intermittent to let him know she could use some money.

"A flower seller ought to have one for herself."

He hailed a little girl selling roses. *"Une rouge,"* he told her. When the girl handed him a red one, he pricked himself on a thorn.

"To flirt with a rose is more dangerous than to flirt with an orange, milord."

"No more dangerous than to flirt with a fan."

He put his finger to his mouth and sucked the dot of blood.

"Lucky finger," she said.

The waiter served them. She felt the first oyster slide down her throat.

"Do you come here often?" he asked.

"I used to, a long time ago." When she came up to his crotch, and pleaded with her eyes for people to buy oranges.

"Then I'd be obliged if you would enlighten me. Who are these people?"

His innocence must be a ruse. Well enough. She could play along.

"Look there," she said, "at that English jockey swigging beer and ogling the women. He makes more than that Russian prince in lilac gloves."

He chuckled. "Do you know them?"

"No, but I wouldn't mind."

"How do you know he's a prince?"

"The pink lining folded down over the top of his boot." She winked to show she was just making it up. "Those three Catalonian women are hankering to dance. Their men are at the billiard tables. You could help out the ladies."

"I don't speak Spanish or Catalan."

"You don't need words. Dancing is a language by itself."

"So are your eyes a language, and right now I prefer the words they're telling me."

"See that lady wearing a bustle? If those false cheeks were made of real flesh, they would have broken her back. And the man yapping at her shoulder in those starched trousers, stiff as what's in them? See his hungry look? He's fair itching after her and doesn't know how to pace himself."

"You're quite the *flâneuse,* mademoiselle."

"Looking is free entertainment."

She recognized Jemmy and Picklock, two thieves from Montmartre, and turned away from them. She didn't want them swaggering up to her and spoiling things. "See those two behind me in the tweed jackets? Rogues from the Butte. Don't let them near or they'll pick your pockets as sure as I'm sitting here."

"They seem respectable enough."

"Upon my soul, they're ogres in and out of Rochefort. Petty crimes, mostly. There's plenty wickeder."

"Angèle!" Jemmy circled around her one way, Picklock the other. "Fancy seeing you here on the Champs-Élysées," Picklock said in a voice as slick as oil.

"Out from the underbelly of Pigalle for a change?" Jemmy wore that leer of thinking his reputation made him powerful.

Milord of the gardenia grasped her arm and propelled her away. "Excuse us. The lady wishes to dance."

He ushered her through the gate to the dance floor, paid two sous, and they joined a polka, careening in a circle, bumping into other spinning pairs and laughing. Couples swirled around her. A waltz followed. He drew her closer to steer her, and she noticed his gold watch chain, his eyes taking her in, the strong fragrance of his gardenia unleashed in their turning, his clipped beard grazing her temple. He prolonged it with a third dance, the dizzying redowa-polka. She felt like she was flying.

When they came back to the table, Jemmy and Picklock had moved on.

"That was right gallant of you, and I don't even know the name of my *cavalier à la fleur*."

"Marcel Olivier."

"You're not a baron, are you?"

"Why do you ask?"

"That song, '*Ah, J'la trouv' trop forte.*' I could sing it for a coin."

"I'm all ears."

> *At the Ball Mabille between two dances,*
> *A young man said he was a baron.*

He offered me a townhouse and carriage
As proper setting for my good taste.

She paused to blow kisses to two men at the next table, and then re-sumed singing.

Lowering my eyes, I went toward him,
Voilà! Here's something new,
I spied some scissors in his pocket.
The baron was just a shop assistant.

"Bravo, mademoiselle. You should be onstage."

"I was a few times. Once I sang the role of Venus in *Orpheus and the Underworld* at the Théâtre de la Gaîtě. It was only a small part, but I danced the cancan in the finale."

"You are a woman of many surprises."

"You can bet your boots on that."

"Then you are a professional."

He drew a coin out of his pocket and slid it across the table to touch her hand. It was a gold louis worth twenty francs.

"Oh, aren't you a regular patron of the arts!"

The two men from the other table added three-franc écus.

"*Oh, là là!*" She gathered them up, laughing, and leaned toward him, pushing one shoulder forward, offering him her décolletage. "*Merci, milord,*" she said and kissed the air close to his neatly trimmed beard.

"Truth to tell, I'm not a professional *anything*. Let's say I'm a miscel-laneous individual. Isn't that the definition of Montmartre—a colony of miscellaneous individuals doing miscellaneous things to keep alive? Times are hard for miscellaneous people."

"I wouldn't know."

"North of place Pigalle you'll find a butcher who plays the trumpet at a cabaret, and a trapeze artist who writes poetry."

"And south of Pigalle?"

She wrinkled her nose. "South of Pigalle, they just work and eat and drink."

Near them, a young Zouave in a tasseled fez and blousy red trousers, an embroidered vest, and a wide green sash was bragging about his adventures in North Africa, becoming loud and obnoxious. The regulator in long black tailcoat shook his finger at him. "Quiet down, monsieur."

"I didn't come here to be quiet," the Zouave bellowed. "Time enough to be quiet in my grave. Look again at all the empty glasses of my listeners before you tell me again to be quiet."

"Mark my words," Angèle said in a low voice, "if he doesn't close his head, he'll be tapped on the shoulder and invited to leave."

He quieted down for the next song, "Alsace and Lorraine," sung at least once every evening here and at the Ambassadeurs and the Eldorado. People stopped talking and stood as though it were an anthem when the music mounted and the *chanteuse de la maison* belted out:

> *You will not have Alsace and Lorraine,*
> *And in spite of you, we will remain French!*
> *You could germanize the plain*
> *But our heart, you will never have it!*

And to prove it, the musicians began the long prelude to Offenbach's quadrille and cancan from *La Vie Parisienne*.

Above the cheers, the impresario shouted, "*Avancez, Messieurs et Mesdames*. A quadrille is about to begin."

A surge of people squeezed through the wickets, and Mademoiselle Irma, the famous *cancaneuse,* mounted the stage. Angèle grabbed Marcel's hand and pulled him between tables and people. He dropped the sous into the box again, and they joined three other pairs to make their square.

All eight jigged forward to meet their opposite and skipped back, executing the five figures until the music signaled the freer *chahut*. Shouts erupted all around them. Men danced as if the workings of their bodies were out of order. Limbs attached with elastic bands flopped about uncontrollably. Angèle and all the women shook their skirts from side to side, raised them in a tease, kicked to the side, the front, the side. One woman in their quadrille launched a kick that knocked off the hat of her partner when he bent forward.

On the stage around the musicians' pavilion, the dancers in the chorus line lifted their skirts high in the cancan, revealing a froth of ruffled organza against black-stockinged legs, kicking high, and then holding the kick above their heads with their hands, pirouetting, cartwheeling, sinking to the floor in the splits, springing back up again, while the crowd cheered and mimicked them.

The music was too spirited for her to contain herself. Angèle pirouetted and pranced, first with low kicks, then raising her knee and letting go a half kick, not high enough to show the bandeau at the top of her white stockings, but enough to make her chignon come undone.

"*Dansez,* milord!" she urged in a throaty voice. "Let yourself go!"

Marcel cavorted too, looking astonished and letting out one *"Mon Dieu!"* after another as the music mounted faster and faster, until the wild whoops of the crashing finish.

"Bravo, milord!"

He held on to her waist with both hands as they wobbled back to the table, hot and out of breath. "I've surprised myself," he said.

"One must dance the cancan when one can," she said.

He signaled the waiter for more champagne. They touched hands and drank and watched the mazurka, the *galop,* the *grandpère,* and they joined on the sedate Boston. She liked its free, sliding movements which made her feel graceful, and its advance and retreat which was flirtatious. What couldn't be said could be sung, and what couldn't be sung could be danced.

On the table, his hand covered hers. "When I saw you alone in the *promenoir,* I thought you looked sad," he said. "How wrong I was!"

"No, you're a smart one. During the barcarole, I ran up against a face that reminded me of someone. Near to shook the stuffing out of me."

"A tragedy?"

"For many people."

"Do you want to talk about it?"

She tapped her glass with her fingernail, considering. Telling it might get him to digging in his pocket, but it was cheap to use Père l'Epingle for a coin.

"It's not the type of story you're likely to hear in your circles."

"I am a republican. I ride the omnibuses. If it's about a human being, I'd like to hear." He slid another gold louis across the table. "Tell me."

Mon Dieu! Forty-six francs altogether. Now she had to tell him. It might sound fake, it was so woeful, and he'd think she made it up. Put a tarnish on the evening, that would. She had to treat it with pussy gloves.

"It's about Père l'Epingle, a ragpicker I used to know in the ragpickers' colony of the Maquis." She looked at him, taking his measure. "Where I grew up."

He didn't bat an eye.

"Father of the fatherless, he was. A clean, gentlemanly old man." She took a quick gulp of champagne. "They called him Père l'Epingle out of respect. He could pick a silver pin out of a heap of rubbish."

"An enviable talent, in his line of work." He tilted his head. "And in life, I suppose."

"True as tears." She took another drink. "When I was a little girl, he moved into the quarter and began to help the ragpickers. He organized their picking territories and settled their quarrels. He set up areas for burning garbage and for latrines. He brought medicine when there was cholera. Everybody in the Maquis called him the Governor. When he was sickly, the whole ragpicking colony surrounded his shanty, wailing up a racket until he came out and told them he would live. He gave me the very hare skins I slept on."

She finished her drink and looked off to the pretty couples spinning around the pavilion under the colored lanterns. All that pleasure and prettiness. Who was she, really, to be here when she carried the Maquis in her veins? Its piles of filth. The refuse of Paris, stench, mud, dampness, ugliness.

Marcel took her hand in both of his. "Finish the story," he murmured.

"Last Sunday, when I was having a pretty time posing, he hanged himself from a tree."

His hand grasped hers tighter.

"He had kicked over his basket beneath him and had used the cord that strapped it to him as his noose." Her voice cracked. "In his coat they found a photograph of a beautiful woman in jewels and finery."

"Even ragpickers are capable of noble love."

"That's right good of you to say."

He drew her head onto his shoulder, and what she'd been holding in all week gave way and she dropped a tear or two until she remembered her part in it. She raised up.

"They buried him the day before yesterday. A fine coffin they pinched from the morgue of Montmartre. I did the flowers. The usual white chrysanthemums weren't good enough. I threw in my week's wage and added white roses, white carnations, white fleurs-de-lis. Père l'Epingle deserved everything clean at last."

"I'm sure they were beautiful."

"I was all to bits over it the whole week. Lost my rudder, I guess you could say."

"Perhaps I can make you forget for a while."

"That you have, milord." Milord, not Marcel. To keep it business.

"Shall we take a walk?" he asked.

They strolled along a gravel path. She darted to a swing hanging from a tree, stood on it, and he made it go. At every swing toward him, she lightened up a little. He tried to kiss her on each pass, but she teased him by turning her face away at the last instant.

"Smile at me, milord. Better than that. *Voilà,* like that." He caught her and lifted her off the swing and took his pleasure with a kiss that sucked the sadness out of her.

They sat on a bench overhung with vines. "I came tonight," he said, "thinking I would just watch how other people lived. You've taken me quite by surprise. Is your name really Angèle?"

"Yes."

"It's too perfect. May I ask your surname?"

"Montmartre. Surnames mean you belong to a family or a man. All I belong to is Montmartre."

She let him kiss and touch, and she'd be a liar if she said she wasn't enjoying it.

They went out onto the avenue. Here was the moment. By the code of Mabille, he could just drop her a coin and disappear. That would be fine with her, but maybe she could mine a little deeper. Such a sweet cuss he was. She could give him another quarter of an hour. His elbow pressed her hand against his side to keep her walking—down avenue Montaigne past the dark boutiques, to stand above the Seine on Pont d'Alma. It was a signal, a turn in the evening. He was not going to hustle off with her to a *hôtel de passe,* which made her breathe more easily.

The gas lanterns along the four arches of Pont des Invalides upriver cast golden lights in the water like sea creatures wiggling with life. Music from a floating café concert rolled softly toward them. Below them, the stone head of a Zouave on the bridge pier honored their role in the Crimean War. She thought of the Zouave at Mabille. Mighty glad she was that she didn't have to endure that bounder to earn her trap money for Auguste.

A crowded pleasure boat, a side-wheeler, tipped down its steam pipe and slid under the bridge in the darkness. Murmurings from below came up to them.

"Do you think the people on that boat are slipping through their lives without noticing how excruciatingly beautiful everything is?" he asked.

"My, you are a sentimental one."

He lifted her chin. *"Au plaisir de vous revoir,"* he said, a wish to see her again.

Now, that was something else again.

"Will you come to the Mabille next Saturday?" he asked.

"I can't say."

"Is it too much to ask that a fine evening be repeated?"

"Yes. A body can't do things over again."

"In your words, I've been 'all to bits' for too long. Tonight was the first night I attempted to find my rudder." His hand petted her cheek as if she were a cat. "A thing is never cherished so much as when a man lacks it."

"Or a woman."

"I know you're probably expecting me to take you somewhere. Is it so terrible that a man tired of grief steps slowly into life again?"

Now she understood what the black border on his white handkerchief meant. A brave fellow, to enter the stream of life again. He pressed another coin into her palm. She didn't look, but it was bigger in her hand than the others. It had to be a Napoléon III fifty-franc piece. He'd come prepared. Not conscience money. Sadness money. The story must have twanged his strings.

"To keep you off the streets until Saturday, just in case."

She'd made no promise, but she wouldn't mind it.

He kissed her forehead. "It's nice to think I'm of some use."

"For me too. A tit for a tat."

He hailed a horse cab and paid the driver to take her home.

CHAPTER TWENTY-SEVEN

Allons! To Work!

U nder the maple tree, Auguste watched Angèle's eyes flash with zest.

"Close your eyes and open your hand," she said.

"But then I can't see you." Or Aline as soon as she was on the bridge, he thought, but he obeyed and Angèle dropped into his hand two three-franc écus, then a louis.

"If this came from where I think it did, it won't make me happy."

"Never no matter, that." She dropped another louis.

"I don't like to think—"

"Shush up. Give me a clean hand." He clenched his fist and she forced it open and dropped the Napoléon III.

He opened his eyes. "Angèle! No! I can't accept this." He tried to give it back but she put her arms behind her and backed up against a tree.

"It's my painting too."

He wasn't so bourgeois yet that he couldn't appreciate Angèle's brand of lusty nobility. And she wasn't so loose that she would do this for anyone else. She probably reveled in doing it for him.

"Slice it however you like, it wasn't earned the way you think. It was *given* fair and square at Jardin Mabille without having to use a *hôtel de passe*. Such a good sort, he was. So don't take the shine off the apple. It's good for a woman to know what she's worth once in a while. It perks me right up to think I'm of some use."

He felt his resistance melt into gratitude. "You've given me something no one else could do."

"Pocket it quick. Antonio's coming."

Antonio leapt down the steps from the footbridge. "Did you get a new model or is *l'enfante terrible* coming back?"

Auguste grinned. "You'll have to wait and see."

"Aha! That means there's someone new."

In a few minutes Pierre and Paul arrived. Pierre held up a bottle of anisette. "A peace offering," he said.

"No need, but we'll enjoy it."

They sat on the lower terrace and drank the anisette until Charles and Jules came. Still no Aline. No Ellen, and without Ellen, he had no hope to see Émile again. When Gustave and Raoul arrived in their boats, Auguste sent everyone off for a sail. He paced the bank and crossed the bridge and came back to help out on the dock—something enjoyable to keep himself occupied. Couples and families rented yoles, young men rented *triplettes, périssoires,* or monotypes with one sail. *Coucou, Lutin, Mouche, Sans Souci*—one after another the boats went out, about twenty of them. Still no Aline.

Père Fournaise brought the steam excursion launch out of the boat garage and sounded the whistle. He'd mounted a banner prow to stern: *Fêtes Nautiques, le 5 septembre.* Auguste helped the ladies and children board and Alphonse managed the lines. Fournaise rang out a tune as the launch pulled away.

"You're providing an important service here," Auguste said.

In the channel, two jousting barques with eight rowers each bore down on each other, the jousters standing on their platforms with lances in position. One jouster was sent flying into the water.

"That's Hugo who knocked him off," Alphonse said. "We call him The Bull. He'll be my strongest competitor."

Auguste squeezed Alphonse's biceps. "Then what do they call you? The Elephant?"

"Hippopotamus. My first name is really Hippolyte."

"I'll put my money on you, so you'd better get out and practice, but not today. I need you for positioning the new model in front of you."

"Next week. I'll practice next week."

"There are only two weeks left."

And still holes in his painting. Still the problem of the flying terrace and the thirteen figures. He rolled and lit a cigarette and took a few puffs.

Alphonsine was chatting with the group under the arbor, the friends of the sailboat *Le Palais*. When their meal was served, she came over to him.

"I felt sure she'd come," he said.

"Go upstairs. Paint something. I'll watch."

"You don't know what she looks like." He snuffed out his cigarette.

"Oh yes I do. I know a Renoir girl when I see one."

"You're a Renoir girl, top to toe."

"What's her name?"

"Aline Charigot. She may have a little dog with her."

Upstairs he rolled the easel out onto the terrace. He had repainted Alphonsine's face and Alphonse's hat during the week which made him feel a little better. Light. Ah, light. Pure radiance. It made the river lavender and pale ocher and aqua and white. It made the sailboats shimmer. It made the grassy hillock on the opposite bank glow a yellow-green. It softened the lines of the railroad bridge and made everything vibrate with life. With this brilliance of heaven come down to earth, how could he have thought to abandon this painting?

The *Nana* and the *Iris* returned and everyone came upstairs.

"Eek! What happened to my face?" Angèle said in mock horror. "And my hat! After all my bargaining at the Marché du Temple!"

"You'll get it back," he said. "I need you to turn more toward Gustave."

"If I looked at him any closer, I might devour him."

"I'll give you your eyes and mouth back today too. Don't worry."

Louise came upstairs. "Shall I have Anne serve the entrée now? It's *terrine de caille* with radishes."

He looked toward the bridge. "Can you wait awhile?"

"If I wait too much longer, the dining room will fill and she'll have to put you off and that will cut into your painting time."

"Just a little longer."

"The man doesn't know what's good for him," Louise muttered to Alphonsine. "Paint the fruit today. It won't last," she said on the way down.

"Another anisette all around?" Pierre said and began pouring.

"Who is this girl we're holding lunch for?" Paul asked. "Anyone I know?"

"Maybe." He didn't want to talk about her in case she didn't show up.

"Maybe she'll bring a man to be our fourteenth," Pierre said.

"You said she might bring a dog?" Alphonsine gestured subtly to a middle-aged woman all decked out in a mauve dress weighty with ruffles promenading with a bulldog on a leash. A child chased a duck right in the dog's way and the dog let out a deep bark. The child screamed and ran off, but the duck just waddled on methodically down the bank and into the water.

"No, Alphonsine, that's not her."

Alphonsine giggled. "Lucky for us."

Another barking commotion erupted at the steps of the footbridge. The lady tried to hold back her bulldog and, on the end of a little terrier's leash, Aline tugged and shouted, "Jacques Valentin Aristide, mind your manners."

The little dog kept up his ferocious yapping and lunging at the bulldog until the big dog backed away.

Auguste leapt down the stairs and bumped into Anne. "You can serve the quail now," he said as he ran outside.

Four leaping steps took him to Aline. "You gave me a scare, you know."

"I'm sorry. Jacques has a shrill bark when he gets riled up."

"I meant when you didn't come and didn't come."

Color rose to her cheeks. "I'm sorry about that too. I would have come sooner if I'd known how to do buttonholes."

"You mean you . . . ?" He watched her pirouette, showing the drape in back, pins everywhere. "The dress of a *canotière* through and through. You look like a picture, except for one thing. You rode third class, on the open-air deck. You've got specks of soot—"

"Oh, no! After all my good washing." She stamped her foot.

He took out his handkerchief, dipped it in the river, and dabbed it on her cheeks and forehead. It reminded him of Alphonsine washing his face. No doubt she was watching this from the terrace.

"There. All clean."

He turned toward the restaurant. Ten heads in a row inclined toward them like tenpins, watching. Twenty hands gripped the railing.

Aline scooped up the dog in her arm and they went upstairs. Everyone was awkwardly silent, staring at her until Auguste, raising her hand, said, "*Messieurs-dames,* I present Aline Charigot, our new model and friend."

Everyone welcomed her at once. Jules pulled out a chair for her.

"And our second new friend, Jacques . . ." Auguste added.

"Jacques Valentin Aristide d'Essoyes sur l'Ource," Aline announced.

"A mighty big name," Gustave said, "for a mighty small dog."

"But mighty is as mighty does," Aline said.

"A toast." Charles held up his glass. "To Mademoiselle Aline. Savior of the painting."

Pierre refilled their glasses, and everyone chorused, "To Aline." Aline's peachy cheeks turned rosy.

"*Que le tableau vive!*" Angèle shouted. "*Vive le tableau!*"

"*Vive le tableau!*" everyone shouted, including Jacques, in his own way.

"*Vive nous,*" Alphonsine added.

Louise and Anne swept in with the quail terrine, and Aline said, "I'm so glad I got here on time." She took a thick slice and began eating before everyone was served. "Excellent, madame."

Louise folded her hands across her ribs. "Ah!" she said and left.

"You should have started this painting with her a month ago," Paul said.

"I know. I'm sorry I didn't."

"Did you have to go to the country to find such a wholesome lady?" Raoul asked.

Auguste and Aline looked at each other and laughed.

"No, I only had to go twenty steps across the street from my studio."

"You have the distinct accent of a Burrrrgundian, lady," Raoul said.

"I come from Essoyes, just across the line in Champagne. My family owned a vineyard. Paris may be the jewel of France, but Champagne is the heart."

"*Huée!* Listen to her roll those *r*'s," Gustave said.

"Give me one week with her and I'll have her speaking like a Parisian," Angèle said.

Auguste chortled. "You'll have her speaking like you!"

"Maybe I don't want to speak like a Parisian," Aline said. "Maybe I want to speak like myself."

Deftly she broke off a morsel and lowered it to the dog. Gustave noticed and smiled. Watching his friends welcome Aline, Auguste saw that there was a greater harmony than that of color. Now *everyone* was there for him.

When Anne was about to clear the platters, Aline held up her fork with a "Tut tut," and took another slice. "Tell Madame it was too good to pass up."

He exchanged delighted looks with Alphonsine, knowing this would puff up Louise.

Evidently Louise wanted to get another look at Aline because she served the main dish herself, announcing, *"Côtelettes d'agneau à la forestière,"* and placing one platter right in front of Aline.

"Oh, là là! With mushrooms, potato balls, and bacon," Aline said. "It smells delicious, madame."

Louise flicked Auguste on the shoulder. "You can bring her here anytime."

"If you had come earlier, we would have been pleased to take you out for a sail," Raoul said.

"Oh, I wanted to, but my buttons and hems wanted sewing. As it is, I'm all itchy with pins," she said and dropped a morsel of lamb in front of Jacques Valentin's nose which he gobbled up before it reached the floor.

"You mean to say that you made that dress by yourself?" Angèle said.

"I know it's plain, but Auguste told me I needed a dark blue dress and I didn't have one."

"Child, you should have gone to the secondhand clothing stalls in the Marché du Temple near Les Halles. It's the saving grace of the Jenny l'Ouvrière class. Why, most every thread that touches my lily-white skin is a reach-me-down from rue du Temple."

"You mean rue du Crime?"

"The same," Angèle said.

"I thought it wasn't safe."

"Oh, kitten, they only call it that because of the crime dramas in all the theaters along that street. Don't let it scare you none. Bargaining with the *marchands* is an art. Some merchants think people are dumb enough to believe them when they say, 'Would you look at this pink satin gown, now. It was worn at Versailles only a fortnight ago by the Duchesse de Poulemouillé.' It's a game. You oughtn't to care, if it's a right pretty frock."

The color went out of Aline's face. "All this work and worry for nothing!" she wailed, collapsed a little, and let out an "Ouch!"

"Your dress is lovely," he said quickly, "and I greatly appreciate you making it. And suffering through pinpricks too."

"Don't go at night," Angèle went on. "Gaslight makes everything look better. You look at it the next day and it's a rag. Let me take you so you don't get lost in the maze. There are five alleys of frippery and another dozen of hats. You can't reach for them yourself, though. You say to the *marchande,* all polite just like you were on rue Saint Honoré, '*S'il vous plaît, madame,* would you take that off the peg? Let's have a squint at it.' Most like it'll set you back six francs, but Mesdames Pauline of boulevard des Capucines and Zulma of Millefleurs on the rue de la Paix won't even hand you one for a try-on for less than thirty."

"Oh, I forgot about a hat!"

"It goes like this," Angèle said. "'Here's a sweet little duck of a white velvet toque for seven francs fifty,' one *marchande* said. After my act of hemming and hawing, I slapped four in her hand and that's what you see on my head this very minute."

"Does it make a difference that I don't have a hat?" Aline asked Auguste.

"You should have a *canotier* for the painting." Auguste looked from Aline to Alphonsine.

"I've got an extra one you can use," Alphonsine said.

"There. See? No need to worry," he said.

She tipped her head at him. "You look a far sight better than the last time I saw you." She turned to Gustave across from her. "He looked roughed up awful on Tuesday morning."

"That reminds me. Angèle, you don't happen to know a fellow by the name of Jimmy, do you?" Auguste asked.

"You mean Jemmy? Jemmy and Picklock. Picklocking is their talent."

"So is mugging. I came into their acquaintance up at place du Tertre, and stumbled down the Butte with an empty wallet."

"I didn't think they would sink so low. Wait till I see them. I'll sic Aline's pup on them to tear flesh from bone."

"Actually, you already saved me from a worse fate. They recognized me as your friend, and left me beaten in the gutter."

"Another sign that the painting lives," Paul said triumphantly.

It would be more likely to if he got to work. He barely lived through the meal, and then Alphonsine served wine-soaked cakes called *galettes* in the shape of pinwheels like the ones sold under the windmill in Montmartre. He knew why. To remind him of his success with *Bal au Moulin de la Galette*. To urge him on.

"*Merci,* Alphonsine. You're a true *collaboratrice.*" He hoped she knew that what he meant was, *I love you for thinking of this.*

After the dessert Aline lifted Jacques Valentin onto the table and practically kissed him, which shocked Charles into a paroxysm of Russian epithets. Amusing to see Charles unable for once to control his surroundings.

A delicious little being, this Aline. A sprite. He imagined taking those first luscious strokes that would put her in Circe's place. He couldn't stand it any longer. "*Allons!* To work!"

When they assumed their poses, he watched her fluff up her skirt to show the poufs drawn across her hip. She winced when a pin pricked her. The drape was the only decorative detail on her dress, and the borrowed *canotier* was plainer than plain too. He adjusted her shoulder so that it was in line with Alphonse's hand on the railing. It was the first time he touched her and it felt momentous, that little bone on the top of her shoulder under the fabric.

He sketched in her shoulder, arm, and torso. Her cool blue dress showed well against the warm washes of pink, lavender, and pale ocher of Alphonse's singlet, and her turned-up nose was well defined in profile against his belly. His brush flew from palette to canvas by instinct, from Aline's face to Angèle's and back to Aline's, from her dress to Alphonsine's skirt to Charles's coat and back to her.

There was only one thing wrong. The dog kept distracting her so she couldn't keep still. Trying to catch her when she resumed the pose after each interruption was as irritating as trying to catch Circe. Was there some jinx on the chair?

When a crowd of people came back on the launch, carousing on the lower terrace, the dog went into a fit of barking and Aline had to hold him in her lap to quiet him. When that didn't work she stood him on the table cooing to him until he calmed down. It was an endearing pose and would make an appealing genre painting in and of itself, even if a tad sentimental.

He had sworn after painting Madame Charpentier with one of her children sitting on their snoring hound that he'd never paint another dog. Confound it. That just might be the solution.

"Can you hold him like that on his hind legs?"

"Depends. Will he get a model's fee?"

"I think he's already eaten it," Gustave said.

"I'll try. What if he piddles? It would be a shame, such a nice cloth."

"Just watch him." He had a thought that amused him. "Figures, still life, landscape, *and* an animal! Zola, eat your hat!" he bellowed.

He liked the way the tips of her fingers were buried under his fur to hold his wiggling body, like fingers thrust into a man's hair. And her interaction with the dog gave Gustave something to adore. The composition was working better now, with sight lines connecting people. He painted in a fever of excitement until he realized he was holding his breath. He put down his brush and palette and gazed at her. He caught Alphonsine looking at him instead of at Raoul.

It was too confusing, this woman thing. He called for a break.

"I—I think Jacques Valentin needs to . . ." Aline hurried the pup downstairs, saying, "Ouch! Ouch!" on the way.

Pierre said in a low voice, "A tasty morsel, that one. I can see it now. You're going to make love to her with your brush."

"As I do with all the women I paint."

CHAPTER TWENTY-EIGHT

An Errand in Paris

After the light faded and Auguste couldn't paint anymore, Alphonsine suggested that they go to Le Bal des Canotiers. "Papa can take us in the launch," she said, knowing he'd enjoy being Admiral of the River. Everyone except Charles agreed to go. A riverside *guinguette* was too rustic for him. Under Papa's banner advertising the Fêtes Nautiques, they sang "Les Canotiers" on the way. Papa kept time with the steam whistle, which set Jacques Valentin to yipping.

The small orchestra was already playing. They walked through the rose garden and found two free tables under an arcade of flowering vines. Gustave ordered Asti Spumante for everyone, a musty, sparkling wine.

"I like it here," Auguste said. "Women don't wear corsets."

"But they smoke cigars," Antonio said.

When a mazurka, a ladies' choice, was announced, Alphonsine hesitated a moment too long. Aline asked Auguste, which was only natural, and he followed her like a hooked fish. Alphonsine turned to Gustave who was already grinning, waiting to be asked. She felt lightheaded as they spun around, his arm firm on her waist. They bumped into Angèle and Antonio, and changed partners. Later, Aline danced the *chahut* with Raoul, imitating his wild, tipping steps and crazy kicks, ending with a military salute. Everyone stopped to watch.

All the men took turns dancing with Aline, while Auguste sat back and watched, swinging Jacques Valentin's leash in time to the music. Joy was written all over his face. "It's her initiation into the group," he said to no one in particular.

Yes. *Nous* included Aline now.

When Paul was waltzing with Aline, Auguste said, "She barely touches the ground. They were made to dance together. I'd just step on her toes. Look how he's adoring her. That would make a fine painting."

"What would you call it?" Alphonsine asked.

"*A Dance in the Country,* of course."

She could see it would make a lovely painting, but she was a girl of the country too. *Nous* was turning sour. A moment later, she was ashamed for thinking so.

The evening ended with a farandole in which the string of dancers, holding hands, skipped between the tables and around the trees. Pierre and Angèle held up their arms to make an arch and Aline threaded the needle and came around to make a circle, ending with three hops to the traditional, *"Oui, oui, oui!"* only Aline said, "Ouch, ouch, ouch!" which made everyone laugh.

They left on the small steam ferry boldly named *The Great Eastern* because it plied the east channel to the rail station in Rueil. The *pon-pon-pon* of the pistons pounded in her head. They lingered at the station, and those staying waved from the platform to those leaving, who waved back from the train windows as if they were going on a long voyage. Alphonsine felt the way one feels just before an ending.

"Take care of our ladies," Raoul shouted.

On the walk across the bridge to their sailboats, Raoul and Gustave couldn't stop talking about Aline. All afternoon and evening she had heard it, and had watched everyone watch Aline. It was too much. She flicked the back of her hand against Raoul's shoulder. "You're like a pack of schoolboys."

The next day rain pelted the river. Alphonsine ran out to the garden to save some roses from ruin and arranged them in a vase. Since there were no customers in the dining room, Auguste set up a small canvas.

He let out a long sigh. "It's relaxing. It doesn't need the tense concentration that painting models does."

"Oh, go on. You can't tell me that you were tense yesterday. You were painting like a child plays."

"But I wasn't reckless. When I paint flowers, I can be reckless. I can make a petal have this tint or that, go this way or that, however it suits me. I can spread pigment in swirls, or dab it, or whisk it, like a feather. I can even smear it on with my finger if I want to. Working on this will keep my hand loose so I don't make the big painting too tight."

He mixed red with white on his palette. "Such pleasure paint gives. This will be for my mother."

"Guy was right. Your eyes do see *la vie en rose.* Now."

By midafternoon he'd finished and borrowed an umbrella to take the small painting to his mother in Louveciennes even though the paint was wet. It seemed a strange time to do that, walking in the rain, sheltering the painting with the umbrella, but when he felt like doing something, he did it.

The next morning, despite the possibility of more rain, Alphonsine had to go to Paris. Putting off her errand any longer might make her intention fade. As she rode on the train, she knew exactly where she would go, if she could forget her own wishes enough to do an act of self-denying love. But first, since she hadn't been to Paris in a while, she thought she might go to see the hat shop. She took rue du Faubourg Saint Honoré, a street she loved for the ironwork of its balconies, like black lace, she had told Louis. Or was it Alexander, who worked in iron? At place de Ternes, she saw the café where she and Louis went on summer evenings for a *digestif* after dinner. In winter, they ordered *petite marmite,* a soup-stew she loved, served in an earthenware pot. She felt no sadness at the memories. It seemed as though it had all happened to someone else. How good that her love for Paris had not been spoiled.

On avenue des Ternes, she passed the *boucherie* that had rationed horsemeat during the Siege, the sheet music store where the pianist worked. And there was the stoop, the door in the alcove, but the sign said *Jacques Verniot, Épicerie Fine.* The window displayed jars of jam, tins of pâté, olive oil, grenadine, wines. Her eye passed over them quickly and went to the stone floor of the alcove. She remembered the stain, a concave hexagon, the shape of France, but saw no trace of it. She opened the door and looked down. No stain on the wooden floor inside either. History had been scrubbed away.

"*Bonjour, madame,*" she heard.

She greeted the man behind the condiment counter wearing a daisy in his buttonhole, and imagined a loving moment when his wife put it there.

"*S'il vous plaît,* monsieur, how long has this shop been here?"

"Just four years, madame."

Then the man who bought the hat shop after the war had kept it only half a dozen years. She had hoped to see the same display tables she had dusted every day, the same hat stands, but that was foolish. Things change.

"Why do you ask?"

"My husband and I had a hat shop here once."

"Monsieur Lequeux?"

"No. Before him. *Papillon et fils.* Before the war."

He smiled kindly at her, with the crinkles of his pale gray eyes more than with his mouth, and invited her to have a look around. The floor still creaked in the back left corner where Louis had his desk. The sound filled her with him, a pleasant feeling, not a sad one.

If the musician still lived above the shop, she would take him something. She surveyed shelves of syrups, chutneys of exotic fruits, spices, foie gras, tins of macaroons and madeleines, olives from Provence, honey from Languedoc, fruit compotes from Gascogne, mustard from Dijon, caviar from the Aquitaine, a wall of sausages from Auvergne. Madeleines. She'd gone to La Madeleine the day the Prussian left. She would give the musician madeleines.

"Do you know if an old musician still lives above the shop?"

"I'm sorry. I don't know."

"Do you ever hear a piano?"

"No."

It was too bad. It would have given her a reason for coming. Still, it was hugely satisfying, this abundance of fine food right where she and the soldier had survived on rat broth and horsemeat morsels. At least on one level, France had recovered.

"You have beautiful displays. It's a fine shop," she said.

"*Merci.*"

She wanted to buy something for the models' luncheon. Something entirely luxurious, something that spoke of regained joy. She stopped at a display of chocolates under glass. *Les Bouchons de Bordeaux.* Chocolate corks filled with cognac. They'd love them, but Auguste would know a deeper meaning. Corks in the current that carried him on.

She bought two boxes, gave the shop one last look, and knew she didn't need to come here again. She opened her umbrella and stepped out into light rain. The paving stones gave off a sheen. Paris was polished and fresh.

Where next? She ought to go to the Marché du Temple to do the errand she'd come for, but not yet. Ah, she knew. The Louvre.

At the end of the Salon Carré, an enormous painting shouted at her to come closer. *The Marriage Feast at Cana* by Veronese, one of the artists he had mentioned. Here was his inspiration. The end of a sumptuous meal, with grapes, goblets, even a little dog on the table. Did Auguste know that? They were eating sugared fruits. She would buy some for their last luncheon. Nineteen centuries ago, this feast. She felt part of something timeless.

She went in search of the other painters he'd mentioned, and in the eighteenth-century gallery she found a painting by Watteau called *Embarkation to Cythera.* The information plaque explained that it depicted a *fête galante,* people on their way to spend the day on the isle of Cythera, called the Isle of Love. Near a statue of Venus, couples were dallying under the trees, and cupids floated above them. She sucked in her breath. Chatou was the modern-day Cythera! And she was hostess. In another painting in the same setting, a woman was swinging on a swing under a tree. It gave her an idea: two swings under the maple trees along the bank.

She looked out the window and saw that the rain had stopped. If she was going to do what she had come for, she'd better do it now when she felt her role most keenly. It would require a generosity of spirit she didn't know if she had, but it was for his painting. She had seen one man's dream of an airy marvel die. Now she could help to make another man's airy marvel live, more beautifully. She left the Louvre at a clipped pace, still not knowing if she would betray the painting or betray herself.

She passed the vegetable stalls of Les Halles, sparse at this hour, and slowed as she approached the Marché du Temple. In the maze of narrow alleys, she found the frippery stalls where she used to buy millinery supplies to decorate hats for the shop. The future flashed before her—Auguste painting Aline dancing with Paul at Bal des Canotiers, both men adoring her all the more in the hat that she, the hostess of the isle of Cythera, had decorated for her. If she had earned any grace for loving France's enemy as herself, giving a gift only to show how good and generous she was to a rival would diminish that grace. She would make the thing, but when the moment came to give it, she wasn't sure if she could.

There was Madame Tiret with a feather bird in her hair, so squat she could barely see over her piles of silk flowers and feathers. She had to use a hooked stick to get the bolts of lace stacked on shelves behind her.

"Do you remember me?" Alphonsine asked. "I used to buy ribbons and flowers from you and Monsieur Tiret." The woman looked at her curiously. "A long time ago. Monsieur Tiret used to call me *la dame aux roses.*"

"Ah, yes. He liked you because you looked over everything and always ended up buying roses."

"Along with other things. Please tell him hello from me."

"I would if I could. He was executed in Père Lachaise Cemetery."

"The Commune!" She imagined them lined up against the cemetery wall, and then crumpling. "He was always kind to me."

It shook her to hear this, but Madame didn't blink. She told her as though the wound had closed and the scar was only a faint shadow. She understood now, after seeing what had been the hat shop, how that could be. So much of life we can't control, she thought. We must accept the cork we are and stay afloat, and bob gaily when we can.

She picked out a meter of tulle to gather up around the hat, three silk poppies, red-orange with black centers for the front, for gaiety, and three small white roses for the back, for remembrance of Monsieur Tiret.

"These will make a fine hat to set off your pretty face," Madame said, wrapping them in newspaper.

"It's not for me. But it is for a pretty face, even prettier now."

Chapter Twenty-nine

Aux Folies-Bergère

In the steamy basement of the Folies-Bergère, Ellen stepped out of the dressing room she shared with Charlotte, her substitute who had made it possible for her to model on Sundays. Now it was her turn to help Charlotte, even though her plan was risky. The sooner she began, the sooner Charlotte would be taken care of and might be able to come back to work before Auguste finished his painting. She just had to be careful about whose help she asked for. She knocked on the Egyptian dancer's door, but since Mademoiselle was being dressed in her twelve-twelve, twelve meters of veils and twelve pounds of bangles, spangles, metal breast cups, chains, anklets, and toe rings, Ellen told the dresser she'd come back later.

She went to Désirée and Clotilde's cell, the dancers representing the Loire and the Rhône in her mimodrama, *The Rivers of France.* She closed the door behind her and said quietly, "I'm gathering a collection for Charlotte."

"How is she?" Désirée asked.

"Not well. Complications. Pains and bleeding."

"Ah, rid of one problem but cursed with another," Clotilde muttered. "Did they use soap or wormwood?"

"Both," Ellen replied. "And then they made her run around the inner courtyard to bring it on, until she fainted."

"Little ninny," said Clotilde.

"It's true, then," Désirée said, "the rumor that those buildings in the Batignolles were designed with inner courtyards just for women in trouble."

"She can be sewn up if she goes to a hospital," Clotilde said.

"She doesn't have a lover to pay?" Désirée asked.

"Apparently not one who covers his liberties with coin," Ellen said.

Désirée gave four francs. Clotilde shot her cellmate a scoffing look, and dug in her drawstring bag until she found a five franc coin. She dropped it on Désirée's four francs so that it made a solid clink. Ellen snickered. Competition boiled in the Folies' corridors.

"This is against the rules," Clotilde said.

Ellen gave them both a sharp look. "I know. And I know you have no reason to snitch."

Désirée held up her hands as if to show they were clean. *"D'accord."*

Ellen went on to the dancers representing the Seine, the Rhine, and the Dordogne, saving Charlotte's reputation by saying she had a miscarriage. Then she started on the other mimes, Sun, Moon, Star, and La Duchesse d'Amboise, and the Greek Goddesses, Euphorie and Eurythmie, who gave her five each, but her time ran out. She had to get in costume, a brown rag of the Ferryman's Daughter. Thirty-six francs. It was a start, but she'd hoped for larger donations. The more people she had to involve, the more chance of some telltale opening her mouth. She lifted the cracked floor tile, hid the money, and put Charlotte's chair in front of it draped with Charlotte's soiled silk wrapper. She applied clown white to her face and overlaid that with pink rouge, exaggerated eyes, and cupid's bow mouth, then applied the white to her arms and hands, and waited for the caller to come for her.

When she got to the wings, the overture to the mimodrama had already begun and the rivers were dancing. On cue she stepped onto the stage and transformed herself into the poor Ferryman's Daughter. Her father forced her to be a pickpocket, but she fell in love with the Distinguished Traveler from whom she was supposed to steal, and ran away with him. He took her on escapades to all the rivers of France. On a Rhine barge, the Prussian Braggart asked for vin d'Alsace. Stealthily, she contrived to serve him vinegar. At the Roman temple at the source of the Seine, a spring called Sequana, she was made to think that her homespun dress had become a golden gown. On the Loire, the Distinguished Traveler

took her to a ball in the Chateau d'Amboise. At the Rhône delta, the
Cowboy of the Camargue carried her off on a wild horseback ride, and
the Distinguished Traveler who loved her was left in misery.

She danced and swooned and expressed every emotion of love and
delight with her body and performed witticisms with her hands, but
the people in the loges aimed their opera glasses at each other, and the
swarms in the *promenoirs* beyond the orchestra seats were too busy flirting to appreciate her. If only she could spill out words to reach them.
Words that would shine and sparkle. Funny words, brilliant words,
immortal words. As a mime, she could act her heart out and it wouldn't
matter. The people of Paris came to the Folies for something else.

"Lousy house tonight," she muttered to a stagehand in the wings,
angry instead at the constraints of mime. Alone for a moment in the
dark, she clenched her greasy white fists. Why was it that what we
couldn't have was sweet beyond measure? Words, for example, or Sunday afternoons along the real Seine with friends, or untangled love, or
peace of mind. Especially peace of mind.

She descended the narrow iron stairway from stage level to the cells
just as the Cossack dancers in red pants and black boots were going up,
taking all the room. She bent backward over the railing so they wouldn't
brush against her white arms and swear at her if her greasepaint came
off on them. In the corridor, Bruno, the knife thrower, leered at her and
backed her against the wall with his sword. He lifted her skirt with its
point and barked out a hoarse cackle. What a reptile! She splayed her
fingers right in front of his face, mimicked his laugh, ducked under his
sword and escaped to her cell.

Slumped on the chair before her dressing table, she slathered on cold
cream for the nightly ordeal of wiping off her hands, arms, and face.
Her calendar stared back at her. Six days late. No. Seven. At this point,
she'd welcome a cramp as a blessing. Seeing Charlotte in such pain and
hearing every sordid detail of what she'd gone through had sent her
into a slough of worry.

A tap at her door made her jump. It was Émile, the stage door concierge whom she'd brought to Chatou, the one-night lover, the one per-

son she didn't want to see. In the mirror, she saw her black eyeliner smeared into a gray streak down her cheek. She looked like a ghoul. So what? It was only Émile.

"Did you go see her?" he asked.

"Yes."

"Well? How is she?"

She kept working on her face. "Feverish."

"Will she get better?"

"If she goes to a doctor."

"Will she?"

It was irritating, how he pressed her about Charlotte every day.

"Only if I collect enough money and take her. I've got to get back to Auguste's painting, so I'm hoping—"

"You're only doing it for that reason."

"That's not true."

With a feeling in her chest like she'd swallowed a grape whole, she remembered her promise to Auguste and Monsieur Ephrussi that she would try to bring Émile again to solve the problem of the missing fourteenth person. Seeing him standing there with his mouth hanging open like a hound dog stopped the question in her throat.

"Will you meet me at Café Tortoni when I get off?" he asked.

"I'm too tired."

"You've said that all week."

"I've got my acting lesson in the mornings, and I'm rehearsing a new pantomime in the afternoons. It's exhausting. I have to fall flat like a board, and squirm along the ground for cover whenever I hear drums and cymbals imitating the Prussian guns, and that's supposed to get a laugh. I hate it—the idea of it, and doing it. Do you know how hard it is to do a dead fall a dozen times an hour?"

Émile came toward her and wiped under her chin with a sponge. She clenched her teeth. He backed her against her Sarah Bernhardt photograph on the wall and pressed himself against her. She pushed him away. "I have some worries, Émile. I need some time. And I've got to do more collecting tonight."

With a cocky look on his face, he opened the door and swept his hand through the air like an usher. "Then go, Mademoiselle Charité. If you change your mind, you know where to find me."

She brushed past him. If she collected enough to ensure Charlotte good treatment at the charity hospital, it might relieve her enough that her monthly would come.

She went to the Egyptian's dressing room. She didn't know her name. In the cells, no one knew each other's real names. They existed in a smoky underground barracks where they knew each other's stage names and cell numbers and costumes and acts—Paradise of Forbidden Pleasure, Famous Courtesans of History, Nine Naughty Nuns. She went to the Spanish Twins, Carmen and Carlotta, with oiled black hair wound into identical knots, and made them swear to secrecy, which they did in unison. She went to Mademoiselle Flambeau, so flamboyant that even the Cossacks made way for her. She found her crying, her Japanese kimono falling open revealing everything.

"Oh, that Monsieur Sari! I could scream! He changed my act and now I have to wear a sequined dress that covers my breasts. And on top of that, my lover has exhausted me."

Ellen gave her a big sigh. "When it's bad, it's bad all around." Then she told her about Charlotte.

Mademoiselle rummaged in her alabaster jewel box for coins, muttering, "Poor child, poor child."

Ellen went to Mademoiselle Zénobie, the lead *cancaneuse* who currently had the glad eye of Duval, the theater manager. She earned ten times what the chorus girls did, but she only gave three francs, picking them out of her silk purse one at a time and dropping them into her palm as though they were insects. She sprayed absinthe in her mouth from a crystal atomizer and said, "Stupid girl. She should have been more careful."

Ellen cringed, feeling as though the comment was aimed at her. She couldn't do any more tonight. In the corridor on her way out, the mime who played the Distinguished Traveler fell into step with her. At the stage door, Émile gave her a look shot with suspicion.

"Too tired tonight?" he muttered to her as she passed.

On the corner of rue Richer, the mime pressed a ten-franc coin into her hand. "For Charlotte," he said and went off in the opposite direction.

"Who told you?"

"I don't remember," he said over his shoulder.

On Saturday morning Ellen had her *café au lait* and baguette outdoors at Café Saint Jean on place des Abbesses in Montmartre. It was a peaceful haven shaded by chestnut trees near Charlotte's flat. All week she had been collecting. All week she had been counting—money and days. She'd been sleeping fitfully and had arrived at her acting lessons listless and uninspired. Every day Émile had pestered her about Charlotte. Every day the dresser with sly, creeping hands slipped her another franc, keening in an oily voice, "For Charlotte, my kitten," or "For my little mouse." Now it was Saturday, day eleven, and she had no acting class or rehearsal. Across the street in the small triangular park, children were swinging on the swings. Their innocent cries sharpened her worry.

When she mustered the courage, she took the collection to Charlotte, and found her worsened, her skin yellowish.

"Look! Look what I have. *Voilà!*" She poured out the coins onto the quilt.

"What for?" Dazed, Charlotte scooped them up and let them fall.

"For you. To go to a hospital."

Charlotte raised herself up on her elbow. "From whom?"

"Everyone."

"Émile? Did Émile contribute?"

The name stung. His interest in Charlotte stung. His badgering insistence stung. Sordid truth slashed through her like Bruno's sword. What a fool she'd been. What a rat he was.

For a minute she could only look at Charlotte's piteous form beneath the quilt, not at her face. She doubted if she could ever look her in the face again.

"Let's get you washed up."

She supported Charlotte down four flights of stairs and paid a boy with a donkey cart to take them to place Pigalle. Charlotte sat on the edge of the fountain while Ellen hailed several hackneys before one was free to take them to the Hôtel Dieu. It was the charity hospital on the Île de la Cité, caring for the poor since the twelfth century. On Pont Notre Dame, Charlotte looked out the window at the wash barges strung out along the quay. "My mother used to work there," she said. "Two hundred washers work on that *bateau-lavoir,* l'Arche Marion. It's the most prestigious."

Ellen took Charlotte's hand in both of hers. "I'm sure it is."

"And my father worked at the *bateau-lavoir* for the omnibus horses."

On the steps to the Hôtel Dieu, a woman more pitiful than Charlotte with a baby wrapped in her shawl held up her callused palm. Seeing the mother not even raising her eyes from the child gave her a stab of cold fear.

"She sure picked a lousy place to beg," Ellen muttered. She couldn't understand why the woman hadn't stationed herself near the entrance to Notre Dame just adjacent. More likely offerings there.

"Can we give her something?" Charlotte asked.

Ellen dropped her a fifty-centime piece and took Charlotte inside to the cloistered garden and had her sit on a bench while she registered her with an elderly nun at the wicket, paid the donation fee, and gave Charlotte the remaining francs.

"May I go in with her to see that she's settled well?" Ellen asked the nun.

"That's not necessary. We'll take over from here." The nun wrapped Charlotte's hand in the crook of her elbow and led her down a corridor.

Charlotte looked back, her eyes dark with fear. "Will you come back to see me? They'll make me well and then I'll do your part and you can go back to that painter."

"Yes. I'm sure every day you'll get a little better."

"Come soon." Her voice quavered against the peal of the cathedral's chimes.

"I will."

Coming out onto the square, Ellen couldn't avoid the beggar woman with her gaunt cheeks, the baby with crusty blood under his nose. Maybe a baby was the last thing that woman wanted too, at one time, but the look in the mother's sunken eyes told her she would never toss that baby. To think she may have something in common with that poor woman was enough to give her the cramps. She hoped.

She had done what she could for Charlotte, but autumn would be here and gone before that girl could step onto the stage.

There was only so much summer. The end of August already. She could take a little time. She sauntered along the river, crossed the roadway of Pont Neuf, and descended to the leafy point of the island facing downstream like the prow of a ship. It was pleasant and cool with the river very close on three sides of her. On the left, the dark, gold-ribbed dome of the Institut de France housed, among other academies, the Académie Française, which set the standards for language, and therefore literature and theater. As long as she worked only for the Folies, those gold ribs kept her out of the life she longed to live.

Two old men on folding stools were fishing with long cane poles. That is, they were in the act of waiting for a fish. "Have you caught anything yet?" she asked.

One man said, "When I was a boy."

The other man chuckled. "Not yet today. We're waiting."

"One can always hope," she said, turning to gaze at the dome.

Was it only at the end of life that one had the capacity for patience and peaceful relaxation? She was prepared and waiting too. Leaning against a chestnut tree on the very point of the island, she yawned and felt herself go limp, felt her shoulders drop, her arms hang, her mouth slacken, her eyelids half close. She sensed the movement of the water, silken and cool, on both sides of her, the flow through Paris and around a few bends to Chatou. She felt a tightness in her belly squeeze and let go, then the moist loosening. *Grâce à Dieu!* She walked briskly back to the bridge, up the stairs quickly, down and up again, to bring it on, to be sure. She crossed the river to the Gothic Church of Saint Germain l'Auxerrois and thought about how many women since the Middle Ages had prayed behind that rose window for the very same thing she had been waiting for. Yes. It was unmistakable. Relief flooded her.

Through blurry eyes, Paris was beautiful. She loved every kiosk,

every paving stone, every pigeon she passed. The café terraces on boulevard des Italiens were filling, and at Café Tortoni, a waiter was placing pansies in glass bowls on cream-colored tablecloths. *"Charmant,
monsieur,"* she said as she passed. A little girl trotting alongside her
mother bobbed a red balloon bearing the word *Louvre,* an advertisement for the department store, Le Grand Magasin du Louvre. *"Elle est
très jolie,"* Ellen said to the mother, who responded with a smile. Seeing
a little boy playing marbles alone, Ellen crouched, took a marble, and
shot it toward another. It went astray. The boy did the same and his
tapped hers. *"Bravo! Tu es un champion!"* She stood up. Words! She
could say lovely words to all of them, smooth and melodic.

Onstage that night, her arms were fluid with feeling, her hands elo-
quent with love, her fingers alive with new witticisms. She wrenched
applause from the grand horseshoe-shaped theater, took a deeper bow
than usual, and descended the iron steps breathing hard, loving the Folies after all.

The stage manager stopped her in the corridor. He's going to congratulate me, she thought.

"You owe a fine," he said.

Her stomach cramped. "What!"

"For gathering a welfare collection."

"Where is it written? Show me in my contract."

"It's understood as policy. The more people solicited, the larger the
fine."

"How do you know what I'm doing?"

"Some people are loyal to Monsieur Sari."

"Who snitched? Mademoiselle Zénobie? Mademoiselle Flambeau?"

"No."

"The Distinguished Traveler?"

"No."

"Who, then? Émile?"

The manager glanced down the corridor. "Someone of impeccable
honor."

"Émile. He's lower than an ant. That's just personal vendetta. You
go and call Monsieur Sari. I want to hear it from his own lips."

She strode toward her dressing room but stopped at the bulletin board listing fines.

Balthazar Rasmakov, late for performance, 5 francs.
Lulu Lagrange, disturbance in the wings, 2 francs.
Carmen and Carlotta, quarreling during rehearsal, 50 centimes each.
Hyménée Baudouin, indecency onstage, 8 francs.
Ellen Andrée, gathering a collection, 20 francs.

"Twenty francs! That's extortion!"

She flung open the door to her cell and stood a moment stunned and staring. Charlotte's poster of Jeanne Samary, Charlotte's hairbrush wound with her black hair, her own dear dressing table. She removed her makeup quickly and changed into her street clothes.

Behind her, a knock on the doorframe. Monsieur Léon Sari loomed in his black evening dress and ruby studs. "Monsieur Duval tells me you have some objection to the company rules?"

Cold fear shot up from her toes. "I have some objection to a fine imposed for caring about a fellow performer."

"There are reasons for rules."

"You only make it against the rules because you don't want people discussing how stingy you are. If you'd given her a paid leave, I wouldn't have made the collection, and you would have earned some respect around here."

"You're telling me how to run the place? An operation of more than two hundred performers? A little *mimeuse* is presuming to know what's best for the Folies-Bergère?"

If she said one more word, it would send her on a road she might not be ready for. Could she, the daughter of a department store clerk, actually find a place on the legitimate stages of Paris? Her fingernails dug into her palms.

"I know what's humane. And I know what's inhumane. It's inhumane not to help a hard-working, loyal worker when she's in trouble and it's inhumane to prevent people from showing that they care about her and it's inhumane to demand that the *trapézistes* throw their baby in order to give the audience a two-franc thrill and I won't work for such an inhumane man. Not someone who makes a joke of the war either. So that's it. Drop the fine, drop the rule, and let them throw a rubber baby the way they've done before, and I'll work till my heart bursts and you'll never hear a peep from me. Otherwise, you'll have a hole in *The Rivers* come matinee tomorrow."

"Impudent rebel."

"Your choice."

"What's come over you, Ellen? You've never been a problem before."

Hearing him say that threatened to sink her. For five years she had thrived under his guidance.

"You'll be nothing without the Folies."

"Wait till you see me in the Odéon."

Sari grabbed her costume for the Ferryman's Daughter and back-handed Monsieur Duval in the stomach with it. "Get that Blanche girl, that choice piece who dances in Forbidden Pleasure, get her fitted into this and bring her to the practice room. Immediately."

Their patent-leather shoes pounding up the iron stairway rang in her ears.

Trembling, she looked around her dressing room, her second home. She swept her cake white and grease pencils, her cold cream and sponges, her brushes and lipstick into a hatbox. She wrapped her curling iron and spirit lamp and alcohol in a towel and then in her kimono, and stuffed the bundle into her carpetbag with her stage slippers and her autographed picture of Sarah Bernhardt. She rolled up the posters advertising her in *The Rivers of France,* took one last look down the corridor to the iron stairway, and went the other way.

At the stage door, Émile looked smug until he saw all that she was carrying. "What happened?"

"Weasel."

She shouldered the door open herself and stepped out into the dark street.

In a matter of hours, it would be Sunday.

CHAPTER THIRTY

In a Closed Field

Paul buttered his bread and took a thoughtful bite. In an hour, Auguste would be expecting them. He looked around at the Café Nouvelle-Athènes where they always met on Sundays before going out to Chatou. He gripped the cool marble edge of the very table where he'd written the Mardi Gras story. That it should come to this—absurd.

"When was the last time you handled a pistol?" Pierre asked in a low voice, hunched over a letter on the table.

"In Algeria, just after the Prussian War."

Pierre scoffed. "Nine years ago."

"I had a quick hand."

"Then. This is now. I tell you, you're a fool. Can't you pay him off?"

"I tried that last year."

Pierre gulped his *café*. "This has been seething that long?" He pushed away from the table. "I won't have this on my conscience."

"I'm not asking for that. I'm just asking you to go with me."

"Does Auguste know this?"

"Not exactly. I was hoping to arrive only an hour late."

"A fine fix you've gotten yourself into. What's the man's issue?"

It was so petty he hated to recount it. "Her name is Gabrielle," Paul said quietly. "It started with a satiric piece I wrote for *Le Petit Journal* about the behavior of some unnamed women at a masked ball at Mardi Gras. I described their costumes and their methods of keeping their lovers' affections at white heat. One Robert Douvaz took offense, see-

ing his mistress in my remark, this Gabrielle who wore a costume similar to one I had described. I had known her, indiscreetly, on one occasion.
She keeps coming back to me. I beg her not to. She comes anyway, steals
some little thing from me and taunts him with false evidence of her
infidelity to stir his ardor."

"Then you're a dupe."

"Not by choice." Paul ate another bite.

"So you agreed to this encounter?"

"I wouldn't say that. It's just better to have half a chance than be
bludgeoned to death in a Montmartre alley."

"He's threatened that?"

"In a manner of speaking. Several times. Once when I was with
Auguste."

"Then what makes you believe he'll actually do it?"

Paul tapped the parchment. "This is the first written cartel."

Pierre read it again. It was written in flamboyant calligraphy.

Monsieur Paul Lhôte,

Being that you have compromised Mademoiselle Gabrielle Carême
by giving her the lie in the public press, be prepared to engage in an
encounter to justify your words Sunday noon in a closed field at
Résidence Balfour, hard by Epinay-sur-Seine on the road to
Villetaneuse.

Robert Douvaz, Appellant.

"Puh! This is ridiculous!" Pierre blurted. "That article is long forgotten."

"It's just an excuse. He hates me because he thinks she loves me. I
don't give a damn about her."

"But this is the modern age, not the *ancien régime*."

"Not for him. Not for plenty of men from his class."

"Can't you take it to the authorities and have him arrested?"

"They would never do anything about it. Currently there's no law
against dueling." Paul chewed on his bottom lip. "It's wearisome to second
guess every man approaching on the street whenever I go out at night."

"You're too bloody calm about it."

"Fascinating word choice, Pierre." He finished the bread and sipped his *café crème*. "I've been taking exercise with a fencing master."

"Little help that, if he chooses pistols."

"It's not his choice, if he goes by traditional rules."

"And if he doesn't, you can't see worth a rat's ass, and here you sit eating your breakfast just like you were going on a little boat ride."

"Douvaz is a big target."

Pierre glared at him. "Your humor is ill-timed."

"I saw well enough during a sandstorm in Algeria. The Zouaves taught me some maneuvers." Paul folded the letter and put it in his breast pocket. "What's so awful about dying is that you don't get to do anything anymore. No more roaming under the streets of Paris. Just lying there. I hate sleeping on my back."

"Stop. I can't stomach it." Pierre bolted out the door and around the corner.

Paul lit a cigarette and waited, giving him his privacy. Sweat trickled down his neck, irritating him. He mopped it with his handkerchief, and lay his palms on the table to feel its coolness. Coolness had saved him on his third escape from the Prussian camp. And again when some urchin pulled a knife on him in the bazaar in Algiers. The greater the danger, the greater the icy calm. He wanted it to be over, regardless of the outcome, but the only way for it to be over was to go through it.

In a few minutes Pierre returned, and wiped his mouth and chin on a napkin. Paul shoved his *café* toward him and Pierre finished it off.

They went about the grim task of hiring a hackney coach and securing a surgeon to accompany them, and the three of them arrived at Epinay-sur-Seine, on the loop north of Argenteuil, well before noon. On a Sunday morning no shops were open. At the peal of a bell, villagers came out of the church. Pierre inquired after the road to Villetaneuse and the location of Résidence Balfour. The driver found what fit the description in open farmland far away from other dwellings, a large derelict country house overgrown with vines reaching up to the mansard roof. One of the four chimneys had been damaged and several of the upper windows were missing glass. Apparently no one lived inside. There was an unkempt orchard on one side and a broken stone path on the other that led to the rear of the house. Two closed carriages were already there.

Paul instructed the hackman to wait. He took the path. Pierre followed with the surgeon carrying a case. At the rear of the house was a crumbling stone enclosure with an iron gate. Pierre opened it for him. Inside, what had once been a garden was now grown rank and weedy except for a swath freshly scythed stretching down the length of the enclosure. The reality of it made him suddenly aware of his pulse. *La piste,* it was called, according to his fencing master, with tables at both ends. At one of them, Robert Douvaz stood with a number of men in top hats. Douvaz and three others approached.

"I am heartened to see you've arrived, and in good time," Douvaz said.

Jesus! The bastard was going to play it for all its worth.

"I am glad to see you well," Paul replied. Obligatory crap. He summoned the calmness that had saved him in the past, and it reassured him.

Douvaz introduced one man as Monsieur Balfour, master of the field, another, Monsieur Roy, as his *parrain,* or godfather, and another as a second. "The gentlemen to the rear are my witnesses and a surgeon. I see you have brought your own."

"Have you a second?" Monsieur Roy asked.

Paul looked at Pierre whose eyes opened wider before he nodded.

"This is Monsieur Pierre Lestringuèz, who will be my second only in matters of preparation, not in execution."

"Understood," Roy said.

Monsieur Roy read the cartel and asked for his response.

Paul cleared his throat. "The article which you deem injurious to the mademoiselle was intended as a generality in the tone of humor, Horatian, not Juvenalian, and was not directed at her. Nevertheless, I am prepared to proceed."

Roy folded the paper and clasped his hands behind his back. "It falls on me to state the conditions and procedure. The encounter is to be executed with pistols of equal weight, equally fitted with a hair trigger,

which have recently undergone thorough and equal cleaning of parts."
He nodded to the second who retreated to the table and brought the
pistols on a tray. "However," Roy continued, "only one of them will
carry a bullet."

Pierre looked at him in astonishment.

"Combatants shall stand back to back and take ten paces," Roy said,
"then turn to face each other and fire at the call. Only one firing shall
constitute the affair, regardless of outcome."

Pierre indicated with a tilt of his head to retreat to their table. "This
isn't a duel," Pierre said under his breath. "It's a game of chance. You
can't be serious to go ahead."

"It's no worse than fifty chances in a hundred."

"You infuriate me. I will not assist in this."

"Tell them we demand the right to choose a different weapon. It's
custom that the challenged has the right to choose."

"It's a farce, and you know it. You're a fool if you let it go further."

"Do what I say."

Paul and Pierre approached the other men in the center of the field.

"Your proposal, and it is only a proposal, is highly irregular," Pierre
said. "To be an honorable duel and hold any meaning in society, both
parties must be equally armed. We demand our right as the challenged
to the choice of weapon, as is customary."

"You have no *parrain*," Roy said. "If you had, he could negotiate.
Negotiation is not the role of a second."

Pierre turned to him and murmured, "How about Raoul?"

Paul nodded.

"Hold off. I will find a *parrain*," Pierre said.

"We will give you one hour."

"I need two. Our godfather will be the honorable *Baron* Raoul Barbier, *ancien Capitaine de la Cavalerie de France*."

Roy and Douvaz exchanged a grave look. "One hour and a half,
with five minutes' grace period," Roy said.

Paul and Pierre clasped hands and Pierre ran out of the closed field,
yelling at the hackman to get in.

CHAPTER THIRTY-ONE

Not One *Canotier* Song

Auguste watched Gustave's larger boat, the *Inès,* come into the dock too quickly and at the wrong angle. Alphonse had to push away with all his force to keep it from slamming into the pilings.

"I've been out to see Claude," Gustave called out and stepped off the boat. "He says he's through with Impressionist exhibitions."

Gustave plopped into the closest chair on the lower terrace. Auguste sat down opposite him so they could speak quietly.

"He says he's distraught by the arguments and hasn't sold enough at our shows for him to continue there. What's worse, he's demoralized about his painting. He admitted that he could hardly bring himself to finish canvases that don't satisfy him and only please a few people. He even talked about giving up painting and trying something else."

"Trying what? All we know is painting."

"He told me that even though he's hurt by Degas calling him a turncoat, he's going to submit to the Salon again next spring."

"So am I!" Auguste said. "Don't you see? If the jury admits us, it will be a triumph for the whole group."

Gustave opened his hands in a gesture of not knowing. "I wrote to Pissarro to persuade him to join in an exhibition of the original group without Degas' new tribe. It would show us the public response to *our* work, separate from theirs."

"With Degas?"

"No. He'll refuse a show without his friends. We've fallen into two camps. Irreversibly."

He let Gustave's sentence hang in the air. No response could mend the crack in Gustave's hope. "What did Pissarro say?"

"He said that no matter how great the difficulties, he was going to stick with the Impressionist exhibitions."

Auguste shook his head slowly. "With a wife and four children to support? There's a point of being too noble."

"He even wants the Impressionist group to grow, so he's not opposed to more of Degas' followers joining. Or to Raffaëlli's prescriptions of subjects."

"Is that any surprise? He's a socialist."

Gustave hunched over the table, his cheek on his fist. "He's making a mistake."

"What about Berthe Morisot?"

"She'll stay with the original group, but Mary Cassatt won't."

Auguste was almost afraid to ask. "Sisley?

"He's been evicted. With his wife and children. The Charpentiers came to their rescue to move them to another lodging."

Auguste leaned back in his chair. "Well, you're just a bundle of good news, aren't you?"

"Sisley says we isolate ourselves too much, and that we're still far from being able to do without the prestige of the Salon. So he chose the Salon for next year."

Auguste felt responsible for some of this. He was the one who had convinced Claude that if they showed three years running at the Salon, then up-and-coming progressive dealers like George Petit might take their paintings. Maybe he'd been wrong to sway him. He hadn't meant to cause such a schism.

Gustave scratched at a spot on the table. "The group isn't ours anymore."

Auguste lay a hand on Gustave's arm. "No. It isn't."

Under his *canotier,* Gustave looked a little pale. "Are you feeling all right?"

"So-so."

"The models are already upstairs, except Pierre and Paul. Ellen came."

"With Émile?"

"No."

"You've got to do something about that."

"I know." Auguste stood up. "Are you coming?"

"After lunch. I have to go over the rules for the jousts with Alphonse. I'll try to eat a little something with him."

Anne served the duck *pâté* to only seven people. Aline was here, this time with a white ruffle around the neckline of her dress. A lovely detail to paint. But no Charles. No Émile. No Jeanne. And now, most worrisome, no Pierre or Paul. Paul would have told him if something intervened.

"You look perky as a bluebird with that ruffle," Angèle said to Aline.

"The Marché du Temple, just as you said. *Sacrebleu,* but it's a confused tangle of alleyways. I got lost getting out of there. I nearly cried going around and around until a crippled man selling old shoes set me straight."

"It's a fine ruffle, and I'm going to like painting it," Auguste said.

"I showed the dress to the dressmaker I work for. She raised my pay by fifty centimes a day and is going to give me more work."

"Not quite a gold earring, but we're right glad," Angèle said.

"It meant a fair something to me." She let her country speech spill out a touch of defensiveness.

Her simplicity appealed to him. She was at the stage when a young woman feels some latent power in her beauty but is unschooled in how to use it.

Anne and Alphonsine brought the main course, veal this week, and Alphonsine sat down in Paul's place to eat with them. "We're so glad you're back," she said to Ellen in a proprietary way that amused him.

"I'll be here from now on. I can come on Saturday too."

"No matinee?" Auguste asked.

"I quit the Folies."

He choked on his seltzer water. Angèle put down her fork. Alphonsine's hand went up to her mouth. Everyone turned to look at Ellen, stunned, realizing the risk she'd taken. It could mean the crashing finish to her career, or it could signal a leap upward.

"You're really a Folies girl?" Aline asked.

"I was."

"A dancer?"

"A mime."

"The best *mimeuse* Paris has ever had," Auguste said.

"Why did you quit?" Aline asked.

"The audience at the Folies doesn't care about the nuances of pantomime. They applaud more for dancing blue poodles than for human emotion. They laugh at farmyard noises of animals in heat, at songs picked out of the gutter, not songs of wit. I'll sell flowers on Pont Neuf if I have to."

"You'd better think twice about that, dolly," Angèle remarked.

"What was it like, working there? All that dazzle and glamour." Aline waved her forkful of veal back and forth on her last words and Jacques Valentin followed it, mesmerized, swaying his head.

"Huh! I wouldn't call cramped underground cells dazzling. Freezing in winter, stifling in summer, so hot that your makeup slides down your face before you ever get onstage. Your skin chapped by cake white. Callers cueing you too late. Congestion in the corridor, your costume torn by a passing sword. Gruff, lecherous men. Unpaid rehearsals that go on till dawn. Only enough time for a croissant and an apple before performances."

"Oh," Aline murmured.

"I hated my new mimodrama, *The Siege*. The indecency of showing breasts and derrière I can ignore, but this was indecent in a hurtful way. We had to fall forward like boards at the boom of drums imitating Prussian guns. People breaking their noses to take cover was supposed to be funny. The producer thinks it's a way to show that Parisians have put the Siege behind them. I see it as a disgrace to those who died."

Auguste checked Alphonsine's reaction. She was stricken for a moment, but recovered and managed to say, "I agree."

"What made you stay, then?" Antonio asked. "Money? Curtain calls?"

"Catcalls, you mean. I was just hoping that someone would notice me."

"Un amoureux?"

"No! A chance to act in a legitimate theater where people come to see performances of real literature and not just to prowl the *promenoirs* for a thirty-franc whore. I want to be in a play instead of in a trivial entertainment. I want to say beautiful words, brave words, unforgettable words. Like Sarah Bernhardt gets to say in *Phèdre*. Words of wit and passion and truth. I want to be a human being onstage, not a cardboard cutout."

"Commendable of you," Jules said solemnly. "To Ellen!"

They raised their glasses. Ellen blushed at the outpouring of support.

"I'll be first at the ticket window to see your debut," Raoul said. "I love theater. Maybe I'll become a critic so I can write rave reviews of you."

"We all wish you well," Alphonsine said.

"I'm glad you're free of it," Auguste said. "The Folies are too tawdry for you."

"Don't say that to my face, Auguste. It was my life. I loved it."

An awkward moment. Angèle stepped in with, "Of course you did, and rightly too. And now we're going to love to model." She signaled to Auguste and Antonio to bring out the painting.

While he was still wheeling it, Ellen cried, "Oh-h!" gliding up and then down the scale. "It's so far along."

"It better be," Auguste said.

"I see the real bottles and glasses on the table," she said, "the real people, but the painting is so much more intense and beautiful."

"Mm," Jules murmured. "Translated into art, at least Auguste's art, we are all more beautiful. That's why we come. To feel beautiful."

He heard heavy footfalls on the stairs and swung around to look, but it was only Gustave and Alphonse, not Pierre and Paul. They weren't just detained. They weren't coming. Paul's reckless side meant he could be anywhere, doing anything. Auguste hoped to God Paul hadn't antagonized that bruiser at the cabaret again.

Just as everyone took their places, Alphonsine ran down the corridor. "Don't start!" she called back to them. She reappeared wearing a strained smile and was holding something covered by a tea towel. Standing by Aline, she flung off the cloth like a magician and revealed a *canotier* decorated with a clump of red-orange poppies in front, tulle around the brim, and white rosebuds in the back.

"It's for you," Alphonsine said. "To wear in the painting. And to keep."

"For me? I can't believe it."

That instant with both women, flushed and glowing, Aline's pretty mouth a perfect O, Alphonsine about to burst, with the hat between them, all four hands on it, what a picture. What a moment. He felt responsible for it, which made him both happy and sad. Not exactly sad. Concerned. There was only one of him.

"Thank you!" Aline said.

Alphonsine tipped him a glance that had something more pointed in it than the joyful complicity he had come to know. It issued a demand. She deserved more than Aline's quick thanks.

"She did that herself, Aline," he said. "She used to decorate hats in a high-class shop in the seventeenth *arrondissement*."

"It's very pretty. I've never had such a hat."

"Put it on," he said. "Like this, so we can see your face." He tilted it back. With his hands on it, he felt he was touching both women at once.

"I like the poppies. A nice choice," Gustave said to Alphonsine.

"You look ducky, darling," Angèle said. "There's nothing like a new hat to perk up a woman, body and soul."

"Look at the bridge!" Jules said in alarm.

Pierre was running across it, dodging people in his way.

"That's dedication," Antonio said.

"No," Angèle said. "He just doesn't want to miss the dessert."

Pierre ran up the stairs shouting, "Raoul. We need you."

"Where's Paul?" Auguste demanded.

Instantly Raoul followed him out, and they both ran back across the bridge and into a waiting hackney which sped off at a gallop.

"What do you make of that?" Alphonse asked.

"Some sort of joke, most likely," Auguste said. A knot formed in the pit of his stomach. Gustave's wan face showed he didn't believe him.

He waited some time to calm himself, and set to work on Aline in her hat in profile against Alphonse's torso so Alphonse could go back to tend the boats. He got the froth of her ruffle against Alphonse's belly, her waist in front of his white pant leg, the dog's head, neck, and paw against his raised thigh, Alphonse's broad hand on the railing against her back. And now the most exquisite, a tendril of her reddish blond hair tickling Alphonse's knuckle. Alphonse was a fool if he wasn't enjoying it.

"All right, Alphonse. You can go. I'll finish you during the week."

Alphonse nodded and left.

Auguste scrubbed Ellen's face with turpentine so he could reposition it between Jules and Charles. The glass up to her lips darkened the skin beneath it. Soft blue-gray for the foot of the glass to harmonize with Jules's shirt. He would add white around the rim and paint her silver ring and bracelets later, when he would highlight spots all over the canvas.

Père Fournaise came upstairs and stood to the side of him. Auguste felt the pressure of his presence.

"What was all that about?"

"We don't know," Auguste replied.

Fournaise looked at the painting. "You'll be finished soon."

"Not today, if that's what you're asking."

"The Fêtes are next Sunday."

"I know, I know."

"I can come on Saturday," Ellen offered. "All day."

"How about the rest of you?" Auguste asked.

"Both days. One to pose. One to enjoy the Fêtes," Jules said.

"You don't think we're going to miss watching Hercules in the jousts, do you? I'd rather miss my own wedding day," Angèle said.

Auguste chortled. He couldn't imagine such an occasion.

"We can start early and work until you finish," Jules said.

"I can only come in the afternoon. I have to work half-days on Saturdays," Aline said.

The person he needed most. He turned to Fournaise. "Is it all right if I paint Saturday?"

Fournaise hesitated.

"Yes!" Alphonsine declared.

"*D'accord*," Fournaise said and ducked back downstairs.

Alphonsine's expression was triumphant. Auguste gave her a look that contained his thanks, and went back to work on Aline's dress, the drape of her polonaise sweeping around her hip. Her naked hip under that swirl of fabric.

"You seem so far away when you're painting," Aline said.

The only way he could be closer was if he used his fingers instead of the brush.

"What are you thinking when you paint?" she asked in that slow drawl of hers.

"About how nice a streak of lavender-pink would look against the lighter blue on the back of your shoulder where the light hits it." The public answer, nonetheless true.

"You don't see us? As people?" Aline asked.

"Yes. I see how slight changes in color create the shape of your cheek. And I see how the edge of your hat brim fits neatly between the lines of Alphonse's body."

"He sees you like a carrot," Alphonsine said.

He took it as a reminder of all that had passed between them.

"Is a voice telling you how to make each part?" Aline asked.

"It *is* my voice. It's also my heart, my brain, and my loins."

"Is that all you think?" Aline asked. "Only those kinds of things?"

"No. I think about being brave."

His fingers cramped in their grasp of the brush. He had to set down his palette to slide out the brush and massage his fingers to get them pliable again. He went downstairs.

"Leave him be," he heard Gustave murmur.

Alphonsine watched Auguste walk up the path to the north of the island, still working on his hand. She choked up seeing him break off a branch with his left hand and whip it against a tree trunk.

Paul was in some kind of trouble. She couldn't do anything about that, but she could do something for Auguste, to ease him, even for a

short time. She had to think. Only something that occupied his senses
would distract him from his worries.

Gustave lit a cigarette and Jules lit his pipe and Antonio poured
more wine. Angèle's hand on her glass was unsteady. Antonio sat down
and stroked her wrist.

Aline picked up tubes of paint one at a time and made shapes with
her mouth. It was apparent that she was trying to fix the letters in her
mind and link them with the smears on each tube.

"What's this called?" she asked, holding one.

"Vermilion. The color Alphonsine chose for the flowers on your
hat," Gustave said, acknowledging what she'd done. Did Gustave know
at what cost? Did she, even as she gave it? Aline did look pretty in the
hat. She thought of it a new way—it would be something of her own
creation in the painting.

"Ver-mil-ion," Aline said slowly. "Vermilion. That sounds nice."

Couldn't Aline read it off the tube? It came as a shock. Aline would
have a long way to go to understand his art like she did. That she should
be jealous of someone so unschooled seemed ridiculous, but that gave
her little comfort.

"What's in those cups?" Aline asked.

Gustave explained.

Aline pointed to one thing after another, asking their names. Easel.
Scraping knife. Palette knife. Palette. Gustave was amused, but Alphonsine saw deeper. She had wanted to find fault with Aline, but
couldn't. Aline knew her deficiency and was preparing herself.

"P-A-L-A-T?" Aline asked, spelling out the word.

"P-A-L-E-T-T-E," Gustave said.

"It stands for an idea," Alphonsine said. Before Gustave could sup-
ply a word in their little game, she said, "harmony," meaning more than
color harmonies, but her mouth strained to say it.

Auguste thrashed through foliage to get to the river. He crouched on
the bank and dipped in his hands, working his fingers in the cool water,
rubbing them. The passing of ripples made his knuckles appear hid-

eously large and his fingers unnaturally curled. He splashed the image away. Too appalling even to tell Dr. Guilbert. The future too harrowing to put into words. He cooled down his face and let the water stream under his shirt collar.

He would have lost his composure if he had stayed on the terrace. Too much at once. His fingers, Alphonsine and Aline with the hat between them, the group breaking up, his own precipitation of that, Claude even thinking of giving up painting, Degas' accusation that he was betraying the group with his selfishness.

And Paul missing, Pierre too hurried to say. If it was the brute in the cabaret, then it was a question of triangles. Two men and one woman. Two women and one man was another sort of problem. Who was he to judge? He didn't know which direction the current was taking him.

And his painting limping along with no clear way to anchor the terrace, the thirteen people on a barge. Thirteen. What had Pierre said? Thirteen at table meant someone would die. If Paul was in trouble with that hothead . . . He ran back.

Upstairs, Aline set down a tube quickly and picked up her dog and held him against her chest as if he were a shield. "I was just curious how verrrmilion is spelled."

"Can you get Émile to come on Saturday?" he asked Ellen.

"That rat! That flimflammer! That monster! Consider him dead."

"*Madre di Dio!* I think the lady has an opinion," Antonio said.

A blow to the stomach. He sank onto the chair, not daring to say what he was thinking.

"Palette," he heard Aline whisper to Jacques Valentin. "P-A-L-E-T-T-E," puffing the letters right at the dog's nose.

Instinctively he painted, but without joy. When the light faded he was glad to stop. None of them wanted to leave. Alphonsine brought up a bottle of *eau-de-vie de mirabelle,* the yellow plum brandy made by orchardists along the river, and a box of Bouchons, cork-shaped chocolates. She was trying. Perhaps too hard. It made him feel obligated. She thought too much.

He rolled his shoulders, folded himself up on the chair, and examined the painting. Coming along. Coming along. Far enough to lay in the foliage in dry strokes to harmonize with the colors already there. He would do that tomorrow. The tops of some trees were turning the same yellow-gold as the straw hats. Autumn was coming. He swirled his *eau-de-vie* and watched the clear liquid catch the light. Everyone was waiting to know, hardly speaking, checking the bridge. Antonio's hand covered Angèle's on the table.

"You've got the *Inès* today," Jules said to Gustave. "Can eight fit?"

"Five."

"I'll stay here in case they come," Auguste said.

"Alphonse won't let them leave," Alphonsine said.

"I said I'm staying." He needed solitude to nurse his worries.

Aline sighed. "I've never been on a sailboat."

Antonio made rowing gestures. "I'll take a yole with two ladies."

"Ellen and me," Angèle offered. "Just to lark around between the bridges." Her voice was flat.

"What about Jacques Valentin?" Aline asked.

"Tie him on a short leash to the tree nearest the dock," Alphonsine answered. "Alphonse will watch him."

Gustave stood up. "Let's go."

When Auguste saw them piling into the boat, he dashed downstairs to join them.

Aline sat next to him close enough that her dress lay over his pant leg and her arm brushed his. Alphonsine and Jules sat across from them. It was a smooth, slow sail without any thought of the sailing regatta two weeks away. They were riding low in the water. With five people, Gustave was being cautious.

"Will you take the helm?" Gustave asked Alphonsine. He looked a little green.

She answered by popping up and changing places with Gustave. She was closer now. His foot could touch her toe.

"Oh, it's so alive," she said, grasping the tiller.

So are you, Auguste thought, noticing her alert scrutiny of the sail, her eyes scanning port and starboard, forward and aft. Aline alert too, turning in all directions, excited to be on the water. Alphonsine statuesque at the helm. Aline restless, grabbing on to her skirt, her hat. One woman's eyes calm and narrow, checking the telltales in the leach of the sail for any shift in the wind, the other's eyes wide at the novelty of passing up rowboats. One face serious, the other gay. One sweet mouth silent, the other sweet mouth issuing soft breathy sounds. Four round, peachy cheeks. Delicious skin under chins. Smooth competent hands with a needle and thread. Smooth competent hands with a pair of tweezers. One who would be pliable, one who was already formed. One almost losing her hat. Better that he hold it. Her reddish blond hair now blowing against his face. Adoring one through the other's hair. Seductive, this luxury of pleasures. How could he indulge himself when his good friend might be in danger?

When the boat heeled a bit, Aline cried out and grabbed his arm. When the gust passed and the boat leveled itself, she let go of him and laughed at her fright. Alphonsine noticed and brought in the tiller to sail closer to the wind. The boat heeled more sharply which pitched Aline into him, and she held on to his arm, not letting go this time. Alphonsine gave him a subtle, knowing look. Why had she done that, thrown Aline right into his arms? Was she trying to take the big worry off his mind for a few minutes? Could she be that selfless? Damned if she wasn't one complicated woman.

What would it be like to live with so complex a woman? One who did accounting and read literature? She might interrupt him to talk about Madame Bovary's vanity or some damn thing, and he would be drawn out of his own contemplation of a painting. Such a woman might want to be too involved, might even interfere with his work. He had to remind himself that his love of women had a lot to do with the quiet, domestic atmosphere they created, like his country-bred mother did.

They sailed in short tacks up and down the river, turning just beyond each bridge. After every train from Paris, they came about to check the footbridge. Each time they passed the yole rowed by Antonio, they exchanged a few words, but no one sang a *canotier* song.

Shadows of trees stretched like dark fingers across the water from the western bank. They stayed out a long time, not knowing what else to do, never going as far upstream as the tip of the island, but once they went downstream to La Grenouillère to listen to the music from the barge dance floor. The little round island connected to the bank and the barge by two precarious catwalks was crowded with people dressed for a Sunday stroll, surrounded by swimmers just the way Auguste and Claude had painted it. Its banks were shored up with pilings so it looked like a wheel of cheese.

"Do you know what they call that little island?" Auguste asked.

"The Camembert," Aline said, as though proud to know. "It looks so jolly from here."

"It's also called the Flower Pot," Jules said, "and the women are the blossoms."

"You've never seen it from the water?" Auguste asked.

"I can't swim. Géraldine can. You should go swimming with her."

"But I don't want to." He faced away from Alphonsine and whispered to Aline, "I want to swim with you."

Alphonsine brought the boat about and sailed upstream. When they passed under the railroad bridge, he spotted Antonio rowing for shore furiously.

"Look on the *passerelle!*" Angèle shouted. Ellen pointed with both arms. Antonio rowed like an engine.

"Faster! Faster!" shouted Angèle, paddling furiously up to her elbow.

Pierre and Raoul and Paul waved wildly from the footbridge. Both boats sent up a cheer.

"*Vous voilà! Vous voilà!*" Auguste yelled out, emptying his lungs till there was nothing left, and holding up a fist.

Gustave brought the boat to the dock.

"You owe it to us to tell us what you were up to," Auguste demanded.

"And it better be good or he'll have you poached," Angèle yelled.

"Upstairs," Raoul said.

Everyone, including the two Alphonses, filed through the outdoor tables filled with customers, hurried up to the terrace, and crowded around one table, leaning in. Paul's nose wasn't straddled by his spectacles.

"You tell them, Raoul," Pierre said.

"No," Raoul said. "Paul should. It was his affair."

"For the love of God, somebody tell!" Auguste said.

"I was in a duel."

"Merde alors!" Angèle said.

Antonio's arm went around her shoulder.

Ellen and Aline gasped. Alphonsine's face lost its color. Gustave looked about to faint.

"That's what I dreaded," Auguste said.

"Not by choice," Paul said.

Fournaise poured all three men an *eau-de-vie*. Paul's hand was steady as he took it. Pierre's trembled.

"That fellow at the cabaret?" Auguste asked.

"Yes, the idiot and his plague of a woman. Curses on both of them."

"Why did you come tearing in here earlier?" Alphonse asked Pierre.

"To get a godfather," Pierre said. "To negotiate Paul's way out of pistols with only one of them loaded. To get Raoul's swords."

"I have a pair of light rapiers from my cavalry days with a lively whip to them." He patted Paul on the back. "Just a few words of advice, a reminder of some moves, and he took the field."

"Was it a long engagement?" Antonio asked.

"Yes," Paul said.

"Describe," Antonio said.

"You tell it, Raoul. It's a blur to me."

"An inauspicious opening when his opponent, Douvaz, beat Paul's blade aside and attacked," Raoul said.

"Paul parried?" Antonio asked.

"And riposted with an ill-aimed thrust. Douvaz countered, but Paul changed the rhythm so that a *coup passé* by Douvaz threw him forward."

"The result?" Antonio asked.

"It unsettled him enough that it put Paul in the aggressor's position for a series. He did a fine feint that slid along Douvaz's blade nearly to the hilt, but Douvaz dodged and countered with a Russian lunge. His thrust missed but showed he meant no game. Paul tired him until Douvaz slowed enough for Paul to execute a *coup extraordinaire,* a deception that passed so quickly around Douvaz's tip that he couldn't follow and Paul thrust home. He performed admirably."

"And Douvaz?" Auguste asked.

"He won't be a problem again," Raoul said. "A deep wound just above the hip. His surgeon was on the field in a flash. He's in the hospital by now."

"Wishing he'd kept his foul trap shut," Angèle said.

"No. Unconscious, I would guess. It's not likely that he'll be promenading for a while."

Silence spread over the group as the seriousness set in. No one moved.

"Where are your spectacles?" Auguste asked.

Paul's hands went up to his eyes. "They flew off, I guess."

"*Mon Dieu,* you must be dazed not to notice," Auguste said.

"I hope you don't want to go back and get them," Pierre said.

"Are you crazy? I never want to go near that bloody place."

Fournaise refilled his glass. Pierre shoved his forward too.

"It's a deadly relic of Romanticism," Jules said. "A . . . a pernicious vice that makes for . . . a horrible frolicking. It's . . . it's downright Greek."

There were a few feeble chuckles at the poet struggling for words.

"Italian," Antonio corrected.

"It's wrong that people think manhood requires such irrational displays," Gustave said.

"Was he dark, hairy, hot, impetuous?" Jules asked. "Did he have a deep voice, a ruddy complexion above a healthy beard? Those are the clichéd expectations of the bourgeois taking on the comportment of the aristocracy of former times. Or was he attempting to compensate for their lack? Was he puny?"

Pierre snorted. "Not puny at all."

"As big as Alphonse," Auguste said.

Père Fournaise stood up and laid his hands on Paul's shoulders. Alphonse leaned across the table and grasped Paul's forearm in his big hand. Aline held her dog to her chest and stared at Paul.

After a while of just sitting, Alphonsine said quietly, "We're going to pose for the last time Saturday morning if you can come."

Paul raised both arms above his head. "I'll be here!"

CHAPTER THIRTY-TWO

The Deal

Gustave rearranged the apples and peaches in his large, stemmed compote. He could build a revealing still life with them. His brother's compote sat far away on the vast ebony dining table. A quirk of Martial's, to keep their fruit separate. Martial had been gone for nearly a week. Gustave didn't know where, or when he'd be back. Typical of their bizarre brotherhood, each of them rowing his own boat, neither one exchanging thoughts about painting or music, yet living in harmony next to each other. Vacancy hung in the air.

He filled two faceted crystal carafes with water and set them diagonally. They reflected brilliantly on the polished wood. He set down two bottles of wine, wine glasses, and water glasses, asymmetrically, as far apart as the table would allow. They had touched them, his other brother, René, and his mother, with their hands and with their lips. He set out no plates or silverware to suggest a meal to come.

He had painted a similar arrangement a few years earlier with René and his mother absorbed in their food. Something about the silent apartment urged him to revisit the theme. This would be his own luncheon painting, different than his first, different than Auguste's. Their places would be empty. Only their glasses existed now. Gone. René at a young age, a premonition of his own future. He bent down to pet Inès, and set up his easel.

His mood paralyzed him. He often suffered in composing until the painting was under way, but this time was worse. He couldn't paint this today. He went into his bedroom to change clothes and gazed at his *Floor Scrapers,* indulging himself. Such fineness in other male bodies. He lusted to have that kind of beauty himself. He put on a cravat and a cream-colored summer jacket to try to feel jaunty, fed Inès and Mame, his cat and dog siblings, and left for Gare Saint-Lazare to take the train to Chatou.

He found Auguste on the terrace painting the railroad bridge in the rear of the boating party. He had adjusted the angle of the opposite bank to get in a couple of inns with red-tiled roofs.

"All it needs is the *Inès* heeling to starboard," Gustave said. "When Paul Durand-Ruel sees this he's going to hock his furniture in order to snatch it up."

"My, my, look at you all decked out. Going to a garden party?"

"Appearances can be deceiving."

"What's wrong?"

"What's wrong? You act like I hadn't told you anything yesterday. The group. I'm so heartsick I can't even paint."

"Then row, or sail, or keep me company while I paint."

Gustave slumped in a chair. That was one thing about Auguste. No matter what was happening, he worked. As for himself, he allowed for distractions of sailing, boat design, stamp collecting, long dinners out.

"I wouldn't say this to anybody," Auguste said, "but I think someday I will have wrung Impressionism dry. I'm beginning to see that if a painter works only in these wispy strokes, eventually he'd have nothing more than momentary effects, and would lose the ability to convey subject matter."

"You're talking like Zola."

"You won't run that risk of losing definition, but I might."

"So might Claude." Gustave lit a cigarette. "I don't know if I can organize another show next spring." He tried to say it casually, but it came out pinched.

"Do you have to know now, on a day as beautiful as this? Autumn is almost here. You ought not to waste a day."

"I'm not. I'm going to see Durand-Ruel."

Auguste chortled. "You must be misinformed. His gallery's only five blocks from your house. What are you doing here?"

"I want you to go with me."

"Why?"

"To see if he has any interest in putting together the next group show. To feel him out about Degas' cronies."

"Why do I need to go with you if I'm not going to exhibit in it?"

"Because he's the most important dealer in Paris. It's time he knew about your painting. And because you understand the problem and can express it in a logical way. You're smart, if you haven't noticed."

"You're joking. I need a Larousse encyclopedia on my lap in order to keep up with you when you're expounding," Auguste said. "But I'm not a fighter."

"That's just it. You're not as likely to get emotional as I am. You're unflappable and I'm irascible."

"Well, that last is true."

Auguste used up the paint on his brush and began cleaning it.

He felt better just being with Auguste. At the station, he pulled out two tickets from his pocket, first class, to keep his jacket clean.

"You were pretty sure of yourself. Two tickets," Auguste said.

"I was prepared to make an ass of myself pleading until you agreed."

On the train, Gustave asked, "Did you have a nice time with Aline in the boat yesterday?"

"Just a little too cozy."

"You have your hands full with two women all of a sudden."

"Feast or famine. You wouldn't consider taking one, would you?"

Gustave chuckled. "You've got to handle it on your own, I think."

"Time will do that for me. In a couple weeks I'll be back at my studio. Until then, it could get downright complicated."

Gustave saw nothing new on the walls of Paul Durand-Ruel's gallery. Delacroix, Daubigny, Corot, Millet, as usual. But the second room surprised him. "Ho-ho! Look at this. Sisley on all four walls. Good for Alfred!"

As soon as Durand-Ruel saw them, he broke away from a conversation and held out both arms. "My friends! Welcome."

To Gustave, Durand-Ruel's skin looked pink against his stiff white shirt collar and his precisely trimmed mustache. He was shortish, like him, but unlike him, heading toward stout. They shook hands. He smelled of cologne.

"I hear you're at Chatou painting a gigantic thing," he said to Auguste.

Auguste snapped his head sideways at him. "Gustave, did you tell him?"

He held up his palms.

"Charles Ephrussi, I think it was," said Durand-Ruel.

"How have you been getting along?" Auguste asked.

"To be candid, if I hadn't grown up in the trade, I wouldn't have survived the battle against public taste. In some circles, I'm still considered a madman. But the climate is improving. And both of you?"

"The group's in trouble," Gustave blurted.

"I'm somewhat aware." He ushered them into his private office hung with drawings by Delacroix. Tufted velvet chairs were set in a half circle around a carved easel for private showings.

Durand-Ruel offered them cigarettes from an ornate silver box. He took one, but Auguste said, "Ready-made cigarettes? That's a little like a kept woman. No, thanks."

"Then a cognac for both of you?" Durand-Ruel poured from a cut crystal decanter that reminded Gustave of his abandoned still life.

"Gustave means there is new contention in the group."

He let Auguste explain the split and the impasse about the next show, but he couldn't keep silent.

"Degas is the crux of it. He insists on bringing in his gang of camp followers. More than a dozen. He sent me this list." Gustave handed it to him.

Durand-Ruel looked it over. "Nearly the same as the list he sent me."

"We've actually splintered three ways," Gustave said. "The original group intent on exhibiting in an Impressionist show, as before—Pissarro, Berthe Morisot, Guillaumin, and if you wish, Gauguin. And the originals who have submitted or will submit to the Salon—Auguste, Monet, Sisley, and Cézanne. And now Degas' string of quasi-Impressionists— Forain, Raffaëlli, Tillot, Vidal, Zandomeneghi, the Bracquemonds, and Mary Cassatt, together with the rest of his list. If they're admitted as participants in an Impressionist show, that will outnumber the original group. Raffaëlli flooded our last exhibition with thirty-seven paintings to the ten or fifteen by each of the rest of us. It will only get worse next year."

"You haven't placed yourself," Durand-Ruel said.

"I will when I know how you stand," Gustave said. "Degas has immense talent and I admire his work as much as ever, but I'm less and less able to cooperate with him to keep the group cohesive."

"There's been some name-calling," Auguste explained, his shoulder jerking. "And arguments over whom to admit and what to call themselves now on the posters."

Hearing it that way, Gustave felt ridiculous.

Durand-Ruel put his elbows on his ostentatious Louis XIV desk. "Someday, it won't be important that you get along. You won't have to organize your own exhibitions. That's not your job. Your job is to paint."

"But for now I need to know how to proceed with the next group show, or whether to proceed at all," Gustave said, massaging his damp palms against the carved arm of the chair. "How do you stand? Don't feel pressed to include me. I know I provoked public outrage in the last show."

Durand-Ruel snorted. "All of you have at one time or another." He aligned the inkwell, the rolling blotter, the small clock on his desk. "I'll help Degas with a sixth Impressionist show if he wants my help. My salons are committed, but I can get exhibit space on the boulevard des Capucines."

"Following his list?" Gustave asked.

"Yes."

That landed like a cannonball in his gut. He couldn't believe it had come to this. A troupe of toadies sucking away their most enthusiastic dealer.

Gustave leaned forward, squeezing both arms of the chair. "Tell us honestly. What do you think about their work, these disciples of Degas?"

"Not scintillating."

"Then why support them?" His voice rose to an embarrassing squeak.

"Call it self-interest. Degas will sell."

"And his tag-alongs? Do you really think they'll sell?"

"They offer a combination of some Impressionist characteristics with sharp realism and anecdotal subjects. To some, it will appeal."

"It will dilute pure Impressionism," Gustave said.

"Is that so important? So does your work, at times. But Monet will hold up that end."

"No, he won't," Gustave retorted. "He's given up the group shows. He told an interviewer that the little band became a banal sprawl when it opened its doors to first-time daubers. Do you want to be seen as representing them? That does us no favors. Being *hung* alongside them doesn't either." He felt feverish, and Auguste had been cool as a clam. "Say something, Auguste."

"Cézanne thinks that hanging our work with theirs will halve our prices," Auguste ventured.

"Do you?" Durand-Ruel asked.

"I hold with Cézanne. I'm out of it." Auguste lifted his hand. "I took a big step forward as a result of showing at the Salon. It's a matter of not losing what I've gained."

"Understood," said Durand-Ruel.

Auguste went right on. "There are scarcely fifteen collectors in Paris who appreciate a painter who isn't in the Salon. There are eighty thousand who won't buy even a nose if the painter *hasn't* shown in the Salon. I've got to live. That's why I send two every year."

"Two a year aren't enough to live on."

"That's why we need a show," Gustave said. "I'll give my all to mount and fund it, only if the participants are selected on the basis of proven artistic merit *in line with our original goals.* If Degas wants to take part, I say let him, but without the crowd he drags along."

"He won't agree to that."

"No, I daresay he won't."

"You have to face it, Gustave. There's every sign that Zola was right in saying that a cohesive Impressionist group no longer exists."

He felt a twinge in his chest, and wondered if Auguste did too. "Then a tragedy has happened right under our noses."

"No tragedy," Durand-Ruel said. "The time will come when you won't need the group. Your styles are diverging anyway. You won't need the Salon either."

Auguste guffawed, but Durand-Ruel ignored it.

"There's a better way. For Monet and Pissarro and Sisley too."

"Which is?" Auguste prompted.

"First, listen to my reasoning. Your boldest work hasn't been shown at the Impressionist shows, and can't be shown at the Salon, so the most innovative work being done in France is either sold among yourselves or to a few friendly buyers or not sold at all, and that does nothing for the ultimate acceptance of the new art."

"Are you saying I'm wrong to buy up the choice pieces?" Gustave asked.

"No. I'm just saying that the time for independent group exhibitions *and* Salon validation is over. The manner of exchange of art is in the throes of a huge change. As important as the change from aristocratic patronage to the bourgeois Salon." Durand-Ruel laid his palms on his desk, fingers splayed. "And we're in the middle of it.

"In this change the dealer is essential. Not just as a *marchand de tableaux* as if paintings were shoes or hardware. As I see it, the dealer is a guide to aesthetic taste for the uninformed, a mentor to artists, a banker if need be, an uncle in affection, a publicist, and somewhat of an impresario."

"That's a hefty handful," Auguste said, crossing his legs. "Especially when you haven't bought anything to speak of recently."

"You don't know how I've suffered in not being able to. But the nation is finally crawling out of recession, and more and more people are coming in ready to buy. I must have stock—1881 will be a year of acquisition for me."

"Then what are you waiting for?" Auguste asked.

"Here's how I see it. If I consider your current work salable, and I have no reason to doubt otherwise, I will soon be prepared to enter into a relationship, not picking and choosing individual paintings, but buying all a painter's output, as I did with Manet years ago when I could afford to."

"How soon?" Auguste asked.

Durand-Ruel raised an index finger as though asking for patience. "I have a new friend, a new player in art circles named Feder who has made a good amount of money available to me, so I immediately bought Sisley, whom I thought needed it the most."

"That's good," Gustave said.

"Each year the authority of the Salon is undermined more and more, thanks to the general dissatisfaction with government institutions exposed by the war and the Commune. It's not in the Salon, it's in the marketplace that your names will be writ in gold. The franc spent at a dealer's gallery will be the arbiter of taste."

Gustave felt queasy in the stuffy room and needed a glass of water.

"What my father did for Delacroix, I can do for you. Under this arrangement . . ."

Durand-Ruel stopped abruptly and poured another round of cognac, as if to dramatize what he was about to say. Oh, he was a master showman, all right.

"You'll have to commit all of your works to me."

Durand-Ruel leaned on his desk toward Auguste and poked at the air in his direction with a silver pen. "Case in point. You did an oval portrait of Marie Murer, and her brother only paid you a hundred francs. That's shameful. Vastly less than what I could have gotten if you would have gone through me."

"But she promised to put it in a Louis XV frame from Grosvalet's."

Durand-Ruel rolled his eyes. He was right to. It was a ridiculous reason, but so like Auguste.

"Irrelevant. With proper management, which you obviously don't know a thing about, Auguste, your paintings will become prime investments. But it won't work without total commitment."

"Would we have the right to accept commissions for portraits and room decorations?" Auguste asked.

"Yes."

"What if I want to keep something? Or give it away?" Auguste asked.

"Let's say, five a year, but without the right to sell them."

"And the Salon?" Auguste asked.

"The Salon's a dying institution. Your group gave it its *coup de grâce.*"

"That doesn't answer his question," Gustave said.

"You can continue to submit two, as you've been doing. And I can exhibit yours that I buy wherever I see opportunity. Don't you see? That means all over France, and Belgium too. I've got contacts in England, and I'm working toward getting the financial backing and influence of Mary Cassatt to hold an exhibition in New York someday."

"Some year, you mean," Auguste said.

"Granted, it will take time. I have a feeling the American public won't laugh. They'll buy, moderately at first, but it will grow. And here's another idea—single-artist exhibitions. The day will come when they'll throng to my gallery to see a whole show of you, another of Monet, another of Pissarro. Can't you see that?"

"No, frankly, I can't," Auguste said.

"Can't you see now that all this squabbling over poster design of a single exhibition is ridiculous and small?"

Now Durand-Ruel was looking at him, not at Auguste, and he did feel small. His aims were small, and Auguste's were big. Durand-Ruel's were even bigger.

"It will be out of your hands. Let Degas have his exhibition. You come to me," Durand-Ruel said. "Or I'll come to you, to your studios."

Gustave saw it clearly now. The die was cast against his idea of a purist exhibition. He felt some vital energy drain out of him. He lost track of what they were saying in the happy memory of Auguste working with him on the 1877 exhibition—doing the publicity, writing the invitations, discussing each painting, designing an arrangement on the walls, working through the night and being surprised at the dawn of a new day. How happy he had been to provide the funds for the expenses, to feel part of something important.

He was going to lose this, the very thing that had given his life meaning for the last half dozen years.

"At the Maison Fournaise? A dozen figures?" he heard Durand-Ruel say. "When can I see it?"

"When it's finished."

"Not even the moment before the last brushstroke?" Durand-Ruel cajoled. That was his way of operating, jollying people into selling and buying so everyone came away feeling they'd made a good deal. Durand-Ruel was an expert at it.

"Soon."

"And my arrangement?" Durand-Ruel asked.

Gustave let Auguste answer. He suddenly didn't care whether his own paintings sold or not.

"I've never been able to know the day before what I'll do the next day," Auguste said.

A good response, under the circumstances. They got out of there into the fresh air of the street.

They stopped at Gustave's apartment to get Mame and walked toward the Jardin des Tuileries. He could tell by Auguste's far-off look that he was going over Durand-Ruel's proposal, but the breakup of the group was what churned in his own mind. The sight of Durand-Ruel saying no to his proposal and yes to Degas', without blinking, without an apology, cold as the eye of an enemy soldier, flashed in his mind. What a dour pair they were, Auguste and himself. Who would lay out his feelings first?

"He's a hybrid," Gustave said. "Aesthete, businessman, politician."

At the garden café in the Tuileries they ordered *glorias,* sugared *cafés* with brandy, and an assortment of pastries. He stroked Mame's back until she settled beside him.

Auguste said, "I knew at the time I was being rooked when Murer bought that portrait of his sister, but my rent was due."

A heavy silence settled on them. Their pastries were served, but Gustave couldn't eat. Auguste started with a mocha buttercream square. Eating seemed to hearten him and he spoke to the point first.

"What bothers me is that giving an exclusive leads to speculation."

"It might benefit you in the long run," Gustave said.

"He wants a monopoly and that opens the way to lower prices. He cornered the market on the Barbizon painters. He owned their souls, in fact."

Gustave sipped his *gloria.* "A gentleman's way to snatch the best of a painter and expect lifelong gratitude."

Auguste rubbed the side of his nose. "With that power, he could force collectors of taste with moderate resources out of the market and sell only to rich clients who know nothing about art."

"Men who buy pictures like shares of stock," Gustave added.

"I despise the idea that paintings are investments," Auguste said.

"Why not hang a Suez Canal stock certificate on the wall? A one-page slice of world shipping, bound to go up in value, and it lends prestige in the meantime. Especially if it's framed in that Louis XV frame you coveted."

"What's a painting by comparison? You can't funnel ships through it."

Gustave smacked the table. "I've got it! We'll go there and paint it. We could make a deal that for every ten thousand shares the investor would get a genuine Renoir of the canal if they preferred loose strokes that Zola would criticize, a Caillebotte if they liked a tighter image, that Zola would criticize."

They laughed at the ridiculousness of it.

Auguste took a bite of rose-shaped chocolate *duja,* and then another. "Mm, try these."

"I visited George Petit's gallery." Gustave paused, not wanting to destroy Auguste's moment of pleasure, but he thought he'd better tell him.

"Well? Out with it."

"I heard him say to a gentleman that Durand-Ruel is constantly on the verge of ruin, that he only gives the impression that he's rich."

"Then we shouldn't put all of our hens in his sack. Think where we'd be if there were paintings from the group hanging in every progressive gallery in Paris. Our movement can't be made to seem only a whim of Durand-Ruel."

Auguste wiped his mouth with his napkin, took a bite, and continued. "What's to prevent him from leaving our paintings to his children if he wants to? Or what if he has more financial setbacks, and Petit or other dealers don't, and we've sold our souls to Durand-Ruel? We'll be ruined."

"And what's to attract the public to a one-man gallery show compared to a large exhibition of all of us that would get press attention?" Gustave asked. "What if he sends all our work to America? What good would that do us in Paris?"

"What if what if what if." Auguste finished the pastries and his *gloria*.

"Degas won't organize under my terms. I won't under his. Point-blank, tell me. If I tried to mount an Impressionist show without Degas, would you exhibit?"

Auguste rolled a cigarette, lit it, and took a couple of puffs.

"Come on. Don't keep me waiting."

"Point-blank. No." Auguste stubbed out the cigarette. "I don't even know whether I'm an Impressionist anymore."

"Then let them have their exhibition. I don't have the stomach to fight it." His mind flew backward. "Degas was my mentor when I started. We used to be comrades."

Two women came to sit at a table near them.

"Would you look at the *nénés* on that one," Auguste murmured.

"Damn it, Auguste. Stick with the issue."

Auguste ordered another *gloria,* grinning to the waiter idiotically, and leaned across the table. "I hope I die before I reach the age when I can't take any pleasure in seeing a woman and imagining her on a rumpled bedsheet."

"I wouldn't worry if I were you."

Gustave finished his *gloria*. It felt warm and smooth going down, a comforting sensation. He was worn down by being the stretched cord holding the group together. What was he actually doing *artistically* to preserve the group identity? Not much stylistically. Only his subject matter and his perspective on *la vie moderne*. That and his funding and his skills for organizing and promoting, but if Durand-Ruel could deliver on his promises, his own help would be less needed. Where would that put him? A willing organizer with no one to organize.

On the way to the river, Auguste said, "I had a bizarre dream last night. I had gone to sleep thinking of Paul Lhôte. In the dream I was in the Salon the night before it was going to open to the public, in front of my boating party, and all the jurists stood in a row, hands across their chests. They all had the same cravats and the same face, as hard as stone. Unreadable. I shouted epithets at them, but they were deaf. The floor was heaving like I was in a boat on the ocean and I was dueling with Zola, but his sword was longer than mine."

"*En garde!*"

"Then Zola changed into Degas and Degas' sword was sharper than mine. Then Degas became Raffaëlli, and Raffaëlli's sword was only a wooden ragpicker's hook."

"Did you skewer him?" Gustave executed a fencer's lunge.

"Right through his gut."

"Ah, bravo!"

They chuckled, but inside, Gustave shivered.

They took the steps down to the quay to watch the pleasure boats go by, the unloading of barges, the bargemen calling out to each other, the young men stripped to the waist on the horse-washing barge. He liked the feeling of Auguste standing next to him, shoulder to shoulder, appreciating with him the green water bronzed with highlights of ocher and gold. On the opposite bank, beyond the quay wall draped with ivy like a green shawl, the ruins of Palais d'Orsay burned by the Communards shone pale yellow in the low-angled sunlight.

"Look there, Auguste, across the river. Proof of what Durand-Ruel said. Old institutions torn down." Auguste only grunted.

He unleashed Mame and threw an imaginary stick to see her run along the quay looking for it. If he lived right on the river in Petit Gennevilliers, Mame would have the right sort of place to run. And he wouldn't have to pass a gallery window every time he stepped out of his house.

At the beginning it was so spirited—the late-night talk in Café Nouvelle-Athènes, praising each other for a new motif or an original composition, loving each other's brushstrokes, rejoicing in every small victory, feeling no divisions among them despite the individuality in their work, working shoulder to shoulder, advancing on the bastion of tradition as a solid force, *Montez la garde! Avant-garde, à gauche, gauche!* Taking them on eye to eye, sword to sword, with *esprit de corps, Marchons, marchons!*

"Gone," he said, facing the river.

Auguste shot him a look of alarm. "That's a hard thing for you to say."

"We've lost something precious."

CHAPTER THIRTY-THREE

Love Made Visible

Auguste tried to ignore everything going on around him to finish painting the faces of Jules and Ellen and Paul, but Pierre and the two Alphonses were hammering a raised platform for vaudeville. His other friends were hanging Chinese lanterns under the arches and swings from the maple trees, Alphonsine's idea.

Merchants were erecting their fish-fry tents and booths for the sale of flags, straw *canotiers,* and paper parasols. An amusement fair was being installed along the Chatou bank with a carousel, a gymnastic apparatus, and games of chance, and a beer garden was being hammered together at the Giquel yacht works. The firemen's league was loading fireworks onto a small barge anchored to the Rueil bank. Only Gustave, painting a schedule of activities on a large board, was quiet.

All morning Auguste had been calling up his models as he needed them, but the one he needed most, Aline, was just now hurrying across the bridge, carrying that silly lapdog. Couldn't she have gotten here a half hour earlier? It might make a world of difference. The good light wasn't lasting as long.

She came upstairs out of breath. "Have I missed lunch?"

"We wouldn't start without you, knowing how you and your furry companion like to eat," Jules said.

She had added a wide red velvet band around her square neckline and a double band of red down the front of her dress. *"Très chic!"* Auguste said.

Aline traced the band with her fingers. "Do you like it?"

The trim defined the lines of the dress and set off her figure. The red made her face more rosy. She wore coral-red earring studs this time. With the money from Angèle, he'd been able to pay Aline. It had gone to good use.

"I love it."

When everyone came upstairs to eat, Angèle took one look at Aline and said, "*Oh, là là!* Aren't you a smart one! The rue de Temple?"

"*Bien sûr!*" Aline said, and the *r* rolled out down the river.

"Just one *r* will do, not three, if you want to be Parisian," Ellen said.

"Maybe I don't."

"Good for you, *chérrrie,*" Auguste said.

Louise came upstairs with Anne to give her usual announcement. "If you'd wanted your luncheon on Sunday," Louise said, "you would have gotten only a slice of pâté on an empty plate. We'll have our hands full in the kitchen tomorrow. But today I'm all yours. The *entrée* is *barquettes de fruits de mer.*"

"Oh, I love puff pastries," Aline said.

What food didn't she love?

"They're in the shape of *périssoires!*" Ellen cried.

"Of course." Louise huffed and puffed and moved her arms as though she were paddling.

"With green beans as paddles," Pierre said.

"For tomorrow's races." There was a lilt to her voice. "Picked from my cousin's garden when they're needle thin. They have the best taste then."

"I think this calls for participation. I'm feeling lucky," Paul said.

"You bet your life you're lucky," Angèle said. "You were especially lucky last Sunday."

"What do you say, Pierre? Shall we enter the *périssoire* races?"

"*Périssoire* comes from the word perish, you know," Pierre cautioned in a deeper voice than usual. "Oh, all right."

Aline was the first to take a bite."Oh, madame, I've never tasted such delicacies. I wish my mother could have a taste. She adores shrimp."

"Come into the kitchen before you leave and I'll wrap some up for her."

"Oh, *merci*, madame."

Alphonsine asked the women to help decorate the musicians' barge with lanterns and put up streamers in the dining room. The men would help Alphonse anchor a sailboat's boom over the water for the balancing game.

"And who'll help me finish this painting?"

After a while, Louise served the main course. "*Faisan, chasse du pays sur choucroute.*"

"Oh, madame! How did you know?" Aline said. Before she could say another word, Gustave and Angèle and Alphonsine fell into a fit of laughter. "Pheasant reminds me of home. We used to have it every autumn."

"And sauerkraut, sausages, and carrots too. A wild guess—you adore them, don't you?" Gustave asked.

Père Fournaise came up the stairs with two bottles. "To be properly tasted, pheasant must be accompanied by a deep red burgundy."

"I'm going to gloat to Charles about what he missed," Jules said.

"Why such a special meal?" Paul asked.

"For Auguste," Fournaise said. "So he'll have the energy to finish the blasted thing today."

"He can't," Pierre said. "He needs a fourteenth model. How about you, monsieur? Then we can wrap it up today and be out of your way tomorrow."

Fournaise backed away shaking his head. "Not me."

"Then you've got to find someone, Auguste," Pierre said. "You keep putting it off, but it augurs ill for us, and for the painting."

"*We defy augury!*" Jules declared, his fist in the air. When Pierre gave him a look of annoyance, Jules added sheepishly, "Hamlet and I."

"Can't you just do without a fourteenth?" Raoul said.

"And leave thirteen figures around a dining table?" Auguste said. "Raoul, you don't know a damn thing about art."

"That's not my job. My job is to pick the winning horse. You'd be pathetic at it." Raoul ate a few bites and said, "Aha! I have an idea of someone just right for a boating party."

"Who?" three voices chorused.

"Maybe I shouldn't say. I don't know a damn thing about art."

"For God's sake, Raoul. Out with it."

Raoul whispered something in Ellen's ear and a mischievous smile came over her face. Ellen whispered to Angèle, who whispered to Antonio. Pierre leaned across the table and Ellen whispered to him.

"That would work!" Pierre said. "Unless it's one of us."

"That's not likely," Raoul said. "None of us are in more than one race. The rower who earns the most points from all the races is the champion."

"Would someone mind telling me what you're concocting? It is my painting, after all."

"We think," Ellen said with excitement in her voice, "that for the painting to be a true luncheon of *canotiers,* the champion *canotier* of the Fêtes should be in it."

"That might be someone I don't even know."

"Come on," Paul said. "It's not like he's a major figure. He's just a face. You don't have to love him."

Everyone looked at him with eager expressions, waiting.

"This is a piece of art. It's not a lottery."

"A champion horse is a piece of art too," Raoul said.

"Here's a solution, Auguste. You're stubborn if you don't accept it," Pierre said.

Raoul said to Fournaise, "Monsieur, you can offer the chance to be in a grand painting of the rowers of Chatou to the winner when you award the *Coupe du championnat.* He can decline, of course, but it's an honor he can't refuse."

"And I can decline too if he turns out to have a mug like a horse."

"No, you can't!" Gustave shouted. "You've avoided filling in that face in order to convince yourself that you're not finished so you could keep going over it. You'll muddy it up by overworking it if you're not careful. This is *exactly* what you need. To make you stop. If you keep working on it, the change to autumn light will play havoc with what you've done. You've got to finish and let it go. The champion rower is the face, and that's that."

"All right, all right. I just hope to God he isn't a gargoyle."

They cheered and laughed and whooped in one raucous sound.

"Thank God," Pierre said.

To cinch the deal, Fournaise brought out a bottle of *eau-de-vie de poire* that he had made from pears grown in their own garden, and Ellen produced a box of Turkish rahat loukoum, jellied candies covered in powdered sugar.

"I regret I must interrupt your gastronomic delight in order to finish what we came for," Auguste said.

They resumed their poses with an air of excitement for having supplied the answer.

Auguste drew out some strands of Aline's hair at her forehead and temple—slowly, to prolong the pleasure. He arranged the folds of her skirt, running two fingers deep in the furrows. The shadows formed by the polonaise transformed the inward folds of cotton flannel into velvet.

"All right, try to hold that little pup still now."

She stood Jacques Valentin on his hind legs.

"Bring him closer to you. That's it. Perfect."

The dog's little nose was visible now against the white of Alphonse's shirt. When the time came for highlights, a white speck in his eye would link them. His rump showed through the short goblet. There were so many colors in the fur, the same colors as Raoul's coat, but here he wouldn't blend them. He would let them be distinct. Ha! An Impressionist dog! A tendon in Aline's hand lifted and caught the light. Also Impressionist, but in a different way.

The dog rested a paw in that sweet hollow below her velvet neck band. Desire to kiss that tender, vulnerable spot moistened Auguste's mouth, pulsed in his throat, tingled his hand. With his wet brush he touched her there on the canvas, and left a tuft of fur.

Ever since he'd painted his first woman on a plate, a face floating on a white sea, a goddess in his thirteen-year-old eyes, he'd set out to find her in the flesh, paint her in the flesh, know her in the flesh even before he knew fully what longings, what surrender, what sensations that would produce. Ever since that first *femme idéale* he'd been looking, relishing the search. And here she was, bloomed to life. The muse of his youth had come to tease him with a fey look directed at Jacques but meant for him. Was it the twenty years between them that made it crack his heart?

With Aline, he felt he was getting close to the best of his capacity. He could paint her forever, until twenty years would shrink to a pinprick of time. Aline was Margot and Lise and Nini and Isabelle and Anna and Henriette and, yes, even Jeanne. All of them in her, and then he came to Alphonsine, who was not funneled into Aline. She was distinct and individual. None like her was ever fashioned.

Now here was Aline, posing for him. Her lips, narrow but full, even fuller when she puckered up to kiss Jacques. The waste of a *dog* being that close to them. It should be him.

Where should he place a first kiss? Right cheek or left? Temple? No, too avuncular. Chin? No, too odd. Ear? No, too precious. Hand? No, too courtly. There was no other place but where his desire demanded. Full on the mouth. And if he could wait, it would be a time and place where she would welcome it and might even press back, and all desire, all thirst would make her forgetful of the twenty years, and exquisite touch would meld them. He pictured it, he would paint it, and thus he would possess it.

Jacques whined. That was the difference between the man and the dog.

"Set him down. I've got him."

"What will you paint now?" she asked.

"Sh. Let me enjoy this."

With his brush loaded and juicy, he pushed the wet tip gently into the hidden folds of her skirt, deep blue-violet folds such as had never seen the light of day, and stroked again and again, pushing farther, gently, wet into the wet already there, a rhythm faint at first, then intensifying, an expectation, a tightening, a rush. He knew he was loading his darks as well as his lights, and that was going against the Académie training that all the Salon jurists upheld like the catechism. He was tempting fate, but he was powerless to resist stroking over and over the dark furrows of her skirt, caressing her hidden secrets with the thick, oily paint a lubricant, violet and dark and moist, building up and up as he went down and down into the folds. This would have consequences. It could mean a Salon rejection, and what dealer would take a painting stamped with the Salon's big red *R* on the back? *Refusée.* Refused, as refuse. Trash. It could mean that he was, after all, painting only for his own pleasure as he had told Gleyre at the Académie as a young man. Down and down he went.

He could play like this till dark. With a jolt and a tremor, he pulled himself back. Now was his last chance to paint her surroundings with her. His brush flew, hunting for places to touch down. These very important moments to see it all together. Everything popping out now. Her sleeve seen through the tall goblet. Dragging the red of her velvet trim over the wet blue to blend the edges. A hunk of ruby in a glass. The rhythm building now in the repeats of colors. The poppies the same red as on Alphonsine's sleeve, the bow at her waist, the band on Paul's hat, the edge of Angèle's collar, the red of her lips, of Alphonsine's, and of Aline's new earring which hinted at some complicity—all red enough to sing out like a bell.

Aline's brilliant white ruffle, white sweeps around her saucer. Scrubbing off a narrow trail of her blue sleeve behind her goblet to make the edge a more luminous white. Streaking it on. Globs of white in the base of glasses to create protrusions to catch light and send it back. More later when these globs dried. The white of the silver spigot on the cask, and of Ellen's silver ring and bracelets. And the white of Angèle's pearl earring. A nod of gratitude to Vermeer. Angèle, his own girl with a pearl earring, with her face and throat as smooth in its blending of hues as any Vermeer.

And tinted whites. Lavender- and green-white on the tablecloth rendered in distinct Impressionist strokes revealing reflected hues in the shadows, not just in gray as the traditionalists painted shadows.

This was his own individuality, this combination of styles on one canvas. It pleased him to the marrow of his bones.

Onward with more tinted whites, blue-white on Angèle's frilled chiffon collar, frothy, as though her neck and head were emerging from some whipped dessert. Brilliant white for the front of Gustave's shoulder, lavender-white for the back of his shoulder in the shadow of his hat. And the white of Raoul's collar, of Antonio's, and of Jeanne's cuffs, bright enough to take the viewer's eye deeper into the picture.

And a white highlight in the dog's eye. "Hold him up again." She did, and he caught it with his smallest brush. A rush of air poured out his mouth and he felt for a chair behind him.

He was satiated by this feast for his eyes, and needed to reflect on every morsel of the painting when he was calmer, and alone.

What was left besides the fourteenth face? The deepening of shadows, more and thicker white highlights, more red touches, a balancing, an accent here and there, and especially a brightening if indoor light failed to bring out the colors as he saw them now—he still had that to do, and that made him strangely happy, not to be finished. But the gnawing problem that could kill the whole thing still shouted at him. The problem that had kept him from painting this three years ago when Fournaise had put up the terrace. How to allude to the building. He would be a target for ridicule if he didn't solve it. He felt the attack coming in his joints.

"I have to finish later, in the studio. It will be viewed inside, so it has to work inside."

"Then you're through with us?" Alphonsine straightened up. Her mouth tightened to an ambiguous Mona Lisa smile, and her forehead became a torture of grooves, every part conveying something different. In her face he realized what finishing the painting might mean to her. He felt himself break in two.

He hated to answer. "Let's just say we're finished working as a group."

Angèle shouted, *"Youpi!"* Pierre swung his hat. Jacques barked. Paul raised both his arms and shouted. "And I was here to see it!"

Mère and Père Fournaise rushed upstairs. Everyone stood up to look.

"*Oh, là là!* Beautiful, Auguste. Just beautiful," Louise said with a quaver in her voice, her hands palm to palm against her mouth.

"That's us," Aline cried. She held up the puppy. "Look, Jacques Valentin Aristide d'Essoyes sur l'Ource. That's you!"

"It *is* different than Manet's scenes," Ellen murmured. "He only shows separate people in cafés. This looks like I was talking and just took a sip."

"Our man Renoir leaves the disintegration of society to Manet and Degas and Raffaëlli," Gustave said. "Here we have genuine sociability."

"My children. My beautiful children." Louise was getting sloppy. She raised her apron to fan herself and wipe her eyes.

Fournaise went downstairs and came up with two bottles of champagne. He poured. They raised their glasses. "To Auguste," Fournaise said.

"To Auguste," everyone said, more seriously than their usual toasts.

"There's a poem I've been trying to remember," Jules said. "For you, Ellen, since you said the painting is lovelier than the reality."

> *We're made so that we love*
> *First when we see them painted, things we have passed*
> *Perhaps a hundred times nor cared to see;*
> *And so they are better, painted—better to us,*
> *Which is the same thing. Art was given for that.*

"Beautiful words, Jules. Thank you," Ellen said.

"Isn't that dandy," said Angèle. "We're *la crème de la crème* to have a poet in the house. You made that up right now just for us?"

"I didn't make it up at all. An English poet did. Robert Browning."

"Aw. You could have lied and I would have drunk another glass to you."

"I have one question," Aline said. "May I have my mother see it?"

Hardly the most important person to show it to. "Yes, but not in Camille's *crémerie.*"

Paul peered at the painting. "This catboat here, let's call it the *Inès*. And this sloop coming in to dock, let's call that . . . What are you sailing in the regatta, Raoul?"

"*Le Capitaine.*"

"Then that one is *Le Capitaine*. And this narrow little racing *périssoire*, this'll be Guy de Maupassant's." He chuckled. "Now we've got all the Maison Fournaise participants represented by their boats except Alphonse."

"Right," Alphonse said. "Where's my jousting barque?"

"Tied to the dock waiting for you to practice, so get at it," Paul said.

"You know, you have some Venus quality in Angèle," Gustave said.

Auguste snickered. "That old Titian, he's always pinching my tricks."

Louise patted her heart. "You paint what you love, don't you?"

"A man always does his best work out of love, madame."

Dear, droll Louise. She had glimpsed the truth. Art was love made visible.

CHAPTER THIRTY-FOUR

À La Grenouillère

Auguste sat staring at the painting, heavy with the problem of giving the terrace a context. His mood had plummeted.

Aline came up the stairs. "Are you going to sit there forever folded up like a grasshopper? Everyone's out on the barge putting up glass lanterns."

"The critics will crucify me if I don't come up with a solution."

"To what? What will they say?"

"Another vagary of an insurrectionist painter attempting to present modern life but giving us a fantasy instead. Once upon a time a party of happy people was riding on a magic carpet over the countryside and they came to a river and landed in some trees." He closed his color box. "All this work may come to nothing. Worse than nothing. A setback. And the most important dealer already knows about it."

Aline sat down close to him. "Didn't you have a fine time working on it today?"

"Yes, I did."

"Then let that be enough for now," she said softly, a different way of addressing him. "Hold on to that and let's go for a walk. Or a swim. Will you teach me?"

He popped up from his chair. "Yes. Right now."

"I don't have a boating costume."

He could ask Alphonsine. . . . No. "We'll rent one at La Grenouillère."

They walked the narrow spit from the isle of Chatou to the isle of Croissy. Aline picked a sycamore sprig with broad leaves and used it as a fan.

"After a rain we had that same dank smell by the stream near our vineyard," she said. "I should think there would be mushrooms here in the spring, and soon, the yellow chanterelles that smell like apricots. I used to find them at home. Oh, I do miss the Aube. In summer the cuckoos roosted in our trees. They're so clumsy. When I was little I tried to scare them so that instead of calling, 'goo-koo,' they would call with three sounds. 'Goo-koo-koo.'"

He felt himself becoming bewitched. His mother spoke like this of her country origins outside Limoges. "Tell me more."

"Oh, it's so pretty when the red poppies come out, and the wild roses and columbines on the slopes and the grapes growing on chalky hillsides near where the Ource meets the Seine. The waterwheels cranking in a rhythm and the ducks quacking in their gullets and water reeds rustling. You'd like it."

"I suspect I would."

Shouts from La Grenouillère made Jacques bark. Swimmers splashed and dove in the roped-off area. Rowers in the green rental rowboats with red stripes yelled the boaters' greeting, *cric,* to other boats answering *crac.* Not another person could fit on the little island called the Flower Pot.

"I hope they know how to swim," Aline said, "because someone's going to be knocked off."

Two *grenouilles* in bathing bloomers sat on the bank with their knees up, spread widely, chatting to each other, waiting for male attention—*loulous* of the suburbs making La Grenouillère a modern Cythera.

He paid for a bathing costume for Aline and she went to the ladies' dressing cottage among the trees while he changed in the men's. When she came out, she took small, hesitant steps. She was rounder than he had imagined. Apparently she couldn't resist a dish of white beans and lard.

She tied Jacques Valentin's leash to a tree and walked two steps into the water. "The mud squishes between my toes. Like grapes in the vat."

Several more steps put her knee deep. Three more and she cried, "Oh!" as the water reached the top of her inner thighs. She giggled in embarrassment at the new sensation. "I'm used to bathing in a pan."

In deeper water, her bathing costume filled with air. "Oh, no! I'm a balloon!" She beat down the billowing blouse. "It's a mighty strange feeling, water all around me at once."

"But you like it, don't you?"

"Oh, yes. My father took me to the source of the Seine once. It's only a trickle coming out of a crack in a hill. He said that once there was an old, old temple to the river goddess Sequana. That was the first name of the river, he said. It goes underground and gurgles up again in a narrow stream. I jumped back and forth across it. And here I am, right *in* it!"

She soon began mimicking the young people playing around her, cupping her hands together and splashing him.

"Some day I will paint you, just like that, splashing someone."

Nude, like an Ingres nude. Not choppy strokes, but smooth gradations. He glimpsed a painting direction arriving unbidden.

"Only if you can catch me." She ran away in the waist-deep water, and he caught her. In the instant between two heartbeats, he could kiss her before she knew what was happening, but he was afraid she would think him a nervy old man.

"Do you want me to teach you to swim, or do you want to splash me till I drown?"

"I want you to teach me to swim."

"Then you'll have to come out deeper."

The bottom fell away, she lost her footing, and her hands grabbed for his neck. Holding her by her waist, he walked backward into deeper water until she couldn't touch bottom. She cried out and giggled, flailing.

"I've got you." Now she was dependent on him. "Relax. Lean forward."

His hands were under her, supporting the mound of her belly and her ribs, a bold indiscretion any other time. Her buoyant breasts grazed his arm. He whirled her in a circle. Her hair floated in patterns like golden sea grass, like filaments of silk moving in graceful unison.

"I should have tried this long ago," she said.

"No, you shouldn't have. Today is the right time."

He showed her how to take a stroke and flutter-kick. She learned quickly, which was disappointing because she didn't hold on to him as tightly.

"You have strong arms," he said.

"That comes of hoisting buckets as soon as I could work the pump."

"I'll bet you can wring a chicken's neck too."

When she became tired, he brought her back so she could stand, and showed her how to float face-up, with his hand supporting her shoulders and the small of her back. The thin cotton of her bathing costume clung to her breasts, and her nipples stood firm and perky in the cool water.

At what moment would she know that he wasn't merely performing an avuncular duty by teaching her to swim so that if she ever got bounced off the Flower Pot she could save herself? At what moment would she know that those pouty lips drove him crazy?

Now. He drew her to him and kissed her wet mouth, succulent as a berry, kissing from her mouth down her neck. He took a deep breath and went underwater to nuzzle her belly, holding her by her hips. Her hands pushed him away and then relaxed. He held his breath until he had to thrust himself upward for air. Lowering himself, he blew bubbles that lodged between her breasts.

"You sure can swim like a fish. Wait till I tell Géraldine."

"Then Camille will know, and that means your mother will too."

"Oh, no. That can't be."

When he saw her shiver, they went back to the bank. Her costume stuck to her in folds. A nude. Yes. Someday. They lay down in a sunny patch of grass.

"Do you know why I like La Grenouillère so much?"

"Because you're a fish."

"Because it's the Moulin de la Galette of the suburbs and the very spot where Impressionism was born. It didn't have a name then, but we knew we were discovering new ways to paint. It's hallowed ground for me here. We had a jolly time that summer even though we didn't eat every day."

"How do you do it? Paint, I mean."

"I look at something. It makes me happy. I paint it. It's a handicraft."

"Like woodworking?"

"Yes, I'd say so."

"My father made things of wood. A table and chairs."

"You take a man who makes something himself, start to finish, from idea to the last sweep of his hand across it, now, that's a happy man. He can look at it, use it, pass it on to his children. He's happy."

"I don't think my father was."

"A factory worker making only chair legs never gets that satisfaction. He's the unhappy one."

"Finishing chairs wasn't enough. My father was unhappy."

"How do you know?"

"In the country, when people have black thoughts they go to a barn to dance the *ronde* or to a *veillée* on winter evenings where the women sew and the men repair tools. My parents went often, but it didn't help."

He wasn't going to make the mistake he did with Margot, not taking an interest in her background.. "Tell me about them."

"Once my father picked me up, set me on his horse, and climbed on behind me. We rode to the top of a hill. He asked me if I could see the sea. I laughed and told him I only saw rows of grapevines and the house and the hills. Then I asked what he saw. 'The sea, another coast, other hills, mountains, other cities,' he said. I thought he was playing a game with me, but no. He was preparing me.

"The next day when I woke up, he wasn't in the house, wasn't in the vineyard or the pressing house. His horse was gone. He never came home."

"I never imagined." He took her hand and stroked the back of it.

"Maman thought he left because she nagged him about bringing in mud on his shoes one too many times."

Auguste had done the same thing, to the infinite displeasure of Madame Bérard. He sympathized with the man.

"You've never heard from him?"

"We waited through several winters and tried to keep the vineyard going with my cousins' help. Then Maman thought we'd find him in Bercy, where the wine comes into Paris from the east. So five years ago we moved here to look for him. I cried all day when we left. It cleft my life in two parts, before and after, like a cleaver going through a melon. Whack. I wobbled for a long time after that."

"You didn't like Paris?"

"The bigness made me feel small. I couldn't sleep for the noise at night. Maman got a post as a seamstress and put me out to work as a laundress. After work every day she dragged me around looking for him. We rode omnibuses on the upper level so we could search better. People gave us mean looks. We didn't know women weren't supposed to climb up there. At the slaughtering yards in La Villette, Maman asked, 'Have you seen a man named Pascal Charigot, middling tall if he weren't so bent, eyes spaced wide like a Dutchman's, a large brown mole beneath the left one?' It was so embarrassing. I hated it.

"But whenever I'm in a café, I sit so I can look out the window, just in case he might walk by. I have dreams of walking down a street or buying fruit in the Marché de Saint Pierre, and there he would be, coming right toward me."

"You never found him?"

"A letter came to the vineyard and my aunt sent it to my mother. He was in America. In a place called North Dakota."

He glimpsed the vacancy her father left in her life. Until now, he had only seen her cheerfulness, just as he had with Alphonsine at first.

"I wonder if he ever wakes up thinking he might have made a mistake. If he had died instead, it would have been easier on Maman. There's something natural about death. There's nothing natural about a father leaving a vineyard his great-great-grandfather planted and a family he loves."

Auguste couldn't blame the man for having the wanderlust. He had the courage to make a clean break from a carping wife. Would the daughter slip into the mother's nagging nature?

He could never take her to Madame Charpentier's salon, to any of the other *hôtels particuliers* where he had commissions, to the Salon or to Durand-Ruel's gallery. She might blurt out some rustic impropriety fit for a barn. He would be leading a double life.

She was too young. He too old, too unstable in money matters. He had visions of Monet unable to feed his pregnant Camille, forced to beg from Charpentier and Zola, and of Sisley's wife packing up in the night, time after time to avoid landlords. He was far from ready to settle down.

Maybe, by a stroke of luck, the painting would earn enough for him to travel. Nearly forty years old, and he had not seen the frescoes of Raphael. He had not expanded his *oeuvre* beyond Paris, the Forest of Fontainebleau, the Seine. Now was the time, when he was unattached. He was going to chase the light. He would experiment. He would be his own man.

Another man might snatch her up in the interim. She was ripe as a grape at picking time. It was all moot anyway if he couldn't solve the last problems of the painting and his career shriveled because of it.

"Do you see differently than normal people?" she asked.

He laughed solemnly at himself. "Maybe. Look at that skiff under that tree. Don't think of objects. Think of colors and shapes. What do you see?"

"A green boat, a green river, a green tree. Like that?"

He shook his head. Never to a dinner where art would be discussed. But what dinners did he attend where art was not discussed?

"Not quite."

"Then, what?"

"An elongated shape pointed and curved up slightly at one end, the shape revealed as gradations of different greens. Behind it, shifting patches of deep green and blue and yellow-green and white, with a shimmering red line repeating the solid one on the long green shape. A vertical column of brown edged in ocher on one side, reaching upward and dividing, angling up to a textured fullness of greens and yellows touched in places by ocher and gold."

"Doesn't all that seeing wear you out?"

"Try again."

She squinted. "I see some great old maple trees that have been here longer than anyone. Honorable trees, as honorable as old grapevines."

Yes, differently.

Their spot of sun had gone. Shadows of trees stretched fingerlike across the water. Gooseflesh rose on her arm. It was time to get dressed. He paced at a respectable distance from the ladies' changing cabin. The sun was sinking. Already a few clouds bloomed in shades of rose and soft orange and cast violet shadows on the river in spots. It would be a dazzling color show.

"Aline, hurry," he said outside the cabin. When she came out, he grabbed her hand. "It'll be over in a few minutes."

She untied Jacques and he hurried her through the little wood to the western bank of the island. The incandescent globe rested momentarily on the poplars across the channel, then winked between their branches, shooting shafts of orange light right through the translucent blue-green surface of the river.

"The sun is rolling toward America," she mused.

Solemn, he would call her expression at that moment if he had to find a word. When he looked skyward again, the pale orange had become rose and he had missed a stage in the color change.

"Don't move." He crawled away from her and lay on his stomach at a little distance. "Now I can see you against the changing colors."

She was quiet and still, for him, he thought. The sky cast a ravishing rosy light over her shoulders and turned her deep golden hair to bronze. He tried to imagine what it would be like to watch her go about her domestic tasks, and to have this display of double beauty at the end of every day.

He crawled back and lay on his side facing her. He could press himself against her, if the yappy terrier would let him. Anticipation pulsed. He never experienced anything deeply unless he was able to touch it. He made a move. Jacques growled.

"I won't hurt your mistress. I promise."

Jacques countered with a bark. Aline scooped him up and he quieted.

Auguste passed his fingers over the grass. "See, Jacques? What I want to do isn't anything more than this. She'll hardly feel it." He would go through a long, slow dance, building a history before he touched her sexually.

What Madame Charpentier and Camille saw in him was a need to give himself to a living, breathing being, someone real, not colors on a canvas. To give himself in a way he'd never done, in this case, by withholding himself for the sake of the woman. He was beginning to grasp the difference between pleasure and happiness. It was another plane, beyond adoration and sensuousness, a country new to him. At this stage of life, he'd better just lean into love, because if he fell, he feared he might break a hip.

"I want to paint you again. Let me name the ways. On the bank about to get into a yole with someone, let's say Gustave. Dancing at Bal des Canotiers."

"With the baron?"

"No, waltzing with Paul. In a garden, reading." Her face turned pink at that. "As a nude in the sunlight, your hair streaming over your shoulders like the great Renaissance paintings of goddesses. Someday. When you're ready."

"You mean when my mother is ready."

"Then begin getting her ready now."

"She doesn't want me to run with a painter."

"We won't run. We'll stroll, and enjoy every step."

He brushed his hand across her ankle, the outer bone and the inner, fixing the shape in his mind. Jacques perforated him with his beady black eyes. His hand moved slowly upward to where her ankle became calf.

Jacques barked and she drew her leg away. "I have to go home. Maman is expecting me before dark."

"Ah, yes, *la mère* whose affection I must win. I could begin tonight."

"No." She stood and picked up her dog.

"Might I accompany you to the station?"

She nodded, already walking.

He would do more than that. He would ride the train with her to Paris, and hope that she wouldn't lose her willingness when they left the mystique of the river world and entered the gaslit streets fanning out from Gare Saint-Lazare before arriving at his atelier. Instead of walking back through the Maison Fournaise, they took the steam ferry from La Grenouillère to Rueil. On the water he looked south beyond Bougival to Louveciennes. Twilight softened the edges of everything. "From the bridge at Bougival, you can see the aqueduct on the hill. Whenever I see its row of arches, I think of Italy. I need to go there someday, to see the art of the Renaissance, and to paint."

"You won't know how to talk to them." Her words were clipped and final.

"Sometimes I feel so restless I can't stand myself. I want to go to Algeria too, to find that southern light that Delacroix painted."

"So you're going to become a wanderer too?" An edge to her voice cut through him.

The approaching evening folded the river, the ferry, and the two of them into a shadow. He slipped his arm around her waist. "Not yet. I'm not a wanderer yet. Right now I'm going with you." In the gloaming, he couldn't tell whether her eyes said yes or no. The alternating stiffness and relaxation of her body told him that she wasn't teasing him. She was genuinely conflicted. At Rueil-Malmaison he waited with her for the train and stepped into it behind her.

"No. Don't. Stay here." She pushed him back down the steps and the conductor closed the door.

CHAPTER THIRTY-FIVE

Les Fêtes Nautiques

Alphonsine sang softly. *Today is Sunday. . . . Hurry, rowers, get the oars ready!* the song urged. She *was* hurrying, putting on her best blue dress, a Parisian dress on the verge of being too chic for the country, but this was the day of the Fêtes, the most important day of the year at Chatou. She fastened a dark blue velvet ribbon around her neck for Alphonse's team.

In the dining room, she watched Auguste grab Maman around the waist and swing her in a dance step, and then he did the same with her.

"It's a busy day, young man. I don't need your foolery." Maman's eyes sparkled even as she said it.

"It's *exactly* what you need. Today especially." He tipped his straw boater at a rakish angle and sashayed outside singing, *"Ohé! Ohé! Ohé!"*

"It'll be sad to see him go now that the painting's finished," Maman said.

"No, it isn't. Not yet."

"Of course, you might lure him to stay longer."

"Maman, sh. Don't talk that way."

"He's been just like another son."

"Stop it."

She had made mistakes. If she had spoken to Circe privately, if she hadn't sent him off to Paris to find another model . . .

She went outside where Uncle Titi was setting up the *grenouille* game, a wooden box with openings in the top around a ceramic frog with a gaping mouth. It was a tossing game. People won chits to spend in the restaurant according to what hole their copper disc fell into.

"Let me try it," Auguste said. He tossed, and by God if the disc didn't land right in the frog's mouth with a clink. "Ha! Do you think that's enough to erase one-hundredth of my bill here?"

"Do you think Papa's actually going to make you pay all of it?"

Alphonse asked Auguste to help him carry out more tables and chairs.

In a few minutes she felt someone behind her squeeze her waist with both hands. She whirled around and Raoul gave her a kiss on both cheeks.

"First to arrive gets to kiss the ladies," he said.

"Aren't you the proper *canotier.*" For once he wasn't in his suit jacket with his brown felt bowler, but white canvas pants, the traditional blue-and-white-striped jersey of a *canotier,* and a flat-topped boater.

Auguste came up from the cellar carrying two chairs and greeted Raoul as though he hadn't seen him in years. "Are you the first to arrive?"

"Aline isn't here yet, if that's what you're asking," Raoul said.

Auguste scowled and turned to get more chairs. Raoul called after him, "Today's the day your *quatorzième* will be named." He lifted his shoulders and made a face as if to say, *What's the matter with him?*

The rail line had doubled its service and people were staking out viewing places on the Rueil bank and the island. They promenaded. They browsed the booths strung out on both banks. They rented yoles. They laid out picnics. They filled the restaurant. All the things Alphonsine loved would be happening today.

She gave out blue and red ribbons for people to show what teams they were supporting in the jousts. An organ grinder cranked out a tune, and his monkey dressed as a *canotier* collected sous and put them in his tiny straw hat. Several pedal boats decorated with garlands of paper flowers came up from La Grenouillère along with the usual green rental rowboats. Accordion music came across the water from Auberge Lefranc.

Auguste sat with the models—all except Aline and Charles and Gustave—under a maple tree at water's edge, crossing and recrossing his legs, watching the bridge and smoking. She brought him a tin ashtray.

"Are you concerned about who will win the spot in the painting?" she asked. "Who the *quatorzième* will be?"

"Among other things."

A racing scull crossed the river from Auberge Lefranc with four people rowing in rhythm to their song:

> *The jolly* canotier *is rowing hard*
> *Digging his own path with his strength and his oars.*
> *On the throne at the rudder, just like in a palace,*
> *Sits one of his women.*

Everyone on both terraces joined in as the boat floated close.

"Start another," Alphonsine prompted.

Angèle started the *Marseillaise des canotiers,* and the team of rowers took that song downriver to the next *guinguette.*

Alphonsine turned and saw Gustave, sporty and chic in blue trousers, expertly tailored cream-colored jacket, the blue silk cravat and flat-topped boater of the Cercle de la Voile à Paris, and a blue breast banner identifying him as the vice president of that prestigious sailing organization. He stepped onto the platform to register the racers, and was mobbed by contestants. Auguste and the models gathered to size them up.

Angèle said to Auguste, "You don't look like the jolly *canotier* in the song. What's wrong?"

"I don't feel anything for these fellows."

"Don't get all herky-jerky about it. It's just a face."

"Yes, yes, just a painting," Auguste said. "Just a chance to turn my career one way or another."

Alphonsine began to feel Auguste's nervousness herself, especially when she saw a man from Bougival with a huge hook of a nose and pink, scabby skin sign up for four races. Auguste gave her a sinking look.

"You'd better hope this Monsieur Le Hook capsizes or rams someone and gets disqualified," she said.

Raoul registered for the one-man *périssoire,* Pierre and Paul registered for the two-man sculls, and Guy de Maupassant registered his team for the two-man sculls, the *triplettes,* the four-man sculls, and registered himself for the slalom course of the narrow open-hulled *as,* the most difficult craft to maneuver.

"Are you crazy? Your arms will fall off," Pierre said.

"You put a boat in front of him, he can't stay out of it," Alphonsine said.

"If I let one of my boats go unused today, she'll say I have too many," Guy said.

A trumpet announced the parade arriving from Bougival. Alphonsine hurried inside to get Maman. Papa in his nautical suit and mariner's hat led off, mounted on Uncle Titi's horse draped with a banner with the words *Le Grand Admiral de Chatou.* She loved seeing him ride in for a festival he had started from nothing. He scanned the crowd for Maman, whose face was alive with pride, her eyes moist, beside herself with adoration.

The mayors and councilmen of all the river towns that had jousting teams followed on horseback, wearing tricolor chest bands. The *gendarmes* and firemen came next, then the acrobats turning cartwheels, a vaudeville troupe, and the former jousting champions in their white shirts and pants with red or blue cummerbunds. The band brought up the rear playing a march.

The mayor of Chatou mounted the platform to welcome everyone. The band played Offenbach's Barcarole, and the vaudeville troupe did a skit using a flat cutout of a gondola. Papa pantomimed cracking a wine bottle against the prow and bellowed into a megaphone, "*Que les courses commencent!* Let the races begin!"

"Let the choosing of a *quatorzième* begin!" Pierre echoed.

Uncle Titi ferried Gustave and the racing master out to the anchored barge that was both the starting point and the finish line, since all races went upstream and then back. Over a megaphone Gustave called for *canotiers* of single-man *périssoires* to take their positions. She liked the authoritative sound of his voice, stronger than his usual deference. This was his day too.

Raoul stood up. "Wish me luck." He leapt onto the dock in an awkward, tipping plunge and Alphonsine gasped, but he managed to get into a boat.

"He's not a *canotier,* is he?" Ellen asked.

"No, he's a cavalier," Auguste said. "But if he can win this, he'll have a chance at the championship, and if he wins that, since he's in the painting already, I can choose my own *quatorzième!*"

Gustave announced, "*Canotiers,* take your mark!" the racing master shot the starting gun, the *canotiers* dug in their paddles.

Raoul kept up on the upstream, but lost position at the turnaround. Alphonsine cheered for him until the end, but he didn't place. A man from Guy's team who went by the name of Tomahawk won first and Monsieur Le Hook from Bougival won second. Raoul came back grinning and exhilarated. "Just wait until next week when I have wind in my sails."

"A lot of good that'll do me this week," Auguste said.

The two-man *périssoires* were next. Pierre was standing to stretch.

"Ask Alphonse to put you in *Lutin,*" Alphonsine said. "It's the lightest."

"With a name that means wanton and roguish, are you sure that's the best boat for us?" Pierre asked.

Alphonse came up from the dock to advise them. "Paul, you take the forward position. Come up with the turning marker on your right. Pierre, you backstroke on the right while Paul does tight forward strokes on the left to turn you tightly."

"*Bonne chance,*" Alphonsine said.

Guy appeared wearing white blousy pants, a red waist sash, and a maillot of blue and white stripes. "Today, my name is Loup d'Eau Douce." He growled and showed his teeth.

"Well, then, Freshwater Wolf, are you racing in the two-man sculls?" Raoul asked.

He growled an exaggerated *"Oui,"* half animal, half human, a demeanor that fit with his bushy mustache, and gestured with his thumb over his shoulder. "With Petit Bleu."

Alphonsine laughed. Petit Bleu was his friend Jean. "Bravo, Jean. You chose the name of the best wine in the Île de France. From Argenteuil."

"Forget the wine. Pour us some victory champagne now," Guy said. "We'll be back before the bubbles are gone."

Alphonsine stood on her toes. Gustave called out, "Take your marks." The gun went off, the trumpet blared, the crowd shouted, *"Oh hisse! Ho!"* and Guy and Jean shot out in front of all but Le Hook. The two boats stayed bow to bow until the turnaround, and Guy and Jean nosed ahead to finish first. On the dock they shook hands all around and Pierre and Paul came back to the table with their arms slung over each other's shoulders.

"Guy and Petit Bleu are good possibilities," Ellen said. "Not bad-looking."

"But Guy and Auguste have no use for each other," Alphonsine said.

Between every two races there was a break, and immediately the water was filled with yoles and pedal boats. The impresario bellowed out the virtues of *canotage* while mimes accompanied his words with buffoonery.

Out of the milling crowd stepped Aline. As soon as Auguste spotted her, he maneuvered his way to her side and brought her to the group.

The trumpet on the barge struck a fanfare and Gustave announced the *triplettes,* sculls for three rowers and a coxswain. Guy's team came in second. That meant his teammate, Tomahawk, a big blond fellow with hair like a haystack and a thick neck, was a possibility.

"Do you have any yellow paint left?" Alphonsine teased.

"Very funny, mademoiselle. I'm going to die laughing," Auguste said.

Anne served eel stew to Guy's team. Alphonsine poked Guy on the shoulder. "That's for your energy. There's a surprise riding on these races." He ate quickly and was off for the four-man race.

"If Guy's team wins, Tomahawk just may be our *quatorzième,*" Pierre said.

"And if they don't, I could have Monsieur Le Hook," Auguste said. "What a happy choice."

"But Le Hook's team has a handsome fellow in the fourth seat," Ellen said. "I wouldn't mind *him* gazing at me in the painting."

Le Hook's team and Guy's team with Tomahawk in the second seat shot off ahead of the pack.

"I'm betting for Guy," Raoul said.

"That would set Tomahawk as a possibility in the painting, depending on whether he's going to race in the slalom," Pierre said.

"Tomahawk is a brute," Paul said. "I'm rooting for Le Hook."

Le Hook gained on the return, and when they approached the finish, Le Hook and Guy were prow to prow.

"*Allez,* Guy! *Allez!*" Raoul yelled with some of the models.

"*Plus vite,* Hook! *Plus vite!*" yelled Pierre and others.

With some misgivings, Alphonsine took up Raoul's chant for Guy. In the last ten meters, Guy won by half a length, and Raoul went wild, cavorting and lunging, saving himself from falling just in time.

The band played dance music while the race master set up buoy markers for the side-by-side slalom courses. Loud conversations crossed each other on the terraces, knives and forks clattered on plates, absinthe, madère, and orange-flavored bishop spiced with cinnamon and nutmeg flowed, and champagne corks popped at every table where there were winners. Alphonsine circulated among the tables to congratulate all the contestants.

The slalom of the narrow *as,* the most precarious, was a highlight second only to the jousts. At the last minute, Paul signed up.

"You're crazy," Pierre said.

"I'm feeling lucky."

"Have you ever paddled an *as?*" Pierre asked.

"No. How difficult can it be? Just dig and drag, left right left?"

"Ha! You'll see," Alphonsine said. "Just don't lean."

All the boats bore a racing name for the day. Guy's was *Le Barbare Joyeux,* and he did look like a jolly barbarian with that outrageous mustache, and that small tongue of a beard below his lower lip. One was *Double Pression, Tapped Beer,* and Tomahawk's was *Le Jupon Léger, The Loose Petticoat.* Le Hook's was called *Quel Chahut, What an Uproar,* referring to the dance. Paul's was *La Verseuse, The Coffeepot,* the kind with the side handle, liable to overturn.

"Oh, bad luck for him," Pierre said.

"Brave *canotiers*," Gustave shouted. "Take your numbers."

Two boats competed side by side in each race. The gunshot cracked.

"And they're off, ladies and gentlemen, galloping nose to nose," Raoul shouted.

"This isn't a horse race, Raoul," Alphonsine said.

"No, lady, but it is a competition," he replied. "Who better than me to announce it?" He pretended to hold a megaphone. "Curving to the right, left, right, like snakes slicing the water."

She and Aline laughed. He was swaying back and forth to the rhythm of his announcing.

"As close as they can get to the markers. Tomahawk in *The Loose Petticoat* leads by a nose, holds her lead on the turnaround. *Tapped Beer* scrambles at the turn. Tips. Rights herself. Presses on. It's *Loose Petticoat* by a chin, a neck. *Loose Petticoat* holds the lead for three more turns, two, one—and it's *Loose Petticoat* by a neck, the winner in race one, and Tomahawk is one step closer to being the champion in the painting."

"Ugh!" Auguste groaned. "A neckless pile of hay smack in the middle of my painting."

"Race two," Gustave announced. "*The Coffeepot* versus *What an Uproar*. Take your mark."

This was Paul's race so they all cheered for him, but he had trouble keeping his prow straight even in the setup.

"It doesn't look good," Pierre said.

"Le Hook in *What an Uproar* shoots off," Raoul shouted. "He stays close to the course. Paul in *The Coffeepot* swings wide, passes the first buoy, swings left, passes the second. *Uproar* pulls ahead. *The Coffeepot* oversteers, grazes the buoy, tips, rights itself. Paul's still in, still in, friends. Oops! No, yes, he's still in but wobbling. *The Coffeepot* approaches the turnaround, tries a tight turn. *The Coffeepot* tips. The brave *canotier* digs in his paddle, too hard. He tips the other way. *The Coffeepot* pours him head first into the river. *What an Uproar* wins by default."

"Oh, no!" shouted Aline. "Does he know how to swim?"

Raoul continued. "A yole is dispatched to retrieve the unlucky *canotier*. He refuses the offered oar. He swims, ladies and gentlemen, swims to the bank and climbs up, red-faced and grinning. Grinning, ladies and gentlemen!"

Paul came to the table shaking off water. "I was just getting the hang of it."

"Be glad you're better with the sword than the paddle!" Pierre said.

Such a man, this fellow Paul, Alphonsine thought. He didn't brood over what might have happened in the duel. He threw himself into life again.

Guy was next in *Le Barbare Joyeux*. He skimmed each buoy neatly, pulled ahead, danced arabesques on the water. "*The Joyous Barbarian* wins his race, but that's not all, ladies and gentlemen," Raoul said. "The finals are yet to come, pitting the three winners against each other."

Tomahawk won against Le Hook, and in the final race, Tomahawk kept Guy a half-length behind on the upstream. Auguste groaned miserably the whole time, but Tomahawk swung too wide and Guy paddled like a maniac and won. Adding his points from all races, he took the championship. On the platform, Papa anointed *The Joyous Barbarian* with the Rowers Championship Cup, *Coupe du championnat des rameurs,* and "a chance to appear in the championship painting, *Les canotiers de la Maison Fournaise!*" and the band played "La Marseillaise."

Alphonsine and Auguste looked at each other. "Well, it could have been Tomahawk," he said.

Alphonse's big jousting event, *les joutes à la lance,* was next.

"If he doesn't win," Alphonsine murmured, "he'll feel he let Papa down. And they'll both be raving mad that he spent Sundays posing instead of practicing."

"A fine thing to tell me now," Auguste said.

Teams of eight rowers, one helmsman, and one jouster were dressed in white with either blue or red sashes. Wearing canvas shoes with rubber soles, the jousters strapped on their padded shields and took up their three-meter lances equipped with flat leather discs at the forward end.

The two heavy wooden barques, the red and the blue, were waiting at the barge, each one having a *tintaine* at the stern, a raised platform two meters above the water where the jousters would stand. Uncle Titi ferried the teams to the barge so they could hear Gustave announce the rules.

Papa stood on the dock, and Maman came out to stand beside Alphonsine.

"Alphonse is worried about Hugo," Maman said.

"I can understand why," Pierre said. "He's bigger than Alphonse."

"You can write an article," Paul said to Antonio, "for your journal in Milan."

"Good idea. This will be entirely new to them."

"Jouteurs sur les tintaines," the master of the jousts called, and the first two teams, from Bezons and Bougival, stepped into each boat and the jousters mounted the platforms.

"You can write that for more than a century," Paul said, "the sons of the lance have observed the same ritual, adapted from medieval tournaments."

"I see. The horse replaced by the barque, the field by the river," Antonio said.

"But the ardor, the bravery, and the challenge remain the same," Paul said. "This keeps alive *le patrimoine,* our national cultural heritage."

Far enough apart to build up speed, at the trumpet's blare, the rowers bent to their oars like machines, and the water churned behind them.

"It looks like they'll ram each other," Antonio said.

"Yes, sometimes that happens," Pierre said matter-of-factly.

A thud, and one jouster was shoved, but he kept his stance. The barques were rowed to the opposite starting marks and charged toward each other again. In a powerful blow, the jouster from Bougival was thrown back and tumbled into the water. Cymbals crashed, tambourines rattled.

"Now what happens?" Antonio asked.

"Two new teams take their places," Paul said.

Croissy with Hugo the Bull on the *tintaine* beat Petit Gennevilliers. Argenteuil and Chatou were next.

"Alphonse is up against Jacques the Red," Alphonsine said. "He's a vegetable farmer, a big show-off. It would be Alphonse's worst humiliation to lose to him."

The oarsmen plowed the water and *La Barque Rouge* got a quick start, but *La Barque Bleue* dug in and gained speed.

Raoul took up the role of announcer again. "The best-known jouster, Alphonse Fournaise, nicknamed the Hippopotame, stands solidly on the *tintaine,* lance in the air, muscles taut, ready for the colossus in red. Rumor has it that Hippopotame has not been at practice. He's been lounging on the terrace for weeks, posing for some painter. We'll see whether he's got what it takes to send this wiry farmer flying. First encounter, Jacques thrusts his lance and it grazes Alphonse's shoulder. He tips, he rights himself. No score. Second encounter. Alphonse plows into Jacques' stomach. The man doubles up, remains standing. Third encounter, neither combatant is willing to yield the *tintaine.* It appears to be an impasse. Bout four, and Jacques the Red breaks his lance against Fournaise's shield."

Alphonsine winced. Maman cried out. Alphonse was pushed backward, but he thrust forward his arms. Bent-kneed, he righted himself.

"Five bouts," Auguste said in amazement.

"Once more the master of the jousts bellows, *'Allez-y!'*" Raoul was shouting now. "They meet. They clash. The blue lance pounds into the shield of the red-sashed jouster. He's shoved backward. One leg lifts. He teeters. He's out of control. He's *in* the water, ladies and gentlemen. *In* the water indeed."

"Bravo à vous, Jouteur Bleu!" Angèle sang out, which started a chant that spread along the bank. Even Maman yelled it.

The winning teams Bezons and Croissy fought, and the winner, Croissy, remained to take on Chatou.

"This is the one he's worried about," Auguste said. "Hugo the Bull. A bruiser and a fighter."

Alphonsine held Maman's hand.

"I hope he won't get hurt." Maman's voice quavered.

"Oh hisse! Ho!" The barques drove at each other, and the *Barque Rouge,* skewed at an angle, rammed Alphonse's boat. Alphonse was thrown off balance and fell to his knees, but he stayed on the *tintaine.*

"Point against *Barque Rouge,*" Gustave declared.

"He's tired. He wouldn't have been knocked down otherwise," Maman said.

They heaved at each other again. Alphonse broke his lance against

Hugo's. He took up the spare for the next bout. Both of them delivered blows. Neither was unboated. On the fifth encounter Alphonse heaved forward his lance, perfectly timed, expertly aimed to strike Hugo's shield off center, spinning him off balance and sending him flying. The splash drenched rowers of both teams.

Earsplitting cheers rent the air. *"Bravo à vous, Jouteur Bleu!"*

"Nice try, fatty," Pierre shouted.

The band played a fanfare, and Uncle Titi ferried Alphonse's team ashore. Alphonse raised his lance over his head with one arm and held it aloft all the way to the dock. The crowd made way for him and slapped him on the back as he strode up to the platform, the lance still over his head. Papa, with chest puffed up like Alphonse's, bellowed, "True to old traditions, Chatou takes the honors of the day. Alphonse Fournaise is declared the champion!" He presented him with the *Coupe du championnat des joutes à la lance*, and the band played "La Marseillaise" yet again.

Guy's and Alphonse's teammates and their friends together with the models took over the upper terrace for the victory champagne.

Alphonsine tugged at Auguste's sleeve as they went upstairs. "Guy can decline and that would free you. I know the two of you aren't on easy terms."

He didn't give her a clue to what he was thinking.

On a big silver tray on the table sat *la pièce montée*, an enormous mounded dessert awarded the winners every year, a boat of cream puffs, stuck together with caramel. Above it in almond *nougatine* was the sticky Arc de Triomphe, ordered from Paris. Guy got the first taste, Alphonse the second. Papa poured champagne amid general rowdiness.

"Now we have two champions in the painting," Ellen said.

"And it's painted by a champion painter of Chatou," Papa said.

She felt her throat constrict. She tried to say to Guy with her eyes: *Refuse politely.* She had another solution.

"Tomorrow?" Auguste asked Guy.

"I'm a workingman during the week. It will have to be very early."

"Fair enough."

Her mind tumbled and boiled.

They all settled down to enjoying the dessert.

A drunken *canotier* leapt onto the iron grille to the terrace, reached through the bars and lifted Ellen's skirt. Gustave pulled her away and Alphonse hurled himself over the railing onto the rogue and carried him, flailing and throwing punches, to the bank and tossed him into the river to hoots of laughter from his teammates.

The small orchestra on the barge played Offenbach's Barcarole again and people began to promenade along the bank. The music gentled the crowd as twilight approached. A second barge for dancing was towed to the middle of the river, and Uncle Titi ferried people back and forth.

Maman nudged Alphonsine in the small of her back. "Go and dance."

She went downstairs and let Uncle Titi take her. Everyone was changing partners. Alphonse was dancing with Ellen, and Angèle was with Raoul. She waltzed with Paul, with Antonio, and then with Raoul, lurching along. He was so gallant and had been so entertaining that she said she would cheer for him as well as for Gustave the next week at the sailing regatta. But it was Auguste she really wanted to dance with. She felt he owed it to her. A dance. What was a dance, after all? Lasting only a few minutes, a privacy of two in a swirling crowd, an opportunity for something to pass between them.

But no. He danced only with Aline. Alphonsine stood there with hope, angry with herself for having that hope. Despite feeling so dispensable, she wanted him to come to her. She waited through a *gavotte,* but when people started a *chahut,* she stepped onto the launch to go back. At that moment frivolity didn't suit her mood. As Titi ferried her back she watched each dancer imitating an animal. Kangaroos, gazelles, horses, cats all moved in a frenzy under the colored lanterns.

She found Maman sitting at a table on the lower terrace, and gave her a kiss on her temple. "This must be the first time you've sat down all day."

"Alphonse was magnificent," Maman said in a dreamy way. "Why aren't you dancing?"

"Oh, I was."

"Then go back."

"I'd rather watch from above."

"You've given up, then?"

"Maman, I would marry him if he asked. I would forget being a widow faithful to my husband's memory. I would even live with him without marriage. But I won't stand on that barge another minute."

Maman's hand grabbed hers. She squeezed it, and went upstairs. There was only one winner in a joust.

A few people remained at the tables quietly enjoying the evening. She stood where the terrace railing wrapped around the building away from the customers. Lights on the dance barge vibrated when the orchestra played a polka. Their colored reflections in the water shook in time to the pounding feet. In between each dance, the music of crickets, the water like black satin, the lights on small boats winking like fireflies, the stars, no moon. Somewhere in the winking night, all the models danced. Darkness enveloped them as light had done when Auguste painted them, and she among them. Who would be hurt if she just went on loving him?

Fireworks shot up, illuminating the sky like stars that couldn't contain themselves, and rained down on the water in shards of light.

Gustave came upstairs and stood beside her. "You have the right idea. This is the best place to see the fireworks."

Oil lamps lit up couples gliding in yoles. Others without lights slid along in secret until a burst of sparkles gave them momentary form and life.

"Did you enjoy the day?" he asked.

Yes and no.

"I always do on the day of the Fêtes. This year especially."

The no had to do with waiting on the barge. Not even one measly dance. Everything else was a yes.

"You were a fine race official."

"I liked doing it."

After watching the last of the fireworks spring wide in a fan of glowing sparks, Gustave said, "The river has something here it doesn't have for me in Paris."

"What's that?"

"Peace."

CHAPTER THIRTY-SIX

À l'Atelier

Aline forked three green beans into her mouth.

"Delicious, Camille. Aren't they good, Maman? They taste like home."

"*Oui.*" Her mother made it sound like it cost her something to agree.

"Straight from the Aube," Camille said, "grown the Burgundian way, like vines in stony soil. Every so often I can get them at Les Halles."

"And cooked with bacon too," Aline said.

Maman didn't respond. Ever since she hurt her by saying that it wasn't just painters who abandon women, but men with vineyards too, her mother refused to talk about home. She felt awful about it, but kept trying.

"Well, now, look who's here," Camille said, putting her hands on her hips and looking out the window of the *crémerie*.

Auguste! And Maman right here. She swallowed without chewing. He walked in and pulled up a chair to their small table without waiting to be invited. Maman stiffened, set down her fork, and gave her a warning look.

"What are you doing in Paris? The painting isn't finished," Aline said.

"I came to give you your modeling fee. You left without it Saturday." He laid two five-franc pieces next to her plate. "And I came to invite you to see my studio. It's just across the street. I have some paintings there I'd like to show you."

She glanced at her mother's icy look of command. "This is my mother, Madame Mélanie Charigot."

"Enchanté, madame," he said, taking off his boater.

Why did he have to do that? Now Maman would think he looked old enough to be her father.

"And you, madame. I would be honored if you would come to have a look."

"A painter's studio? Never. And neither will my daughter."

"I will, Maman. Monsieur Renoir might want me to pose again. I daren't lose the chance."

"No, Aline. We will not be going."

She had been waiting for just the right moment. She reached in her drawstring bag. "Hold out your hand, Maman."

Maman gave her a look of suspicious annoyance.

"Do it, Mélanie," Camille said.

Maman didn't move. Aline took her wrist and turned her hand palm up, and put something small in it. Her mother stared down at the newspaper wrapping. Since Maman wasn't going to unwrap it, she tugged the edge of the paper herself. A thimble rolled out onto Maman's palm. "Silver. You always say your brass one turns your finger green. I bought it on rue du Temple. Put it on."

"You shouldn't be spending money frivolously."

"Why, that's a proper thing for a daughter to do," Camille said.

Aline put it on her mother's middle finger. "There. It fits good and tight."

She finished her meal, and said, "I *am* going to Monsieur's studio." She picked up Auguste's two five-franc coins and set down two one-franc coins of her own so that they made two clicks, for her mother's meal as well as hers. "It would be nice if you came too."

She felt Maman's hand squeeze her knee under the table. She gave her a moment, stood, and walked out the door on wobbly legs, leaving Auguste to make amends. Stepping off the curb and crossing the street, she felt as though she were crossing to a different land.

Auguste caught up with her. "Well played," he said and walked up to the concierge's wicket. *"Bonsoir, monsieur. S'il vous plaît,* my mail?"

The man looked her over like he was peeling an onion and she felt cheap.

"The higher in the building, the less respect from the concierge. Take a deep breath. I'm on the sixth floor. That's how they designed these apartments. Painters' studios on the top, with large windows for light."

He paused at the third-floor landing and ripped open an envelope. "Aha. Finally." He snapped a banknote against his palm. "From a friend named Deudon. For the painting."

"He's buying it?"

"No. For the painting's expenses."

The higher she climbed, the more anxious she felt. She'd been cruel again to Maman. She hadn't meant to be. Maman's fear for her was like a tendril on a vine. If she let it grow, it would strangle her.

He opened his door. She stopped in the hallway. Maman's warnings about painters blared in her mind. This was a mighty big difference from being with him at the river where there were other people around and she could scream if she needed to. All the confidence she had felt at the river left her.

He chuckled in an understanding way. "Come in. I won't do anything you don't want me to. I promise."

How many times had he said that to women he lured up here? Stepping across the threshold might mark another cleft in her life.

"I can't. I shouldn't have come. Jacques hasn't been out all day."

"Your sweet mother can tend to Jacques Valentin Aristide d'Essoyes sur l'Ource."

Hearing him say the whole name softened her. From the doorway she looked into a large dark room empty in the middle. An easel to hold paintings. She knew the name now. Two sunken armchairs and two cane chairs against a wall. A table. A low divan. She drew back. That must be where he made them lie, his naked women. She grasped the doorframe. Vaguely, as if from a distance, she heard him say something. He put his arm around her waist and eased her inside and shut the door. It closed with a click. Maybe it locked. She was trapped.

He raised the shades of a whole *wall* of windows. The room became filled with light, much lighter than any apartment she had ever been in. Now she could see paintings hanging without frames and leaning in stacks against the walls. Some were pictures of the country and the river, but more were of beautiful women in elegant dresses that even Madame Carnot would be proud to have made. How could he want her?

He turned the paintings outward, leaned them against the furniture, and laid some on the floor. He moved about like a grasshopper, springing from one to the other. She couldn't make her feet move, couldn't say a word out loud.

But to herself, she said, *Mon Dieu.* My life has just begun.

Another cleft. She wanted it at the same time that she was afraid of it. Modeling was a good bit better than being a seamstress. If Maman kept to barking about her running with a painter, she wouldn't turn over one franc of the money she earned, but she'd be sure to tell her the amount.

"You don't have much furniture for so big a room."

"I only want what is strictly necessary. Light is necessary. Furniture is not."

She saw a painting of the Flower Pot island with people on the plank bridge, near where they had lain on the grass. The easy feeling she had then came back. He had listened to her tell about Papa and the vineyard, and then he had to go and make her nervous by crawling his fingers over her ankle.

"The floor won't cave in if you step on it. See?" He hopped from one foot to another in a funny way. "Come. Have a look."

Slowly, she circled the room and stopped at each painting. The women were so chic. She saw one of a woman sewing. She could pose for one like that.

"Who is this?"

"Nina Lopez. She didn't have a father either."

"I *have* a father. There's a difference." Her annoyance carried over to how she asked about a model in a blue dress in the next painting.

"Henriette Henriot, an actress I knew a long time ago."

"What about this one in a rowboat?"

"Lise. I painted that near Chatou."

"Why didn't you ask her when you needed someone in your painting?"

"I don't know where she is."

Abandoned. She saw again her mother's arm flung backward. All these women, one after another, abandoned. He had used them up. He may even have left some with children.

There was one of Alphonsine with her shift off her shoulder. That made her nervous. Did she really want to be his model with her shift off her shoulder? She couldn't remake herself. She wanted to be *something* to him, but she would never be more than second to his love for painting. She would never have all of him. He couldn't keep painting *her* the rest of his life.

She saw a painting of him folded up with his feet on the chair. "This is my favorite. Because it's of you," she said.

He stepped behind her and laid his hands on her shoulders. "A good friend painted that. Frédéric Bazille."

"Once you were walking right down the middle of rue Saint-Georges with two men, and you were all carrying paint boxes. All of you wore your hair long, which caused a stir in Camille's *crémerie,* where Géraldine and I were watching out the window. We pretended to place bets on which of you would be famous. 'The middle one,' I said. 'He has a serious look.' That was you. Maybe the man who painted this was one of the others."

"How long ago did you come here?"

"Five years ago. When I was fourteen."

"Then it wasn't him. He died in the war."

"Oh."

She circled the room a second time. "Did you love these ladies?"

"I love all the women I paint, in some measure."

That wasn't what she meant. She stopped at one of a man and a lady cozy together reading a book. That cut her out. This same lady was trying on a hat in another painting. "Who is she?"

One of his eyebrows curved. "Margot Legrand."

She took a risk. "Did you love her?"

She waited, frozen, until he answered.

"Yes."

There it was. The truth of Maman's fears. Every painting of a woman in this room made every minute she stayed here more dangerous. She darted to the door.

"Wait! Stop!" He took hold of her shoulders. "Fifteen minutes. That's all I ask. Please, stay." He took her hand and led her toward the divan. "Sit."

She felt her knees bend.

"Your mother has a powerful hold on you," he said.

She traced the stitching on the upholstery with her fingernail.

"Is she a seamstress too?"

"Yes."

"So is mine. You can tell her that. She's as strong as steel, just like yours, but soft as swansdown inside. And my father was a tailor."

"But you're not. Did you ever want to be anything other than an artist?"

"Don't call me that. I'm a workman of painting. It's a trade, something humble. Artists think of themselves as intellectuals. They follow rules of schools. I trust my hands and eyes more than my mind."

"But did you always want that?"

"For a while I thought about being a singer. I used to sing in a choir at church and the choir director thought I should study opera. He became a famous composer. I love his *Ave Maria*. You can tell your mother that too."

"Sing me something."

He blushed in such a sweet way. He looked like he was trying to think of the perfect song.

"Some other time."

"But you didn't want that? To sing for a living?"

"My parents thought painting china would be more steady. They were from Limoges, the porcelain-making city, so they were more comfortable with that."

She looked again at the paintings. "Didn't you ever study how to do this?"

"Oh, yes, at the École des Beaux-Arts, like everyone else. I was always the last one to leave the studio so I could pick up discarded tubes of paint in the hope to squeeze out a dab. You can tell your mother how thrifty I was."

"She would only think you were poor."

"A group of us left because we wanted to find a new way, and new subjects."

"And did you?"

"Yes, but the group is splitting up. There's a lot of turmoil about art in Paris these days. Gustave is in despair over the arguments."

"Are you?"

"They're hurtful." He stared at the paint-spotted floor. "Sometimes I don't know who I am as a painter. I don't know whether I should paint what I want to or paint to make a living."

"Can't you do both?"

"It's more complicated than that."

That shut her out. Another way of saying she was too simpleminded to understand.

"I'm like a cork in the river, bobbing every which way, not knowing what I'm looking for."

She pictured what her mother would say: *I forbid you to tie yourself to a painter without a sou to his name, a confused one at that.*

"Just paint. Whatever way you want to. You make it too hard with all that thinking."

"At what point is a painter ready to free himself from influences? I need to go away somewhere to think hard. Maybe after this big painting."

"Papa was made that way, not content to live out his life in one spot. And look, he abandoned us."

"This is traveling for a purpose. I need to see the Titians in Venice, the Raphaels in Rome, and to discover the sources of Delacroix's colors in Algeria. That's the way it has to be."

"So paint." She flung out her arm. "Go to Italy. Go to Algeria. America. Wherever. I don't care."

It came out harshly, and he looked stunned. Of course she did care.

She saw that he had to paint to live. He had to paint to breathe. He was made to paint just as grapevines were made to produce wine, and if this traveling was part of being a painter, she had to let him be him. That was something her mother never learned about her father. She would rather have Auguste go away now, before anything happened. If he came back, he might be more likely to stay. She didn't want an unhappy man pining for another place.

"If you come back, you might want to paint in Essoyes. Mother still owns the farmhouse. It would be a nice place for you to paint. You can paint whatever you want there. The quiet is so lovely. The peace. You won't be bothered by painters' arguments. Just paint what you see. The trees, and the rows of grapevines climbing over the hills. Streams. Waterwheels. Wild violets and lilies of the valley."

If she could get him to come to the Aube, then she'd be there if Papa ever came home. Otherwise, Papa might never find them.

"The Seine isn't the only river," she said. "The Aube is twice as wide and of a green so whitish and shimmery you would swear it was lit from below."

"You knew that would intrigue me."

He rubbed the side of his nose. "To be so isolated, one has to be strong."

"You are strong."

"I wouldn't be able to do without Paris. I'd feel cut off from my friends, the cafés, the entertainments, the boulevards, the galleries. The Louvre. The pulse of city life. Our movement."

"You won't have the pulse of city life in some African desert."

"But I'm coming back."

That's what she wanted to hear. She studied his face and couldn't find in it any hint of deception.

"Write me a letter, and I'll be at the station."

What had she said? She would have to learn to read it! She watched his eyes moving slowly to every part of her face.

"Kissing you in the water was lovely," he said.

"So was swimming."

"We can do that again." His eyes and his voice were so serious.

"I'd like that."

Even if she only had a part of him once in a while, it would be better than nothing. She had to give in order to receive. That was true, city or country.

He pulled away. "I promised your mother you would be home in an hour."

"What did she say to that?"

"She said it was one hour too long."

"I thought you wanted me to come here to make love to me." The words spilled out before she could catch them.

"I already have. With my brush."

She looked down at her lap. "I didn't mean that way."

"That's the last thing I want to do now. I just want to be close to you."

She had been too blunt. Too countryish. When a man takes a woman into his barn, she knows what to expect. Apparently Auguste was not like that.

"This time was just for you to see the studio. Not to paint you. Not to have relations with you. The proper time will come."

She was confused and embarrassed and a little relieved. "Then you don't want to paint me naked." She didn't know whether to hope he'd say yes or no.

"Of course I do, but you have to understand. The nude is a painter's highest aspiration, my earthly paradise in fact, but a painter doesn't do it with just anyone or on a whim. Someday I will, when you're ready and I'm ready. I'm not now. I've been seduced by color and I have to reacquaint myself with line before I paint you nude. That may take me a long time."

That made her feel dumb again. They were from different worlds.

"That's why I have to go to Italy. To learn to paint you as Raphael and Titian painted nudes in the Renaissance."

"My mother said it would come to this. She said that every painter wants you to take off your clothes, and after you model bare, you painters use up a woman and then abandon her."

He didn't laugh at her, but he didn't deny it either. His hand stroked her hair and came around to her chin.

"Some things have to be resolved before love can grow roots or bear fruit. Next time, bring your mother with you."

"You're asking for trouble."

"No. I'm asking for resolution."

"And if she won't come?"

His lips touched hers, softly at first, and he pressed her to him. She felt the top bone in his spine at the back of his neck.

"Then I guess you can't come." He breathed into her mouth, "Find a way."

CHAPTER THIRTY-SEVEN

So Brief a Pair

Alphonsine was eating lunch on the lower terrace with her mother when Gustave bounded down the steps from the footbridge wearing a smile as wide as a frog's.

"Is Auguste here?" he asked.

"I see that you're dressed as a gentleman should," Maman said. "It's about time, after two months of wearing your undershirt around here."

"*Tch, tch.* Just as your own son does, madame."

"Guy hasn't shown up to pose for two days, so Auguste is painting downstream from the railroad bridge," Alphonsine said. She was annoyed at Guy but hoped for a different solution.

"It's good for him," her mother said. "He's been moody."

"Well, then, I won't bother him. I just wanted to tell everyone that I bought a piece of property in Petit Gennevilliers."

"You did it!" Alphonsine smacked her hand against her cheek. "You actually did it."

He jingled a ring of keys. "I signed the papers yesterday."

"We'll almost be neighbors," Louise said. "Both Alphonses will be so happy."

"I wanted to show it to Auguste."

"You can show me," Alphonsine said.

"With pleasure."

. . .

They took the train to Asnières and switched to the Montigny line, which had a stop across the river in Argenteuil. He had a look of utter contentment as they rode. She felt content too.

"I thought you'd be out practicing for the regatta, not buying houses."

"Whenever I sail by this house, I can't keep my mind on sailing. You were with me when I decided."

"I was? When?"

"We were watching the fireworks. I said the river gave me peace."

"Ah, it does that. You can come to it with a turbulent mind and feel the peace enfold you."

"The most exciting period of my life is coming to a close," he said.

She was shocked. "Why do you say that?"

"The contention among the painters. I don't have the constitution for it. This will be a retreat to simpler pleasures. Gardening. Sailing. Designing a racing yacht."

"Not painting?"

"When I feel like it. For me."

They crossed the Argenteuil road bridge on foot. At this stretch of river, the Argenteuil bank had a wide, tree-lined promenade, large estates, and a few small factories. The Petit Gennevilliers bank was more rustic, with boatyards, and summerhouses nestled in orchards.

Gustave pointed to a short, narrow dock. "That's mine. I'll have a larger one built, and I'll keep the slips in the Argenteuil marina until I can get a large boat garage built."

Set back from the bank, the house had a steeply pitched roof of red tiles, two gables with windows and wooden balconies. A wide chimney ran the length with four chimney pots.

"I'll plant a garden down to the river with trellises and a rose arbor."

"With what kinds of flowers?" She thought she might prepare a basket of seed packets and bulbs as a gift.

"I want dahlias, lilacs, irises, lilies. I'll build a greenhouse with a hot-air stove so I can propagate orchids. Claude and I have some ideas about how to do that. There's a gardener's cottage and a wood behind."

At the front door he sorted through the keys. "This is the first time I've been in it since I signed the documents."

"I'm honored," she said with a little curtsy.

"It hasn't been kept up, and the rooms are all empty, but try to imagine what it will be like repainted and with furniture and paintings."

The central parlor was large and airy and looked out on the river. "The bigger paintings will hang here, but . . ." He led her into another reception room. "Here's where I'll hang Auguste's *Bords de la Seine à Champrosay*. And here will be Claude's *Régates à Argenteuil*. And here Sisley's *La Seine à Suresnes*."

"You'll feel just like you're out on the water."

He nodded with quick bobs of his head. "Exactly."

"How many paintings do you have?"

"About fifty by others. Plus almost everything I've ever painted."

"I can't wait to see them."

"Mine too?"

"Yours especially."

"They're odd. So people say."

"They won't be to me. They're a part of you."

He stopped his circuit of the room and turned to her. His cheeks lifted, and creases fanned out from the corners of his eyes, as though she'd said something unexpected, welcome, and important. Maybe there was possibility here, right under her nose, and she'd been facing the wrong direction.

They walked through room after room on each of two floors above the ground floor.

"The best view is from the upstairs studio, but you'll have to climb a ladder."

"I don't mind."

The studio was a separate structure built in the shape of a hexagon. Two wide bay windows let in light from two directions into a large open area. He positioned a ladder up to the loft. "Be careful. I'm right behind you."

It was hard to climb the ladder without stepping on her skirt. She had to lift it and hold on to the ladder at the same time. When he opened the shutters, the river stretched like a glittering blue ribbon in both directions. The promenade at Argenteuil, the Argenteuil road bridge, the marina, and the Château Michelet with its pointed towers all within one view.

"It looks like a painting, right from here. Tell me you'll paint it."

He took a few minutes and gazed out the window. "Maybe someday. The château is owned by the president of the Cercle de la Voile à Paris."

"Then it's only fitting that you live across the river from him."

"You've heard your father speak of Chevreux and Luce, the boat builders?"

"Of course. They're famous around here."

"They're building a new boatworks, the biggest on the river, right in Petit Gennevilliers. I think eventually I'll give them some business."

She whirled around and found him grinning. "A new boat?"

"A seagoing racing yacht so I can enter the big coastal regattas too." He let out a breath that seemed long-held. "I'm going to like it here."

"You're going to *love* it."

A fresh, new hope rose. She might be invited here from time to time. "I'm so happy." *For you,* he could take it to mean, or for herself. He went to the ladder and descended partway.

"Be careful. I'll be just a few steps below you. Face the ladder."

Her skirt prevented her from seeing where to put her feet. She hesitated at each step until she felt his hand on her ankle guiding her to each rung, a caring intimacy.

"I'm down," he said. "You have four more steps."

Her heel caught her skirt hem and she shook her leg to free it and lost her footing and fell. He caught her, and held her for just an instant, until she righted herself and her feet were on the ground. He almost pushed her away as though she were hot to the touch.

"Are you all right?" He backed away with an odd expression on his face.

"Yes."

"Don't tell Auguste. He'll think I was irresponsible to take you up there."

"Of course I'll tell him. How else could I describe the view?"

On the way back in the train, he said, "I'm going to be content here for the rest of my life."

"Anyone would be," she said.

"No. Not anyone. Not Auguste. He's restless. One thing leads him to another. When he is painting a landscape, he loves water against a bank of trees. He loves a boat and its reflection. He loves what light does. If he's painting a woman, he loves her. If he is painting a still life, he loves each petal. He may look at it afterward with joy that he and it and the light collaborated to make something that never existed before, something composed of all three, but the moment he finishes it, he goes on to something else."

"Or someone else? Is that what you mean?"

"He keeps himself alive by the next subject and the next and the next. Any woman who thinks she can command all of his attentions will find herself unhappy."

She had surmised as much, particularly after Aline arrived on the scene, but to hear it laid out like that was something else.

"I've seen what you've been doing," he said in a gentle voice. "Insinuating yourself into his life by assisting with the painting in so many winsome ways."

His tone wasn't accusatory, but it held something inauspicious.

"That can get irksome to a man if it's overly present or heavy."

The sting.

"I can't seem to hold back."

"Not that he's given any indication of feeling that way. I just thought you should know."

"Does this have anything to do with Aline?"

"No. I would tell her the same thing."

"You don't have to worry. One more session with Guy, and the painting will be finished. He'll go back to Paris." She couldn't control the pique in her voice. It wasn't the truth of what he said that pricked, but the fact that he felt he needed to say it.

He laid his hand on her forearm. "I'm learning too that pleasure can be spoiled by expecting too much from it."

She nodded in acquiescence, not in agreement.

When the train approached Asnières she said, "You don't have to accompany me the rest of the way. You can go back to Paris on this line." She stepped onto the platform. Speaking with all the affection she felt for him, she said, "Thank you for showing me your house. It's perfect for you. Remember, I'll be cheering for you at the regatta."

She lingered on the footbridge, numbed by Gustave's well-intentioned counsel. Still, she was so happy about his new house that she wanted to tell Auguste. She headed downstream. Under Alexander's metal arches leaping across the river, she thought how tied her family was to the bridge. Alphonse had been in the unit ordered to blow it up so the Prussian army couldn't use it to enter Paris, her father depended on it for his business, Alexander had designed the repair of it and killed himself right here. A love that fierce, and she hadn't fully recognized the truth of it, or accepted that it could come to her. She should have known from Louis that love was too precious to waste.

A train passed overhead on its way to Paris. In the quiet that followed she heard Auguste humming on the other side of the stone piling and the thick foliage. She recognized the tune. Béranger's "Garret." She sang the words in her mind.

> Yes, here's the old room where I roughed it so long
> In the penniless days I ne'er cease to regret,
> When a scapegrace of twenty I lived but for song,
> A few cheery friends, and the charms of Lisette.

A dart shot through her. Auguste was already thinking of his own garret studio in Paris. She sang the words softly to his humming:

In the prime of life's spring-tide, ne'er taking account
Of the world and its ways, or what Fate had in store,
How gaily up six flights of stairs would I mount.
Ah, give me my youth and a garret once more.

The humming stopped.

"Alphonsine?"

"That's truly your song, you know."

"Where are you?"

"In a spot I own more than anyone."

"Come here."

She squeezed her way between bushes to his easel. On the canvas, beyond a small meadow done in feathery pastel strokes, Alexander's green ironwork threaded through the upper branches of two flowering tamarisk trees in front and a third one behind, the blossoms mere smudges of rose and white, with poplars rising in the distance. Under one of the trees, barely discernible, stood a man wearing a flat-topped *canotier.* She could imagine him to be whomever she wanted.

"A companion painting!" she said. "The terrace painting you did of me looks at the railroad bridge from one side. This from the other. A man in one and a woman in the other. The railroad completes the story."

Auguste gave her a wary look. "What story?"

"Just Parisians on the train coming out to our island of Cythera, for pleasure."

"Where did you learn about Cythera?"

"In the Louvre. Watteau's paintings."

"You surprise me."

Good. Aline would never have made the connection.

"More blossoms," she said. "To make this spot a happy place."

With a deadpan expression, he came toward her and lifted his brush to her cheek as though he were going to paint it. She backed away. "No, silly. On the canvas."

He flipped the brush so that the handle was toward her now. "Do it. Add one more."

"Do you mean that?"

His deadpan changed to mock exasperation.

"Why?" she asked.

"For pleasure, of course." He held his palette toward her and pointed to a smear of rose. "Lick up some of that. Feel the wet gooeyness of it."

He put his free hand around her waist and drew her toward the painting.

"Where?"

"Wherever you want. A collaboration."

That lovely word. She aimed her brush. "Here?"

"*D'accord.*"

She daubed the paint on a branch that rested against the bridge.

"A blossom for him," Auguste said. "Perfect."

She handed back the brush. This was far better than a dance.

That's just what they had done this summer—danced around Gustave and the Prussian and Alexander and Jeanne and Aline with light, uncertain steps.

"Gustave bought a house in Petit Gennevilliers. Right on the river."

A scramble of emotions darkened his face. "I thought he might, but not this soon."

"What's wrong? You should be happy for him."

"I am, if that's what he wants. I'm just concerned about what it might mean. His state of mind."

"He was over the moon about it. It's a perfect place for him."

She told him all about it, and about going up to the studio loft and falling off the ladder.

"The instant he saw I was on the ground, he practically shoved me away as though I were made of hot coals."

He set down his palette and brushes. "I wouldn't recommend you to be overly fond of him. For your sake."

"Why? Is he hiding a model with a quaint Burgundian accent?"

"That's just it. He isn't. He never has. His models are mostly men. He has strong feelings for them, and for his sailing crew and boat builders and friends in Paris. His need for intimacy is taken care of by men, *chérie.*"

"I don't believe—"

"When have you ever seen him with a woman?"

"I . . ." The reality descended. "Never."

Air escaped her lungs but would not come back. Her appalling blindness shamed her, her transparency embarrassed her. "I never thought."

Auguste drew her against his chest. "I'm sorry."

She felt his breath coming through her hair on the top of her head. This moment, enfolded in his tenderness, had to last her a long, long time. He didn't seem anxious to pull away. She felt his hand stroke the top of her head and his fingers trail through her hair, for the pleasure of it. His doctrine. That big-knuckled hand that created beauty, that was beauty itself, was anointing her with affection.

How does one end a moment like this? It would kill her to feel him pull away. She had to be first. In a moment. One moment more. Yes. Now.

She drew back. The lines in his forehead contorted, the furrows from his nostrils to the corners of his mouth plowed deeper, and his cheeks were more hollowed. He had aged. Two months and he had aged.

"Thank you for telling me. It saved me from embarrassing myself, and him." She glanced at the painting. "And for letting me add a blossom for Alexander."

"Gustave is going to buy it."

"How do you know?"

"Just a feeling. Your blossom will be in his house."

As if to say, *But you won't. You'll have to be satisfied with that.* She felt the tingle that comes just before tears, and mastered it the instant it rose.

"Go back to work. You've got to finish the sky before the light goes. I just wanted to tell you about his new house."

She drew back and tried to make a graceful exit between the bushes.

She took a *périssoire* and paddled upstream, splashing herself in a hurry to get away. The willows were weeping yellowed leaves into the eddies.

The quieter, more reflective season was coming soon, when she would sift through events and try to rein in her imagination from where it was accustomed to roam. Bare to the waist in the moonlight, Auguste had said she shouldn't regret anything done out of instinct. Despite Gustave's warning, despite Auguste's revelation, she felt no regret for hoping, or for loving, regardless of the return.

She stepped out on the bank where the lovers' bodies had lain. She had called their death beautiful. She had thought Héloïse's love for Abelard beautiful too. But Héloïse was a martyr. Maybe to be insouciant, like Angèle, was a better way to negotiate love.

A wine bottle lay on the bank and a cork was lodged in the reeds. She picked it apart, dropped the pieces, and ground them into the earth with her heel.

She lay down on the grass near the rill and became absorbed in a silver sheet of water spilling over an exposed root, creating colonies of bubbles that separated into pairs as they traveled across a small pool, so fragile they clung to each other, so brief a pair, and took the plunge together over some rocks to disappear in the river.

CHAPTER THIRTY-EIGHT

The Awning

Early Thursday morning, Auguste squinted into the sun rising over the rooftops of Rueil to the east and waited, his patience thin. Against the sun's glare on the terrace, the skin under his eye was ticking off the minutes.

Alphonsine sat beside him, pulling apart a croissant. "Another *café*?"

"If it doesn't mean anything more to him than a niggling obligation, I don't want him in it," Auguste said.

Guy hadn't come on Monday or Tuesday, and Alphonsine had given the excuse that he was recovering from his bout of drinking and the exhaustion after his rowing exertions. Probably true, but on Wednesday he had come down from his upstairs room bleary-eyed, and saw Auguste waiting to paint him. "Oh, I forgot. Sorry," Guy had said. "I can't do it today. I'm already late for work. Tomorrow. I'll do it tomorrow."

"Yes, another cup, if you please," Auguste said and watched Alphonsine descend the stairs, her back straight. If his caution about Gustave had wounded her at all, she didn't show it.

When she came back with the tray, she looked so lovely in a rose-colored dress that he felt torn in two. A river blossom herself. He wanted to paint her again. Not nude. Never nude. Not a classical figure. An Impressionist one, painted with all the tenderness he felt for her. River nymph and Parisienne, she would always remain a part of this Impressionist world. Aline was different. Her deep country origins made her belong to all time, or timelessness in the classical sense. Alphonsine was color, whereas Aline was line. Maybe a woman wasn't too different from a painting direction.

"If he doesn't show up in ten minutes, will you let me paint you instead? Downstairs in the dining room in soft light in front of the blue wallpaper with an open fan in your hand?"

"No."

"Why not?"

"One painting at a time, Auguste." She sipped her *café* thoughtfully, her head tipped down to the creamy brown liquid. "How important is it to resolve the problem of thirteen?"

"With thirteen, I may as well cart it back to my studio in the dark of night and never let a soul lay eyes on it except me."

"Then I have a solution." Her voice had lost its spirit. "Paint me out."

He slammed his cup into the saucer. "What? You don't mean that."

"Put boats on the river where I am and fill in Émile's hole with Charles's jacket. Then you'll have twelve."

He puffed air out his mouth. "How can you say such a thing? You're the soul of this place."

"So are boats on the river." Her eyes had a look of resolve. Regardless of how ridiculous it was, she was sincere in offering a heavy sacrifice.

"I know you mean what you say, and I appreciate your offer, but that would spoil the painting for me. I can't consider it." The tightness in her face softened. "Besides, it wouldn't solve the problem of Ellen left alone. Without a man there, she'll end up being the solitary drinker I promised her she wouldn't be. It would introduce a different mood."

"Loneliness in the midst of gaiety." Her voice, coming from some deep place in her, disturbed him.

"Yes. The sort of despair Degas and Manet have painted in cafés. You know that's not my intent. But thank you. And thank you for your collaboration through all of this."

Only when she nodded could he draw his eyes away to the painting and the area of raw canvas. "I like the idea of a face tucked in there. It would be a spicy surprise."

"Then if he doesn't show up in ten minutes, I'm bringing you a mirror and you can paint yourself."

"Not a chance. Here I am," Guy said, coming through the doorway, his arms out to his sides.

"I had almost given up on you," Auguste said.

"I'm good for my word, but I don't have a lot of time."

Then forget it, he felt like saying. He positioned the painting and told him where to sit.

"Alphonsine, will you sit in Ellen's position, so he has someone pretty to look at?"

She gave him a mock stern look and sat down.

What was he to do about that reddish scrub brush Guy called a mustache? It was so broad and thick that it overpowered his face and made him look like a small walrus. He would fare better with the ladies if he put it on his head and moved that puny tuft beneath his bottom lip to under his nose, for a civilized mustache. He would not have a dragoon leering at Ellen in his painting.

This early in the morning Guy had to look straight into the sun. It made him squint. This wouldn't work.

"This glare will play the devil with my work. Let's try unrolling the awning," he said.

The sun still glared under the scallops at its edge. He waited.

"The longer you wait, the less time you'll have," Guy said.

"I have no choice."

When the sun rose higher, the awning diffused the light so Guy didn't have to squint.

This was it! Of course it was. The solution! He had never used the awning because it cast a shadow over the terrace with the sun overhead or to the west, but by inference, the awning was attached to a building. It conveyed that they weren't floating on a magic carpet.

"I've got it!" he shouted.

In his excitement, he left off painting Guy, whom he'd hardly started, and mixed ultramarine with white and a touch of the soft greens and rose madder to lay in the awning supports again where he'd painted over them, greener against the foliage, bluer against the river. In the early stages, he'd just considered them as vertical place markers. Now he constructed the horizontal rods too.

But he didn't have enough space for all of the awning. Just a suggestion. Right over the sky he'd already painted, he laid in long sweeps of coral for the flat part of the awning, contrasting stripes of yellow where the sun beat directly on it, dulled to a warm mauve gray in parts. And where the scallops hung down, the contrasting stripes flirted with various pastel tints depending on how the breeze moved them and made them catch the light in pale lavender-gray, blue-gray, and pale yellow washes. To catch them as they fluttered, that was the thing, and to make each one a different curve to show them moving, to show that there was a breeze making those sailboats skim across the water.

Some of the scallops would cut off the continuous line of the railroad bridge. He would have to sacrifice that. Covering over the riverscape he'd painted was a shame, but this was the only way he knew to resolve the problem. Ho-ho, he had it now. Zola's claim that the Impressionists remained inferior to what they undertook was bogus.

"Bogus, Émile! Suck your words!"

"Who are you talking to?" Alphonsine asked. "Émile isn't here."

"Wrong Émile, *ma chérie.*"

"I've got to go," Guy said. "My office is waiting."

"*D'accord.* I'm much obliged," Auguste said, looking at the awning developing on the canvas. "Much obliged. You solved a problem for me."

Guy took a look at the painting. "I don't see how. You've hardly got me there at all."

"Enough. I'm much obliged."

"See what I mean, Alphonsine?" Guy said. "The man sees through rose-colored glasses."

"And why not? He's the painter of happiness."

Auguste let his arm sweep left to right across the canvas even as Guy was leaving. He was conscious of Alphonsine watching but neither of them spoke. They didn't need to. She was with him and his brush was flying.

Half an hour and he'd overlaid the landscape with stripes. Alphonse's hat just touched the awning flap. So did a sail. Good. It helped to enclose the group. But now the back looked cramped. He took up his scraping knife.

"What's wrong?" Alphonsine asked

"Nobody's face. The top hat's a little too tall."

He tried to shave off a couple of centimeters, but it was too dry so he had to paint over it thickly. This was the third position of that hat.

"Why didn't I see this earlier? *Quel idiot je suis!*"

As soon as he'd redefined the top hat, he saw that he'd have to lower Jules's hat and head. When he'd done that he saw that Alphonse's hat was a bit too high. He painted awning stripes above it to lower the crown.

The higher the sun, the more translucent the awning became, and the more warmly Alphonsine's skin glowed. That would happen all over the canvas. He asked her to take everyone's positions, one at a time, and he found more places for a subtle wash of coral—on Alphonse's face, Raoul's ear and just under it, Antonio's cheekbone, Pierre's nose and cheek, warming up the whole painting.

"It's the crowning touch," Alphonsine said.

"Not quite. White highlights along the edges of glasses and bottles, and thick white pigment in the bottom of glasses will be the crowning touch."

He felt chagrined. The champion rower wasn't there. The space was blank.

"Now can I bring a mirror?"

"Only if you'll let me scrape a decade off my weathered-wood face."

"Your discovery today already did that. Just in time for you to paint yourself there. It's what I've wanted all along."

Then he'd been wrong about her. She wouldn't interfere in his work.

"It's a kind of signature. You'll be in good company," she said in a lilting voice. "Veronese did the same thing in *his* feast painting."

A surprise, her knowing this.

She planted a sudden, firm kiss on his mouth, a loud smack like Angèle would do, and darted away to get a mirror.

CHAPTER THIRTY-NINE

The Last Luncheon

The regatta would start soon. Auguste paced along the bank. No Aline. No Paul. He peppered Pierre with questions. Pierre knew nothing. Every trainload of people without Paul thickened his misgivings. A fine thing this was, making them imagine another duel.

Aline's lateness had to be intentional. It made him doubt himself. He had pushed himself on her too much, she thought he was an old man, she didn't care for him, he was a fool for thinking she might. Madame Charpentier was right, it was wrong of him to keep chasing after young models, she was only nineteen. He couldn't stand still. He couldn't sit.

He rolled a cigarette. Under a maple tree, Ellen made a comic-tragic face and said, "Our last luncheon." He caught a glimpse of the more authentic disappointment of Alphonsine. His chest collapsed with heaviness. He didn't want the end of the painting to mean the end of the delicious closeness they had shared during the making of it. He wouldn't say he could not have accomplished it without her, but it was a far sight more enjoyable with her. He hoped she knew that. He couldn't imagine not coming back to paint her again, and to enjoy the family, but he had to be careful. He had to be realistic. He had to be independent, for his painting. There was a moral risk in leading on either one of them.

Père Fournaise came outside and offered to take everyone to Argenteuil in the steam launch to watch the regatta begin.

"Give us a little while. We've got two more to come," Auguste said. "In the meantime, I'd like to settle up my account."

"You're leaving us?"

"This evening, but I'll be back soon to transport the painting. And I'll come to paint from time to time. You'll always be my good friends."

He counted out Deudon's money, knowing that it wouldn't cover everything.

Fournaise held up a hand to stop him at three hundred. "I'll call it even if you let me do one thing. It has to do with the painting."

"Sign your name to the thing?"

"Let me show it to my customers. The place will be packed after the boats come across the finish line here."

"It's still wet. It can't be moved."

"I'll guard it myself with Alphonse. One on each side, on the platform."

He liked to live with a painting privately for a time to make sure of it before he exhibited it. "It's not finished."

"Finished enough. It'll do my business a great favor."

Angèle overheard. "Don't be a fusspot, Auguste. We deserve to see it."

"If it be not now," Jules said, *"yet it will come. The readiness is all."* Jules crossed his arms and smiled smugly. "And we're ready."

"It has two surprises in it now," Alphonsine said.

Her reminder of the awning made him agree.

Pierre flung out his arms. "In one grand moment the world will be astonished."

"Oh, is that a welcome for me?" Aline said, brushing past him from nowhere and stepping into Pierre's outspread arms.

"You vixen. Don't tease me coming late all the time," Auguste said.

Louise came running out of the restaurant. "Don't eat a thing in Argenteuil. I want you good and hungry when you come back."

"Don't worry, madame. I'm always hungry. I'm sure the luncheon will be *le plus extraordinaire!*" Aline said.

He thought she chose her words just to end her sentences with *"rrr."*

"If we wait any longer, we'll miss the start," Fournaise said.

Auguste checked the bridge again. No Paul. "All right. We'll go."

They passed dozens of yoles jockeying for good viewing positions. Sailboats not in the races tacked back and forth. Accordion music poured out from a floating wash barge turned into a *guinguette* for the day.

Fournaise docked the launch along the Petit Gennevilliers bank so they would have the best view from the road bridge. The whole basin, two hundred meters wide, was lively with boats flying the colors of their series. The series one boats with red pennants, seven catboats under two tons, and Guy's rigged *périssoire,* were positioning themselves behind the imaginary starting line. Auguste explained to Aline how the boats were classified into five series by weight, with each series having a different start time five minutes apart. The boats competed with the others in their class as well as vying for the grand prize. Aline ignored him.

The horn blasted and the little boats skimmed along downstream at different points of sail, Guy keeping up with the others.

"Monsieur Fournaise, why is that blue boat going the wrong way?" Aline asked.

"It overshot the starting line before the gun and has to go back to start again," Fournaise explained.

Why didn't she ask him? He could have answered as well as Fournaise.

With the wind coming upriver from the southwest, the boats had to change courses often to go downriver, but they were nimble and the river was at its widest here. It would be more difficult for the bigger boats. Everyone darted to the downstream side of the bridge to see them emerge. One heeled over so far its sail caught water and pulled it over. Guy deftly changed his course to avoid the sail lying in the water.

"It's possible Guy could win this championship too," Auguste said. But Gustave needed it more, to get through the crisis he was suffering. If Guy won, they would both be impossible to live with, for opposite reasons. Sailing meant so much more to Gustave than to Guy.

Crossing the bridge again, Alphonsine explained to Aline, "Gustave has three boats in the regatta. Two of them are in this blue series, the *Iris,* his catboat we've been using all summer, sailed by his friend, and his new cutter, the *Condor,* sailed by his brother Martial."

"Where's Gustave?" Aline asked.

Auguste opened his mouth to answer, but Aline turned to Alphonsine who told her that Gustave was in his biggest boat, the *Inès*.

Christ! He had held back with her in his studio, acting the gentleman, and had felt right in holding back, and this was what he was getting for it? Exclusion? What had gone wrong? His talk of Italy? Something her mother said? She was conflicted, poor thing. But, then, so was he.

The *Iris* had a good start but lost position going around the far bridge support. "*Ohé, ohé, ohé,*" he called down to Martial. If Gustave didn't win in the *Inès*, it wouldn't be such a loss as long as one of his other boats did.

The third series, yellow, had already started, and there, cutting swiftly through the water right toward them close-hauled, was Raoul at the helm of *Le Capitaine* heeled to leeward, and hiked way out over the water on the windward rail, Paul was waving his cap over his head in wild circles and shouting, "*Plus vite, plus vite!*"

"Faster, faster," they shouted back.

"Thank God," Auguste said.

"I'm bringing him luck," Paul shouted.

"If he falls out," Pierre said, "another boat could run him over."

"That's one man who knows how to squeeze the most into one life," Angèle said.

"Not one life. Nine," Auguste said. "Like a tomcat."

The fourth and fifth series started together. Fournaise explained that the fourth series flying green pennants, Gustave's class, was the largest of the centerboards and leeboards, above six tons, and the fifth series, two oceangoing yachts with fixed keels, were considered the fastest. Those two, *Miss Jane* and *Miss Helen,* had sailed from England for this race. "That may spell trouble, two of them."

"Why, monsieur?" Aline asked.

"One might run interference so the other can win," Fournaise said.

Auguste could feel the breeze getting skittish. Gustave had a good start in the *Inès,* but so did *Le Palais, Jupiter,* and *Le Rouge-et-Noir,* the three others flying green pennants. Of all the boats, if *Le Palais,* Gustave's longtime rival, took the lead, that might topple his spirit. In his recent mood shifts, Gustave might get so discouraged he wouldn't sail well. *Miss Jane,* flying a white pennant, pulled ahead of all of them, with *Miss Helen* close behind.

Auguste ventured a comment to Aline. "See how Gustave's boat is gaff-rigged? That gives him more sail on a short mast, and that's an advantage."

She didn't respond. Why couldn't women be more straightforward? Like men. Or like Alphonsine. She never played games. But then, she was more than a decade older than Aline. Aline had some growing up to do. Well, fine. He would watch the race.

"Plus vite, Inès!" Auguste shouted when Gustave came within earshot. Gustave glanced up but was more intent on watching the angle of sails of the lead boats, *Le Dragon* in Raoul's series; *Jupiter,* which had a long record of wins; *Le Palais,* supported by the group that commandeered the tables under the arbor; *Le Rouge-et-Noir,* the biggest boat; Raoul in *Le Capitaine;* Guy in his *périssoire* with that handkerchief of a sail; and the two English boats.

"Eight boats to pass. I just don't know," Auguste said. "Aline, you were born near the source of this river. You must have some influence with the river goddess."

"Sequana!" Her expression brightened and she gave him a genuine smile.

Aha! He had reached her. Relief poured out of him.

"Then it's up to you," he said. "Start praying."

She grinned and put her palms together.

Gustave set his course with his sail in tight to overtake *Miss Helen* with her sail way out, and slid past her close to the far bank. Auguste saw that *Miss Helen* needed to tack soon, and heard the captain shout, "Hey, skipper, I need some sea room."

Gustave ignored him, and *Miss Helen* had to let out sail in order to avoid the bank until after the *Inès* passed.

"Good man! He does have his heart into it," Auguste said.

When all the boats had passed under the bridge, the group boarded the launch which motored upwind, hugging the eastern bank, and overtaking the sailboats which had to zigzag against the wind.

"I'm worried about Paul," Pierre said. "Can you stay just ahead of him so we can see if he falls out?"

"I have to stay ahead of the lead boat," Fournaise said.

The racers crossed tacks, maneuvering for each other's wind. Two kilometers down the course, Auguste felt the wind shift and that left some boats in irons, their sails flapping. Gustave noticed and trimmed his sail, but *Miss Jane* was still in the lead by a fair distance.

Auguste saw the tall dredger along the windward bank cut off the wind of some boats. Raoul hugged the opposite bank until the mudflats, which snagged some boats whose captains didn't raise their centerboards. The huge *Rouge-et-Noir* sailed right alongside the dredge but didn't lose much speed because her mast was so tall. She cut a deep hollow on her leeward side and Gustave sailed right into it, riding her wind shadow with just a meter of space between their hulls.

"What's he doing that for?" Fournaise said.

"He's pinning her and making her skipper nervous," Pierre said. "If *Le Rouge-et-Noir* decides to let out any more mainsail, her boom could get fouled in Gustave's shrouds."

"No. It's his clever way to keep up his own speed passing the dredge," Auguste said. Just past the dredge, Gustave began his tack in the *Inès.* "See?"

"A bold move," Fournaise said.

The wind shifted again. Gustave tacked instantly. The cumbersome *Rouge-et-Noir* couldn't stay ahead. *Le Dragon* fumbled the tack. The *Inès* took it to starboard. "Good going!" Auguste shouted.

Now he was trailing *Jupiter, Le Capitaine,* and *Le Palais,* which were behind *Miss Jane* and Guy's *périssoire* looking like a matchstick compared to the big boats. The *Inès* and *Jupiter* were headed to cross courses. Neither was giving way.

"Are they going to crash?" Aline cried.

Pierre scratched his beard. "Possibly."

Auguste gave him a look. "What a thing to say."

The boats missed each other by an arm's length.

"He's got bravado, our man Gustave," Pierre said.

"He's got skill," Auguste added.

At the point of the island, two boats were forced down the commercial channel and had to come about to maneuver into the eastern channel.

"*Ohé,*" Auguste shouted. "Now Raoul only has to catch *Le Dragon* to win his series." Whatever tack Raoul took, there was Paul leaning far out over the water to keep them stable with the boat heeled sharply, its sails full.

Le Palais was on a broad reach. Her boom, extended way out on her port side, caught on a hazard pole marking an underwater obstacle which yanked the boat around and plunged the bow into the muddy bank.

"*Sacrebleu!*" Fournaise said. "He knew that was there."

Le Palais lay crosswise to the river, a danger to other boats. Her crew scurried to disentangle the boom and push off from the bank. *Jupiter,* sailing wing on wing, both sails out wide on opposite sides of the boat, had to haul in quickly to avoid *Le Palais,* and lost her wind. The *Inès,* coming up fast behind, nearly clipped the stern of *Le Palais* as he passed. The skipper of *Le Palais* shouted angrily at Gustave.

"Gustave is sailing like he owns the river," Auguste said.

"Well, he does, at least a stretch of the bank," Alphonsine said.

Now the *Inès* and *Jupiter* were bow to bow. One and then the other crept ahead. All four larger boats overtook Guy's *périssoire.* The *Inès* left *Jupiter* behind and was gaining on *Le Capitaine* and *Miss Jane.*

"It's just a horse race now," Fournaise said.

They disembarked at the dock and found Charles Ephrussi in his top hat.

"Just in time, Charles. Just in time," Auguste said.

The *Inès* came alongside *Le Capitaine,* so far heeled to windward that Paul was getting quite a ride, bending backward over the rail and getting splashed full in the face.

"He can't stand to be in a race without being right *in* the river," Jules said.

"Fly, Gustave! Fly, *Inès!*" Alphonsine called.

"Raoul, get your ass moving!" Angèle shouted.

The *Inès* pulled ahead across the invisible finish line. Cheers on both banks were deafening. *Miss Jane* was close behind, then *Jupiter,* and Raoul and Paul in *Le Capitaine.* Paul thrust both fists into the air and shouted, "Just call me Monsieur Bonne Fortune!"

"Some are born great, some achieve greatness, some have greatness thrrrust upon them!" Jules shouted back, his fist in the air.

Angèle and Pierre began the song "Le roi des régates," proclaiming Gustave the king of the regatta to whom even the frigates must salute, and the crowd joined in.

The skipper and crew of *Miss Jane* were the first to shake Gustave's hand. Alphonse *fils* was ready with an uncorked bottle of champagne for Gustave and Raoul and Paul, who upended it right over his mouth.

"I figure the course required about twenty tacks, wouldn't you say?" Alphonse asked.

Gustave blew air out of his mouth. "It felt like forty."

The supporters of *Le Palais* cheered when it arrived, its bow muddy, but Henri, the skipper, was obviously humiliated. Word of the mishap spread quickly and Henri's crowd retreated under the arbor.

The president of the Cercle de la Voile à Paris mounted the platform and gave out the medals. The skipper of *Miss Jane,* Guy, Raoul, and Gustave each received one hundred francs and a silver medal for winning their series, and Gustave received the *Prix d'honneur,* an *objet d'art* valued at five hundred francs, the president announced. As Gustave held aloft an ornate silver cup mounted on an onyx base, Henri, the captain of *Le Palais,* put one foot on the platform and held up a bottle of brandy.

"Armagnac Cames," Henri said. "But not just any Armagnac." He draped the bottle in his boat's flag and held it out to Gustave.

"Take it quick," Angèle shouted.

"Ah, it's Clos de Moutouguet," Gustave announced and held up the bottle. "Two *objets d'art. Merci beaucoup!*" he said with a broad smile.

When they stepped down from the platform away from the congratulating crowd, Auguste saw Gustave slip his winnings into Louise's apron pocket.

After much slapping of backs, they pulled three tables together on the lower terrace and Loüise served caviar on small glass plates with tiny mother-of-pearl spoons. "This is to be eaten with contemplation—"

"And champagne!" Aline said as Anne brought out a tray of crystal stemware. "Champagne from home!"

Everyone watched Charles lay the bowl of the spoon on his tongue and close his mouth, his little finger extended. When he said, "As fine as any in Odessa," Louise nodded definitively, one nod.

Gustave, Raoul, and Paul received congratulations from everyone in the restaurant and on the promenade. Paul was beaming through it all, singing snatches of *canotier* songs.

"They're not the only ones to be congratulated," Ellen said. She waited for their attention. "I've been accepted to the new Théâtre des Arts, a true literary theater that will change everything. It will be dark during performances so there won't be any moving around. No *promenoirs.*"

"How are men going to find their women of the evening?" Angèle asked.

"They won't. They sit in one spot and *listen* to the play."

"Unbelievable," Raoul said.

"The plays will either be by new writers or foreigners. For Ibsen's *A Doll's House,* we'll have real furniture onstage, real food. Even the style of acting will be realistic, just how people really speak."

"An artistic revolution," Jules said.

"This is certainly worth a piece in *Le Figaro,*" Raoul said. "It could be the start of my life as a theater critic."

"All in good time, Baron," Louise said as she laid down a platter of *couliabac,* salmon with mushrooms and dill baked in brioche dough. "First you can be a critic of the *cuisine de la Maison Fournaise.*"

"This originated in Russia, you know," Charles said.

Fournaise himself laid down a second platter. "It's one of my favorites. It's folded with *crêpes* and tapioca and covered with a *velouté* sauce. She started yesterday. I'm going to have to join you." He sat at the head of the table and served it. "Go lightly. There's more to come."

"I've never known anything like this existed," Aline said.

Louise watched Charles take a bite. At the first forkful, he emitted such a loud moan of pleasure that she clapped her hands over her mouth and left.

Gustave announced his move to Petit Gennevilliers. "After I get settled I'm going to sail the *Inès* to Le Havre."

"You mean our local races are too easy for you?" Auguste asked.

Gustave's cheeks colored. It was good to see him happy for a change.

Soon Louise and Anne brought out the second platter. "*Boeuf Richelieu* in Madeira sauce," Louise announced.

"*Mamma mia,*" Antonio said.

"The *couliabac* was for Gustave, for taking honors, because his boat swims like a fish," Louise said. "The beef is for Auguste. You have to guess why."

Auguste admired the roast surrounded by braised lettuce hearts, château potatoes, baked tomatoes, and stuffed mushroom caps. How carefully she'd laid out everything, alternating colors to make a pattern on the enormous oval platter.

"The platter is a palette! You paint with food, madame," he said.

Père Fournaise uncorked a bottle of Chateau-Yquem and poured.

Auguste ate and drank heartily, and began to relax. Raoul pretended to paint his plate with his fork, screwing up his face and splattering the imaginary paint. Aline and Alphonsine laughed together uproariously. He loved to watch both of them equally. How he wished he could be two men.

He had more things on his mind than women, though. There was still the issue of what he would do now. There would always be that issue. Some days what he chose to do wouldn't make a smidgen of difference, and other days his whole life might change. Tonight might be one such time.

The dessert was *poires Belle Hélène,* pears poached in vanilla syrup served on vanilla ice cream with chocolate sauce and brandy. It slid coolly down his throat while Angèle sang the *Amours divins* aria from Offenbach's *La Belle Hélène.* Fitting. Not only was the dessert the rage on the boulevards when the operetta opened, but it was his favorite operetta.

"*All* our women put the Queen of Sparta and Troy to shame," Auguste said.

"Isn't it time to open the Armagnac?" Angèle asked, tipping her head onto Antonio's shoulder. "Too much wine makes the skin blotchy."

"The perfect time," Gustave said and poured slowly, all around.

Charles raised his glass to look across it. "A fine mahogany color with an amber surface." He brought it to his nose to smell the *montant,* the strongest aromas. "An abundant nose, not for the faint of heart." He swirled it gently and watched it coat the glass. He raised it again for the second nose, the full bouquet. "Vanilla, plum, and spices."

Charles waited until everyone had enjoyed the aromas. "The perfect sip is always the first."

"You're wrong," Angèle said. "The perfect sip is the one you're sipping."

They toasted Gustave. Charles sipped. "Ah, semisweet."

"With a long, deep aftertaste of prunes," Raoul said. "A far sight better than your young brandy in that country cask, you'll have to admit."

Fournaise took another sip, not willing to accede so quickly. After the third, he nodded. *"D'accord."*

Auguste almost laughed at them rinsing their gums as though it were a mouthwash. Someone behind him tapped him on the shoulder. He turned.

"Jeanne!"

Dressed as in the painting.

"Ellen told me you were almost finished," Jeanne said.

"You came to pose?" He let that hang in the air. "I've done without you."

"Is it here?"

"Yes."

Make her ask. Even though he was dying to see if the awning worked the way he needed it to, he wanted her to ask.

"I'd like Joseph-Paul to see it." She gestured to him standing off to the side. "After all, we're going to have a big wedding in December."

She got the reaction she wanted, dropping that plum of information. Congratulations flew across the tables.

Auguste was too full of the sensations of well-being to feel injured.

He took another sip of the Armagnac before he said, *"Félicitations,"* kissed her blithely on the cheek, and shook Joseph's hand.

"Another toast," Paul said, and poured two more glasses.

"The painting, Auguste," Jeanne said.

"All right. The painting."

Fournaise and Alphonse carried it onto the platform with the back toward everyone, and Gustave brought the easel. Chest out, chin raised, Fournaise commanded attention by his posture. People all over the grounds quieted. Gustave gave the nod, and they walked it around to set it on the easel.

Applause burst forth from all sides and made him reel.

"The awning!" several voices cried.

"Holding out on us. You might have rolled it out the first day and saved ourselves some sunburn," Angèle said.

"I needed the light."

Gustave pumped his hand. "It works! We assume it's attached to a building we can't see. Bravo!"

Looking at it now from a distance for the first time, he saw that the divergent diagonals of rail, table edge, and awning contained and united the figures as a group. "Why don't simple answers occur to us in the beginning?"

"Because we have to wrestle them out of some bedrock within," Gustave said.

"True indeed," Jules said. "I'd venture to say the prodigious effort required is what makes any true artist suffer. As the bard says, *With what he most enjoys, contented least.* That necessity of torment sets the artist apart from the nonartist, in all fields."

They understood. Despite his principle that he wouldn't do anything except out of pleasure, the vision had required such effort that anguish and emotional exhaustion were inevitable. He'd had no choice but to endure it in order to give the painting a future.

"There hasn't been such shimmering opulence in a painting since the Venetians," Charles said.

Jules nodded. "The whole thing is a symphony of colored vibrations. Thousands of tones and touches give form by the subtlest of gradations."

Swimming in a sea of compliments, Auguste let his pleasure swell and realized at the same time how physically exhausted he was, how tight in his muscles, how stiff his joints. But he'd had the idea always before him expressed moment by moment in the spirit of his friends, and that had sustained him. Nearly two months, eight luncheons, counting today's, a couple dozen tubes of paint, five women, nine men, a *mère* and a *père*. The sight of everyone who had helped him flooded him with joy. For two months the models had been his and he had been theirs. He felt a culmination of his life this far.

His search for the perfect composition, the perfect stroke, the perfect colors, model, woman—did he dare think he had found them? In the morning, or in some distant morning, would he awake and find it had been a night dream that had teased him into taking an illusion for reality?

Could he ever be as good again as he was this moment? As full of hope? If he wanted to say yes, and mean it, he would have to change. With this painting, he had carried Impressionism as far as he could. At least with figures. The recognition descended as his eyes filled. He had created a revolution that left him out.

The crowd was abuzz, matching the figures in the painting with the models who reveled in their images. Jeanne's husband looked miffed. He was outside the frame. Auguste chortled. What did he expect?

"Who's the mystery man in the center looking at me?" Ellen asked.

"Everyman, *chérie*." He watched her expressive face show her delight. "A painting requires a little mystery, some vagueness, some fantasy. When you make your meaning perfectly plain you end up boring people."

"What a wonderful meal those people must have just eaten," Aline murmured.

"It's more important than a pleasant lunch, Aline," Alphonsine said in a pinched tone. "It's the evidence of the healing of France, and Maison Fournaise has played a part as much as Emélie Bécat singing 'Alsace and Lorraine.'" She turned to him. "It sends out a blessedness because we're in a state of grace on that piece of cloth."

It was dear of her to think that, but to his mind, the moment any painter becomes conscious of a message, the work loses its seductive power to unveil any more discoveries. Still, if grace involved love and good deeds, she was right to feel its blessings.

"True indeed, Alphonsine," Jules said, nodding thoughtfully. "The light of history is glancing off our shoulders."

"It's terribly bourgeois, though," Charles remarked.

"Look again," Jules said. "These aren't safely married couples re-peopling France with children. They're not at church on Sunday. They are, *we* are the fringe element that makes the bourgeoisie nervous. We're enjoying ourselves too much."

Charles threaded his fingers through his beard in a contemplative way. "Some *flâneur* of the future will look at our faces, hats, and clothes and will deduce our relationships, our occupations, our domestic lives."

"They'll have a great deal of guessing to do," Jules said. "But what doesn't take any guessing is Auguste's own identity in all of us. That's where genius lies, in the flashes of revelation that go from the painter through the subject to the viewer."

A crewman of *Le Palais* weaved his way toward Auguste. "Nice painting you've got there."

"Thank you kindly."

"Some fine-looking women. You've probably laid every one of them. How long did it take you? To paint, I mean."

"Twenty years."

Gustave snorted. Others laughed.

"It's true!" His voice rose. "I've been working toward it for that long."

The man swayed. "You've got a lot of paint on it. How much did that cost you?"

"A couple hundred francs."

The man put his face right into his. Auguste backed away. The man reeked of wine. "You expect to get that much out of it, then? How much do you get?"

"Plenty." Auguste puffed out air back to him. "I paint pornography in the brothels, so I get as much as I want. My success there is so big it's astounding."

The man's friends hooted and he staggered off.

Charles stepped up alongside him. "I want to warn you that someone you know is coming to see the painting today."

"Not another one like that duffer."

"Someone important."

Auguste groaned. "Zola?"

"Guess again."

"Not Degas, I hope." He didn't want to have to spar with that porcupine.

"If you take your eyes off your painting for a minute, you can see for yourself."

There in the back of the crowd was Paul Durand-Ruel.

"You sure aren't one for giving a man much of a warning. How did he know to come today?"

"I told him." Smugness seeped through Charles's voice.

"But it's not finished."

Durand-Ruel made his way through the crowd and shook his hand. "Astonishing."

"It's not finished."

Auguste introduced him to everyone. They acted like excited children anticipating the praise of a schoolmaster.

"Keep in mind that I'm not finished."

"Radiant," Durand-Ruel said. "These women could not have been painted by anyone else. They have that roguish charm that only you can give to women."

"I only paint what they give me."

"The sly, soft eyes of this one tipping her head coquettishly, the archness of her smile. And the pert little nose of that one, her petulance, absorbed in her dog but knowing that Gustave is adoring her. The feline charm of this one looking through the glass. And the black gloves to this one's ears, forcing us to speculate what she doesn't want to hear."

"You must agree that the composition is brilliant," Charles said, his words tumbling out. "Look at the woman holding the dog, how her shoulder and upper arm connect with the boatman's hand so the line of both their arms enclose the group on the left, and the standing man's arm and Gustave's back enclose it on the right."

"Yes, I see," Durand-Ruel said.

"And Gustave's hand lines up with Angèle's, the woman looking at him," Charles said. "And the two hands on the chair on the right, the titillation of that."

"Not to mention the moments of bravura painting," Durand-Ruel said. "The luscious still life. The face through a glass is far lovelier than Vermeer's attempt. The young woman loving her little dog—you're quoting Fragonard there. And the languor of the one leaning on the railing is pure Ingres. You've given the masters a rebirth in Impressionist style and subject."

Ah, good. His debt to the painters he loved was evident. His whole body released its grip.

"Marvelous, the stories you hint at in the interactions," Durand-Ruel said.

"There is no story. It's only a moment."

"With this, the modern genre painting has fully eclipsed history painting, and art will never be the same again," Durand-Ruel said. "You come to me before you offer it to anyone else."

"It's not finished."

"It will be a devil to sell, though."

Auguste bristled. "Why, after what you've just said?"

Durand-Ruel raised one eyebrow. "I might love it too much to let it go."

A turbulence in his chest made him put his hand there. He turned away a moment so the stinging behind his eyes wouldn't brim over.

A second later he turned right back. "I want it exhibited, Paul, not just hanging in your dining room for a dozen people to see. I want *thousands* to see it."

"Hundreds of thousands will. They'll come great distances to see it."

Aline and Ellen and Angèle and Jeanne had all arranged themselves in a row, with Alphonsine in the middle, their arms linked, their faces beaming. A chorus line. He was overcome.

"*Toutes mes chères femmes.*" The words came out in a higher pitch than normal. All his dear women, each of them brave in her own way.

"What do you want people to see when they look at this painting in years to come?" Durand-Ruel asked.

"The goodness of life."

Or, he could have said the painting of love, and the love of painting. It amounted to the same thing.

Yet, to him, it seemed an image of all things that he was eventually going to give up, maybe sooner than he had thought. His insouciance, the bohemian life, Impressionism. The painting was a directive proclaiming new challenges ahead.

There was no remaining still, in art or in life.

Alphonsine felt a chill as she watched her father and brother carry the painting inside. For some moments, she was adrift in a haze of noise and movement. She tried to steady herself by watching yellow leaves fall into the river. Soon the trees would be bare skeletons. Eventually Auguste's friends, her friends, drifted upstairs to the terrace, feeling some ownership, she supposed. It was a charmed circle no one outside could enter or understand, not even this dealer who would own the canvas but not their thoughts.

For them, the memory would be more full and vivid than the weeks themselves had been when they had been living them, swept up in the swirl of the process too intensely to reflect on it. Only upon the completion of the painting, and hearing people speak about it, could they comprehend that they had been a piece of something more complex and more far-reaching than their own single parts in it. It humbled her at the same time as it thrilled her.

Daylight stole away. Dusk in autumn came subtly, but this one was all too sharp to her. What had blossomed here one magical summer would be no more. A thing exists, and then it does not, and a new thing is born. His hands became the work and the work became them, all the models together. But when the painting would go beyond Chatou, it would become a different thing, a piece of human history, no longer only theirs. She would feel the void. Auguste wouldn't. His thoughts were already weighty with the next.

The great moment of her life was almost over. Her contribution would go unrecognized, and she would have the decades ahead to relive the beautiful liquid days when Pierre-Auguste Renoir created a masterpiece on her terrace.

She went upstairs to be with them one last time. Gold and silver lights winked on in Rueil and on boats still on the river. The time for leaving approached. There were sweet words. Embraces. Goodbyes. She knew the finality of them. Auguste said he would always be indebted to her. Beyond that, his moist, penetrating eyes said what he couldn't put in words.

Her moment of keenest sorrow sucked the breath out of her—Aline and Auguste walking across the bridge away from Chatou, and Aline, with little understanding of its importance, carrying Auguste's color box that had once been Bazille's.

She gripped the railing and felt an arm reach around her and draw her to his side.

Papa.

CHAPTER FORTY

Incandescence

Another man is lost to me, the fifth in my life, if I'm to count Louis, Alexander, Gustave, and Maurice. The fifth, most dear, most enduring. Auguste died yesterday.

At his villa in Cagnes-sur-Mer, the article in *Excelsior* said, the third of December 1919, a year after the armistice. I've just read again, here by the river, how three months ago his friends carried him in a chair through the Louvre, opened just for him, to see for the last time Veronese and Watteau and Delacroix, Titian, Boucher, Fragonard, Rubens, and Ingres, his favorites returned safely from their wartime hiding places.

Oh, his last words. Apparently his maid had gathered wild anemones on the hillside above the Mediterranean Sea, and for several hours he lost himself in the mysteries of painting flowers, and forgot his pain. Then he motioned for someone to take his brush, and murmured, "I think I'm beginning to understand something about it."

For nearly forty years, knowing that he was in the world painting what he loved had to be enough. Mine was a distant love, not as sensuous as Héloïse longing for Abelard for fifteen years, but as steady. She and I share one thing—the helplessness of desire. Like her, I can send my love *To him who is specially hers, from she who is singularly his,* even though the outward manifestation of it existed only briefly. Perhaps now that he is beyond the breach, this love stretching into the unknown will be easier for me in the years I have left.

He'll be buried in Essoyes, Champagne, alongside her. Aline, I mean. It had taken him ten years and the birth of two of his three sons before he made his relationship public and married her. Gustave had told me that he'd kept her a secret until he was ready to settle down, and she had been content with that. I have a feeling from the way she applied herself to learning P-A-L-E-T-T-E that she used that time wisely.

I went to Durand-Ruel's gallery once to try to see the painting, and learned that their sons Pierre and Jean were both seriously wounded in the Great War, another cataclysm of cruelty, and Aline, ill herself, had undertaken the arduous journey from one son's hospital in the southwest to the other's in the northeast to plead with the doctors not to amputate Jean's leg. What she saw must have devastated her. When Jean was out of danger, she went home and collapsed, passing away a few days later with three more years of war to go.

As soon as the armistice was signed and train service began again, I went to Les Collettes, Auguste's villa in the South, my need to see him pulsing as strong as ever. I won't say he cried, but his eyes pooled when he saw me. He was more emaciated than ever, the hollows of his cheeks were deeper, and his hands and legs were paralyzed. It was a shock I tried not to show.

He was surrounded by paintings affirming that beauty was still all-in-all to him. I recognized Aline in one, gray-haired, motherly, stout under a flowing dress, her hand cupped under the belly of a newborn puppy. He said only two things about her, that mercifully she had died without knowing it, and that she had given him peace and time to think. I was glad of both. Then he added, almost as an apology to me, that all currents bring a person to a final safe place, and that he was right to rely on what happened naturally.

His nurse and his cook carried him in a wicker armchair across a rough path overhung with bougainvillea to a small studio. "If I had to choose between walking and painting, I would much rather paint," he said.

Completely made of glass and warmed by an oil stove, the room was surrounded by bare olive trees that storms and age had made into weirdly shaped skeletons.

In a feeble voice, he said, "I can roast my rheumatism in the sun here, and feel like I am painting *en plein air.*" He let out a long, fluttering sigh. "The light here opens my eyes to eternal things. In the spring, the orange trees, roses, and wisteria will all be blooming. My earthly paradise."

I prayed that he would live to see it.

An unfinished canvas of gold and white chrysanthemums in a green ceramic vase was nailed to a mechanism that could roll it up and down so the part he was working on would be within reach. I watched in agony as his nurse slid a brush between his index and middle fingers, and cushioned it with a cotton pad against the hollow of his palm, which was bound to keep down the swelling.

I ached for him, gaunt and crippled as he was, in his gray felt carpet slippers, as intensely as when he was young and wiry. I held his palette, but what I wanted was to touch his hands, the thumbs permanently bent against the palms, the frozen fingers twisted toward his wrist as weirdly as the olive tree branches, the knobs of knuckles stretching the skin. I yearned to cradle them in my palms. I loved his hands, so small and brittle.

He must have guessed. After painting awhile, he let me change the brush his nurse had inserted. His skin was as thin as parchment. I was afraid I would tear it, like the bandaged place on his wrist had torn. Slowly I slid one brush out between his rigid fingers and worked the other one in.

Once in place, he pointed with the brush to a ladybug resting on a white petal. A high, soft sound, like a bird's sigh at twilight, issued from the space between his thin lips. "Out of the whole world where he could have flown, he came here so I could paint him. That's God."

He reached toward the canvas slowly and placed a red dot on a petal, unerringly, without a support.

"There, now. That little bug belongs to me. You see, one doesn't need a hand in order to paint."

He groaned, trying to shift in his chair. "Why did they have to make a thin man's sit-bones so pointed?"

The heads of the chrysanthemums bent forward, tired, but there was adoration for them in his eyes. Each stroke applied with pain-racked fingers showed his intoxication with those blooms, his awe at the miracle of their being. In his desire overcoming pain in the service of beauty, he was radiant.

"A painter should be dead if he can't paint," he said.

That led us to speak of Gustave, how he had withdrawn from the Paris art world after his move to Petit Gennevilliers, how he designed racing yachts and had owned ten boats at one time or another, and how he had won nearly every race he entered at Argenteuil and on the coast at Le Havre and Trouville. I told Auguste that he had become Conseilleur Municipal of Petit Gennevilliers. Whenever the town needed streetlights, paving, or uniforms for the fire department, he paid out of his own pocket. Easier that way, he had told me.

"That sounds just like him. Awful that he died just before Durand-Ruel's big show of his work. I think he retreated intentionally from the attention."

"I went to it," I was quick to say. "How beautifully he painted *périssoires* on water."

"He made one important mistake in his life. Undervaluing his own work. He didn't include a single painting of his own in his legacy to the Louvre. I insisted that one be added."

"Which one?"

"The one of workmen in bare torsos scraping a parquet floor."

"Ah, yes. I understood then, seeing it, why you had warned me."

A thought clouded his eyes then. "I had to fight to have his collection accepted by the Louvre. They took barely more than half of it," he said, something between pain and fury in his voice. Apparently he hadn't made peace with some things.

Nor had I. "There was a woman who lived in a cottage on his property, a housekeeper, perhaps," I said. "Maybe he did need a woman after all."

Auguste lifted a shoulder in a minute shrug.

I didn't tell him that every year on All Souls' Day, I laid roses on Gustave's grave in Père Lachaise Cemetery. Roses. An idea. Fidelity. Like Héloïse after all.

We shared what we knew about the others. Raoul did become a theater critic. Jules moved to Germany and then to England where he married, returned to Paris and died a few months later, at twenty-seven.

"The obituary said he cast a great influence on some poets outside France—Ezra Pound, T. S. Eliot, and an Irishman named Yeats," I said.

"That's a kind of immortality."

He was silent a few moments, and then said, "Angèle came to see me once with a husband. She had become proper. 'He knows I posed for you,' she said, and then she added in a whisper, 'but he doesn't know that I used to say *merde.*'" He chuckled in a tender, bemused way. "Scratch a bohemian and you find a person yearning to be a bourgeois. There was hardly a hint of that raw, earthy vitality. A shame. In a way, she had sold herself."

In a moment his eyes turned serious.

"Jeanne acted for ten years after that summer," he said, as though the painting marked a division in his life, "and became an officer of the Académie Française. She had finally convinced Guy de Maupassant to let the Comédie-Française produce his story 'Yvette' for her to play the lead role, but she died three days after he agreed. Typhoid fever. Two thousand people followed her coffin to the cemetery, I among them."

"I thought of you when I read the obituary," I said.

He looked at me a long time, blinking. His mouth opened, closed, and then he asked, softly, "Did you ever have a lover?"

I was pleased that he wanted to know.

"Yes. A painter."

Auguste's eyes opened wider and out of his mouth came a rising "Oh-h." I took it to mean approval.

"Maurice Réalier-Dumas. He painted me sitting at a table by the riverbank under a maple tree, and created frescoes of the four ages of man on the Maison. In the dining room, his comical murals of storybook characters in a jungle remind me that it was a happy time, those ten years. He was fourteen years younger than I was. His pious parents forced him to give me up as inappropriately old, but the longing to be precious to someone was satisfied and lost its hold on me. I have your kiss to thank for that. It freed me from the claims of the past."

He patted me on the arm with his curled fist.

"Loving your neighbor as yourself is a complicated thing," I said. "Saving the life of an enemy was easier than decorating a hat and giving it to a rival. What made that difficult was the belief that there wasn't enough love to go around. But I found there is."

He nodded. "There always is."

I still live on the island in the great river that flows through the bosom of France. I kept the Maison open for twenty-five years after the painting. Thousands of reenactments of the pleasure Auguste recorded took place there. It had been a part of the healing of France once. I wish it could be again, after this generation's calamity.

Two weeks ago, I heard a motorcar stop alongside the Maison. I went out to the side balcony. The driver opened the rear door, where Auguste sat alone. It took all my self-possession not to leap down the stairs to smother him in an embrace. He would have to make the first move, if only a tiny gesture or a word.

I could say there was yearning in his eyes, but I suspect I was only seeing my own, mirrored in his face. Whenever I've tried to enter imaginatively into another person's life, Auguste's or Aline's, for example, I found connections that lifted me above mere personal perspectives to a higher contemplation. In that instant, as he sat in the motorcar, I saw his life and his life's work as one great, open-armed cry of love.

Without a word, we only looked. We were linked in a way too pure for words.

Let go. Let him go, I told myself. Eventually he murmured to the driver to close the door.

I've come to think that if doing something simple or silly can give a person pleasure, then, by God, do it. So, with the article still in my hand, I came out this evening in the early twilight, sat in the swing on the bank of the Seine, backed up as far as I could, and swung forward, sailing out over the timeless eddies and the ducks in pairs, so I could feel that moment of weightlessness, that suspension of all earthly ties. I pray that's what Auguste is feeling now, and Gustave, and Louis, and Alexander, and Aline too, all of them enjoying that sweet bodiless flight above a river bathed in winter light. A cork may swirl in an eddy or rest in a tangle of reeds, but only for a time. It passes on to other, unknown pleasures.

I'm remembering now our last conversation in the South of France. "Do you see all the years behind you? Each one?" I had asked.

"Yes. I've painted all of them."

"Then time must be continuous for you."

"Like a river." He blinked uncontrollably. "I still love all the models I ever painted, women and men, so they are all alive to me."

With his frozen fist resting on my arm, he slowly brought his face close to mine. "Honors shower me from every side. The Maison Fournaise painting wins praise wherever Durand-Ruel shows it. Today's artists pay me compliments. They find my position enviable. But I don't have a single real friend."

It seemed too late, too obvious, too trite for me to say, *You have me.* Instead, I reached into my handbag and took out the cork. He couldn't hold it, so I let it lie in my palm on his lap. "The cork from the first bottle opened on the first painting day. For you."

His face contorted, and a tear bubbled over the tic beneath his eye. That communion we had felt at Chatou enfolded us again.

"At least a dozen paintings I did of you and you never let me paint your breasts. That was a sin, you know, not letting me. I was on the verge of tears when you refused."

I laughed, amused by his pouting.

"I suffered intensely from being deprived of seeing something I knew would be beautiful."

I shook my head. "When will you get over your obsession with breasts?"

"Never!" he declared, sensuality brightening his eyes. "They're divine. Just like clouds."

The incandescence that glowed hotly when he painted the boating party flickered back to life. That ought to satisfy me for another forty years.

Author's Note

Renoir finished and signed *Le déjeuner des canotiers* in 1881, and Paul Durand-Ruel purchased it on February 14, 1881, sold it to a Parisian collector, but reacquired it early in 1882. Contrary to Renoir's wish, though Renoir did eventually acquiesce, Durand-Ruel showed it in the seventh Impressionist exhibition in March 1882, and later in London, Zurich, and New York. It was never shown at the Salon. Durand-Ruel kept it for the rest of his life.

After his death, Durand-Ruel's sons sold the painting to Duncan Phillips in 1923 for his Phillips Memorial Gallery in Washington, D.C., now known as The Phillips Collection. Exulting over the purchase in a letter, Phillips called it "one of the greatest paintings in the world . . . a masterpiece by Renoir and finer than any Rubens. . . . Its fame is tremendous and people will travel thousands of miles to our house to see it. . . . Such a picture creates a sensation wherever it goes."[1]

The identities of the models are true, with the exception of the last face painted, which is still in question, with possibilities being either Guy de Maupassant or Renoir himself.[2] An extensive technical examination made by the conservation department at The Phillips Collection reports that the repositioning of the figures and the late addition of the awning were executed as I have narrated them.

For the sake of the narrative, the actual dates of certain events were adjusted by a few months. We can assume that his broken arm was out

1. Eliza E. Rathbone et al., *Impressionists on the Seine: A Celebration of Renoir's "Luncheon of the Boating Party"* (Washington, D.C.: The Phillips Collection, 1996), 231–234.

2. Benoît Noël and Jean Hournon, *La Seine au temps des canotiers* (Paris: Les Presses Francili-ennes, n.d.), 74.

of the cast when he began the painting. Most but not all sources have reported the date Renoir became acquainted with Aline to have been just prior to his commencement of the painting. The identity of the model for *La balançoire, The Swing,* is reported to be either a different Jeanne than Jeanne Samary, which I thought would be confusing, or Margot Legrand. For the purposes of my narrative, I chose Margot.

For the portrait of Alphonsine painted to pay Renoir's debt, I chose *Alphonsine Fournaise, fille d'un restaurateur de Chatou,* actually painted in 1879. Its background of river and railroad bridge fit my narrative better than *Portrait of Alphonsine Fournaise,* 1880, executed in an interior with a plain background that offered me no narrative link.

Sources disagree as to whether Angèle posed for *Sleeping Girl with a Cat.* Barbara Ehrlich White in *Renoir, His Life, Art and Letters* and François Daulte in *Renoir: Catalogue raisonné* affirm that she did. It is my fiction that a study for *Two Little Circus Girls* was sold to the very real clown, Sagot.

Apologies to Monsieur Mullard for my use of Julien Tanguy, a more colorful character, as Renoir's pigment supplier. Certainly Renoir patronized both shops during his long career. Renoir owned several bicycles and one steam-powered three-wheeled cycle in his adult life; he suffered two falls, the first in January 1880. The second, from a bicycle in Essoyes, was thought to have contributed to his later incapacity. Angèle riding the steam-cycle and its subsequent sale to Alphonse Fournaise were my inventions.

Other than these occasions, I have not departed intentionally from known fact, but have taken the novelist's license of invention where no facts are known. I take my cue from Renoir: not all of his models were as lovely as he painted them, and we do not feel cheated.

A large portion of Gustave Caillebotte's collection, along with *Alphonsine Fournaise, fille d'un restaurateur de Chatou,* can be seen at the Musée d'Orsay in Paris. After being closed a number of years, La Maison Fournaise is open as a restaurant with its terrace shaded by a striped awning. Part of the building houses Le Musée Fournaise, featuring work by those who painted this stretch of the Seine.

Acknowledgments

I am deeply grateful to the authors of two books in particular: Eliza Rathbone, Katherine Rothkopf, Richard Brettell, Elizabeth Steele, and Charles Moffett for *Impressionists on the Seine: A Celebration of Renoir's "Luncheon of the Boating Party,"* published by The Phillips Collection; and Jean Renoir for his biographical memoir, *Renoir: My Father,* which gave me the flavor of Renoir's voice and opinions.

I am indebted to the following biographical works: *Renoir: The Man, the Painter, and His World* by Lawrence Hanson; *Renoir* by John House, Anne Distel, and Lawrence Gowing; *Renoir et ses amis* by Georges Rivière; *Renoir: An Intimate Record* by Ambroise Vollard; and *Renoir, His Life, Art and Letters* by Barbara Ehrlich White.

For art-historical information, I especially thank Anne Distel of the Musée d'Orsay, whose scholarship I found in many texts. I also thank Robert Herbert for *Impressionism;* T. J. Clark for *The Painting of Modern Life;* Gabriele Crepaldi for *The Impressionists;* Anne Galloyer for *La Maison Fournaise: table des canotiers;* Benoît Noël and Jean Hournon for *Les Arts en Seine* and *La Seine au temps des canotiers.*

I am indebted to Colette for her colorful sketches of Paris music halls, including the fines charged performers in *The Collected Stories of Colette;* to Guy de Maupassant for the story Raoul Barbier tells Alphonsine, adapted from "Sur le Seine" or "En Canot"; to Edward King for *My Paris: French Character Sketches,* which gives his eyewitness description of Jardin Mabille and the tribute money that changed hands there; and to Jean Renoir for the item of Angèle "doing a boulevard" for Renoir. Ross King's monumental *The Judgment of Paris: The Revolutionary Decade That Gave the World Impressionism* was particularly helpful in explaining the workings of the Salon and the events of the Franco-Prussian War and the Commune.

Limitations of space prevent me from mentioning the many other published reference sources. For a complete bibliography of works consulted, please see www.svreeland.com.

Several curators gave me their insights into Renoir and his work. I especially wish to thank Monsieur Jean Habert, conservateur-en-chef des peintures, Musée du Louvre. I am grateful to Madame Anne Galloyer, Conservatrice du Musée Fournaise, Île de Chatou, who answered graciously my many questions. Thanks also to Patrice Marandel and Stephanie Barron of the Los Angeles County Museum of Art; Nannette Maciejunes, Director of the Columbus Museum of Art; and Stephen Kern, formerly of the San Diego Museum of Art.

Karen Brown, Marna Hostettler, and Jo Cottingham of The Thomas Cooper Library of the University of South Carolina and Dyanne Hoffman, formerly of the University of California San Diego Libraries, were my magical links to books and materials I could not have accessed otherwise. I wish to thank Françoise Courgabe, Conservatrice de la Bibliothèque historique de la Ville de Paris, as well.

For help in preliminary research, thanks go to Gayle Vreeland, and to Caroline Olivier for works in French. For all things pertaining to sailing and regattas, profound thanks to that spirited champion yachtsman, Craig Mueller, as well as to sailing enthusiast Terry Cantor. I am deeply grateful to artist Gerrit Greve for sharing generously his understanding of Renoir as a painter and as a man; to Dennis Sanders for his painter's perspective while in Paris; and to my lively team of location scouts and photographers in Paris, Betty and Jan-Gerrit van Wijhe. *Merci à* Madame Noëlle Desplat, Edmond Ballerin, and the members of Association Sequana on Île de Chatou, which restores and builds reproductions of period boats, who made it possible for me to go boating on the Seine, see the spots immortalized by Impressionist painters, and imagine the races and river life.

For their critical reading and insightful commentary, I thank John Baker, Judy Bernstein, Julie Brickman, Mark Doten, Kip Gray, Jerry Hannah, Nan Kaufman, and John and Cheryl Ritter; and for his careful copyediting, Dave Cole. For all things French, and for her precise editorial advice, I am grateful to Madame Babette Mann, my window on French culture and sensibility. Enthusiastic appreciation goes to my energetic, supportive, and keen-eyed editor at Viking, Kendra Harpster, who grew along with me on this project. Especially and always, I thrive under the warm and wise counsel and editorial acumen of my agent, Barbara Braun, to whom I am deeply grateful.

A PENGUIN READERS GUIDE TO

LUNCHEON OF THE BOATING PARTY

Susan Vreeland

An Introduction to
Luncheon of the Boating Party

Library Journal says of this novel, "One of the most significant paintings of the Impressionist period is Renoir's *Luncheon of the Boating Party*, and it's hard to imagine that a novel could do it justice. Yet this new work from Vreeland does just that." It reveals the mysteries of the painting with all the life, color, vibrancy, and subtlety of the painting itself. In the painting, Renoir depicted a group of Parisians on a restaurant terrace overlooking the Seine near Paris. In the novel, Renoir and these same revelers take us into their own lives—behind the scenes at the Folies-Bergère and to artists' studios, cafés, cabarets, salons, and regattas—while reflecting tumultuous changes as Paris careens toward modernity. With the impending and agonizing breakup of the Impressionist group and a huge change in the marketing of art imminent, Renoir faces a double crisis in art and love.

In *Luncheon of the Boating Party*, Susan Vreeland, an exquisite and passionate chronicler of art throughout history, takes the reader through the process of painting by way of Renoir, the many models in the painting, and the relationships he had with them—a complex mix of paint, color, and texture as well as the personalities of the myriad men and women in his life. The progress is always the main issue, revealing the artist's difficulties and ultimately his triumph, but the models' lives display such French cultural issues as the residual trauma of the Franco-Prussian War and the Commune, changes in marriage traditions, the rise of feminism, the decline of old institutions, the yearning for personal expression, and the explosion of creativity in the arts: journalism, music, and literature.

Renoir had wanted to paint boaters on the terrace of La Maison Fournaise in Chatou for years. With the nineteenth-century advent of "le weekend," Parisians flocked to the boathouse and restaurant to rent rowing skiffs, eat good food, and relax with friends and family by the river. Throughout the 1870s, Renoir often visited La Maison Fournaise to enjoy its convivial atmosphere and rural beauty, and to paint scenes nearby. In the late summer of 1880, simultaneously realizing that the light was perfect, and acknowledging the gravity of Zola's charge that the Impressionists "remain inferior to what they undertake," Renoir put into action his plan to paint. But the complexity of his idea for the painting and the time constraint of the season gave him just two months— only seven or eight Sundays—of good light. He had to hurry.

Forgoing any preliminary sketches or oil studies, Renoir went straight to the canvas. Now he had the setting, but he needed his subjects. Renoir wanted to construct a painting about modern life—the new, liberated freedom of *la vie moderne*. The patrons of the Maison were a ready blend of people from different classes and occupations: artists, actors, writers, society women, seamstresses, and shop girls. He assembled fourteen men and women—some of them friends, some of them lovers, some he'd never met before— into a vibrant portrait of modern society.

Through meticulous research, Susan Vreeland has used the known information to create their personalities and stories, and allows them to reveal the issues of their lives in their own voices, issues that bear witness to the complex texture of Parisian society. We hear Angèle's earthy slang and appreciate how she negotiates the bohemian world of Montmarte. We palpably feel Alphonsine's fear that she would never be loved again, Paul's reckless lust for life and the irrational forces that threaten it, Gustave Caillebotte's anguish at the contention between groups of painters. We empathize with Ellen, the mime of the Folies-Bergère, in her longing "to say beautiful words, brave words, unforgettable words." Above all, we feel Renoir's struggle in meeting the challenges of this ambitious painting, and can taste his yearning as if it were our own. We come to understand his answer that what he wanted people to see in the painting, was "The goodness of life," and we agree that art is "love made visible." Ultimately, the novel is a feast of intense creative endeavors, and one comes away from it convinced of the vital importance of aesthetics in a fully lived life.

A Conversation with
Susan Vreeland

Why did you choose Auguste Renoir's Luncheon of the Boating
Party *as a subject for a novel? Does it have some significance to you
personally?*

There are many reasons. *Luncheon of the Boating Party*, owned
by The Phillips Collection in Washington, D.C., has served
Americans as a symbol of France and French culture, both of
which I love, and is as evocative and triumphant an image as that
other emissary of France, the Statue of Liberty. Besides being the
central masterpiece of the art movement that changed the look of
art forever, it represents the qualities of the French soul: joyous
friendship, appreciation of beauty, verve, and the intoxication with
life. It invites us to ask ourselves: How can one live a life so filled
with beauty and so rich with pleasure?

Some part of me came alive in front of this painting the first
time I saw it. I glimpsed more than the aesthetics of another
culture—I saw a lovely, enticing range of cultural attitudes to
discover. I sensed that a study of this painting would lead me to
an exploration that was bound to enrich my life. The painting
suggested a *supplement d'âme*, something more in the soul, another
region ultimately more important than what can be quantified in a
methodical assessment of one's life. It was, in fact, the French *art de
vivre*. At that moment, I felt possessed by the yearning for creative
expression, just as, I was later to discover, was keenly felt by most of
the figures in the painting.

What is the painting about? In part, it's about the tantalizing
riches of the senses. It invokes sensuous experiences beyond the
visual: the feel of the breeze on the skin, evidenced by the fluttering
scallops on the awning and the sailboats making their way
upstream; the fragrance of the fruit that fills the nose; the taste of
wine that enlivens the palate; the feel of one's surroundings—one
woman's fingers in a dog's fur, the sun on another one's back; the
sound of songs sung by boaters as they row past, and by the models

to each other. They are sucking pleasure out of everything, valuing the last taste in the glass and the colors surrounding them, noticing the look in someone's eyes and engaging in spirited exchange.

One looks at the painting and envies for an instant the characters' capacity to fill themselves with pleasure, to grasp the fleeting present and hold it as one might hold a small bird before letting it go. The painting is imbued with this encouragement to notice delicious details in life, to value the moment, and each other. Seen in the press of high-speed living, it seduces us and urges us to stop and look and listen and taste and feel—and, ultimately, appreciate. At its best moments that's what fine art can do if we let it work on us.

Such a gift from Renoir to the ages! One must clasp hands before it in awe. My novel is my way of living in the painting, learning its lessons of the art of living, and ultimately disseminating its spirit and its sensibilities.

This painting is packed with beautiful figures interacting. Did that influence your choice of this painting as a subject?

Indeed, it did. I saw tremendous story potential in these appealing characters, flushed with pleasure and enjoying a summer day on a terrace overlooking the Seine. They teased and captivated me. However, Renoir took pains not to suggest a specific story and attested that he was only depicting a single moment in that summertime of Impressionism. That begs a novelist to create a story—and how rich it could be with all of those characters from different social classes. Renoir's composition poses intriguing questions about the people and their relationships that I knew I must answer. For example, why is that woman in the upper right covering her ears? What is being said that she doesn't want to hear? Or is she cupping her ears so she can hear better? Whose hand is that around her waist? Does the girl playing with the dog know that the man in the boater opposite her is admiring at her? Why do two men wear singlets and another a top hat, and what is the top-hatted man saying to his friend? And what is the big fellow thinking as he surveys the scene? Oh, so much to decide. It was exhilarating, and I found myself living that vibrant life captured in this moment.

As I researched Renoir's life and the lives of the models, his very real friends, I saw that the issues of their lives reflected the artistic, intellectual, and social climate of the time. I could use their personal stories to expand the novel from merely a story about a man painting a picture to a multilayered narrative revealing the essence of a time period, the explosive, rapidly changing late-nineteenth century in Paris, the world capital of art and style and pleasure and, because it's French, love.

Renoir painted fourteen different individuals. What sources did you consult in your research of the models posed in the painting? Why specifically did you give narrative voices to only seven of the models? What made you choose them over any of the others? And how did you come to speculate on their innermost thoughts and feelings?

I started with a wonderful book produced by The Phillips Collection, which owns the painting: *Impressionists on the Seine: A Celebration of Renoir's "Luncheon of the Boating Party,"* by Eliza E. Rathbone et al. It identified the models and provided some information about each of them. Then I did individual research about them in other books. For example, biographies and critical studies of Jules Laforgue indicated his proclivity toward quoting Shakespeare. I read his poetry and art criticism, as well as that of Charles Ephrussi, in his *Gazette des Beaux-Arts* to learn his assessment of Impressionist painters. Ellen Andrée's performance history revealed her career as a mime to have taken a turn when she joined an avant-garde theater. I read accounts of the Folies-Bergère and applied aspects of it to her. I searched the archives of the Comédie-Française in Paris to learn what plays Jeanne Samary was rehearsing and performing at the time the painting was made, read them (they were by Molière) to learn what she might have been thinking. I discovered her contested engagement and elopement to Joseph-Paul Lagarde, and so I integrated lines from the plays into her scenes. Bits of description of Julien Tanguy, the art-supply dealer, appeared in several contemporary reports, and his portrait by Vincent van Gogh revealed his appearance. *Renoir: My Father*, the memoir by Renoir's son, Jean Renoir provided recollections of his father's attitudes, favorite sayings, and some priceless bits of humor and sarcasm. Renoir's letters appear in several sources, and subjective accounts of his life by two of his friends—Ambroise Vollard's *Renoir: An Intimate Record* and Georges Rivière's *Renoir et Ses Amis*—were helpful.

Having all fourteen models function as point-of-view characters would have lengthened the novel to unmanageable proportions. I made selections on the basis of what material was available, but more importantly, what that information would allow me to contribute to a portrait of late-nineteenth-century Paris. I chose those whose lives provided heat or conflict, as well as issues that I like to explore. For example, the yearning to express and to create is demonstrated by Gustave, Jules, Ellen, and Jeanne Samary, who would not give up theater for love. Changes in marriage traditions and the roles of women could be illustrated by Jeanne's elopement, which did, in fact, happen at this time. Bohemian life of Montmartre could best be represented by Angèle. I chose Aline, Gustave, and Paul as point-of-view characters because of their importance in Renoir's life. Fortunately, their experiences provided material for a more complete picture of the artistic and social worlds of the time. And I chose Alphonsine because she could be most present, could provide a picture of the losses and trauma of the Franco-Prussian War, and would, I imagine, be attracted to Renoir in part, at least, because his work conveyed the river life surrounding her. The rest is imagination.

Impressionism developed in the 1870s. How did you prepare yourself to write about a different time and place?

By reading, of course. Fiction and nonfiction. My bibliography posted on my Web site indicates that my reading extended far beyond biographies of Renoir and art histories of the Impressionist period. My research included such broad topics as the history of the nineteenth century in France, French society and culture, as well as such specific topics as the Franco-Prussian War, the Siege of Paris, and the Commune; the changes in the marketing of art from the Salon to independent galleries, along with the famous art dealer Paul Durand-Ruel; the practice of the duel; dressmaking and couture of late-nineteenth-century Paris; Baron Haussmann's sweeping changes in the look of Paris streets and squares, Montmartre, and quarters where Gustave Caillebotte, Charles Ephrussi, and Madame Charpentier lived; operas current at the time, cabarets and cabaret songs and singers, dance halls and dances, cafés; *canotage*, the new leisure of boating, styles of rowing craft, the specifics of river jousting, the organization of sailing regattas; transportation and currency; oil paints available at the time, art-supply dealers, color theory, Renoir's palette and his preferred types of brushes; other painters who figure in the novel, Monet, Cézanne, Caillebotte, Degas, Bazille, Sisley; the tension among the Impressionist painters and the eventual break up of the group; publications popular at the time; the French character, gender roles, and early feminism.

I also read literature written or performed at the time: the novels of Émile Zola, the stories of Guy de Maupassant, and the poetry of Jules Laforgue, all of whom are characters in *Luncheon of the Boating Party* who frequented La Maison Fournaise. This gave me a sense of voice. And I searched out and listened to the music and operas and cabaret songs of the late-nineteenth century to give me a sense of the gaiety, the attitudes towards love, and the political opinions expressed in the period.

I had the good fortune to travel to Paris twice for visual research, to walk where my characters walked and feel the rise of the land, the surrounding architecture, the river and its banks, the quality of air. I had two luncheons at La Maison Fournaise, the restaurant just west of Paris where Renoir painted *Luncheon*. I studied French during the three years of writing the book, so that I could read untranslated research and grasp the sound of the language and expressions. I absorbed as many Impressionist paintings as I could, in Parisian museums and in many museums in the United States, and in books, looking for clues to architecture, clothing, settings. All of this was enormously enjoyable to me, and I've come away understanding more of French culture.

What elements in the novel are fact and what is fiction? How do you decide when departures from fact are justified?

With all of this research, I was able to have a large degree of authenticity. The paintings, the identities of the models, the salient events of their lives, Renoir's process of painting, the issues facing the Impressionist group, the places where scenes are set, are all factual. For the sake of the narrative, actual dates of certain events—Renoir's meeting Aline, owning the steam-cycle, and getting his arm out of the cast—were adjusted by a few months. When the identity of a model in another painting was reported as two different women, I chose the one that would enhance my narrative. I would never deliberately change a well-known or significant fact to fit my narrative, but when a detail is of little consequence or extremely hard or even impossible to find, I took the novelist's license to make it work for the benefit of the story. Similarly, when research does not reveal the personality and character of historic figures—Alphonsine, Angèle, Fionie, Madame Charpentier, and Baron Raoul Barbier, for example—I am free to create according to my own delight so long as what I devise is consistent with the time and place and social level of the individual.

In your opinion, what drove Renoir to paint? Were those motivations universal among his peers? Among contemporary painters?

Love, of course. He's French, above all. And he's a sensualist. Love for women, the river, Paris, cafés, color, the physicality of the medium, the act of working, brushstroke after brushstroke, all of these passions kept him painting, through good press and bad, through poverty and wealth, through confident times and self-doubt, through debilitating illness and pain, always yearning to learn more, express more, command more facility, to grasp the elusive play of light, the warm and convivial magic of a moment, the exquisite individuality of a woman or child or blossom, working at it with the devotion of a monk until a matter of hours before his death.

To a large extent, his contemporaries felt similar dedications, but I can't speak for their motivations, or the motivations of contemporary painters. I don't believe any of the painters in Renoir's circle enjoyed the rich gooeyness of the paint more than Renoir did.

Renoir struggled to stay with the committed group of Impressionists. Why do you suppose this commitment lasted as long as it did? What was it about his friendships with Frédéric Bazille, Claude Monet, and Alfred Sisley that was so brilliant?

A bond formed when these artists rejected together the stiff, arbitrary rules of academic painting that had no relationship to the world they saw around them in Paris and in the rural areas beyond. Together, these four left the academy to paint *en plein air* in the Forest of Fontainebleau. They drew strength from each other in forging new painting methods, new and revolutionary brushwork, and new subject matter depicting the present rather than the past, and in finding new painting sites. There were endless hours of discussion and argument in the cafés, especially Café Guerbois and later Café Nouvelle-Athènes, argument being part of the French artistic soul. Nevertheless, these painters had profound respect for each other, and for the work of their precursor Edouard Manet, and their contemporaries Berthe Morisot and Paul Cézanne as well. Seeing a painting by Cézanne in Père Tanguy's art-supply shop, Renoir thinks, *The man pressed on through solitude and howling criticism, finding his ecstasy in laying his individuality on canvas after canvas*, and then says aloud, "With a saint's devotion." Such deep-seated valuing of each other's work and struggles and bravery characterized the core group of Impressionists.

How could he break away from the solidarity that had kept them all going through the lean years? But how could he not follow his own inclinations if they led him in a different direction than theirs? Caillebotte worked with a tighter hand, and Cézanne worked more structurally than in Monet's feathery strokes. They pursued their own way. In the end, only Monet and Morisot remained faithful to the wispy, broken stroke. In order to keep progressing, Renoir ultimately had to follow his own direction. Interestingly, though, the Impressionist stroke resurfaced from time to time all of his life.

Have you found any differences in writing about male artists versus female artists? As a woman, was it difficult to inhabit the voice of Renoir? How did you manage to do it?

I suppose it's easier for most writers to create and vivify characters of their own gender. If Renoir wasn't an artist, with a painter's sensibility and sensitivity, which some think are aspects of the feminine domain, it would have been more difficult. Actually, I rather enjoyed moments when I could have him do something generally termed masculine—like kicking something out of anger, swearing, being coarse. He was no lily-white angel, you know. How did I do it? Ah, that's the office of the imagination.

Do you think the creative processes for writers and artists are similar? How so?

Just as some painters are intuitive in their approach and others are intellectual or analytical, planning out every square inch of canvas, so are some writers intuitive, working scene by scene as though feeling their way in a cave, and others are intellectual, working from a preconceived plan or even a scene-by-scene outline. Of course, this isn't a definitive difference. Rather, it's a continuum, for both the painter and the writer.

What is the value of writing fiction about art? What does it allow you to address?

The value of writing about art is its effect on the imagination. Paintings allow us to inhabit another culture, place, and time period, and address the issues of those time periods that resonate with our own time.

Take the motif of a painting of figures around a dining table. What vastly different insights we get from an Italian depiction of the opulent *Marriage Feast at Cana* by Veronese; Degas' *The Absinthe Drinker*, portraying the vacant, despairing stare of the woman; van Gogh's humble, struggling, yet interacting peasants in *The Potato Eaters*; and Renoir's *Luncheon of the Boating Party*. Each one whisks us into a very different mental and social milieu and asks of us to live these lives for a moment, thus expanding our sense of humanity.

Each time we enter imaginatively into the life of another, it's a small step upward in the elevation of the human race. When there is no imagination of others' lives, there is no human connection, and therefore no compassion. Without compassion, then community, commitment, loving kindness, human understanding, and peace—all shrivel. Individuals become isolated, the isolated can turn cruel, and the tragic hovers. Art—and literature—are antidotes to that.

QUESTIONS FOR DISCUSSION

1. How do you think Renoir's humble beginnings affected his life and his painting?

2. Describe what you think was going through Renoir's mind as he took on the technical challenge of this painting. Was he ready for this? How was he to achieve the perspective? Position the figures? Anchor the terrace? Convey the river below?

3. Besides Renoir, how do other characters explore the issue of creative expression? In whom is this yearning most deeply felt? What effect does the gathering of these people have on each other? While reading this book, could you imagine being a model in the painting? What would it have been like for you? Elaborate on how you would have fit in or not.

4. Discuss the level of commitment each character had to the painting. How did their involvement affect the painting? Do you relate to any one of the characters in the painting *Luncheon of the Boating Party*?

5. How do the separate models' plots act upon the progress of the painting and enlighten a single common theme? Which of the male models is your favorite? And of the female models? Why does each hold a place in your affections?

6. How did the fact that there was time pressure to finish the painting affect its result? Would the painting have turned out differently if Renoir had had more time to work on it?

7. Renoir seems to fall in love over and over again with the two things he most adored: the female form and the riverscape. He saw one woman as color, another as line. Was there something about the season in which he was painting and his relationships with Aline and Alphonsine that contributed to the overall effect of the image?

8. What does *Luncheon of the Boating Party* suggest about finding oneself in life and in love? Is there something unique or universal about the way an artist finds his or her way?

9. In what ways, if any, did the novel surprise you? How do you react to a novel that incorporates real and well-known people as characters? Did anything in the novel affect the way you had previously thought about Renoir? Impressionism? French culture?

10. What in the story of this painting gives you a fresh perspective on understanding and developing the relationships and creative inclinations in your own life?

For further exploration and discussion of *Luncheon of the Boating Party*, please visit the author's Web site, www.svreeland.com, where additional discussion questions and a teachers' guide are available.

For more information about or to order other Penguin Readers Guides, please e-mail the Penguin Marketing Department at reading@us.penguingroup.com or write to us at:

Penguin Books Marketing Dept.
Readers Guides
375 Hudson Street
New York, NY 10014-3657

Please allow 4–6 weeks for delivery.
To access Penguin Readers Guides online, visit the Penguin Group (USA) Inc. Web site at www.penguin.com and www.vpbookclub.com.